Bad Men

BAD MEN

A Western Tale

A novel by:
Michael Kanaly

BAD MEN: A Western Tale

A novel by Michael Kanaly
374 pages

Also by the author:
THOUGHTS OF GOD
VIRUS CLANS
THE VOICE WITHIN
ROOM ONE
THE LONG ARMS

ISBN 978-0692646021
Copyright © 2016 by Michael Kanaly
Key words: buffalo hunters, plains Indians, historic fiction

Design and layout by Rogue Ship Graphics

PILOT HILL PRESS

Vancouver   St. John's
British Columbia   Newfoundland

PilotHillPress@gmail.com

For my grandson, Robert

Bad Men

"Probably all laws are useless;
for good men do not need laws at
all, and bad men are made no better
by them."
-Demonox,
Greek Philosopher

Bad Men

Prologue:

Buffalo Hunters

In the distance a heavy gun boomed. Daniel McCanty's eyes narrowed, his jaw hardened like granite. Hide men, he knew, killing off the buffalo herds. Doing the government's dirty work, helping the likes of Grant, Sherman and Sheridan. He had no problem with hunters making meat, even for the railroad. But the hide men were stripping the herds from the land, taking skins and tongues, leaving the rest to rot. All part of the government's plan to starve the tribes into submission, to open the land for the white invaders. Eventually, to exterminate the Indians and their way of life. And McCanty knew there was nothing anyone could do to stop it. Although he wasn't ready yet to quit trying.

The price of hides was dropping quicker than the Upper Missouri in high summer...and it sure as hell wasn't high summer anymore. The wind was starting to blow cold and hard off the mountains, the morning brought frost as likely as not. Zeb Biggs wanted to get as many skins as possible into his wagons before the snow fell. It was a tricky thing to end the season and get your hides to market before the snow and bitter cold hit, freezing man and wagon into the ice locked ground. He poured a measure of water down the barrel of his Sharps, followed by a grease rag, as he had been taught. A hot, dirty barrel made for a poor shot, and Zeb Biggs was not one to waste a shot if he would help it. Dead buff littered the valley below him, like so many fallen leaves. A hundred or more, by his quick count. He sat amid a pile of shell casings and considered the day, which had been a good one in terms of the hunt. Well, it wasn't exactly a hunt, in the proper sense of the word. Slaughter was closer to the truth. Buffalo Running the old timers called it, as if they didn't care to admit what was actually going on...firing into unsuspecting herds of animals, killing them by the thousands. So Biggs called himself a Buffalo Runner when around the campfires and saloons frequented by those grizzled old sharpshooters.

In the valley, Biggs' two skinners were working the edges of the killing field, back where he'd started shooting this morning. The herd, two or three hundred animals, had wandered some during the day, and those that were left were starting to mill around, as if sensing something might be wrong. It was amazing to Biggs that they just stood there and let themselves be shot. Of course, he took the proper precautions, setting up with the wind in his face, so the shaggies wouldn't smell him. Buff didn't see too well, but they sure could smell. Next, he was careful to pick the look-out animal as his first target. It could be a bull or a cow, usually an older, experienced critter that would warn the herd of approaching danger. This first kill was critical and Biggs made certain that it was a single shot, clean and accurate, right behind the shoulder blade, three-quarters of the way down from the top of the hump. An animal hit there, through the heart and lungs, would generally drop where it stood, a fountain of blood pouring out of its nose and mouth. Strangely, this did not alarm the others in the herd. Biggs considered that maybe they thought the dead animal was just laying down, digesting its grass, as the buff were prone to do. Or that the lead animal had merely gone to sleep. Either way, the rest of the herd went about their business, grazing, milling around. Sometimes a few of the buffalo might realize that their leader was down, and they would cluster around, snorting and bawling, maybe poking at the critter with their horns to try and force it up. But if the herd couldn't see or smell the danger, they didn't know which way to run. With no leader, they would usually just stay put, while death visited them.

If it all worked out correctly, and the shaggies didn't stampede or amble off out of range, Biggs could set up his shooting sticks, supporting the barrel of the heavy Sharps, which weighed in at a whopping fourteen pounds, and work his stand. First targeting the outside members of the herd, those who looked like they might wander off and take the rest of the animals with them. Then as the day wore on, he would target any of the herd when they came into range.

He used a .50 caliber Sharps, which was extremely accurate up to six hundred yards. At that range, he might miss now and again, particularly if the barrel was hot, but he couldn't recall pulling a shot at three hundred yards or under. He would wipe the gun barrel down or pour a measure of water through it, then a greased rag, every four or five shots, as he had been taught by the old Buffalo Runner, Manny Lopez. Biggs had been a surprisingly attentive student, learning well the business of killing buffalo.

"A prudent man will plug his ears with bees' wax before shooting too many rounds," Manny had said in his thick accent, as he jerked the two and a half inch shell into the chamber of his Sharps and pulled the first of the twin triggers to lock the shell in place. Manny used a .50-90 load, that packed enough wallop to drop any animal in its tracks. It was the same load Biggs used, and he was most careful to plug his ears before beginning the day's work of killing buffalo.

For Indians, however, Biggs carried a Winchester repeater in his saddle boot. It was a .44 caliber rim fire, which held twelve rounds, as opposed to the single shot Sharps. Although it certainly did not have the range of the Big Fifty, the Winchester repeater was a fearsome weapon in close encounters.

Down in the valley, about half the herd milled around. The other half would not move again. The two skinners glanced up from their work from time to time, to see what the shooter was doing. They trusted Biggs enough not to shoot them, of course, but there were more than a hundred carcasses to be dealt with, and a good skinner could pull maybe fifty hides a day. Anything that didn't get skinned the same day stood a fair chance of being wasted, as it was likely that scavengers would get to the carcass during the night, and render the hide useless.

The skinners, Clayton and Austin Murphy, were proficient in their trade. Like most men in the profession, they did their best work skinning the shaggies by hand. If the killing field was full, like it was today, they would have to employ the mules and horses from the wagons, and yank the hides off with ropes. This was not the best method, as the Murphy brothers well knew, because the hides had a tendency to rip or tear, and thus became less valuable. While they understood this, they had doubts that Zeb Biggs knew the difference between quantity and quality, since the shooter didn't seem to know when to quit sometimes. Or else he couldn't count very well, as brother Austin suspected. But the skinners had hired on for the base pay of fifty dollars a month, so the quality problem really wasn't theirs, other than from a personal pride perspective. And, as brother Clayton often pointed out, they stunk far too much of blood, sweat and dead buffalo to have much personal pride left.

So the Murphy brothers went about their work. The carcasses were stripped. The green hides were piled on one of the two wagons, and taken back to the semi-permanent camp. There, they were staked out for four or five days, then turned so the flesh side was up for another day. After which, the hides were turned daily until fully dried. They were sprinkled with poison to kill the ticks, fleas and lice, as well as other bugs that could eat holes in the hides, ruining them for the buyers.

"You know we're in Sioux territory, don't you?" Austin asked his brother. They were above the Niobrara River, and these were Sioux buffalo they were killing, which made Austin extremely nervous.

"Biggs says the shaggies are migrating animals, so anybody can shoot 'em," Clayton replied. "The Army agrees, as well."

Clayton grunted as he cut away the tongue from a butchered cow. The tongues were smoked back at their dugout camp, and sold separately from the hides. The Murphy brothers claimed the tongues for themselves, as they were sold through traders to the eastern restaurants, where they were served as a delicacy. There was a lot of work involved cutting and preserving the tongues, so Biggs, who operated the outfit, didn't care to have anything to do with smoked tongue.

"The Indians might have something to say about whose buffalo these are," Austin suggested. His brother considered that Austin might be too worrisome for this kind of work.

"Biggs'll keep the injins off us," Clayton said, convinced in the shooter's skill. "We'll be back across the river in a few days."

"Not soon enough for me," Austin declared, confirming his brother's judgment.

Closer, Biggs' Sharps started booming again, forcing the two skinners to redouble their efforts.

"Son-of-a-bitch don't know when to quit," Austin grumbled.

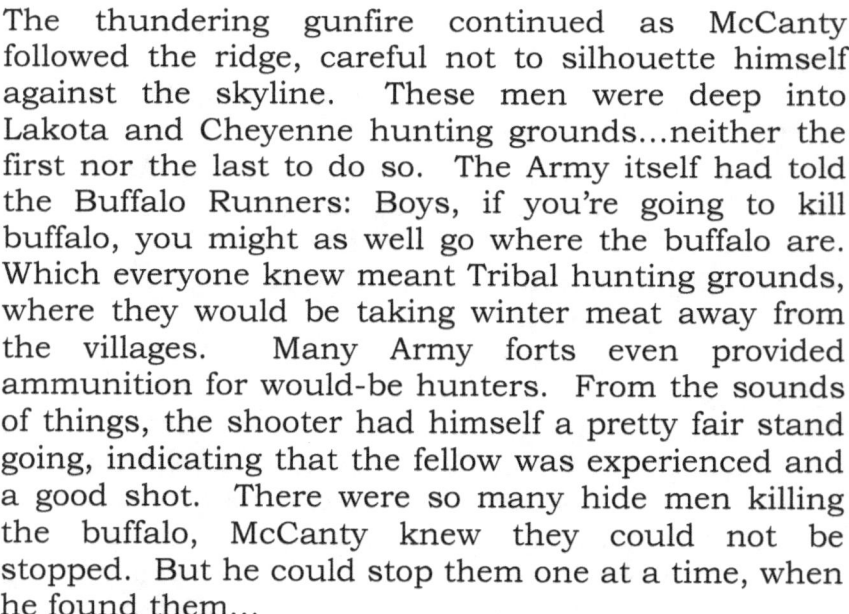

The thundering gunfire continued as McCanty followed the ridge, careful not to silhouette himself against the skyline. These men were deep into Lakota and Cheyenne hunting grounds...neither the first nor the last to do so. The Army itself had told the Buffalo Runners: Boys, if you're going to kill buffalo, you might as well go where the buffalo are. Which everyone knew meant Tribal hunting grounds, where they would be taking winter meat away from the villages. Many Army forts even provided ammunition for would-be hunters. From the sounds of things, the shooter had himself a pretty fair stand going, indicating that the fellow was experienced and a good shot. There were so many hide men killing the buffalo, McCanty knew they could not be stopped. But he could stop them one at a time, when he found them...

With that, he pulled his own Big Fifty from its saddle boot and laid it across his lap, knowing that a man could get into a heap of trouble this way.

"You! Down the hill! What the hell are ya doin'?" McCanty shouted, sliding off his horse, laying his big gun across the saddle. The Sharps, cocked and loaded, the barrel centered on the man below.

"Shootin' buffalo!" Zeb Biggs shouted back, turning now to face uphill. He did not look very pleased to be interrupted in his enterprise.

The shooter had been hailed between shots, as he poured water through his heated barrel, his cartridge chamber empty. This was not by accident. McCanty closed to around four hundred yards of the man, a range at which he was unlikely to miss.

"Takin' food from women and children, as I see it!" McCanty returned. "You're on Tribal hunting grounds!"

"What's it to you?" Biggs yelled back, sensing now that he might be in more trouble than it first seemed, particularly with his weapon unloaded, a situation he hurried to correct. "You're a fuckin' white man, ain't ya?"

"I'm an Irishman," McCanty said loudly, as the man below fumbled with his cartridge belt. "We don't like it when people starve women and children!"

McCanty sighted quickly and fingered the twin triggers. The side hammer dropped, the gun roared. The man below looked startled at the sound, then totally surprised when an ounce of lead tore through his chest and exited out his back, tearing apart his lungs, breaking his spine.

Down in the valley the two skinners shouted, wondering what was going on. Sensing something amiss, they began to run. McCanty answered with two more blasts from the Sharps. Caught in midstride, each of the skinners seemed to fly a few feet into the air, crashing, flailing on the ground, their blood mingling with the great pools already spilled in the yellow grass.

McCanty surveyed the wagon, with its load of green hides, knowing it was likely there was a dugout camp somewhere near, with a stack of dried hides. He would take those hides and sell them, then get the Cheyenne some rifles to fight the coming scourge. But first, he knew a village that could use some meat.

Part One:
Two Towns

"Towns sprang up like weeds.
 Some of 'em thrived,
 Some withered and died."
             -C.J. Brighton,
             Cowboy poet

"We prospered...until we didn't."
             -early Kansas settler

"They miscalculated when they laid
out the town of Cold Springs.
It was cold enough, by God,
but the springs only ran for two
months during the snow melt.
We learned right quick:
You can't drink cold."
             -Moses Altman,
             on the Missouri frontier

CHAPTER ONE

Cherokee Creek

Rufus Gates was generally considered to be the worst hangman west of the Mississippi. His arrival in the town of Cherokee Creek was especially bad news for John Bullis, whose murder trial was scheduled to begin on Monday morning. Bullis had the miserable luck to have shot and killed what had to be the only unarmed card sharp in the entire country. He had known the man to be cheating, and had assumed that anyone who would bottom-deal a poker deck would naturally be carrying a gun of some sort when he reached into his coat pocket. Only he hadn't...just another deck of badly marked cards. Still, Bullis hoped to get off.

But watching the hangman out of his cell window bothered him more than he cared to admit. Rufus Gates was a grizzled man of indeterminate age. Thin and wrinkled, grey stubble, a battered flop hat, and an Adam's apple that jiggled like a yo-yo. He looked like a tall chicken pecking along on the gallows, which was his workshop. He was unmarried and mostly without family, which allowed him to travel freely, plying his trade wherever required. He was known to visit the Upstairs Girls on occasion, but his was an infrequent lust, vastly overwhelmed by what many thought to be an unquenchable thirst. In truth, these same people considered alcohol to be the principal stumbling block in Rufus Gates' practice of his unconventional trade. They were largely mistaken.

It was true, however, that Rufus had been more than a little drunk last month up in Danville when it had been time to see Ben Waite off into whatever Afterlife awaited the well-known horse thief and bushwhacker. Waite, a large man of uncommon strength, did not take kindly to the proceedings, fighting and biting and spitting right up to the time the deputies wrestled him onto the lip of the gallows and got the rope slipped over his thick neck. Still, Waite continued to struggle until Rufus Gates thoughtfully tightened the rope, bringing the big man to attention on the tips of his toes, while Gates finished up his preliminary adjustments.

"You better get this right, you miserable excuse of a hangman!" Ben Waite managed to gasp, his anger at the situation causing him to spit directly into one of Rufus Gates' bloodshot eyes.

Some later considered this to be a severe lapse of judgment on Waite's part, a man of obviously flawed judgment to begin with. But if Gates took offense, he did not immediately show it. He merely pulled a ragged bandana out of his back pocket, wiped his face, and continued checking knots and levers and the like. He did seem to whisper something that on-lookers thought caused Ben Waite's eyes to widen, just as the noose was fixed into its final position and the hood was pulled down over the condemned man's face. But it was a thing that happened so fast, no one could really be sure what took place.

What took place next, however, was frozen into everyone's memory for years to come. As the Sheriff of Danville, James Smith, finished reading the sentence and nodded to the hangman, the lever was pulled and the still struggling form of Ben Waite dropped through the trap door. But the hangman's knot had slipped it seemed and Waite somehow got his hands free, as his body writhed and jerked at the end of the rope. He began clawing at the noose that was slowly...very slowly...wringing the life out of him.

The crowd which had gathered, anticipating, even hoping for one of Gates' legendary botched executions, was nonetheless aghast. As the minutes ticked on and Waite managed to kick his legs free, the screams of the women in the crowd at the base of the gallows rose in crescendo, as Waite clutched frantically at the rope. Although admittedly his attempts were growing more feeble, his gasps for air, seen and heard though the black hood were less frequent. Still, it seemed like an impossibly long time had passed. And even after Waite's hands fell to his side, his feet continued to move, and every so often a terrible gasp would escape the dying man's body. This continued until finally Sheriff Smith felt compelled to rush down the gallows' steps, pulling his large Dragoon pistol from its holster as he went, shooting Ben Waite in the heart at point-blank range.

Some in the crowd were heard to whisper: "About time!" while staring banefully in Rufus Gates' direction. Others, pleased to have gotten their money's worth, adjourned to the nearby bars, or picnicked in the bandstand, where the 4th of July bunting was still up. Most considered that Ben Waite had gotten what he deserved...and perhaps a little more thrown in for good measure. After all, no one, other than a convicted thief and murderer, had been harmed.

"Hey, you're a might early with the gallows, ain't ya?" Bullis yelled out, hearing Sheriff Henry Cobb enter his office at the bottom of the stairs. In truth, the hammering and sawing was unnerving, even to a man of John Bullis' steady continence.

The Sheriff, a large, portly man, poked his head into the stairwell and let out an equally unnerving laugh.

"Only by a day or two, maybe," Cobb said, making the threat sound almost jocular, as he was usually pleasant by nature and in his appearance. He wore a clean, white shirt every day, fresh from the Chinese laundry, with a Bolo tie. He also fancied a grey Stetson, his boots were generally shined, and he made it a point to get clean shaven by the barber every two days. "They're bringing Kaleb Lee over from Granville," he said. "Odds are the two of you will be sharing the contraption."

"What happened to innocent until proven guilty?" Bullis shouted back.

It peeved him some that his guilt was assumed. This despite the hard fact that he had shot an unarmed man in front of a saloon full of witnesses.

"Kaleb Lee has already been proved guilty in a court of law," Cobb called up. "And you ain't far behind."

There wasn't much to say, being that it was true. So Bullis pulled his blanket over his head and tried to block out the sound of Rufus Gates' gallows construction. Bullis' only chance, he knew, lay in the hands of his lawyer, Shamus Young; who was at this moment, spreading the largesse Bullis had scooped from the table during the chaos that ensued after the shooting, distributing those bills and coins into the hands of the jury. After, of course, the lawyer kept a sufficient portion of the mostly ill-gotten gain for himself. While the loss of his stake was disconcerting to Bullis, he figured it would be money well spent if it kept him off the gallows Rufus Gates was building in the town square.

The question of quilt and innocence did bother Sheriff Cobb from time to time. That was to say, if a man was guilty, then a botched hanging had to be taken into consideration when he committed his particular crime. A hanging of any kind, he supposed, as the events at Danville had become common gossip. But there had been an incident or two here in Cherokee Creek, as well. One bothered him to this day.

It started when bounty hunters brought in a prisoner they claimed to be the notorious outlaw, Dancin' Yancy Edwards, complete with wanted poster and reward notification. And sure enough, the fellow matched Edwards' description, right down to having a scar that ran from his eyebrow to his chin. Sheriff Cobb didn't give much thought to the fact that in those years after the Civil War, there was a good number of men with such markings. He also didn't give much credence to the protests of the prisoner, who claimed not be Dancin' Yancy at all, but Zeke Pendergast, a farmer from Butte. Because, the Sheriff figured, Dancin' Yancy Edwards would naturally claim to be someone else. So the reward had been paid and the prisoner held over for trial. Later the Sheriff admitted, at least to himself, it had not been much of a trial. The circuit judge arrived, as he did every month or two. The prosecuting attorney, who traveled with the judge, brought along a couple of witnesses who claimed to be familiar with Dancin' Yancy's illegal activities. After a night of drinking and whoring, mostly at the county's expense, Judge Silas Crump banged his gavel, the witnesses pointed to the defendant and swore they had seen him rob stages and banks and ranch payrolls, as well as shooting anyone who protested, and even some who didn't. Judge Crump asked if this was true; the prisoner denied everything and begged someone to check his story about being Zeke Pendergast from Butte. Unfortunately, the telegraph lines were down again, so the judge shook his head, weighed the evidence, which included several hundred dollars found in the man's boot upon his capture...and banged the gavel again to confirm the guilty verdict.

A few days later, Rufus Gates arrived and began supervising the building of the gallows. The prisoner put up such a fuss, that Sheriff Cobb thought it prudent to send a man up to Butte to check the fellow's story...since the Indians or the weather kept the telegraph lines from being repaired. But the man, who wasn't a deputy or anything, must have gotten lost or drunk, since he never did come back. So they hanged the fellow. The newspaper covered the event. Pictures were taken, before and after. The drop, while not exactly clean, was not terrible. The hanged man did bite his tongue or something, as there was a good deal of blood dripping out from under the black hood over his head. So the crowd had been somewhat placated by the successful conclusion of the proceedings, but Sheriff Cobb had not been able to get the man's tearful protests out of his mind.

Then, two days later, a woman came driving through town with a wagon, demanding to see her husband, Zeke Pentergast. Who, she said, had last been seen traveling to Yankton to sell cattle to the government. Seems some fellow had ridden by their farm, with the story that Zeke was about to be hung through a case of mistaken identity...

A bad few hours ensued, during which the tearful woman identified her husband through the newspaper pictures, the body was dug up to be taken back to the family ranch for proper burial. The town treasury was raided to pay the woman what damages the City Council could afford...luckily, the several hundred dollars found in the famer's boot was still available, along with a few extra horses from the town livery. In truth, although the widow had been understandably upset, the monetary offering seemed to have eased her suffering somewhat, Sheriff Cobb thought. The Sheriff was more than mortified to have been caught up in yet another of Rufus Gates' execution mishaps.

Such things, Cobb thought, followed in Gates' footsteps like some ghostly shade. Although, it had to be admitted that this particular mishap was hardly the hangman's fault.

Things got even more muddled a few weeks later when a letter arrived from someone else claiming to be Mrs. Zeke Pendergast, inquiring as to the whereabouts of her husband. By then, the Sheriff was so confused over who had been hung, who had been paid, that he tossed the letter away without answering, hoping the whole thing would just go away. It did. And after a while, when no more wanted posters came in with Dancin' Yancy's name on them, the Sheriff was able to convince himself that maybe they had, indeed, hung the right man.

"And how does the jury find?" Judge Crump asked, his voice casual. Silas Crump was a white-haired jurist, troubled by frequent bouts of gout. A former lawyer, whose brother-in-law had gotten him appointed to the post of Circuit Judge. Crump wanted nothing more in life than to get his crooked bother-in-law, who happened to be in the Kansas Legislature, in front of his bench. And if he could somehow get the man convicted of a capital offense, Silas Crump would have Rufus Gates hang the bribe-taking son-of-a-bitch. Aw, but that was a dream for another day. His gout was acting up and after two days of testimony, the verdict was clear-cut and obvious in his mind.

"We find the defendant, John Bullis, not guilty, your honor," the foreman said, cringing under the judge's baleful glare.

"Really?" Crump asked, sounding incredulous. "Not guilty, you say?"

"Yes sir," the foreman coughed. "It were unanimous," he said, looking down the line at the other faces in the jury box, no doubt hoping to spread the blame around.

"Unanimous?" Judge Crump asked, wondering if he had heard right. The foreman nodded, the other jury members looked at their hands.

At the defendant's table, Lawyer Young, who was hardly known for his scruples, was smiling and shaking the hand of his client, the shootist and gambler, John Bullis.

"Despite the facts of the case?" the judge asked in obvious disbelief. "Despite the eyewitness testimony that clearly showed Mr. Bullis pulling his revolver and shooting Mr. Harris squarely in the chest?"

"Your honor, this is hardly..." Shamus Young began protesting.

Judge Crump held up his hand, at which the lawyer wisely hushed.

"We believe the shooting was an unfortunate accident," the foreman said, in what was most certainly a rehearsed manner. "William Harris was a known card sharp and cheat, your honor."

"That may be so," the judge admitted, being familiar with Bill Harris' misadventures at the poker table. "But he was, in fact, unarmed when shot to death."

"That was the accidental part, your honor," the foreman said, nodding his head.

"You believe that Mr. Harris being unarmed was an accident?" Crump inquired, his eyebrows pulling together as he tried to follow the jury's twisted logic.

"Seemed that way to us," the foreman said, looking down the line to his accomplices, who all nodded their heads. "If he was going to cheat a man like John Bullis, we're thinking he would have brung his gun with him."

"So it was an accident on his part, that he left his gun in his hotel room?" the judge asked.

"That's pretty much it," the foreman concluded.

"All right," Silas Crump sighed, his head pounding at both his hangover and the obvious miscarriage of justice. Two situations he was intimately acquainted with. "The jury has spoken... however foolishly. Mr. Bullis, you are free to go."

"Thank you, your honor," Bullis said.

"Don't thank me. Thank your crooked lawyer and your idiotic peers," the judge muttered, in what some thought to be a most unjudicial manner.

Outside the Sheriff's Office, Bullis strapped on his Colt, tilted the brim of his hat and headed across the street to Flannery's Saloon, the scene of the crime, so to speak. He was hoping to find another card game, or a seat at the faro table to regain his stake. He was careful, however, not to walk in the shadow of Rufus Gates' gallows.

CHAPTER TWO

Rockville

He rode into town on a copper gelding that looked as dusty and dirty as the man himself. Horse and man with their heads down against the hot, dry wind that blew sand through the town like a midwinter blizzard. The man wore a long duster that might have once been white, but was now the same brownish color as his animal. His hat pulled low over his eyes, a dark bandana tied across his face as protection against the vicious sandstorm. He drew up in front of the Silver Strike Saloon and lurched sideways as he dismounted, clutching his side. He wrapped the reins loosely around the hitching post, pulled a Winchester repeater out of the saddle scabbard and walked the three steps onto the wooden sidewalk that ran the length of Main Street. He paused at the swinging doors of the saloon, clutched his side again, and promptly collapsed into a groaning heap.

It was an occurrence that was odd, even in the rough and tumble town of Rockville, which saw more than its share of odd occurrences. A couple of Good Samaritans from inside the Silver Strike peered out at the fallen man, saw the pool of blood leaking onto the wooden boards of the sidewalk and rushed out to help. They dragged the man, who was not overly large, but unwieldy in his present state, and still somewhat feisty, into the bar, if only so that he could die inside, out of the sandstorm. Jim Warner, the bartender, sent his sweeper boy across the street for the barber, who was the closest thing to a doctor in Rockville. The Upstairs Girls clustered around the fallen figure and several of the barflies eyed the man's boots and Winchester with obvious ill intent. But the burly bartender shooed them away, kneeling beside the man, gauging the extent of his injuries. Warner, who had a lot of experience with such wounds, declared to himself that this was a bad one and the fellow, whoever he was, seemed unlikely to survive. Warner took off the man's hat and laid it under his head.

"I've sent for the barber," he said, which sounded absurd even as he spoke, but the man didn't seem to hear him, so it didn't matter much. "Get back," he said to the Upstairs Girls, just to have something sensible to say. He tried to pry the Winchester out of the man's hands, more to prevent any accidental firing than to lay claim to the weapon, but was startled when the fellow's eyes jerked open and glared at him.

"Just trying to help, mister," Warner said, although the gun was a fine one and would undoubtedly be up for grabs before long.

Beneath a growth of several days' worth of beard, the man's face was ghostly pale, pits and scars amid the leathery features spoke of past violent encounters. It was impossible to give an age to the fellow, but he was surely older, rather than younger, Warner thought. The Upstairs Girls whispered among themselves, commenting on the man's deplorable condition and the hard features of his face. The sweeper boy returned with the barber, Slim Whitmore, whose secondary function, aside from cutting hair and shaving folks, was pulling rotten teeth, setting broken bones, and prescribing the occasional salve for the Upstairs Girls, wiped his hands on a half clean towel.

"What ya got, Jim?" he asked, ignoring the obviousness of the situation.

"Don't know," Warner replied. "Fellow just rode into town and fell down outside. Shot, I'm guessing."

The barber knelt down and began cutting away the man's vest and shirt with the same razor he had recently applied to a Fall River cowboy. Blood ran across the man's side, mingling with the sawdust spread across the Silver Strike's floor, mostly to pick up vomit and tobacco juice.

"Best get me some whiskey and clean water, if you got any," Slim said, surveying the slashing wound in the man's abdomen. One of the Upstairs Girls, Big Jenna, got the required materials from behind the bar. Slim took a slug of the whiskey, before dabbing a bit on his half clean rag.

"Yup, gun shot," he stated, rinsing the wound with a mixture of water and liquor. "See the slits here, how they're slanted? Appears as though he did a passable job of digging the bullet out himself."

At that, the barflies and the Upstairs Girls looked at the fallen figure with new respect.

"Is he going to live?" Jim asked.

"Not likely," Slim the barber pronounced, shaking his head. "He tried to seal the wound...see the scorch marks here? But he's lost a lot of blood. Still, you never can tell. If the bullet didn't nick his guts, or the knife he dug it out with weren't too dirty, he might heal. We'll sew him up and see. Any man who can cut a bullet out of hisself and stick a hot knife inside the gash...well, he's got some sand. A tough old bird, no doubt."

The fallen man's eyes flickered open and he tried to speak, but the words were faint and blurry, like the sun peeking through the sandstorm outside. Slim wiped the sweat off the man's forehead and dipped his rag into the whiskey bottle, pressing it against the fellow's dry, cracked lips.

"Did I get it right, mister?" Slim asked.

"My horse..." the man gasped, ignoring the question.

"We'll take care of your horse," Jim Warner said. "What's your name? Anybody we should contact?"

The last was merely a consideration to a dying man, as Rockville had no telegraph, and quite literally no contact with the outside world, other than the occasional stage coach or haphazard mail service. That didn't matter, however, as the fellow had lapsed back into unconsciousness.

"So what do we do with him?" Warner asked. "Can you do anything for him, Slim?"

"Clean the wound, sew him up, put some cunt salve on it," Slim shrugged. "The rest is in God's hands."

Jim Warner figured as much. "Well, we sure as hell can't leave him here on the floor," he said, irritated that this trouble had presented itself on a Thursday afternoon, with miners and cowboys from the nearby ranches due in tomorrow for their weekly flings.

"We can carry him up to my room," Big Jenna said. As her name suggested, Jenna was a large girl, who had more than once punched drunken cowboys into unconsciousness after they were foolish enough to insult her size. But Jenna had a soft, nurturing side, which made the young cowboys and miners feel comfortable around her. And making a man feel comfortable was what being an Upstairs Girl was all about, Jim Warner knew. Jenna was also the one who regularly took in stray dogs and cowboys who needed mothering. "I can split my upstairs time with Sara."

Warner frowned and thought about objecting, but knew it was useless to argue. They did have to move the man somewhere. It was unseemly to suggest the stables for a dying man. He knew the girls would get cranky and disagreeable if he did, so he and the barflies carried the unnamed man up to Jenna's bed. Where, no doubt, his dying would take days, disrupting the Silver Strike's business in the process. There were, however, several gold coins found in the man's pockets, which Jim Warner promptly appropriated for room and board, and for the eventual burial fee.

Curiously, the man refused to die.

He proved to be as stubborn as his horse. The gelding stood in the street, refusing to move, despite being pushed from behind by Billy Jolin, the sweeper boy and pulled from the front by Deputy Skeet Miller. It was Harv Gorman, the stable owner, who finally led the big animal down to the livery by enticing the beast with a bucket of beer. The horse consumed most of two buckets, then promptly fell asleep in its stall, snoring loudly most of the night.

"Damn horse drinks more beer than me," Harv said, over his own mug at the Silver Strike. "That guy's still on this side of the dirt, huh?"

Jim Warner mumbled in the affirmative, more than a little irritated at the man's stubbornness. Accounts were down with the stranger's occupation of

Big Jenna's bed, and by the amount of nursing being done by all the Upstairs Girls. The man's room and board was rapidly eating up the few coins found on his person, not to mention the cost of keeping the horse in beer.

"I sent word up to the mining camps," Warner grumbled. "The Sherriff's up there settling some claim disputes, and he's supposed to bring Doc Watson down with him."

Watson, who purported to be an Eastern physician, was up in the hills seeking his fortune with the rest of the hard scrabblers. The lure of precious metals attracting all sorts of people these days, Warner knew. No one, of course, bothered to check on Watson to see if he was a real doctor. Mostly because no one cared enough to do so. Out here at the edge of civilization, a man's past was his own business, and few could stand up to close scrutiny. You could be pretty much anybody or anything you wanted. But whatever his background, Doc Watson figured to be an improvement over Slim the barber in the doctoring field. And somebody, Jim Warner thought, had to either cure the fellow in Jenna's bed, or bleed him on his way into forever. Warner didn't much care which way it went. Having helped a few men into forever himself, the bartender understood he couldn't stand up to much scrutiny either.

One of the few who seemed like he might stand inspection was Owen Scales, the sheriff hired away from Owl's Head, when the Rockville mining boom started in earnest last spring, bringing the usual riff-raff, including a small army of prospectors, gamblers, street whores, drifters, and outright thieves. Owen Scales had proved to be a good investment. A hard man, to be sure, but his presence, along with his

Owl's Head reputation, had served to clean things up a bit, at least according to the somewhat lax standards of the Kansas frontier. The gunmen and thieves had mostly seen fit to move on to greener pastures, after several of their kind had been buried in Potter's Field.

Scales rode into town later that afternoon. After checking on his deputy, Skeet Miller, whom he suspected of narcolepsy, since the man could usually be found sleeping at his desk in the jail house, and making sure there were no prisoners locked away for extended periods, Scales settled into a table at the Silver Strike to wash the dust out of his craw.

"Heard you got a boarder," Scales tipped his hat back and grinned at Jim Warner, knowing the burly bartender would be put out at having an unproductive bed upstairs.

"Seemed unchristian to let the fellow die outside in the street," Warner offered, sliding into a chair at the Sheriff's table, helping himself to the bottle set there by Sweet Kate, the Sheriff's regular Upstairs Girl. Sweet Kate was a bosomy redhead, with long curls and blue eyes, possessing a sharp tongue and a temperament to match. Warner saw nothing wrong with his intrusion, since the bottle and Kate were provided free, as part of Scale's compensation package.

"Nobody can accuse you of being unchristian," Scales nodded. "Doc Watson said he'll be in town later this week, or next. He'll be glad to tend to your guest, if the fellow's still with us. You know who it is?"

"He ain't said more than a handful of words since we carried him up," Warner frowned, sensing something in the Sheriff's tone. "Why? You know something?"

Scales winked at his friend. "I might," the Sheriff admitted. "Recognized the horse and saddle at the stable. If he's who I think he is, you might be able to charge extra for the bed after he's gone, one way or the other."

"What exactly are you saying?" Warner asked suspiciously.

"Well, I'll go eyeball him in a minute or two," Scales worked a crick out of his thick neck. "But that beer drinking horse, once belonged to Jake Johnson."

"Jake Johnson?" Warner almost jumped out of his chair. Johnson was a well-known figure on the plains. A former trapper, and a hunter for the railroad, he had turned his tracking and shooting skills into the lucrative field of bounty hunting. He was most famous for killing three men in a gunfight in Abilene.

"Rein that in a bit," Scales warned, glancing around to see if anyone had heard. "We'll need to keep that just between the two of us for the moment."

"You gonna arrest him?" Warner asked quietly.

"Nope," the Sheriff shook his head. "Checked the flyers at the jail. Got nothing to arrest him for. But unless you want every two-bit punk with a gun and an itch to make his reputation swarming into your saloon to kill a famous shootist when he's flat on his back, we'd best keep our cards held tight and our mouths shut."

Warner thought about that for a second or two, gulping down another shot of the Sheriff's high-end whiskey, weighing the threat of violence against the increase in business.

"You might be right about that," Warner admitted, having no wish to catch a stray bullet.

"I am, Jim, believe me," Scales nodded sagely. "Seen it before. Word gets out, and the town'll be flush with low-life pistolerios who'd be pleased to notch Jake Johnson onto their gun handles."

The piano player was making a mess of some song, as he usually did late in the day, before he'd slept off the afternoon beer. Sheriff Scales winked at Sweet Kate, who was greasing the faro table with smiles and encouragement, urging on a few drunken cowboys who had gotten paid early.

"Well, let's go see who this fellow is, with the nerve to be traveling about on Jake Johnson's horse," Scales grinned, quietly checking his Colt before walking up the stairs.

"Slim's got him on a pretty strong dose of laudanum," Warner said, helpfully. "And we put his guns in the bureau. You know, just so nobody gets accidently shot."

"You're charitable and wise," Scales nodded. "I'd sure hate to shoot a man on his deathbed."

But even as he said that, Warner noticed that the Sheriff had his Colt in his hand, as he climbed the stairs and knocked on the upstairs door.

"Jenna's probably with him," Warner said from the bottom of the stairs, with a fair amount of irritation.

The door opened and Big Jenna peered out.

"He's asleep," she whispered, then noticed the caller was the Sheriff.

"I just need to see him, Miss Jenna," Scales said politely.

The fact that he was kind to all the Upstairs Girls earned the Sheriff 'extras' it was said. Free 'extras', Jim Warner often thought, arguing constantly with the Town Council that the Sheriff's excessive appetites, when it came to whiskey and women, should be a part of Rockville's budget. An argument that always fell on deaf ears, much to the saloon keeper's chagrin. Warner conveniently forgetting that he had agreed to the terms, in lue of cash payments to the lawman's upkeep. But who knew the man would be prone to drink and fuck so much?

"You're not gonna shoot him?" Jenna's eyes got wide as her famous hips.

"No, ma'am," the Sheriff said quietly. Though not yet holstering his weapon, Warner noted, coming to the top of the landing. Scales entered the room, studying the unconscious man, who lay under the sheets, a heavy quilt tucked around his shoulders.

Apparently hearing the sounds at the door, the man's eyes flickered open. He blinked, glanced around, obviously trying to clear his vision.

"I think we'll need a minute or two alone," Scales said, nodding toward Warner, who led a mildly protesting Jenna into the hall. Scales closed the door behind them, pulled a chair over to the bed, resting the Colt on his leg. The man seemed to be able to focus his eyes enough to see the star on Scales' vest.

"Can you hear me, mister?" Scales asked, his tone not unsympathetic at the fallen shootist's plight. The man nodded. "I'm the Sheriff, Owen Scales, and I know who you are, Mr. Johnson."

The wounded man closed his eyes briefly and seemed to sigh. Beneath the quilt, Scales saw Johnson's right hand twitch involuntarily, searching for guns that were not there.

"You've nothing to fear from me," Scales said amiably. "I'm an admirer of yours, truth be told. Saw you kill those three men in Abilene a few years back."

In fact, Owen Scales, who was not yet a lawman, had almost involved himself on Jake Johnson's side in the legendary gunfight in Abilene, in which Johnson had faced three men in that cow town's dusty street. Scales had thought the odds to be grossly unfair, but before he could react - Bang, Bang, Bang! The three would-be killers were dead, just that quick, Scales recalled. Bang, Bang, Bang! Their guns were out; two had managed to get a shot off, before Jake Johnson dispatched the three of them with his Winchester. As easily as shooting cans off a fence post. Scales thought then, as he did to this day, that he had never seen a man so cool and calm under fire. Even as the three gunmen had called Johnson out, cursing him for collecting a dead-man bounty on one of their relatives, Jake Johnson had calmly walked to his horse, pulled the Winchester from its scabbard, walked a bit further away from the men and their pistols, and proceeded to shoot them all dead. Bang, Bang, Bang! His legend grew expediently, as he put the rifle back, unbuckled his gun belt and calmly surrendered to an extremely nervous Deputy Sheriff. Since he had killed three men who had already drawn their guns on him, no jury in the world was ever going to convict him of anything but self-defense, so he rode out of Abilene the next day, although he surely could have hung around and collected free drinks at the saloons for days, maybe weeks, Scales considered.

"There's no warrants on you in this part of the country," Scales said, almost pleasantly. "So in my mind, you're free to get well or die in peace. We'll do our best to keep your presence here and your unfortunate condition quiet. All I ask is, if you do recover, you ride out of my town as soon as you're able.   And if you do die, I promise you a nice, dignified funeral."

Owen Scales smiled, believing he had delivered a fine speech, offering what comfort he could to an obviously dying man.   Jake Johnson was as pale as the pillow case on which his head rested.   The stains on the barroom floor and on the sidewalk outside the Silver Strike, testified to the massive amount of blood the bounty hunter had lost.   And God only knew how far Johnson had ridden after he had taken the bullet. Owen was curious as to the nature of that encounter, but Johnson seemed in no condition to discuss the matter.

"Are we in agreement, then?" Scales smiled, and the man nodded, or maybe passed out.   Scales couldn't tell.

But just to be safe the Sheriff went to the bureau and collected Jake Johnson's guns before leaving.   An old Colt single-action, wrapped in its holster, the Winchester rifle leaned up in a corner by the wash basin.   No sense in taking any chances, Scales thought to himself, knowing that the weapons could be auctioned off to cover the burial expenses, with a goodly sum left over, he considered with some satisfaction.

"Take good care of him, Miss Jenna," Scales said pleasantly, as he left.   Jim Warner, who had his eyes on the guns himself, frowned, but couldn't bring himself to say anything.   "Relax Jim, you can sell the man's horse if he dies," Scales grinned good-naturedly.

"Yeah, like anybody's likely to buy that drunk ass animal," Warner growled.

Scales laughed, thinking he might play a little faro with Kate, to celebrate his encounter with such a famous shootist, especially with the man's guns in hand. Bang, Bang, Bang! He hefted the Winchester that had taken down the three gunslingers in Abilene, trying to guess what a weapon like this might bring.

CHAPTER THREE

Cherokee Creek

The dappled grey picked its way carefully down the muddy street, placing its feet as if uncertain what hidden objects or sinkholes might lay beneath the muck. The man, sitting high atop the big grey could not fault the animal. Behind them, the pack mule followed in the horse's footsteps demurely, almost as if it understood that in the event of a sinkhole, horse and rider would be the first to disappear. The mule, the man had long ago decided, was not as dumb as it appeared.

Other animals, apparently used to the soupy path that passed for the main thoroughfare in this shantytown at the edge of nowhere, lumbered by, pulling their wagon loads of supplies, carrying men who seemed to be in a great hurry to get someplace other than here. It was a chaotic place, full of noise and activity, which attacked the man's senses, more used to the quiet solitude of the plains and the mountains, the shadows of which could be seen on the far western horizon. Dogs barked, children ran along the planked sidewalks between the store fronts and saloons, pigs staked out their claims to garbage in the alley ways. Bonneted women walked with their eyes front and their chins set, carrying baskets of goods, past the piano music, the shouts, squeals and general mayhem of the saloons and gambling dens. Scantily clad women, looking provocative, if none too clean, posed and waved from doorways, displaying themselves to prospective customers, including the man on the big grey. He nodded back, touching the brim of his old slough cap. In fact, he was a prospective customer and planned on working his way through as many of the wayward women as possible during the next few days.

More than the whores were noticing him now. Boys were stopping to point, men in frock coats and small brimmed hats were frowning in his direction. He wore fringed buckskin in a time when most men favored factory cloth, or at worst homespun. His beard was long and unkept, as was his hair, both once black, now touched with grey. And he was the sort of man who looked disagreeable, even when he was not. Others, carrying side arms, were glancing at him as he passed, gauging the extent of his threat to their own person. It was a thing he had grown used to over the years. While it was true that other men often saw him as a threat, he was not...unless provoked. And the men who saw him in this light were not innocent, as it was often pointed out to him by his few friends and acquaintances. If provoked, he was not just a threat, he was death incarnate. Other men, mostly fearful men, sensed this somehow...and yet, many of them still provoked him, for reasons Daniel McCanty never did understand.

He nudged the horse into a structure loosely labeled Livery Stable. There he swung off the grey with an easy grace that belied his age. McCanty stood a shade over six foot, but thick through the chest and shoulders, making him seem even bigger. It was also true that his shoulders were stooped a little, his waist thicker than it used to be. He slapped the dust out of his slouch hat, which in appearance was almost as old as the man himself. The livery man blinked his rheumy eyes and stood up from a rickety looking chair by the stable doors.

"Help you?" the man asked, looking upward, blinking as if peering into the branches of a tall tree.

"You got any thieves in this here town?" McCanty asked, deciding not to berate the fellow for his foolish question.

"Thick as fleas on a dog," the livery man allowed, watching as the big fellow uncinched the horse's saddle and pulled a heavy Sharps rifle from the fringed saddle scabbard. Must be a buffalo hunter, the livery man guessed. He was about to ask, but then thought better of it. There were rumors about, and it behooved a man to keep his nose where it belonged.

"Think you can keep 'em from stealing my horse and mule for a couple of days?"

At that, the fellow grinned and nodded.

"They could use a good feed and a rubdown," McCanty said. "You got a boy to do that?"

"Do it myself," the livery man hitched up his pants and spat a stream of tobacco into the dirt. "Two dollars for two days...apiece," he said, sounding as if he was digging in his heels at the price.

"Didn't expect you to do it as a favor," the grizzled old hunter growled a little at the insinuation, opening his pouch, flipping the livery man a five dollar gold piece. "My mule will guard the packs and saddle in the stall with him. It would do to be cautious around that critter. He is not an overly friendly animal."

"Yes sir!" the livery man winked, realizing the old fellow was not some poor panner, who might try and sneak back to steal his animals after losing his stake to the card hustlers at Flanagan's Saloon. There were enough of them in town these days.

Deciding not to inquire about the man's profession, the livery man turned his attention to the horse and mule, subjects about which he was more familiar, anyway. "What's this big fellow called?" he asked, rubbing the horse's neck affectionately.

"The horse is called *Wiconi,* which is Sioux for ghost, on account of his color," McCanty said.

Indeed, the shadowy white along the animal's side did look kind of ghostly, the stable man allowed.

"Mule got a name?" he asked. The mule was a black, slick-skinned animal. Heavy and big boned, but not overly tall. It had long, rabbit-like ears, and a face that reminded McCanty of a large, oversized boot. It was a functional beast, but far from aesthetically pleasing.

"Probably," McCanty said, glancing at the animal. "But he ain't mentioned it yet."

At that, the livery man blinked, not knowing whether to laugh or not. The rough man's eyes told him not.

"Where can I get me a room and a bath?"

The livery man pointed out the hotel, thinking that the bath was not a bad idea. The old fellow smelled like he had been on the trail for a while, although the livery man was not about to suggest such a thing. He watched as the stranger shouldered his pack, the Sharps cradled into the crook of his arm. He thought: There is a man who is on a first name basis with trouble.

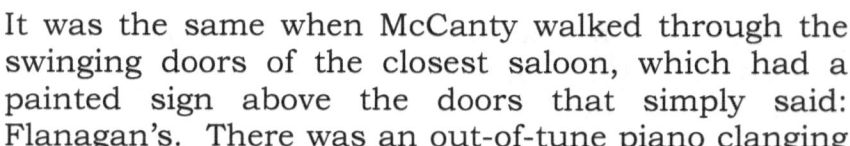

It was the same when McCanty walked through the swinging doors of the closest saloon, which had a painted sign above the doors that simply said: Flanagan's. There was an out-of-tune piano clanging some song, which the bar girls seemed to enjoy singing along with. There was a roulette wheel...rigged, no doubt. Men were drinking at a long plank bar, the usual tables and chairs spread haphazardly about the place, at which dubious card games were in process.

It was, for a Saturday afternoon, a pretty lively place, McCanty allowed, shouldering his way to the bar with his Sharps in hand. Many of the men, he noted, were armed with a variety of handguns. Colt, along with Smith & Wesson and others, provided weapons in such quantities these days that every cowboy and pretend outlaw went about armed. The music hesitated when the swinging doors snapped shut behind him. Men stared, the bar girls glanced in his direction...and he ignored them all, as he usually did, pushing his way to the plank bar. Which, surprisingly, had a three foot mirror behind it, mimicking the big city bars of St. Louis and the railhead cattle towns like Dodge and Abilene. Behind him, in slow, rolling waves, the music and the sound of the saloon regained its volume.

He was an anomaly, he knew, but not such as would halt the afternoon proceedings for very long. A bartender, in a semi-clean shirt and apron, came and pretended to wipe a clean spot for him on the plank bar.

"Whiskey," McCanty said, swinging the Sharps to stand at attention along the length of his leg.

The bartender nodded and poured, once coins appeared from a fringed pouch. The whiskey, not terrible, much to his surprise, burned on the way down, exactly as he imagined it would during the weeks of travel. He gulped the first one, planning to enjoy the second one slowly, when a voice rose above the piano music.

"I have smelled such a stink from dead horses," the voice said, loudly, so everyone at his table could hear. "But never from a standing up, alive man..."

McCanty closed his eyes for a moment, sighed again, and looked into the bar mirror, seeing what appeared to be a middle aged cowhand, lean and narrow, tilt his hat back, staring at him over a hand of cards. The other men at the table chuckled nervously. His tormentor's eyes were hard and dark. Not a cowhand, either, his black clothing just a touch too fancy. And not someone other men trifled with...much like himself, McCanty thought absently.

"I am surprised no one has cut such a harsh tongue out of your head," he growled. And this time the piano music stopped, the bar girls stepped into the corners of the room, and men began to push away from the tables.

The man at the card table dropped his hands lower, beneath the table.

"Injins tried to cut my dick off once," he said, in a voice that was at once a taunt and a snarl. "They couldn't find a knife big enough."

At that, men were scattering. The bartender was edging toward a sawed-off shotgun kept beneath the dish rags for just such an emergency, although the bartender was hesitant to get between two such obviously dangerous opponents...until he saw the ghost of a smile appear on the fringed man's bearded face.

"You been bragging about that thing for years," the big fellow scoffed, staring into the mirror's reflection. "How you been, John Bullis?"

Realizing the joke, men and women sighed in relief. The dark man at the card table laughed and wandered over, reaching up, slapping the rough older man on the shoulder, dust rising from the fringed clothing.

"Pretty fair, ol' hoss," John Bullis said, loudly enough so everyone could be in on the ruse. "Ladies and gents, this here's Daniel McCanty, a genuine, fire-breathing mountain man! Led wagon trains up the Oregon Trail. Traveled this country when there wasn't another white man for a thousand miles."

McCanty, embarrassed at the attention, nodded at the crowd's approval. The Trail was an arduous twenty-two hundred mile journey from Independence, Missouri to the fertile farming grounds of the Oregon Territory, usually made by families in covered wagons. A man who led such a journey in the days before the railroad was looked upon as something of a hero in western towns. His sometimes friend and drinking companion, the gambler and shootist, Jonathan Bullis, who understood McCanty's reluctant hero status, laughed and ordered drinks for them, reaching up to put an arm across the man's dusty shoulders.

"You do kinda smell like a dead horse," Bullis whispered, the stench rising from his friend, watering his eyes. And Bullis was not known as a man who was particularly sensitive about such things.

"I know," McCanty said, frowning himself. "Been on the trail a while. Was about to get a room and a bath, but thought a drink might help the bath go down easier. Anyway, figured I was more thirsty than dirty."

"You must have a powerful thirst," Bullis observed. He waved to the bartender. "Better bring my old friend a couple more drinks!"

At which everyone, including the ripe mountain man, laughed uproariously...

"They sure do make enough racket," McCanty blinked into the bright light of morning. Too bright, he thought, shaking his head, still half-drunk from the night. He had never made it back to Flanagan's Saloon, thanks to a willing wash girl and a bottle of whiskey sold to him by the hotel's desk clerk. Who, he also suspected, sold him the girl, as well. He couldn't remember, exactly. But that was his weakness, his vice... whiskey and whores. And if you're going to indulge, you had to be prepared to pay the price.

The whole town of Cherokee Creek seemed to be filled with the sounds of hammering and sawing. In fact, it was, he saw. Buildings being thrown up as quickly as the lumber could be brought down from the mills. This place was the true meaning of the term Boom Town. The question was, would all this be here in another year or two? Or would it be inhabited by tumbleweeds and coyotes? The townspeople were obviously betting that the good times would last. That roads would be cut across the prairie, maybe even a rail head to ship ore and cattle back east. Odds were generally against all that, but the building went on relentlessly. Human beings were like ants, McCanty thought absently, building their colonies ever outward from the main hive, spreading across the land like a swarm. Thoughts he did not share with John Bullis, a man already suspicious of the roads McCanty's mind traveled down. But at least the muddy soup of a main street looked dryer in the early morning light.

"They are industrious in these parts," Bullis acknowledged with a chuckle. He, too, had seen the remnants of such deserted places when the human swarm moved on.

"And that's a gallows those boys are hammering together?" McCanty asked.

"It is, indeed," Bullis nodded, stopping to light one of the cheroots he favored. "Had me a potentially close encounter with that Rufus Gates fellow just before you come into town." McCanty raised his eyebrows at the story. In truth, it was not unexpected that John Bullis would end up on the wrong end of a rope eventually. The two men had finished breakfast at the hotel and were passing time before the saloons opened. "Instead of me, they're gonna hang an outlaw by the name of Kaleb Lee."

"Wait...ain't it Sunday?" McCanty asked, hoping that in his drunkenness he hadn't missed a day. That had happened a time or two in the past.

"It's Sunday," Bullis chuckled again, reading his friend's concern. "The hanging is Wednesday. That's in three days, in case you lose track."

"Didn't lose track," McCanty growled at the suggestion. "Just forgot to go to church, is all."

"There's still time, I believe," Bullis made a show of checking his pocket watch. "The miners and the cow hands are not early risers after their Saturday night debauchery. But they do have plenty of sins to rid themselves of, so the preachers are a little lax on the timeframe for morning services. Did you sin heavily with that washer girl last night?"

"Might have," McCanty admitted, watching the carpenters throw together their gallows. "What'd Kaleb Lee do to deserve a trip up them stairs...which look none too sturdy, mind you."

"I doubt Kaleb will care much," Bullis said, grinning. "He only has to get up the steps. The trip down will take care of itself. I do believe there's a reason that particular carpentering crew ain't working on one of the merchant buildings. They were in the process of closing Flanagan's last night, when I left in the wee hours. But to answer your question, Kaleb and his brother, Dirk, got caught doing some cattle rustling."

McCanty winced. "Might have done a little of that myself, from time to time," he admitted.

"Ain't we all," Bullis commented, drawing on his cheroot. "The trick is not to get caught with dead men's cows, especially if you happened to kill the rancher and his two sons. Brother Dirk had the good sense not to survive the encounter with the posse that tracked them down. Kaleb made the mistake of surrendering."

"I guess," McCanty said, blinking again into the bright sun. "What time does that damn saloon open?"

"'Bout now, I'm guessing," Bullis stepped on the end of his cheroot, leading the way around the still muddy parts of the street. "You do smell a might better than yesterday," Bullis said over his shoulder.

McCanty grunted, sounding a lot like the pigs that were fighting one another over garbage in the alleyways. The whores, recovering from the rigors of a Saturday night, stretched and rolled their necks on the second story balconies. The pious and sinful answered the call of church bells. The wicked continued their forlorn trek through life. McCanty included himself in the latter group.

McCanty followed, as Bullis led the way to Flanagan's, stepping carefully, trying to keep his Spanish boots clean. He was tall and lean, dressed mostly in black, except for the silver inlay on his holster and a wide brimmed, tan Stetson. Bullis might walk like a dandy, McCanty thought, but knew it would be a mistake to consider him such. The man was quick with both his fists and his Colt. Although Bullis often said that it was not quickness that counted in a gunfight, as much as accuracy and steady nerves.

"There's many a man who pulled his gun first and ended up dead," Bullis was fond of saying, and those listening knew that not a few such men had died standing in front of Jonathan Bullis. "The first shot has to be a center shot." And he would touch his chest to make his point. "If the first shot is accurate, there'll be no need for a second."

McCanty, who had seen his fair share of gunfights, doubted the accuracy of the statement, but was not so impolite to discredit his friend, or so rude as to ruin a good story. But the truth was men like Bullis, who were fast and accurate, were by far the exception. McCanty had seen the high drama of a street showdown end when both the participants ran out of bullets without hitting anything. There was a reason that by-standers scattered when guns were drawn, since a man was more likely to be hit by a stray shot, than by anything fired with serious intent.

The same was not true for his own weapon of choice, the .50 caliber Sharps. Many of his acquaintance preferred the lighter .45 Sharps. A fine weapon, to be sure, but without the range of the .50 caliber, plus McCanty felt the Big Fifty was more accurate. It was true that Mr. Colt's handguns, and those of his competitors like Mr. Wesson and Mr. Smith, were indeed lethal weapons in the right hands...although their range was limited. And yes,

John Bullis and Wild Bill could shoot silver dollars out of the air with them. Hickok and Bullis and a handful of others could kill men quickly and efficiently within that fifty-to-seventy yard range. But if you were standing at the far end of the street, both Hickok and Bullis could fire their pistols at you all day, until their arms got tired, and not have a hope of hitting you. With the Sharps...well, McCanty could shoot the buttons off your vest, if you'd care to stand still for it. He could put one of the heavy slugs into your chest, whether you stood still for it, or not. And he would never be so foolish as to allow either Hickok or even Bullis to pull their weapon on him at close range. Or anyone else who fancied himself a gunman, for that matter. Even though McCanty knew, as did Bullis and Wild Bill, that many fancied themselves in such a light, but few could stand the scrutiny.

McCanty knew his fighting distance with firearms to be measured at four to five hundred yards. If he could put the Sharp sights on you at that range, they could start digging the hole for your remains. But McCanty could be equally deadly at arm's length. The knife he carried at his side, called an Arkansas Toothpick or Bowie knife by some, could be in his hand in an instant. Literally, in the blink of a man's eye. A foot of steel, razor sharp, and lethal as a scorpion. It could be driven into a man's chest, splitting heart and lungs in a single thrust...or it could gut a man, stem to stern, in a single heartbeat. Every man who came within Dan McCanty's eagle-like wingspan was subject to that thrust. Some knew it instinctively, and stepped back. Some didn't, until their friends pulled them away...everyone smiling at what didn't happen in the presence of a truly dangerous man.

McCanty never consciously thought of himself in such terms. True, he was careful about those who he allowed close to him...except for whores, of course. But they were his weakness. He supposed, when he thought about it, many a whore could have killed him whenever she wanted to. Either for revenge...there were some twenty men who had sisters, lovers, nieces or even mothers who might want him dead. Or simply some degraded woman who might be tired of the harshness of life. But he never really believed that would happen. In his heart, McCanty could not convince himself that the things you loved...in his case, whiskey and whores...would ever be so unkind as to kill you. Well, perhaps the whiskey might, as he had seen it wear down and end the lives of many a man. But he knew he was right about the whores, who loved him for his generosity and his genuine feel for them as people. Whores, in McCanty's mind, were the most honest kind of people. They loved you for money and made no excuses for their behavior. While it was true that a banker or a lawyer was the same sort of person, McCanty understood that they were harder to fuck. Whores and whiskey made him happy, and he himself made no excuses for his behavior. The whores understood him. He had yet to meet a banker or a lawyer who did. Although in fairness, he did know a far greater number of whores.

John Bullis, on the other hand, was under no such delusions. Several whores had, in fact, tried to kill him, one or two coming close to succeeding. These events usually the result of promises made, but unfortunately not kept. And most often, his fault, Bullis admitted. Issues of trust, he called them, both he and the whores being difficult to trust. Bullis did, however, trust McCanty to a certain extent...as much as he trusted anyone, he supposed. As a shootist, Bullis respected McCanty's skill, although it had to be admitted that when the two met up, strong drink flowed like water in spring and they were usually too drunk to shoot at anything accurately.

To Bullis, there was something unaccountably strange about Daniel McCanty. A hunter and trapper who carried books in his mule pack...and actually read them! McCanty seemed to know what he was doing all the time, even when drunk. Bullis realized that he himself did not. That he lurched from one troubling incident to the next, without proper regard or thought. Bullis understood that this was a dangerous way to live and wanted to ask the book-reading frontiersman if there was some particular secret to life. Something that he could hold onto during times of strife and confusion. Something that would help explain all the madness and chaos Bullis seemed to encounter. But he was afraid to expose himself to ridicule. Or worse, have McCanty tell him that: "Yes, there was a secret to life, but you had to find it out for yourself." Bullis figured he might have to shoot someone who told him that.

CHAPTER FOUR

Rockville

The good times ended for Owen Scales two days later, when the first bad man rode into town. Not that bad men were unusual in Rockville, but the Sheriff saw right off that this one was different. Hardly more than a kid, Scales thought, watching him ride into town. Sporting a thin mustache and a sneer to make himself look older. A wide hat pulled low and clothes too new and clean for a cowhand. Riding a sorrel horse, with a Mexican saddle. Much too fancy for a working cowboy, Scales concluded.

And when the stranger dismounted in front of the Silver Strike, the Sheriff knew for sure that this was a bad man. His gun hung low on his hip, tied down at the thigh; the kid's eyes as he checked the street were cold and hard. A young killer on the drift.

"Looks like we got us some trouble," Owen Scales grumbled to his deputy, Skeet Miller.

Skeet was thirty, going on fifty. Slow moving and sparse with his words, Scales thought his deputy was working at being an old man, and he was getting pretty good at it, too. Skeet smoked three-cent cheroots, visited the Upstairs Girls once a week; but never with Kate, by unspoken agreement with his boss. He carried an old Navy Colt and slept in the jail's storage room in summer, moving his cot out by the stove in winter. Skeet also made his own whiskey in a still out back of the jail house. Hearing the news, Skeet abruptly decided that this was a good time to sweep out the jail and make sure last night's drunks were sober enough for release.

It was a little past noon, the sun high and bright, the wind had thankfully died down, the sand settled into everything. It would be a hot one, Owen thought casually, rolling a cigarette, smoking it quietly in the shade of the jail's awning. He tipped back in his chair, put his boots up on the rail and allowed himself a few minutes of peace and quiet, as he kept his eyes and ears on the swinging doors of the Silver Strike. Experience taught him that it was better to go into these kinds of situations as calm as possible. He knew he didn't possess that sort of natural fearlessness that men like Jake Johnson seemed to come by so easily. Not that he would ever let anyone know he had moments of fear. That wouldn't do at all. A Marshall in Tombstone once told him: Any man who tells you he isn't afraid of gunplay is either lying or downright foolish. He had wanted to believe that, especially after sneaking off into an alley and emptying his stomach the first time he'd shot a man in the line of duty. He had believed it, in fact, before seeing men like Holiday, Hickok, and Jake Johnson look calmly down the barrel of someone else's gun. Men who he knew were not foolish, although Wild Bill was a notorious liar. But they all had one thing in common — they had ice in their veins when it was time to act. A quality Owen Scales knew he did not possess. But he worked at it over the years, allowing his muscles to relax, his breathing to steady. No one could call him a coward, certainly, and he had killed a man or two in his time, but he had never liked it, and he hoped he wouldn't have to kill the young gunslinger. Hoped the kid, who surely looked dangerous, hadn't come to town in search of Jake Johnson.

Then Billy Jolin, the young bar sweep at the Silver Strike, came running across the street, and Scales sighed, knowing...

"Mr. Warner says you should come right away," Jolin panted.

Scales nodded, took a last drag on his cigarette, tipped his chair back down.

"Maybe you should stay here with Skeet," the Sheriff said calmly. "See if he needs any help sweeping out the cells."

Billy Jolin glanced over his shoulder at the saloon and nodded. The boy showed uncommon good sense, Scales thought, going inside the jail, picking a double-barreled ten gauge from the rifle rack, rummaging around in his desk for a handful of shells. Another thing experience had taught him — if you're heading into a gunfight, bring enough guns. He shoved two big shells into the twin breaches, checked the loads on his Colt, and shouted to Skeet to keep an eye on Billy Jolin for a few minutes.

Dust rose under his boots, like a thin covering of snow in the wake of the sandstorm. A buckboard of timber passed by, heading down to the new construction at the end of Main Street, where buildings were shooting up, replacing the canvas tents from which new arrivals sold their goods to the miners. This town might find itself on the map someday, he thought absently, especially if the rumors on the richness of the silver strike played true. The railroad was pushing its way west, and the Town Council was already writing letters, sending representatives with money to bribe the Rail Barons. There was talk of a new school house, and a permanent church was being built down the street.

Yes, Rockville might have a future, Scales thought, standing for a moment at the swinging doors of the Silver Strike Saloon...and he planned to be around to see it.

The piano player was banging away. The faro table was crowded for three o'clock on a Friday afternoon. Cowboys from the Fall River Cattle Company were starting their weekend binge early. The Upstairs Girls were circulating through the crowd, flirting shamelessly. Sara, thin, wall-eyed, not the prettiest, but she was said to be enthusiastic about her work, and so was a favorite among the cowboys. Jenna and beside her, Lizzie, a beautiful Spanish girl with dark hair and eyes, who made all the young cowboys and miners fall in love with her. Little Anne, with her blonde hair, a tiny sparrow of a girl. It hardly seemed possible that she was old enough to be a working whore, although she had a paper proving her age to be nineteen. Jim Warner doubted that, but you couldn't argue with an official paper, he knew. Besides, when she was in the mood to do so, Little Anne could sing like a canary. Drunken cowboys and miners showered her with money, just to hear her sing a sad ballad, Owen Scales among them. Warner, pushing beer and whiskey through the smoky haze of the room, caught his eye, glanced toward the faro table, where the gun toting stranger was laughing, trying to pull Sweet Kate onto his lap.

"He was asking if Jake Johnson was around," Warner said quietly. Scales raised an eyebrow. "Told him I didn't know the man," Warner shrugged.

The kid glanced up, saw Scales with his shotgun and badge, and sneered once before looking away, laughing too loud and too long at Kate's hesitation to camp out on his knee. Kate saw Owen coming and backed away, shaking her head in the Sheriff's direction. Of course, she was an Upstairs Girl, and certainly not Owen Scales' personal property, but the kid's hands on her infuriated him somehow. As he neared the faro table, the kid stopped laughing and pretended to concentrate on the dealer's cards. His right hand, Scales noted, strayed near his low slung gun, one of Sam Colt's new .45 center fire repeaters. The fact that it cost seventeen dollars new, also stuck in Scales' craw. A week's salary.

"You want something from me, mister?" the kid asked, keeping his eyes on the faro table, his tone suggesting that he did not care to be interfered with. This one had an itchy hand, Scales knew. He warned Kate back to the bar with a glance.

"I'm the Sheriff here and I'm asking who you are, and what your business is in Rockville," Scales growled, returning the kid's surly tone.

"My business ain't none of yours," he said, eyes turning now to meet the Sheriff. Cold, dark eyes, Scales saw. With a depth and meanness to them that was more reptile than human. Scales wondered for a moment if the kid was afraid, or was he one of those ice men who could kill, then continue on drinking and gambling with hardly a passing thought. Didn't matter, Scales considered, quickly deciding he wasn't going to give this one any second chances.

"I'm saying it is my business," Scales growled. "And you best put your hands on the table...now!"

Grinning, the kid did as he was told.

"This now you treat strangers in these parts?" the kid asked flippantly, looking around to see if any other guns were trained on him. "Not very neighborly, if you ask me..."

"I didn't ask you," Scales said, raising the tone of his voice. "I asked you your business here."

"Name's Billy Grimes, and I'm just passing through," the kid said, into the sudden silence that overtook the Silver Strike, as the piano player fled to the relative safety of the bar, and the faro dealer pushed away from the table. The Grimes family was a well-known bunch of rustlers, thieves and guns-for-hire. "Thought I'd have a drink to wash down the dust, gamble a little, and maybe roll around with the whores a bit."

"Well, Billy Grimes, you had your drink and you gambled a little," Scales said, forcing a smile he didn't mean. The Grimes were trouble, he knew. They had a pack mentality...fight one, and you fought them all. "I'm pretty sure there's whores in the next town down the line. I'd suggest you get on your horse and go visit them."

The kid chuckled, cold and harsh, like a stream freezing over in winter. He got slowly to his feet, and Owen took a step back to keep the distance between them. At that, Billy Grimes laughed a little deeper.

"You think I'm afraid of some old man with a big popgun?" he snarled. "That badge don't make you God, you know. I ain't done a thing wrong, and I believe I'll leave your little shithole town when I'm goddamn good and ready..."

Scales stepped forward and swung the butt of the ten gauge at the kid's head. So quick and unexpected, the kid hardly had time to put his hand on the handle of his Colt. The blow landed with a sickening crunch and the gunman went down, spitting blood, trying to shout, but he seemed to have trouble working his jaw. He could only gasp with gurgling sound, as his mouth filled with blood. Still, his hand jerked the Colt out of its holster, but Scales was on him, knocking the gun away with the barrel of the ten gauge. He stepped on the kid's gun hand, grinding it cruelly under his boot heel. The kid managed a scream, as Scales kicked at the fallen man's ribs until he was sure he had broken at least one or two. Kate had covered her mouth, horrified at the level of violence, the other Upstairs Girls were screaming, men were shouting. Jim Warner was coming around the bar, no doubt to try and stop the assault before Scales killed the man.

"What do you think? You afraid of me now?" Scales shouted at the writhing figure under his boot. "You think you might be goddamned good and ready to leave now?"

Disgusted, Scales stepped back, pointing at two nearby cowboys.

"You two drag him out and tie him on his horse," Scales ordered. "Ride him to the edge of town and make sure his animal's got a running head start out of here! Go on, get to it!"

The cowboys jumped to carry out their instructions, dragging the moaning kid across the saloon floor. The rage leaving him, Scales shook his head, stepped over a pool of blood, turning toward a startled Jim Warner.

"Who'd you tell?" Scales asked quietly, but still with a good deal of menace in his voice.

Warner tried not to look guilty, silently cursing that drunken Doc Watson, who had come to tend the wounded man in the upstairs bed.

"It was just Doc," Warner said meekly. "I figured he should know."

"Son-of-a-bitch," Scales whispered, shaking his head. "Well, I'll be goddamned if I let one of those pissant gunslingers shoot me! Put the word out, have the Upstairs Girls tell their cowboys and miners:

Anybody comes to Rockville with bad intentions, this is what they'll get!"

Warner nodded, as Owen Scales turned and walked unmindful through the blood and sawdust, slamming past the swinging doors of the Silver Strike, leaving behind startled whispers and the beginnings of a potentially deadly rumor. Jim Warner doubted the Grimes family would simply let this go.

"I can't protect you here, Mr. Johnson," Owen Scales felt some consternation at that admission, as if it was somehow a mark against him as Sheriff. It had been a week since the young gunslinger had been dragged out of the saloon and put on his horse. Rumors were flying fast and furious. A band of gunmen were supposedly riding up from Texas, kin to the three men Jake Johnson had killed in Abilene. There was also word that the brothers of the kid Scales had assaulted were on their way to Rockville. Although, admittedly, they were looking for the man who had savaged their younger sibling.

"Don't recall asking you to protect me," Jake Johnson grumbled, now sitting up in bed, feeding himself soup.

That was a fair point, Scales considered, eying the supposedly direly wounded man. Doc Watson hadn't given him much chance of recovering.

"The man was treated by a barber, after all," Doc Watson had said, dismissively.

But Johnson seemed better every day. It didn't look like he was going to die anytime soon, providing someone didn't show up to shoot him again.

"Why don't you just bring me back my guns, and let me do my own protecting?" Johnson said.

The request was a reasonable one, Scales knew, but still he was hesitant to arm such a notorious man.

"I don't want a lot of unnecessary killing in my town," Scales replied, more sharply than he intended.

"I have never killed anyone unnecessarily," Johnson's eyes seemed to blaze at the suggestion.

"I'm not saying you did," Scales shook his head.

"Seemed like it," Johnson snarled a little, and Scales thought he caught a glimpse of how truly dangerous the man could be. But Scales had the feeling he was, perhaps, being somewhat unreasonable. It was unlikely, after all, that the man could get out of bed by himself, and he was certainly a sitting duck if anyone with bad intentions made it upstairs.

"I'll bring your revolver back with me," Scales relented, offering a smile.

"And I'll try to keep the killing to a bare minimum," Johnson replied coldly.

"I didn't mean..." Scales began to apologize.

"Yes, you did," Johnson sighed, turning in the bed, trying to find a place that didn't hurt. "And I can't really blame you none. I never counted myself as a model citizen."

"I've got nothing against you, personally," Scales said.

Johnson nodded, closing his eyes against the pain, which the Sheriff thought must be considerable.

"When you bring the gun, tell the Upstairs Girls they're safe," Johnson's voice was little more than a hoarse whisper. "I promise not to shoot any of them."

Scales chuckled at the joke.

"And I'll be on my way soon as I can get on my horse," Johnson said quietly.

"When you're healed," Scales said, amiably. Curious, he decided to press the issue. "So, what happened, anyway?"

"Don't rightly know," Johnson shrugged. "These two fellows must've figured I was an easy target when they jumped me. I guess they figured right," he admitted, rubbing the thick bandage. "They sure got one into me pretty good."

"Did you get a look at them?"

"I did after I kilt 'em," Johnson growled. "Didn't recognize them as having warrants. Their horses had run off and I was gut shot. So I left the bastards where they fell. Likely farmers or Indians have the horses by now."

"Sounds like you were lucky," Scales commented.

The shootist nodded again, drifting off into a laudanum doze. Scales took the empty soup bowl and put it on the bed stand. Downstairs he stood at the bar, wondering what it must be like to be a famous gun hand. To have killed as many men as Jake Johnson, to have all their kin and any two-bit drifter with a five dollar gun looking to challenge you. It would make a man bitter, he decided.

"He ain't gonna die, is he?" Jim Warner came over and interrupted his thoughts.

"Someday he is," Scales said absently. "But probably not in Jenna's bed, unless somebody sneaks up and puts more holes in him than he's already got."

"Doubtful," Warner considered the possibilities. "The girls have taken a shine to him. They're pretty watchful. They make the cowboys check their guns at the bar before they'll take 'em upstairs."

"That so?" Scales said thoughtfully. "Well, I guess dangerous men have their attractions."

Jim Warner nodded and drew the Sheriff another beer. It went without saying that half the men in Rockville considered themselves dangerous, most without any good reason.

"Kate was asking after you," Warner said casually.

"Where is she?" Scales asked, looking around at the mostly empty saloon. The cowboys were out riding herd on their cattle, the miners digging or panning.

"Over at the seamstress," Warner said. "Some of the girls are having new dresses made."

One of the new businesses in town was run by a woman who drove a buckboard into Rockville with a sewing machine and bolts of Eastern material in the back. A sure sign of approaching civilization, Scales thought.

"Business must be good," he said, mostly just to say something.

"Not for Kate," Warner chuckled. "Don't think she's had a handful of customers since you beat the hell out of that kid."

Scales looked up from his beer.

"Appears you're considered a dangerous man these days," Warner nodded at him. "Nobody wants to cross you by taking your girl upstairs."

Owen Scales frowned, taking a moment to consider that statement. Wondering, on several levels, if it was a good thing, or bad.

"Well, shit," he shook his head, unable to decide. "Maybe I'd better go look her up, then..."

Jim Warner grinned to himself, washing glasses, wiping down his bar. There were few things more pitiful, in his mind, than a grown man with woman troubles. And Owen Scales had plenty of trouble, whether he knew it or not.

CHAPTER FIVE

Cherokee Creek

Visits into town...whatever town, however long the visit...were usually a blur of time and events to Dan McCanty. This particular visit was proving especially blurry, given the chance encounter with his occasional drinking companion, the gunman Jonathan Bullis.

Bullis was, like McCanty himself, an odd duck, although he doubted the gunman saw himself in that light. But McCanty did know that both believed the other man to be so. He also doubted that Bullis was aware of the fact that this was usually the case in any pairing of odd people. If you look around and see an odd person, chances are that he or she will be paired with another odd person, and none of them will consider themselves such. It was a thought that McCanty was just starting to come to terms with. This was almost certainly true of human beings, and may well prove so with other creatures. Experiments will have to be done. Theories tested, scientific papers written...or so Daniel McCanty thought, glancing down at the unconscious form of his sometime friend.

McCanty was awake, reading in a chair by the window light of his hotel room. A newspaper, the *National Republican*, laid folded and discarded on the floor at his feet. The paper regaled President Grant's scandalous administration, as if anything else could be expected by a man known throughout the South as Butcher Grant, McCanty thought bitterly. Of much greater interest was a book he had picked up on his last sojourn to St. Louis. It was a relatively new volume, *The Celebrated Jumping Frog of Calaveras County* by someone named Mark Twain. Reading, other than the Bible or the newspaper, was not considered a typical past time on the frontier, but McCanty was not bothered by what others thought...as long as they did not provoke him, of course.

Although, curiously, Bullis did so, almost constantly. Apparently friends, even if they were occasional friends, could provoke him without consequences, he thought, laughing quietly at the times Bullis had annoyed him with his churlish brand of human behavior. And, in truth, he annoyed the gunman as well, he knew. Bullis was known to shoot people who said the things McCanty said to him. And McCanty had violently engaged men for much less than what Bullis said or did at times. For some reason, McCanty considered, that was what friendship meant: You didn't kill the other person, no matter what they said. A curious, but apparently true dynamic.

McCanty chuckled at the thought, and at Twain, who also seemed to understand the churlish brand of human behavior. Bullis groaned, stirring in his sleep, instinctively reaching for his sidearm, which McCanty had prudently removed to avoid any unfortunate drunken accidents. Outside, the last minute hammering continued on Kaleb Lee's gallows.

It was mid-morning on Wednesday in the town of Cherokee Creek and Dan McCanty thought it was like the circus had come to set up their tents.   Main Street teemed with people.   Farmers with their families in wagons, buggies from God knew where, cowboys rode their horses up and down the through-fair, whooping like it was the Fourth of July. Gangs of wild young boys raced themselves along the plank walks between the stores, followed by barking dogs, which themselves seemed to take great delight in the boys' mischief, as they threw fire crackers beneath the feet of unsuspecting women and horses, and even startled the usually unflappable pigs, who owned the alleyways. The livery man came out and yelled at the boys for scattering his chickens, and Sheriff Cobb finally had to shoo the boys off to their mothers when the complaints got out of hand.

But they were soon back, McCanty noticed, this time finding fascination with the recently completed gallows, which stood ominously in the town square.   In truth, the gang of wayward boys were not the only ones drawn to the platform, with its crossbar and traditional thirteen steps. People milled about the structure, some with picnic baskets, as the city fathers had also put up a park bench, a band gazebo, and someone had done their civic duty by planting a shade tree, no doubt dug up from the nearby river bed. Although it had to be admitted that the shade tree, while undoubtedly a fine idea, was not exactly prospering in the sandy soil, away from its natural habitat. It looked straggly and forlorn, as trees go, but seemed oddly to fit the decor perfectly with the somewhat crooked, hastily constructed gallows.

"Nothing brings people out like a good hanging," Bullis observed, drawing on his cheroot, watching the crowd buzz with excitement, as the noontime hour approached, the time set for Kaleb Lee to be sent off into eternity.

"Good for business, I guess," Dan agreed. The town was busier than a Saturday night, with the miners streaming in on an undeclared holiday, and the cow hands apparently leaving their herds to their own devices.

"Them Lee brothers killed and robbed a lot in these parts," Bullis allowed.

"There's a lesson in that," McCanty said.

"Yeah, spread your crimes around," Bullis replied, dryly. "Do too much thieving and murdering in one place, and a mighty big crowd will come out to watch you swing."

McCanty chuckled, then told Bullis about Tyburn in England, where for centuries the condemned were treated to horrendous deaths, being drawn and quartered, after being hung and disemboweled and having their privates cut off and burned before their eyes.

"You are a fountain of information," Bullis said, raising an eyebrow. "Might read me a book yet, if you keep up with those tales."

"Everyone should read at least one book before they die," McCanty said seriously, even though he knew Bullis was joking with him.

At that moment, however, a hush settled over Main Street, and those in the saloons rushed out to crowd the town square, as the church bells tolled the midday hour. The door to the jail opened, Sheriff Cobb and two deputies led a trussed up man out the door and down the front steps. The crowd buzzed with excitement. Kaleb Lee kept his head down mostly, looking dirty and disheveled.

But occasional glances in the direction of the waiting gallows showed his nervousness. He wore plain homespun clothes, his hair long and hanging over his face. He was thin and of average height, this confirmed as the hangman, standing on top of the gallows' platform, strung the rope, measuring the noose to his own height. It did not look to McCanty that Kaleb Lee had ever read a book. And it was for sure too late now. The Sheriff, who nodded at a black frocked preacher about halfway to the gallows, might have. His eyes were bright and alert, anyway, so McCanty was comfortable giving him the benefit of the doubt. McCanty held a high opinion of a man he thought had read at least one book and was willing to believe the Sheriff might have. But McCanty did not count the Bible, which although being obvious propaganda, was clearly a requirement for anyone with the knowledge to read, so he was not able to credit the preacher with a read. Although the man did know his words, as he fell into the death procession at the tail end, reciting from the Good Book as he marched.

The deputies held Kaleb Lee's elbows as the condemned man walked up the thirteen steps, stumbling here and there, as a man in that inevitable situation was apt to do. It was one thing to rustle cattle, to shoot an innocent man and his son...it was quite another matter to stand up to the consequences of your actions, to pay the price in this world and to perhaps meet your Maker in the next, there to explain what you'd done. McCanty was not entirely convinced that was the case, but Kaleb Lee sure looked as though he believed. His eyes, raised now, confronted the noose and the hangman with obvious fear. His body trembled, supported by the deputies who pushed him forward to the edge of the gate-like platform.

The crowd, hissing and booing, catcalling at the man, grew quiet as the Sheriff read the charges and the sentence. In the background, the preacher droned on about God and absolution, no matter how terrible the crimes might be. McCanty was not convinced of that, either, although Lee seemed to take some solace from it, his spine stiffening, his shoulders shrugging off the deputies' hands, his eyes looking defiantly out at the crowd, whom he knew eagerly awaited his death.

"Any last words before sentence is imposed?" Sheriff Cobb asked, looking resplendent and dignified in his fresh white shirt and bolo tie.

Lee swallowed, blinked and nodded, stepping forward out onto the gate which was soon to swing downwards, ending his life.

"I'm sorry about the rancher and his boy!" Lee yelled. "My brother did the killing, not me..."

"You're gonna be sorry, Kaleb Lee!" A woman, thin and wild-eyed, shook off the restraining arm of a relative, and waved her fist in the direction of the murderer.

"Weren't me that killed your husband and boy!" Lee shouted again, even as the grieving widow was dragged back into the crowd.

At that, the crowd hooted some more. The gang of boys lit more firecrackers, startling Lee, who all but slipped off the platform. The crowd laughed, and the condemned man tried to regain his composure. "I didn't kill them people, but I'd sure as hell like the chance to kill the sons-of-bitches who are hanging me today!"

Kaleb Lee stamped his feet in anger. The Sheriff nodded, the hangman came forward and the deputies held Lee in place while the noose was slipped over his head. Lee fought, twisting his head this way and that, snarling his rage at the hangman, much to the mob's delight. When all was in readiness, when the hood had been drawn over Kaleb Lee's head, the preacher ramped up his praying, the crowd jeered and cheered, fathers held their children on their shoulders for the best possible view, women discreetly looked through their fingers. The hangman stepped back, Cobb nodded again, the swinging gate under Kaleb Lee's feet fell away...

The body swung down. The crowd let out a collective sound, somewhere between a gasp and a cheer. And there was another sound, a creaking, cracking noise...as the wooden arm supporting both the noose and Kaleb Lee, sagged and snapped under the weight of the falling body. As Lee continued his fall downward, the supporting wooden arm of the hastily built gallows broke off, following the body to the ground, pulling the rope along with it, as the Sheriff, the two deputies, and the preacher looked on in disbelief. For some reason, McCanty thought, the hangman did not look surprised at all. Almost as if he expected that to happen. After a loud thump and a collective gasp of horror from the gathered masses, all five men still on the gallows peered over the swinging gate to find their victim laying sprawled in the dirt, the crossbar laying over him, where it had broken off, striking the condemned in the head on the way down.

There was, for a moment, silence, which was a strange thing to hear, Dan McCanty thought, considering that there were more than a hundred people gathered in the small town square. They were as stunned as he was, he guessed, after witnessing the oddest hanging he had ever seen. Then one of

Kaleb Lee's feet twitched and he let out a muffled groan from beneath the black bag that had been pulled over his head to spare the faint of heart. But by then, of course, the faint of heart were screaming. Even grown men were shouting. The wild gang of boys were so spooked, they cried out and ran for their mothers' skirts. Beside him, McCanty heard John Bullis whisper:

"Damn..." the gunman said between clenched teeth. "Damn..."

The Sheriff and his two deputies were running down the gallows steps. The hangman was staring at his broken contraption. The preacher was looking at the pages of the Good Book, shaking his head in wonderment. One of the deputies reached Kaleb Lee first, untangling him from the rope, lifting the crossbar off him. The deputy seemed to be treating the man with the sort of gentleness you might expect if a person got run over by a wagon, McCanty thought. Not somebody you were trying to hang only a minute before. They jerked the hood off Kaleb Lee, his eyes opened wide, looking like bird's eggs. He coughed three or four times, his mouth open, gasping for breath, looking wildly around, as if he couldn't quite believe where he was.

The crowd couldn't quite believe it, either. Half of them turned away in disgust, looking for other things to do on this bright, pleasant afternoon. The rest crowded around the partially hanged man, mostly in amazement that he was still alive. Kaleb Lee was slowly coming to that conclusion himself.

"It's a miracle," he said, hoarsely, still gasping. "I prayed for a miracle, and it's happened! I survived my hanging, by God! I survived!"

He turned to the Sheriff now, his eyes blazing.

"Cut me loose, Sheriff!" he said, louder now as he found his voice. "I lived through my hanging! I can't be hung twice for the same crime! Cut me loose!!"

Sheriff Cobb appeared pained, as though he had just drunk some rancid liquor. He looked up quickly, angrily, at the hangman standing now by the still swinging gate. Rufus Gates merely shrugged.

"You can't be *tried* twice for the same crime," the Sheriff said. "The sentence was, you were to be hanged until you was dead."

Cobb didn't look like he enjoyed giving even a man as bad as Kaleb Lee such news.

"We got to do it all again, once they fix this damned contraption..." he said, hitching up his pants, brushing the dust off his white shirt, straightening his bolo tie.

Kaleb Lee blinked...once, twice, as if he could not believe what he was hearing. He looked down, suddenly realizing that at some point he had soiled himself. Tears leaked from the corners of his eyes and to everyone's dismay, the bad man began to sob.

"That...that ain't hardly fair," Kaleb Lee cried. "It just ain't..."

Well, to almost everyone's dismay.

"I told you...didn't I Kaleb Lee!" the widow screamed, then began laughing hysterically, even as she was being led away. "I told you! You're gonna be the sorriest hanged man in all the world!"

The rest of the crowd seemed to have had enough of hanging for one day, as those remaining retired to the saloons, or simply mounted their horses and rode back to their cattle or their farms.

"It ain't fair!" Kaleb Lee wailed. "I already was hung once!"

"Take him back to his cell and get him cleaned up," the Sheriff said to his deputies, his displeasure obvious. Then he turned to the hangman. "And you...get this fucking thing fixed so it'll do its job!"

"I ain't responsible for the carpenters who built this," Gates said, belligerently, squaring his thin shoulders, his eyes defiant. The man had no chin, McCanty saw, and a neck so scrawny it was amazing it held the fellow's large head upright.

Some of the remaining crowd looked like they wouldn't mind if the hangman took Kaleb Lee's place. Or at least be made to test the equipment before the outlaw used it again.

"Get back, all of you!" the Sheriff growled, helping his prisoner to his feet. "We'll finish this tomorrow, if the carpenters can sober up enough to get the job done right!"

Lee, hearing that his sentence would be carried out the very next day, began sobbing uncontrollably.

"I shoulda been with Jesus by now," the man wailed.

Up on the gallows platform, even the preacher looked skeptical at that, McCanty thought, following a now sullen Bullis over to Flanagan's saloon.

"They should just shoot that son-of-a-bitch," Bullis mumbled. "They need somebody to do it, I'm available."

In McCanty's mind, that was not an altogether bad idea.

"Kinda surprised the fall didn't kill him," Bullis commented over whiskey at Flanagan's. Half the men in town seemed to have the same idea: to spend the day drinking. So Flanagan's was jumping like it was Saturday night, instead of Wednesday afternoon.

"Surprised that Lee fellow, too, I reckon," McCanty grinned, then decided he shouldn't be finding amusement in another man's misery, no matter what the other man might have done. "Although the widow seemed to enjoy it."

Bullis laughed. "Overly much, I guess," he said.

Outside came the sound of hammering and sawing, as the gallows was being repaired under the watchful eye of a deputy with a shotgun cradled in his arm. A signal to the carpenters that they were to remain sober until the work was completed. A couple of the saloon whores wandered by, and McCanty bought them drinks. The afternoon passed pleasantly, with whiskey and the company of, if not exactly pretty, at least pleasant looking gals. McCanty was about to take one of them upstairs before supper. A bouncy little thing, with pert breasts and a tight bustle, named Nora, when a loud voice came from the far end of the saloon.

"I know that fellow!" someone said, the words slurred in a hoarse, whiskey laden breath. "The Cheyenne call him Hide Man Hunter. Injins consider him big medicine!"

Bullis looked up, his own eyes slightly hazy with drink, wondering if he had heard correctly. He could tell by the look on McCanty's face that he had. His friend frowned, like he had just found a scorpion in his boot.

"Yes sir, they say that man killed a whole crew of buffalo runners, then brought the hides and meat to a Cheyenne village over by Medicine Butte," the man said, nodding his head to his friends. "I was driving a company wagon out of the Leadville mines.

Heard all about it from the soldiers at the fort there. That's him...the Hide Man Hunter...right over there!"

Several men at the corner table stared in McCanty's direction. One of them got up. A big fellow, taller than McCanty, not as solidly built. But his eyes were hard and his gun was slung low on his hip. Bullis marked him as a dangerous man. McCanty sighed, pushing Nora off his lap, but did not get up to confront the man. The Sharps was leaning in a corner by their table, too far away to do any immediate good. Bullis' hand drifted down near his own holster, just to be ready. McCanty poured a drink from the bottle on the table, as the man crossed the suddenly quiet saloon, to stand over him. Still, he refused to acknowledge the angry fellow.

"That true, what the Teamster said?" the man asked, his voice a low, dangerous growl. "You kill white men and give their hides to the fucking injins?"

McCanty stared at the table, at his empty glass.

"I'm here for the whiskey and the whores...no offense, Miss Nora," he said quietly, easily.

Standing behind John Bullis, Nora shrugged and tried to smile.

"So I'm not looking to kill anyone today, mister," McCanty said, now turning toward the intruder.

And Bullis thought: If that man could read a storm coming in somebody's eyes, he'll be taking a step or two back about now.

"I asked you a question," the man sneered, apparently as insensitive to danger as he was to storms, Bullis thought. "You that sorry bastard they call the Hide Man Hunter?"

"But if I was to kill anyone today, I reckon you'd do as well as anybody," McCanty said easily, as if the man hadn't made the last statement at all.

"You son-of-a-bitch!" the man spat. "You and me, out in the street! Right now!"

Bullis shook his head, knowing that McCanty was now sufficiently provoked. McCanty stood quickly. Much faster than a man his size should be able to move, especially following an afternoon of drinking. Certainly a lot faster than the man standing over him expected...the fellow stepping back, belatedly realizing the misjudged distance, to say nothing of the quickness and power of the big-shouldered, grey bearded man now suddenly in front of him...like an old grizzly bear rising unexpectedly out of the tall grass. Panicked, the man made a fatal mistake, reaching instinctively for his gun.

Bullis, who was himself quick of hand and eye, saw three things happen almost simultaneously...at least they happened too quick for him to follow: The loud-mouthed man's gun was halfway out of its holster. McCanty's big knife was in his hand, the blade plunging downward into the center of the man's chest, as the fellow let out a startled gurgle, a gasp. McCanty twisted the Bowie knife a half-turn with his wrist to ensure a killing blow, and the dead man's eyes glazed. McCanty pulled the foot long blade free, and the man fell to the sawdust floor of Flanagan's saloon.

The quiet stretched out for another heartbeat or two. The entire killing had taken place in the blink of an eye, Bullis thought, making a mental note never to engage in a heated argument with McCanty at close quarters. The barkeep was the first to regain his voice.

"Somebody get the Sheriff!" he yelled.

Bullis knew this was not the first time the man had given that instruction, nor would it likely be the last.

"By God, that man stabbed Joe Bottom!" somebody said.

CHAPTER SIX

Rockville

O wen Scales was standing uncomfortably outside the new dress making shop, with its female garments displayed in a real glass window. He was deciding on the pros and cons of going inside, when Kate swept out of the shop, burdened with boxes of dresses for the Upstairs Girls.

"Well, Sheriff Scales," Kate said, rather coldly, he thought. Her blue eyes seemed to snap at him, her face encased in red curls. She smiled, but somehow did not seem to mean it.

"Kate," he nodded, more distressed when she handed him the boxes and started down the street ahead of him. He had the uncomfortable feeling that everyone they passed was staring, whispering behind his back. It made him feel decidedly undangerous.

"Where are we going?" he managed to ask, when she headed down Main Street, in the opposite direction of the Silver Strike.

"You're taking me to lunch," she said, bluntly, stopping by the doorway of the inappropriately named Russian Tea Room. Another uncomfortable bit of civilization, recently added to Rockville's expanding market place.

There were no Russians, Scales knew, but there was tea and tablecloths and lace napkins. The place was run by two Eastern dandies, both men, who seemed to be trying to bring a taste of culture to a rough-house western town. Scales had no idea why anyone would attempt such a thing. But, surprisingly, the tea house seemed to be doing a thriving business, serving square-cut bread and no liquor. Scales had no idea how they might be thriving. The proprietors, however, seemed to know Kate personally and seated them with a flourish at a corner table, Scales stacking the dress boxes on an extra chair. Kate ordered and Scales nodded that he would have the same. Small bowls of what appeared to be bean and bacon soup arrived, with tea in china cups so delicate he couldn't put his thick fingers into the flimsy handles.

"Jim Warner said you were looking for me," Scales said into her silence. He frowned...the soup, what there was of it, was surprisingly good.

"We have a problem," Kate said, sipping her tea, staring across the table at him.

She looked nothing like her nickname, Sweet Kate. Her blue eyes, which usually reminded him of a deep, clear sky, seemed to pin him like a bug beneath her fingers. But her hair, the color of fall leaves dried in the sun, just touched her shoulders. And despite the firm set of her mouth, Scales thought, not for the first time, that she was the prettiest female he had ever laid eyes on. She wore a rust colored dress, cut just low enough to draw a man's eyes, and let him imagine what the rest of her was like. Owen Scales, who did indeed know what the rest of her was like, had to shake his head to break the trance that overtook him when he was close to her. He wished, fervently, that the Russian Tea Room served red-eye whiskey, or at least beer.

"What problem?" he managed to ask.

"You either have to make an honest woman of me, or make it known that we've severed relations," Kate said bluntly.

His confusion was obvious, and to her credit she gave him time to appraise her statement.

"This is good soup, don't you think?" she said casually, daintily bringing the spoon to her lips.

"It is," Scales agreed, looking down into his empty bowl, the contents of which he had already slurped up. "Kate, I..." he began clumsily.

"I know," she nodded, the bluntness gone now, replaced by the gentleness he knew was inside her. "You don't know what to say. I understand, and you don't have to respond right away, but I thought it best to bring things out into the open. I care about you, Owen Scales, but the plain truth is, we can't go on like this anymore. And, quite frankly, I don't care to. My days as an Upstairs Girl are about over, for a number of reasons. So we need to decide, you and me, where we stand."

Scales felt himself caught between a rock and a hard place, as the saying went. Or a rock and a soft place, he thought absently, looking over the top of Kate's dress.

"I've been thinking about that, actually," he lied, as all men do when caught in similar situations.

"Good," she said, choosing to believe him, even though she was aware it probably wasn't true.

The waiter brought pieces of square-cut bread that had thinly sliced meat between them, topped with some leafy stuff he didn't recognize. The bread slices were stabbed together with toothpicks. Owen Scales had never seen the like of it.

"What the hell are these?" Scales whispered. Kate frowned at the language, but the proprietor who was leaning over the table grinned at him in a most uncomfortable manner.

"They are sandwiches from Miss Elizabeth Leslie's very own cookbook," he said, proudly.

Scales grunted and gamely tried to eat them. They were not bad, he concluded, if one was a woman or an Eastern dandy.

"Have you come to any conclusions?" she asked, when it became obvious he wasn't inclined to continue.

"You know I care about you, Kate," he began, the look in her eyes telling him it wasn't a very good beginning. He sighed, spread his hands out on the table and tried again. "I do, you know...a lot. But I'm just a sheriff in a two-bit town who has to buy his own damn bullets. I own a horse, an extra change of clothes, and I live in a room at the hotel. I got, maybe, fifty dollars in the bank."

She was staring at him, her eyes flashing intensely, waiting for him to say something else. Only he had no idea what.

"I'm a poor man, and I'm afraid I don't have much to offer," he said finally, shaking his head.

"I'm not," she replied.

"Not what?" he asked, confused.

"Poor," she said, almost casually, taking a careful bite of her sandwich. "I have money, Owen. Quite a bit, actually."

"You do?" Scales felt his confusion deepen.

"Yes," she nodded. "There's few things in this world more pitiful than an old Upstairs Girl with no money. I don't plan on ending up that way, so I've put aside a fairly sizeable sum."

"Well," Scales said, wondering where the conversation was heading. He felt like a man lost in the tall grass of the high plains, with no land marks in sight. "So what are you going to do with this sizeable sum?"

"I'm going to use it to get out of Rockville," she said firmly. "I'm heading to a bigger town. Hayes City, I'm thinking."

"What'll you do there?" Scales asked, unable to put away that lost feeling.

"Oh, I'm guessing there'll be opportunities in Hayes," she shrugged. "I'll set up my own place, maybe bring some of the girls with me, if they want to go. As I said, my days as a working whore are about over, but I do know the business end of it pretty well. I'm thinking I'll collect my money standing up, smiling for a change."

She smiled at him, and Scales found himself quite unable to say anything. Unable to break the long silence that seemed to stretch on for forever.

"That's good," he finally found his voice. "Real good."

"I'd like you to come with me, Owen," she said finally, raising her eyebrows at his stunned expression.

"Leave town...my job?" Scales said, feeling the bean and bacon soup repeat. "What'll I do in Hayes City?"

"Well, you won't have to buy your own bullets, that's for sure," Kate said, trying to make a joke. But Owen, she saw, seemed to have left his sense of humor outside in the dusty street. "We can set up a brothel business in town, and use the profits to buy a ranch."

"I'm not much with livestock," he said, shaking his head.

"Then a hotel, or a general store," Kate sounded frustrated with him now. "Don't you see?"

"I guess not," Scales felt pitifully low.

"I can't live here anymore," Kate said sharply. "I'm sick to death of dirty sheets and waking up feeling like a horse somebody's rode too hard. And I'm sick of worrying about you!"

"Worrying about me?" Scales asked, startled.

"Yes, you!" Kate got tears in her blue eyes, and that seemed to make her madder. "Worrying that some drunken cowboy is going to put a hole in you. That some stupid gunslinger is going to see your badge and decide he's going to make his reputation by gunning down the town Sheriff. I'm sick of worrying about every stranger who comes into town with his gun hung low and that cold, dark look in his eyes!"

"Kate..." Scales began, then stopped, realizing now what she was asking. For him to quit being a lawman, which in a way he guessed he understood. But he couldn't see himself as a hotel clerk, or wearing an apron behind the counter of a dry goods store. It wasn't him, and Kate seemed to see that, too.

"Just don't talk anymore," Kate shook her head, more sad now, than angry. And somehow that was worse, Scales thought. "I saw the look in your own eyes when you beat down that boy who was looking for Jake Johnson. I don't care to see it again. And I surely don't plan on staying around here, to see you stretched out in the street, or bleeding to death on the sawdust floor of that miserable saloon! I won't do it, you hear! I won't..."

"Kate," he said, low and sorrowful. He couldn't stand to see the tears welling up in her eyes. He was chagrined to see the owners of the Russian Tea Room glaring at him for making a lady cry.

Kate must have sensed it, too, because she quickly dried her eyes with one of the lace napkins, stiffened her backbone and actually smiled at him.

"I care too much about you to stay here and see any of that happen. So, Mr. Owen Scales, I'm leaving, and I would like nothing more than to have you come with me."

"Kate, I..." he began, having no idea what he was going to say next.

But the moment of indecision was taken out of his hands, as Skeet Miller burst through the doors of the Russian Tea Room.

"There you are!" Skeet said, breathless. This really was the last place he'd thought to look for the Sheriff. "Doc Watson says you need to get up to the mining camp, pronto! There's been a robbery and Doc says a bunch of people are shot up!"

"I'll be back," he said quietly to Kate. "Don't do anything until I get back. Promise..."

Kate nodded, and he was gone.

CHAPTER SEVEN

Cherokee Creek

There was the usual uproar that always happens when a man gets killed. Joe Bottom's companions expressed their outrage, their confusion at what they'd seen take place. After all, getting shot was one thing, but it was far from usual to see a man skewered by a foot of sharp steel. The fact that it had happened in nearly a single heartbeat, threw even more confusion into the mix. But by now, John Bullis saw, the dead man's friends were pushing themselves up from their card table. Although none of them looked to be in any hurry to go near the man in the buckskins, who had so suddenly and efficiently dispatched one of their own. But they were mumbling, grumbling among themselves, each man trying to goad the other to action. Dan McCanty, Bullis noticed, seemed oddly unconcerned, even as he wiped the blood off his vicious looking blade.

Sensing that things might be about to take a turn for the worse, Bullis stood, facing the five men in Bottom's crew. That gave them another few moments of confusion, Bullis saw with satisfaction, even if they were five guns to his one. McCanty's Sharps rifle was still standing in the corner, and he did not seem to be in any hurry to put it into play. Still, Bullis thought, it was unlikely that he could get all five men before they got him. That idea must have finally dawned on at least one of the cowhands.

"That son-of-a-bitch can't get us all," someone whispered.

"That there's John Bullis," another man said, as if unsure of the odds, stacked though they might be.

To reinforce the man's fear, Bullis grinned at him, hand just over the butt of his Colt.

"At your service, sir," Bullis said, calmly. It was this calmness in the face of danger, he knew, that separated him from other men. He could feel it now...the certainty that he could kill at least three of them, and that the others would lose heart.

"Nobody's shooting anybody...unless it's me!" the bartender yelled, balancing a gleaming sawed-off shotgun on the bar. "Everybody just back off and we'll let the law sort this out!"

The men at the card table did not need much convincing, Bullis noted with some satisfaction. The five of them deciding that waiting for the Sheriff was the proper course of action. McCanty had already sat down to finish his whiskey, as he dug into his pockets for silver.

"Nora, be a darling and take my rifle in the corner there...take it up and put it under your bed. I'll be back for it in a day or two."

The bar girl nodded, slipped the coins into her dress and lugged the big Sharps upstairs. The last thing McCanty wanted was some two-bit Sheriff confiscating his gun. A moment later, Sheriff Cobb appeared, toting a scattergun, looking decidedly serious.

"That man stabbed Joe Bottom to death," one of the dead man's friends chirped, pointing to

McCanty, who sat quietly at the table, hands in sight, drinking his whiskey.

The Sheriff grunted, taking the situation in quickly. The dead man had surely been stabbed to death, all right.

"That man drew his gun on my friend," John Bullis said, casually.

"Well, no one could ever credit Joe Bottom with good sense," Sheriff Cobb drawled. He had already come to the conclusion that the dead man was laying there largely due to his own bad temper and a not-so-lightning draw. "You men, take Joe Bottom back to the Bar-T and get him buried. Go on, now..."

Cobb felt their hesitation, knew they wanted revenge on the half-wild man who had dispatched their colleague. Knew also, that they weren't likely to get it with a gunman the caliber of John Bullis declaring the stranger to be his friend. Most likely, more of the cowhands would get killed, a situation the Sheriff wanted to avoid.

"I'll handle this," Cobb gestured with the scattergun, shooing the cowhands on their way.

They started dragging Joe Bottom toward the door.

"For Christ's sake, pick him up," the Sheriff winced, shaking his head at the trail of blood.

"That feller, he kilt a party of buffalo hunters out near Dodge City," one of the men said, once he was safely behind the Sheriff and his scattergun. "White men, and he gave their truck to the injins."

"And the Army thinks he sold guns to them red savages!" another piped in.

At those accusations, Sheriff Cobb raised his eyebrows and looked the stranger over more carefully.

"That true, Mr..." he paused, waiting.

"McCanty. Daniel McCanty," Dan held his hands out. "The only people I ever killed, deserved it."

"OK," the Sheriff nodded, as if accepting the curious statement as true. In fact, he did believe it, mostly. "But I'd say we've had enough blood letting for one night. Why don't you come on over to the jail and spend the night, while I check for warrants and make sure these here cowboys get out of town without being slung over their own mounts. Where are you on this, John?" he made a point to look over at Bullis, who only shrugged.

"Weren't my quarrel," Bullis said, showing his palms.

"I know those fellows," Sheriff Cobb glanced over at the now empty table where the friends of Joe Bottom had been drinking. They were outside, tying the dead man to his horse, grumbling and staring back inside Flanagan's. "They ain't gonna take kindly to this at the Bar-T."

"Then they'll all be stupid and dead, like their friend," Bullis suggested, returning the glares through the swinging doors of the saloon.

"They come from a big spread," Cobb said, not unkindly. "You'd have to kill a whole passel of them boys."

Bullis shrugged, as if he was not opposed to such a suggestion. And, indeed, he wasn't. "If somebody thinks they're just gonna ride up and shoot Dan here, they are mistaken."

The Sheriff nodded again. "Mr. McCanty, you coming peacefully?"

McCanty nodded and stood up, wide shouldered and with an easy grace, like a big cat. Cobb saw right away that Joe Bottom had surely bitten off more than he could chew. And likely the buffalo runners out by Dodge, as well, if McCanty's eyes and fluid movements were any indication. The Sheriff had worked cow towns and gambling dens his whole career. He knew dangerous men when he saw them.

"I'm guessing it was only a matter of time before somebody killed Joe Bottom?" McCanty suggested.

The Sheriff, despite the gravity of the situation, barely suppressed a grin. "I'd have to say that it don't come as a complete surprise in find him in such a state," Cobb returned.

"Didn't think so," McCanty said.

Cobb, a prudent man, took a step back and kept his thumb on the hammers of the scattergun the whole walk back to the jail, relaxing only when the key was turned in the lock and the stranger was safely put away for the night. It had been a busy day, and Cobb was tired. He didn't even mind when John Bullis showed up with a bottle of whiskey, declaring his intention to keep his friend company for a while.

"I got your word, John? No trouble?" Cobb asked. The two men knew each other even before Bullis had 'accidently' shot the card cheat, William Harris. In truth, Cobb had not looked forward to hanging John Bullis, but would have carried out his duty as required. He also understood that if Bullis wanted to bust his friend out of jail, he wouldn't have shown up with a bottle of whiskey, and he wouldn't have willingly turned his sidearm over to the deputy, who was on guard duty because of the condemned man also residing in the jail...for one more night, anyway.

"My word," Bullis agreed.   And the Sheriff nodded wearily. "The deputy here can have a drink?" Bullis asked.

"One," Cobb said, narrowing his eyes.

"Better make it a good one, then," Bullis laughed pouring the deputy a cupful of his redeye whiskey.

"The first ones, I come on in the high grass country, out by the Yellowstone," McCanty said, shaking his head. They were well into Bullis' bottle. Sheriff Cobb had long since left for the night, and the deputy was asleep with his boots on the desk downstairs.   "I could hear 'em shooting for hours," he said, staring into his whiskey. "Boom, boom, boom...I rode to the sound, knowing what I'd find."

Bullis sat quietly while his friend told the story, sitting on the thin bed in his cell. There was sadness in the big man's voice, something the gunman hadn't heard before. Outside, the noise from the carpenters' work grew silent, as they finished their repairs on the gallows.

"I came over a ridge and there must have been a hundred carcasses in front of me," McCanty scowled at the memory.   "I mean, I got nothing against making meat. I shot my share of shaggies, too.   And the tribes I hunted with, they'd take as many of the critters as they could. But there was a difference between hunting and what was happening down there in that valley.   The Indians, they use everything, you know. The hides, the meat, hell even the bones and sinew. But those white men, they was set up high on a ridge, with the wind in their faces, so the buf couldn't see or smell 'em. They just shot and shot and shot. The shaggies kept dropping and dropping and dropping ...more meat than any village could eat in a year. Only these fellows, they didn't care about the meat, only the hides. Two of 'em shooting these big caliber Remingtons, while two knife men worked down in the hollow, cutting the hides on the dead animals, while a third man ripped the skins off with a mule."

"The buffs ain't smart enough to run, unless they can see or smell what's attacking 'em," Bullis nodded. "They'll stand there and graze until they're dead. I don't know...maybe they think the others are just sleeping."

"It was wrong," McCanty said, shaking his head at the memory. "That kind of slaughter...it weren't right. It was like they wanted to kill every buffalo on the plains."

"They do," Bullis said, knowingly. "The government wants to kill the buffalo, cut off the Indians' food supply to force 'em onto the reservations. General Phil Sheridan himself said, 'The only good Indian I ever saw was dead.' His boss Sherman ain't no better."

McCanty growled at that.

"William Tecumseh Sherman," Bullis said. "Named after Chief Tecumseh, a Shawnee, I believe. What do they call that in books?"

"Irony," McCanty replied, especially given that Chief Tecumseh had been an Indian leader who refused to cede his land to the whites in Indiana. "He's still a mean son-of-a-bitch, I hear."

"You hear right," Bullis said. The gunman had briefly fought for the Confederates, before realizing he was on the losing side of a bad fight. McCanty, he knew, had fought in western campaigns for the South during the time of the Great War. His family had suffered grievously when Sherman burned his way through Georgia to the sea. And now that the South had been defeated, the government in Washington was turning its attention westward, to the mineral rich, vast landscapes on which the Indian Tribes currently dwelled.

"So I rode up to those men," McCanty said, continuing with his story. "Asked 'em what in hell they thought they were doing. 'Shooting buffalo,' they said, stopping only to cool down their overheated gun barrels. 'You got a problem with that?' You're goddamned right I do, I said," McCanty took another drink and passed the bottle back between the bars. "You men got enough hides, and I pointed to their wagon, which was already filled. 'Five dollars apiece at the Lincoln railhead,' one of 'em laughed. 'Reckon I'll say when we got enough.' So I stared him down. Reckon you won't, I said."

Bullis laughed, knowing how provoked his friend must have been at that point.

"Then, by God, they turned them big bore rifles toward me," McCanty said, incredulously. "I swear, they were fixing to peg my hide out to dry on that bloody grass, then throw me in the back of that wagon with the other shaggies!"

"Well, I'm glad they weren't successful," Bullis raised the bottle in acknowledgement.

There was silence between the men, as Bullis considered what had been done.

"It was wrong, what they were doin'," McCanty said finally, his eyes hard, making no apologies for his actions. "And I'll kill anyone else I find doin' the same! Have done so, in fact..."

"There's been others?" Bullis asked.

McCanty nodded, not mentioning the Zeb Biggs party, where he had given the hides and what meat he could salvage to the Cheyenne, as the Teamster at the saloon had accused him of doing. He stared through the bars of the cell, as if daring the gunman to disagree with him.

"I guess some would say they got what they deserved," Bullis shrugged.

McCanty poured more whiskey into the jailhouse tin cups, glad that the issue was settled between them. Bullis didn't carry any particular grudge against the tribes, McCanty knew, although he doubted the man would go out of his way to help them. But the tribes were in desperate need of guns and ammunition, if they were to have a chance of holding off Sherman and his troops. The Blue Coats, he knew, were merely the forerunners of settlers, miners, and all the rest. So-called civilized society, which was waiting like a wave to sweep away the tribes. McCanty felt his anger...dulled now by the whiskey, but still there, lurking in the background.

From the other cell, Kaleb Lee groaned.

"I already got hung once," Lee muttered for the tenth time. "It ain't fair..."

"Shut up!" Bullis snapped. "You kilt people... white people, while you was robbing them!"

"Ain't the only one who done that, from what I heard," he said, forlornly.

"You didn't hear nothing!" Bullis warned the man's complaints away. "You shot a rancher and his son. He left a widow and two daughters."

"Weren't me!" Kaleb Lee snapped, angrily. "My brother done that. Stupid bastard! I was just there..."

"That's enough to hang you," Bullis pointed out.

"But I already got hung once," Lee almost let out another sob, which he caught. "I felt that floor fall away. Felt the noose tighten. Thought I was dead," he said, hands moving up to the rope burn around his neck. "Now I got to do it all over again. Ain't fair…"

"Probably ain't," Bullis allowed. "Here, have a drink of whiskey. But only if you promise to stop moaning and complaining."

"OK," Kaleb Lee nodded, rubbing his neck. "Talkin' makes my throat hurt, anyway."

Bullis put some whiskey in the man's water cup, and Kaleb Lee sat on his bunk, knees up, sipping the redeye. At least he was quiet, Bullis thought. But the man's continued outbursts had soured the visit for Bullis and he left directly.

In the night, Dan McCanty heard Lee crying softly. It was very disturbing.

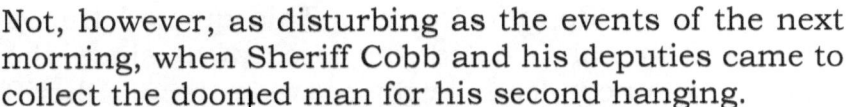

Not, however, as disturbing as the events of the next morning, when Sheriff Cobb and his deputies came to collect the doomed man for his second hanging.

McCanty heard them coming up the stairs, an hour or so after first light. Boots clomping up to the second level of the jail, where the cells were kept. Kaleb Lee heard them, too, and he started to moan and sob. McCanty watched, fascinated, as Cobb and the two deputies paused outside the man's cell.

"It's time, Kaleb Lee," Cobb said, frowning at the prisoner, who was sitting on his bed, eyes wide with terror.

"I already got hung once," Lee whispered, his voice shaking like the rest of him.

"Well, you're gonna get hung again," one of the deputies barked. But he quickly shushed under Cobb's harsh stare.

"That ain't fair," Kaleb Lee sobbed, wrapping the blankets of his bunk around him.

"Fair or not, like it or not, it's gonna happen, son," Cobb said, unlocking the cell door, nodding to the deputies to pull the condemned man out. "Be a sight easier if you'd cooperate," Cobb snapped.

"Easier for you, maybe!" Lee spat. "You ain't been hung once already!"

Getting hung once and surviving to get hung again had certainly taken the sap out of Kaleb Lee, McCanty thought, deciding it was probably a good experience to avoid.

The deputies grabbed Lee's arms, his hands were locked behind him, and he was pulled from the cell. Lee was shouting now, protesting the heavy hands being laid on him, twisting under the deputies' grasp. So much so, that the Sheriff drew his hog leg Colt and tapped Lee behind the ear, causing him to go limp in the deputies' arms. This quieted things some, but it complicated the procedure since the prisoner was now dead weight between them. Sheriff Cobb, having done his part, offered no help. At the bottom of the stairs, the group apparently picked up another member, as McCanty heard the preacher reciting passages from the Bible. McCanty found himself thinking that might have done Kaleb Lee some good if he could have heard them.

McCanty could see out the barred window, into the small square below, where the newly repaired gallows waited, along with a smaller crowd from the previous day. Or so McCanty estimated, since his field of vision had changed considerably since yesterday. Unfortunately for Kaleb Lee, he recovered from the Sheriff's tap on his head just as the deputies made it to the first steps. Coming to, realizing what was about to take place, the condemned man began fighting and yelling, as if this might somehow stop, or at least delay the inevitable. It did not. Lee's efforts accomplished neither.

The deputies, used to the man's weight by now, carried him upward, toward the waiting hangman and the dangling hemp rope. Kaleb Lee was still shouting, as Cobb read the death warrant and the noose was placed around his neck. No one asked if he had any last words. But someone in the crowd sure had some last words for Lee, who was now standing silent, seemingly confused at the edge of the gallows. The thin widow, her young face lined with grief, broke free of the crowd and shouted up at him.

"You miserable bastard!" the woman screamed. "You killed my man and my boy...and now you're going to suffer for it! That's right, Kaleb Lee!" the woman shouted. "You're going to hell! And you're gonna suffer doing it. Scared, ain't ya?" The woman laughed wildly, and seemed on the verge of hysteria. "Yesterday weren't nothing, you rotten boy-killing puke! You're gonna die ugly, you bastard!"

The woman, who was obviously close to madness, shook off the restraining hand of a relative and glared up at Kaleb Lee, who recoiled at her venom and tried to back away. The noose, however, kept him in place and the woman pointed up at him, screaming unintelligibly. Sheriff Cobb, wanting nothing more than to get this execution over with, stepped forward, pulling the death hood over Kaleb Lee's fear maddened eyes, then turned and nodded toward the hangman. Lee's boots were scraping on the edge of the swinging gate, as he tried to back away from the screaming blood-mad woman...when the gate fell way from under him...

Unfortunately for Kaleb Lee, the gate did not fall away completely, as it was supposed to do. It fell downward, then seemed to catch halfway. Lee's boot heels tried to find purchase, as he slipped downward, until it appeared that he was running downhill, even as his feet continued to slip along the inclined gate.

The crowd gasped in collective horror. Sheriff Cobb seemed caught between pushing Kaleb Lee off the edge of the gate, and pulling him back to safety. The mad widow stopped her taunting and was staring fixedly at the half swinging figure, as Lee rotated out away from the gate, feet flailing in midair, then finding purchase of a sort, as his boots encountered the half open gate, and the doomed man tried to balance himself on the wooden incline. But the momentum slid his body downward, until he reached the end of the rope, his feet sliding off the gate, as he seemed to try and run in the air. The black death mask moved in and out, forming a dark circle, where Lee's mouth strained for breath, as the rope tightened. His feet still moved, as if he was actually running somewhere.

The crowd gasped again. The mad widow gave off a high-pitched squeal, and clapped her hands in delight. One of the deputies threw up his breakfast over the back railing. The preacher, who had performed these services dozens of times, was shocked into stunned silence. Sheriff Cobb had his hand on his Colt, unsure whether or not to take mercy on the condemned man and shoot him to end all this horror. But Kaleb Lee's legs were slowing. His feet walked slowly in the air now, gradually coming to a stop and the Sheriff began to breathe a sigh of relief...

When suddenly the body at the end of the rope shivered and twisted. The crowd shouted, the widow squealed with joy, as Kaleb Lee's knees came up to his chest and his body seemed to shoot itself upward, away from the strangling noose, so that it might somehow, someway, draw one last lungful of air. This happened once...twice, McCanty saw. Cobb had his pistol out and cocked. The condemned man's body arced, like a fish being pulled from the water, the feet wiggling grotesquely, the hands behind his back opening and closing, opening and closing...

McCanty, like the rest of the crowd in the square, was unable to turn away, as Kaleb Lee strangled at the end of a noose that was supposed to break his neck during the first drop of the body down the trapdoor gate...but didn't somehow. And Lee swung for another minute, until someone in the square — John Bullis, McCanty saw — stepped forward and pulled strongly on the hanged man's legs, taking whatever life remained in the swinging body.

"Now that was a bad drop," McCanty heard someone say from just below the barred window.

And the mad widow seemed to have enjoyed every moment of it, McCanty thought, as her relatives led her away, her laughter spreading across the square like a chill wind.

Sheriff Cobb appeared at McCanty's cell a few minutes later, looking frazzled, if not outright shaken. McCanty himself felt a moment of uncustomary fear, as if somehow, irrationally, he might be following in Kaleb Lee's footsteps.

"No warrants," Cobb explained. "You're free to go, I guess."

McCanty nodded.

"Joe Bottom had friends out at the Bar-T," Cobb said. "You might think about leaving town."

McCanty had already come to the conclusion that leaving town would be a good idea. But despite it all, there was still the call of whiskey and whores.

"In a day or two," McCanty said.

"How about today?" Cobb suggested.

McCanty shook his head. "Tomorrow, maybe," he shrugged.

"Well don't kill nobody between now and then," Cobb said, staring out the window, where the deputies were cutting down Kaleb Lee's body.

"I'll try not to," McCanty said.

CHAPTER EIGHT

Rockville

O wen Scales let the horse find her own pace along the winding dirt road that led north into the hills, where smoke from the mining camp hung like fog over the scrub pines. He wondered who had been shot, and if the situation had already resolved itself, as these things had a tendency to do. Even so, it was good to get out of town. The leather of the saddle creaking beneath him, the gentle bounce of the mare's gate calming him. In truth, Scales admitted, he was much more comfortable dealing with this sort of crisis, than trying to come to terms with Kate in the close confines of the Russian Tea Room. The high sky above, the breeze in his face, a robbery and shooting to figure out. These were problems he could handle. Not some crying woman threatening to leave him. Try as he might, Scales couldn't understand her. True, he was glad to hear she wasn't going to be whoring anymore. That was a burr under his saddle he never had come to terms with. He had already decided that he could talk her into staying. That her fear of him dying in some unexpected gunplay was totally unjustified. He was always careful about his business, had survived years as a lawman with hardly a scratch to show for it. He was a professional, and it surely wasn't fair for her to pressure him into giving up his trade. She was just out-of-sorts because of the Grimes kid. He knew he had been harsh with Billy Grimes, but you couldn't allow that sort any leeway. That was how a man ended up bloody. Of course, he couldn't explain that to her. Women just didn't understand that sort of thing. And the violence... well, sometimes that was just part of the job. But at the end of the day, it had to be said that he was a careful man. And he took his job seriously. Nobody could doubt that. Besides, he liked Rockville, which was usually a nice, quiet town. At least it was until Jake Johnson arrived, but that was a momentary inconvenience. Once the famous bounty hunter had departed, things would get back to normal. A few drunken cowboys to deal with on Saturday night, some miners to lock up to sleep off their binges. That was about the extent of any trouble he'd had to handle. Hayes City, now that was another ball of wax altogether...

By the time he came to the outskirts of the sprawling mining camp, Scales had decided he'd spend a couple days up in the hills, after he dealt with whatever trouble there'd been up here. Sort through what Kate said, talk with Doc Watson, who besides being at the back end of a bottle most days, was still the smartest man Scales knew.

Scales rode up and hitched his horse in front of the sutter's tent. In the late afternoon, the camp was all but deserted, the miners working their claims down in the valley, where the Whitefish River drained the surrounding hillsides. The camp itself was a rough built place with shacks and tents of all shapes and sizes. There were, at any given time, maybe fifty men working the sloughs, panning the creeks and river banks. A few men, not knowing any better, had brought their wives and kids along. Mostly fleeing worked out farms in the Pennsylvania and Ohio

Valleys, or the big cities of the East. Where, he heard, people lived packed like rats atop of one another, working in factories and mills for starvation wages. Here they ran from one gold or silver strike to the next, hoping to strike it rich. Not many did, of course, but that didn't stop them from trying. Miners were a stubborn bunch, he knew from experience. In a way, you had to admire their gumption, even if they seemed to lack any sort of common sense.

Some kids, toting wood, ran through the dirt paths that passed for streets. A few tired looking women hung laundry from sagging rope lines. In the distance, he could hear the clang of picks and the scrape of shovels. This, Scales thought to himself, was the border of the thing called civilization...the very edge of it. Some said that one day there would be farms and towns and railroads all through this country. Maybe, Scales considered, but he doubted he'd see it in his lifetime.

"Sheriff, good to see ya," said Charlie Wells, who ran the sutter's tent, selling picks and shovels and pan paraphernalia in the camp, stood outside the canvas flaps of his business.

"Charlie," Owen smiled. Wells was a dreadfully skinny man, dressed in wool pants and what once might have been a white shirt. "Doc Watson sent a message. You all had some trouble up here?"

"Had some," Charlie said amiably. "Come on inside, I got a jug of homemade...unless you're sworn to label whiskey."

"Not a bit," Scales grinned. It was true that some would only drink bottle whiskey, particularly after last winter's poisoning, when several men had actually died from bad liquor; none of it, thankfully, traced back to Skeet Miller's still. But Scales supposed anyone could put a label on the most crudely made brew, so it hardly mattered. Unless you made it yourself, it was all pretty much pot luck.

Inside, the cluttered tent was filled with all manner of goods and clothing, some new, some old, all sold at ridiculously high prices. Harness and boots, can goods, sacks of beans and corn meal, hats and gloves and belts. A pistol or two in back of the plank counter, some squirrel guns and an old scattergun. Plugs of tobacco, more sacks of flour, coffee, and sugar. Wells wiped two tin cups with a sour-looking rag and poured from a clay jug he kept under the plank bar. Scales figured that whatever was in the jug would kill whatever might be on the rag. He clicked his tin cup against Charlie's and sipped carefully.

"Whoa!" Scales blinked, feeling the burn run down his throat, all the way to his toes.

"It'll keep the chill away, that's for sure," Charlie smiled back. "Sorry to tell you, but you might have made the ride out for nothing."

Scales raised an eyebrow, pushing his hat back on his head. "Maybe you better fill me in, Charlie..."

Not surprisingly, as it turned out, the miners had dealt with the situation themselves.

"A couple hard cases came into camp last week," Wells poured another round, the Sheriff poked around in his shirt pocket and produced a couple of cheroots. "We get them up here from time to time, as you know. Drifters, mostly. I mean, you can tell a working man right off by his hands."

Wells nodded sagely, apparently ignoring the fact that his own hands barely did more than count money and pour whiskey.

"Anyway, these fellows were asking around about open claims and the like," Charlie continued.

"They camped up above the hills, near the Stony Creek outfit."

Scales nodded. The Stony Creek group was the only professional mining company working the Whitefish strike. Run by Redeye John Baker from the coal county of Litchfield, Pennsylvania, Stony Creek employed a crew of twenty men, and rumor had it that they had hit a vein of high grade silver. Redeye Baker was a busy man, said to be on the verge of making his eastern investors quite rich. He came to Rockville infrequently, mostly to pick up supplies he'd had shipped in at less inflated prices than Charlie Wells' high priced goods.

"So one morning a few days back, the Trawler boys, Jim and Gerald, didn't show up to work on their claim," Charlie said, stopping to sell a bag of corn meal and one of beans to a haggard looking woman with three kids in tow. Scales smiled pleasantly and reached across to pull a handful of sugar candies out of a jar on the counter, handing the pieces out to the grateful kids. Scales winked at them, and the mother spoke up in a harsh, high voice.

"What do you say to the nice man?"

"Thank you," the trio chimed back, and Scales laughed, rolling a nickel in Charlie's direction.

"Those Trawler brothers, they're hard working boys," Wells lowered his voice, getting to the heart of his story. "Their claim is down the hill a bit from the Stony Creek Mine, so Redeye Baker sends a man up to their campsite to check on 'em...and don't you know, both Jim and Gerald are laying there dead, or so Baker's man thought. He runs back to the mine, finds Redeye, who goes up to check. Jim Trawler was dead, alright, shot right between the eyes, while he was taking a leak...or so it appeared. His brother was still in the ransacked tent, gut shot, but still breathing, a little anyway. Blood and gore all over the place. According to Baker, Gerald describes the two hard cases as who done the deed, just before he gives up the ghost. So Redeye grabs his gun and a half dozen of his men, catches the hard cases packing up their gear, finds a poke of gold on 'em...and well, they hung them two right there in the pines. We buried the four of 'em just yesterday."

"Huh," Scales said, shaking his head. In truth, the story was hardly uncommon. The outskirts of civilization, the thought came again. "Well, I guess I'd better have a word with Mr. Redeye Baker," he said, frowning.

"He don't buy much here, but I got nothing against the man personally," Charlie said quietly. "I'd appreciate it if you kept my name out of it. Folks around here, they're speaking kindly of him, protecting them and all."

Scales nodded, went outside and unhitched his horse, drawing a deep breath of fresh air. Charlie Wells had a bit of a strong odor about him. He rode down to the Stony Creek operation, found Baker in a platform tent, working over a ledger book.

"Mr. Baker," Scales announced himself. John Baker, a wide man of obvious strength looked up, saw the Sheriff and cursed under his breath. Baker earned his nickname it was said, not because of an overabundance of whiskey, but rather through years in the Pennsylvania coal mines. He took off a pair of spectacles and waved to a chair on the other side of his desk.

"Guess I was expecting you," Baker said, rubbing his eyes, which were indeed bright red, Scales saw.

"Word is you took it upon yourself to hang a couple of men the other day," Scales took off his hat, knocked it against his leg to shake off the dust. An act which made little sense, he thought absently, since the entire mining camp was awash in dust.

"Murderers," Baker said, unapologetic. "They killed two miners, hard working young men, and we caught the bastards with the boys' poke. Frankly, I don't have the time or the manpower to waste, hauling 'em into town. Then there'd be the trial, more time wasted to testify..."

"Trial being the main word there," Scales frowned, knowing that the law required him to take Baker into custody; undecided, as yet, whether justice required the action.

"I know," Baker shrugged his wide shoulders, kept his hands in plain sight on the desk. "I realize it seems rash..."

"A bit more than rash," Scales commented. "Gerald Trawler, he described the men to you?"

"Exactly, before he died," Baker nodded. "Doc Watson was there, too, to pronounce 'em dead...and Charlie Wells as a witness. We caught 'em and we did what needed to be done. I got a clear conscience about the entire affair."

"Might be you do," Scales acknowledged, knowing that if he did arrest Baker, no jury would ever convict the man. "I'll speak to Doc Watson, but even here on the frontier we expect our citizens to abide by the law, Mr. Baker. And the law says even murderers get a trial before we hang them."

Redeye Baker looked sufficiently contrite, given the circumstances, Scales thought.

"Here's what we'll do," Scales said slowly. "I'll confirm your story with Doc Watson and explain what happened to the Circuit Judge, when he comes through next time. Most likely, he'll see his way clear to let all this pass. By the way, what happened to the Trawler boys' poke?"

"I give it to Charlie Wells," Redeye said, looking somewhat embarrassed. "He's to use it if any of the panners' families are starvin' over the winter."

"Huh," Owen Scales said, more than a little surprised. Redeye Baker was not known to be among the charitable or the Christian. The Sheriff put his hand out, already deciding not to bring the subject up with the Circuit Judge. Baker returned the handshake. The hard hand of a hard man, Scales thought.

"If it happens again, take the time to bring the offenders into town," Scales said coldly. "I'd hate to see you on the other side of things."

Redeye Baker shrugged, as if being on the other side of things was not an unfamiliar situation, and was of little concern, either. He returned to his ledger, leaving the Sheriff to show himself out.

"Truthfully, it was all I could do not to thank the man for saving me the trouble," Scales chuckled, sitting on a camp stool around Doc Watson's fire. Watson was tall and thin, with a close-cropped mustache and wire glasses. He had been a real doctor once, back east, but had fled west to take up prospecting and drinking. These days, he seemed better at one than the other, in Scales' mind. It was rumored that the man had some deeply hidden tragedy that the Upstairs Girls were always trying to figure out. Doc worked off his bar bill by treating the girls for the various ailments and injuries associated with their profession.

Watson laughed, stirring up a pot of venison stew. An old half-breed hunter named LaBonty had brought two deer carcasses into camp that afternoon, when Owen, Doc, and Charlie Wells had been drinking at the sutter's tent.

"Hang 'em out back!" Charlie had yelled.

The old man led his horse around the rear of the tent, then came back to get paid. He held up three fingers, but Wells shook his head and held up two fingers.

"For Christ's sake, pay the man, Charlie," Scales spoke up.

Three, the old guy held up his fingers again.

"Here, I'll buy a hunk of that venison," Doc Watson said, tossing a dollar coin in Charlie's direction. Shaking his head, Wells reluctantly paid up.

"You pay the old buzzard three dollars today, he'll want four tomorrow," Charlie grumbled.

"You could always go hunt your own meat," Owen suggested, knowing that wasn't likely to happen.

"I'd appreciate it if you weren't so involved in my business," Wells snapped.

"If I was involved in your business up here, might be I wouldn't allow you all to go around hanging people," Scales said, dryly.

That shut Wells up for a while, but as the drinking continued, he was soon grumbling about paying the mute too much money.

"That old guy's a mute?" Doc Watson asked and Scales nodded.

"Sort of," Scales said. "His name's LaBonty, a French *voyageur*...forest runners, they used to call 'em. Rowed Manuel Lewis up the Missouri, back in the day, or so it's said. LaBonty got his tongue out."

"His tongue cut out?" Doc Watson exclaimed. "How'd that happen?"

"He ain't never said," Charlie Wells made his version of a joke.

"*Voyageurs*, they would sing when they rowed or pulled those old flatboats," Scales explained. "LaBonty had a mighty powerful voice and one morning a Crow warrior by the name of Broken Snake woke up with a head full of stones, after drinking a passel of ol' Manuel's fire water. LaBonty's singing was apparently too loud for Broken Snake. One thing led to another and before anyone could stop him, that Crow cut LaBonty's tongue right out of his head."

"Mother of God," Watson said.

"They was wild back in the old days," Scales nodded. "And when the other *voyageurs* got finished with Snake, that Crow had to change his tune some."

"Cut out his tongue, did they?" Watson asked.

"Hand, I believe," Scales said. "They was going to go eye-for-eye, but figured an injin don't talk that much, anyway. So they just hacked off his tongue-cutting hand."

Doc Watson looked shocked.

"Yeah, it's a harsh ol' world..."

Doc Watson stirred his stew, with its dollars' worth of venison, considering Scale's remark about Redeye Baker.

"He's not a bad fellow, for a mining boss," Doc allowed.

He and Owen Scales had struck up a friendship of sorts, although they were men with little in common, other than proximity and a mutual enjoyment of potent spirits. The Sheriff knew a good deal about the history of the wild country, which interested Watson, coming as he did from a New England background. Watson kept books of medical texts, and had a folding table in his tent where he wrote in a journal, often retelling Scales' stories about the olden days, although he never showed them to anyone. Scales, on the other hand, could work his way through a newspaper, if given sufficient time, but couldn't remember ever writing a proper letter to anyone. Perhaps, Scales sometimes considered, the two men got along because the exiled doctor was a good listener, or seemed to be when drunk. And the Sheriff, when drunk, liked to talk.

"Kate says she's leaving town," Scales said, as the sun set in red and purple splashes behind the mountains. The smell of cooking fires permeated the mining camp and in the distance someone played an unidentifiable song on a Jew's harp.

"Can't blame her for that," Doc Watson poked at the fire and accepted another cupful of the store bought whiskey Scales had carried in his saddlebags.

"I suppose not," Scales admitted. "She's got ambitions."

"Beats havin' no ambition," Doc Watson commented, and Scales wondered if the man was referring to himself, or maybe both of them.

"Wants me to go with her," Scales said, trying to sound casual. Doc Watson raised an eyebrow, tasted the venison stew and proclaimed it done by spooning out onto two tin plates, hot-handing biscuits from a flat rock at the edge of the fire.

"You ain't a bad cook," Scales said, being used to eating in the sometimes disagreeable tent slop houses in town...when he wasn't lunching at the

Russian Tea Room, he thought, grinning at that bit of foolishness.

"It's the sign of a man who spends a lot of time alone," Watson helped himself to more of the labeled liquor. "You brought good whiskey."

"Sign of a man with a real job," Scales commented, and they both laughed.

"That's so," Watson admitted, stretching out his long, thin legs. "I'm not much of a miner, I guess."

"You should come into town, set up a proper practice," Scales said, seriously. They had had this conversation before and Doc Watson was apparently not in the mood to have it again. He merely frowned and looked up at the stars that were starting to poke through the night sky.

"So, you going with her?" Watson asked quietly. "She's a good woman."

"She is," Scales admitted, mostly to himself. "But I kind of thought I'd grow old in Rockville, you know. If the railroad comes through, it could be a real nice town, with a real future."

"Maybe," Doc Watson sounded unsure.

"What do you mean...maybe?" Scales asked.

"I lied a minute ago," Watson said carefully. "I'm a pretty fair miner, actually. Been at it a while. Pulled more than my share out of the ground in California during the '49 rush. Made more in Colorado along the South Platte fields."

"What are you saying?" Scales asked, suddenly concerned.

"There ain't much left here. I'm thinking this strike will play out before long," Watson shrugged. "Expect I'll be moving on myself in the spring. Maybe out across the Divide again."

"What about the silver vein the Stony Creek outfit's struck?" Scales scoffed, not believing a word

Watson was saying. "They got investors and twenty men digging in that mountain."

"I'm hearing the vein wasn't all they thought it was," Doc Watson shook his head. "Yeah, they're digging up the mountain looking for it, but all they're finding is more mountain. A lot of them boys are talking about moving on."

"Jesus..." Scales whispered.

The countryside was rife with dust-filled ghost towns. Places that boomed for a while, then turned abruptly quiet, as the miners moved on following wherever rumors were whispered about the location of the next big strike. For the first time he thought of Rockville empty, except for the few hangers-on, who refused to let go of their own investment in time and money. He had ridden through those sad, forlorn places. Everybody had, at one time or another.

"Jesus," he whispered again, as the night settled in and the harmonica player stopped his mournful song, filling the air with silence. He knew how quickly such a thing could happen, once the rumors started. By spring, it could be all gone, he realized. The thought startling to him, like a bolt of lightning from a clear sky.

"Might be Kate's got the right idea," Doc Watson said quietly.

"Well, hell, you ain't no fun at all!" Scales said dryly, forcing himself to consider life as Sweet Kate's kept man. It was a mostly unpleasant thought.

"I guess we can drink the rest of your store bought whiskey," Doc Watson suggested. "Maybe I'll become less morose."

Privately, Owen Scales doubted it. In fact, as the night progressed, morose became a common theme.

CHAPTER NINE

Cherokee Creek

"Remind me not to get hung in these parts," McCanty said, returning his knife to its sheath, blinking into the dusty sunlight outside the jailhouse.

"That were a might grisly," Bullis agreed, as he led the way to Flanagan's, where most of the spectators had already adjourned. "But if you do get strung up by that fellow..." Bullis indicated the wiry figure of Rufus Gates, now slicing up several pieces of rope to be sold as souvenirs to those who had witnessed the execution. The saloon keeper at Flanagan's was always a ready customer and kept hanks of rope under glass above the bar, each labeled with the name and date of the last user. "If it comes to that, make damn sure you squirrel away a few dollars to insure the job gets done right," Bullis said, seriously.

"Sharpening the blade, it's called," McCanty said, knowingly. "In France, they have a machine called a guillotine. A heavy blade drops down and cuts the heads off condemned prisoners."

"Jesus," Bullis frowned.

"Those who are going to be killed give a coin or two to the executioner, to make sure the blade is sharp, before it comes down."

"Jesus," Bullis said again. "Hanging...cutting folks' heads off. Why the hell don't they just shoot the poor son of bitches?"

"I got no idea," McCanty admitted.

And there were other nagging questions about which he had no idea, either: Just why did the government not step in, given Rufus Gates' long history of botched executions? Why didn't the Governor, or the City Councils or the various law enforcement personnel demand his removal from the office of hangman? Surely a more competent, more efficient executioner would be in everybody's best interests?

Well, not necessarily, as it turns out.

First off, being a traveling hangman was such a low, ill-paid position, most doubted that any suitable replacement could be found. Secondly, not all of Rufus Gates' executions were haphazard, almost criminally cruel affairs. It was said, not by a few, that Gates could send a man into eternity without the slightest mess or fuss. That, depending on his mood or the state of his sobriety, the much-faulted hangman could snap a man's neck with ease and finesse. That he could send the condemned into the Afterlife like a summer breeze whispering in a fellow's ear. That a man would be gone and in the arms of the angels before he knew his breath had left his body.

All of which seemed to be contrary facts. But, in truth, they were not. Rufus Gates was actually a most adept hangman. Which meant, that if he was not the worst hangman west of the Mississippi, he had to be the most corrupt. He was a man driven by greed, and clearly not at all affected by any sense of conscience. Money, not alcohol was the crux of Rufus Gates' weakness, for he sold his expertise to the highest bidder.

Even given Gates' barely kept secret, the question of botched executions, or seemingly botched executions, came up from time to time. Why was such cruelty tolerated? Again, it was a question of money. The town fathers, the various bureaucrats and politicians, were mostly merchants. They operated general stores, saloons, eateries, had a share of the Upstairs Girls' proceeds, collected rent on rooms at the hotel and boarding houses, stalls at the livery stables. It all came down to a very simple equation: When more people came to town, business boomed and everyone made more money. And nothing brought people to town like the prospect of a good hanging...other than the prospect of a potentially botched hanging. With Rufus Gates in charge of the affair, one never knew what sort of hanging they might witness, so people flocked to town on Hanging Days, afraid to miss what their neighbors might be talking about until Christmas. The merchants, being city fathers and good politicians, had no incentive to replace their bumbling hangman. In fact, the real incentive was to provide Rufus Gates with enough liquor, so he might just mistie a knot or two, forget to grease a squeaky latch, not remember to oil the rope properly...mostly because people came to expect a good show, and it seemed a shame not to deliver one every so often.

It was said by several folks with the best inside information, that the widow and mother of the Lee brothers' victims, sold a half dozen of her husband's stolen cattle and then used the money to bribe the hangman to extend the execution for as long as possible, thus extracting her own brand of brutal justice. The broken crossbar on the first day was no accident, men whispered, declaring it was Rufus Gates himself who got the carpenters drunk, and that he picked out the rotten piece of lumber...all at the widow's request. And that the gate which was supposed to drop Kaleb Lee into eternity had been designed to do a half-mast drop, causing ol' Kaleb to dangle horribly, while the mad widow's taunts and screams echoed through his dying brain.

There was no proof of any of this, of course, and only the widow and Rufus Gates knew the truth of it. Although years later a confession by one Divine Johansson, who was then a guest of an eastern institution for the deranged, seemed to bare out the facts. The woman, it was said, had been driven mad by what she had done, but there was no one alive to confirm or deny the story, as by that time Rufus Gates was parked in the ground in Dodge City, shot to death by the relation of a man whose hanging Rufus had botched. As to why there were no other complaints about the hangman's incompetence in sending the condemned on their way, no one was quite sure. It might have been that business was unusually good on hanging days.

Or it simply might have been that those with the biggest complaint had, presumably, registered their displeasure with either God or the Devil. And given the nature of those involved, it was generally believed that not many of them saw God, and that the Devil, when informed of the Earthly suffering of condemned men was probably in agreement with Rufus Gates' arrangements.

In any event, Gates continued to administer to the convicted with varying degrees of effectiveness for many years, until the above mentioned relative of a dissatisfied customer sent Rufus along to God or the Devil, with most people assuming the latter.

It was a lot of ponder, McCanty thought. Before long, he had retrieved the Sharps from under Nora's bed, and casually informed his friend, John Bullis, of his decision to move on...once the desire for whiskey and whores had played itself out. Which, if past history was any indication, it would in another day or two when the majority of his money was spent.

"Yeah, been thinking about a change of scenery myself," Bullis said, sipping his whiskey, glancing around at the sorry specimens that populated Flanagan's, himself included. Such places grew old quickly, he knew, and once a man or two had been killed, it was usually time to move along. "Any idea where you're headed?" Bullis asked.

"Got some business northwest, in the Territories," McCanty said carefully, not wanting to reveal too much of his activities in a crowded bar.

"I hear your old trading partner, Jake Johnson, is laid up in a place called Rockville," Bullis said. "Shot up pretty bad, they say. Believe it's along that trail."

McCanty seemed surprised at the news. "Jake Johnson is a careful man. It is surprising someone got close enough to shoot him."

"I heard he was ambushed," Bullis said.

"Well, if he survived, I'd bet the bushwackers did not," McCanty said.

"That's what I hear," Bullis agreed.

"Then I guess we'd better go check on ol' Jake," McCanty shook his head. "See what brought him to such a low point that he almost got kilt by amateurs."

Bullis nodded, having heard the stories of the men's adventures. Jake Johnson had been brought up in a Cheyenne village, the offspring of a squaw and an Irish fur hunter, who had found tipi living to his liking. He and McCanty often traded with the Indians, and the goods were not always Army approved, if the rumors were to be believed.

"Gotta go hunt up some buffalo runners on the way?" Bullis said quietly, probing McCanty. Given the previous night's admissions, Bullis decided it might be prudent to inquire after McCanty's plans.

"If I find any," McCanty growled, blinking, realizing Bullis was asking to be invited along, deciding that might not be a bad idea. Bullis was trustworthy, to a point, and he was an excellent hand with a gun, should they encounter any trouble. Which seemed likely, between the Bar-T cowboys, the buff hunters, and the Army, not to mention any hostile Indians.

"Why not ride with me a ways?" McCanty suggested, shrugging. "We can jaw a bit and you can decide how far you want to ride."

"Sure," Bullis said. "I'll ride along a little."

What the hell, he thought, prospects were dim enough. They probably couldn't get much worse.

Bullis realized that McCanty had something in mind that would be dangerous, at the least. Still, he supposed, it was better than hanging around this place, which seemed suddenly small and depressing. Rufus Gates was loudly advertising the bits of hemp from the gallows, and his business seemed brisk. Some of the customers in Flanagan's were ribbing Gates about the botched hanging, which in Bullis' mind was a dangerous thing, because any of the men in the saloon could never be sure about finding themselves on the other side of the law, and the hangman could surely bring about a poor ending. He himself refrained from comment.

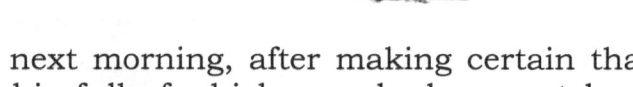

The next morning, after making certain that he had had his full of whiskey and whores, at least for the time being, McCanty left the hotel and headed to the livery stable to collect his animals. There he found the livery owner with his arm in a sling, and in a most foul mood.

"That goddamned mule broke my arm!" the man lamented, his anger increasing when McCanty only chuckled.

"Believe I warned you about that animal's temperament," McCanty said, not unkindly.

"That's the meanest goddamned mule I ever run across!" the livery man gave both McCanty and the creature in question his version of the Evil Eye.

"As I recall, that is what I told you," McCanty said, noticing that the mule was watching the proceedings with what appeared to be genuine interest. Not for the first time, McCanty wondered what the animal was actually thinking. Probably that it would like for someone to open the stall, so it could have another shot at the semi-defenseless livery man.

"I stuck my hand through the stall gate...just for a second, and that devil of a critter swung his big head against my wrist and broke the damned bone!" The man somehow felt it was necessary to explain how he had come by his injury. McCanty thought it might have had something to do with the packs the mule was guarding.

"That mule has killed wolves out on the prairie," McCanty said, getting the packs and saddle together.

"He bit two horses when I corralled him to swamp out his stable," the livery man continued his complaint.

"He don't care much for strange horses, neither," McCanty said.

"I'd like to shoot that son-of-a-bitch," the man remarked, with actual murder in his eyes.

"If you do...don't miss," McCanty said easily. "Nothing makes that mule madder than gettin' shot at."

McCanty could barely contain his laughter at the look in the man's eyes. Fear, mixed with the realization that he had met his match...and that it had taken the unexpected form of a mule. The man stared as McCanty saddled the seemingly docile pack animal.

"He don't seem contrary with you," the livery man observed. In fact, the mule's meanness made him curious. He liked horses and their four legged kin, as behooved a man in the livery business, he supposed. And he did try to understand the animals.

"He knows I really will shoot him if he misbehaves with me," McCanty offered. Which was not exactly true. McCanty had simply learned, after being nipped at a couple of times, not to turn his back on the ornery creature. But the mule did kill wolves if given the opportunity, and was an excellent indicator of approaching trouble on dark prairie nights.

"Hup," the livery man grunted, turning his attention to McCanty's other animal, the ghostly white stallion, which the livery man estimated to be between seventeen or eighteen hands high. He patted the tall horse's shoulder with some affection. "This big fellow, on the other hand, is as calm a critter as I've seen," the livery man remarked.

"Well, he can afford to be calm. He's got the mule for protection," McCanty observed, sliding the Sharps into the saddle sling, slipping the livery man a couple of extra coins for his trouble, which he figured was the point of the extended conversation, anyway. "Get some liniment for that arm," McCanty suggested.

The man chuckled, despite his seemingly grumpy disposition, rolling the coins around in his hand.

"I believe I'll get the kind of liniment that works from the inside out," the man laughed.

McCanty nodded, keeping the mule on a tight lead, knowing it would like nothing better than to take a hunk out of the fast-talking livery man...

"I see you still got that mean ass mule," Bullis said, catching up with them on the road out of town. Even as he made the comment, the gunman reached over and rubbed the animal behind its big ears. "Hello, mule," Bullis said, amiably.

McCanty chuckled and nodded. Dan McCanty found the mule some years back. Or rather, the mule found McCanty when it wandered into his camp along the Platte River one morning at daybreak. Where the animal had come from, what misfortune had overtaken it, McCanty never knew. It arrived, limping, head down, its saddle pack torn, with an arrow punched through the leather, sticking into the mule's shank. It bayed once, pitifully, when McCanty removed the tattered pack and dug the arrow out. Had he known how feisty the creature could be, he would have been considerably more careful. But the mule had most of the fight taken out of it by what appeared to be a Crow arrow, stuck in its hind quarters for a while now, it seemed. McCanty cleaned the wound, rubbed some bear grease on the shank and declared to the beast that it would make a full recovery, for which the mule seemed grateful.

The Crow arrow was something of an oddity, as the mule was most likely an Army animal, and the Crows had thrown in with the Blue Coats as scouts, fighting against their traditional enemies, the Sioux and the Cheyenne. Perhaps the arrow was a result of the mule's meanness, he thought. But McCanty found no markings on the mule's hide to indicate ownership, and so claimed the critter as salvage.

The mule turned out to be a useful companion. It was, of course, a weight bearing animal, only occasionally complaining or balking about its load. And the mule, it had to be admitted, was an unusually good lookout. A lot like a dog, but without all the barking. The mule would alert McCanty to dangers far in advance of what he himself could see, smell or hear. McCanty thought the mule's previous bad experience, whatever it had been, provoked the critter into a constant state of watchfulness. Whatever had happened, no one was sneaking up on that mule again.

For some reason, the mule took to Bullis, tolerating the man, just as it did the horse and McCanty himself. The animal was a continuing source of bafflement to McCanty. In truth, he often suspected the creature might be the smartest among them, now a party of five.

John Bullis was an excellent traveling companion. The man had more stories, more adventures, than any dime novel. Most of them, McCanty suspected, about as factual as those fabricated tales.

"Was down in Le Paso," Bullis was saying as they rode through a sun drenched, unusually hot afternoon. Clouds on the far horizon looked like they might be troublesome, McCanty noted, thinking they had better make camp on high ground. Around them, the grassland stretched out, waving and yellow. A few hills and ridges rose and fell, sheltering the occasional, scattered stands of trees along streams or riverbeds.

"You know, the Bar-T ranch ain't far from here," Bullis observed, interrupting his story. "Might be a good idea to avoid those boys."

"Wasn't planning on asking for hospitality from that bunch," McCanty nodded.

Bullis shrugged, then seemed to remember his story.

"Two Mexican girls," he grinned, mostly to himself, shaking his head at the memory. "One had tits as big and round as bread dough before it's baked..."

Bullis looked at McCanty to see if he understood what was obviously a well thought out image. McCanty nodded his approval, and Bullis grinned some more.

"The other...well, she had these perky little breasts. They looked like they could stand up and sing a song," Bullis said, and McCanty laughed in appreciation. "I confess to a weakness for both kinds of women, and so I took up with the two of them," Bullis admitted. "Not at the same time, mind you. I do have some morals. Also, I figured they might be jealous of one another, so I snuck around with one, then the other. We'd drink tequila and bed down in my room at the local hacienda. It was the life, I tell you! But after a month or so, I was wore to a frazzle, and couldn't stand the sneaking around all the time. So I brung 'em both together, meaning to confess and see where the chips might fall. Well, don't you know, they was sisters, McCanty! Flesh and blood sisters! All this time both of 'em was telling the other about our carrying on! Oh, did we have a laugh over that!" Bullis chuckled, brushing the dust from his hat, as if one or both of the Mexican girls might be waiting up ahead. "But then their father got word that I was defiling both his daughters. That was one mad Mex, I tell you! I got on my horse and didn't stop riding until I hit Texarkana." Bullis paused for a moment, lost in the memory. "I'd sure like to go back to Le Paso again sometime," he said, finally growing quiet for a while.

"So where are we headed after Rockville and what are we gonna do when we get there?" Bullis asked. He was leaning back on his saddle, drinking coffee, lighting a cheroot from the campfire. They'd found a small stand of trees by some slow moving water. Even though the sky was still clear, McCanty insisted they camp high on a knoll and hobble the animals close to the trees.

"You're free to tag along," McCanty said carefully, poking the flames. "But I plan on going pretty deep into the Territories, if I can manage it. Past Fort Sully, up into the high country."

Bullis grunted, staring across the fire at his friend. That was a far piece, and into some very hostile country.

"What's there?" Bullis asked.

McCanty paused before answering. "I got a Cheyenne woman," McCanty admitted. "She's got a sister with some kids, some of whom are Jake Johnson's. I am partial to both, and I figure me and Jake will try to get them out before the Blue Coats make their way that deep into the Territories. Assuming Jake is up to the task."

"So, we talking *wives?*" Bullis asked, startled, even though he thought he was familiar with McCanty's background.

"Sort of," McCanty shrugged. "Not by Christian standards, I suppose, but I gave a lot of ponies to her family. Back in the trappin' days, me and Jake spent some pleasant years together with them women. I go back to winter in that Cheyenne village most years. I'd sure hate to see 'em rubbed out by the Army, or starved by them fuckin' buffalo hunters!"

Bullis nodded his understanding. McCanty's hatred of the buff hunters made sense. It was common knowledge that the government, in particular Generals Sherman and Sheridan, who were in charge of the 'Indian problem', meant to solve the troublesome presence of the Tribes on land Washington wanted open to settlement, by encouraging the buffalo slaughter. Thus forcing the Indians onto reservations, or pushing them into a fight they could not hope to win.

"So you figure the two of you will just ride in, collect your people and ride on out again?" Bullis asked, knowing that might sound easy, but in reality surely would not be so. Even assuming a shot-up Jake Johnson would be healthy enough to make such a journey.

"No," McCanty frowned, his eyes looking troubled in the firelight. "The woman and her sister are in a village headed by a chief named Small Bear.

He can't abide white people. Hates whites with a passion."

"Can't hardly blame him," Bullis observed. "Seeing how the Army, which is mostly white men, means to kill or capture every one of his people, down to the last squaw and babe...no offense meant," Bullis said quickly.

"None taken," McCanty sighed. "I suppose I can see his view, but it seems intolerably stupid to hate everybody who's a different shade from you."

Bullis shook his head and barked out a laugh.

"There might be some fellows down below the Mason-Dixon line who'd disagree," he said.

"Still, don't seem right...or moral," McCanty said weakly.

"Oh, it ain't none of that," Bullis laughed again. "But it surely is the way things are!"

"I guess," McCanty admitted. It was a further reality that a woman he cared deeply about, was in the path of a soon to be rampaging Army.

"So this Small Bear is ill disposed toward whites," Bullis said.

"To the point that he would see his people dead, than in the hands of white men," McCanty replied.

"Including you?" Bullis asked.

"Well, he tolerates me, I guess," McCanty admitted. "We never do see eye to eye, but presents go a long way with Small Bear, particularly the kind I bring. Also, I was friends with the woman's father, Two Eagles, who was the headman before the Army killed him. Small Bear took over the village and moved 'em deep into the high country, as far away from the white invasion as he could get."

"Not far enough," Bullis suggested.

"Ain't no place far enough," McCanty said bitterly.

"So by presents, you mean guns?" Bullis asked, thinking it was a long way to ride, just to get killed by a bunch of pissed-off Indians.

"Small Bear needs guns," McCanty nodded. "If he's going to fight the Army, he needs all the rifles he can get. I bring him what I can, he tends to the woman and her sister when I ain't there."

"Huh," Bullis grunted, stunned by the big man's audacity. Trading guns with the Indians could surely get a man in the deepest trouble possible. Better save some blade-sharpening coins to put in the palm of Rufus Gates, if you get caught, Bullis thought, but didn't say. McCanty surely knew the punishment for gun running to the red man. Johnathan Bullis began to wonder just how far along this trail he was willing to go.

In the night, the mule huffed and blew, and McCanty left his bedroll to check the area. The stars had faded some, as clouds rolled across the sky. It was pitch dark, with no moon. That may have been what bothered the mule, McCanty thought, as he found nothing amiss. McCanty returned to his sleeping robes, resting lightly, with the Sharps tucked beside him like a woman.

The mule let out a sharp baying warning.

"Son-of-bitch!" somebody yelled. "That fucking mule just bit me!"

McCanty was on his feet in an instant. The fire had burned down to a dim glow, but it was bright enough to show shadowy figures moving in behind them. McCanty bent down low, his fingers feeling for the Sharps.

"Nope, you can stop right there, big man," a voice growled from the shadows. The form solidifying, a boot pushed McCanty's rifle out of reach.

Other forms followed, a half dozen men pointing pistols and rifles at he and Bullis, one of them limping, holding a hand to his bloody leg. The leader of this band, a cowboy of medium height, with a wide, cruel grin poking out from under a thin mustache. He wore his gun low, and obviously felt safe enough in the company of his men not to have drawn his weapon.

"Dickie Waters, shootist for the Bar-T," Bullis said, sitting up in his blankets, his hands wisely in front of him. "Considers himself a bad man, don't ya, Dickie? Sneakin' up on folks while they's sleeping..." Bullis shook his head dismissively.

"Why don't I just shoot you in your fast-draw hand for starters, John Bullis, if you don't shut the fuck up?" Dickie Waters said, threateningly.

Bullis just shrugged, as if unimpressed by the threat. But he did keep his mouth shut, McCanty noted. Dickie Waters was indeed a dangerous man. Someone stepped from the shadows and took Bullis' gun belt off the saddle horn under his head.

"Well, is that him?" Waters asked, pointing in McCanty's direction.

"That's him all right," one of the men from the Silver Strike stepped forward and identified McCanty. "That's the man who stabbed Joe Bottom!"

Dickie Waters nodded. "Maybe you'd better let that big ol' pig sticker down, mister," Waters said. "Real easy, if you please."

Seeing little choice in the matter, McCanty unsheathed the knife and dropped it blade first into the ground at his feet.

"What are we gonna do with 'em?" someone asked.

"Wait until morning, then hang 'em," Dickie Waters said, as this was the most obvious thing in the world.

"We should just shoot 'em now and be done with it," the first man suggested, staring at Bullis and McCanty, as if expecting to be shot himself at any moment.

"Naw, let 'em think about it for a bit," Dickie Waters grinned, stirring the fire, throwing some wood on the blaze. "Joe Bottom rode with us. It's only right that we hang his killers."

John Bullis was so impressed by this show of bluster that he rolled over into his blankets and went back to sleep. Or pretended to, McCanty thought, hardly able to believe that even someone like Bullis could take the threat of hanging so casually. McCanty sat on his own saddle, watching as the Bar-T men talked among themselves and boiled coffee. But they were careful, he noted. There were always guns on him and Bullis.

The night wore on. Someone tended to the bleeding man's leg.

"I'd like to shoot that fucking mule," the distressed man growled.

Dickie Waters shook his head. "That there's a working animal," he said, sharply. "We'll be paid in found for the mule and those horses, once we're done here. Although I do believe I'll be keeping that

Sharps for myself," he grinned at McCanty. "Never know, I might want to do me a little buffalo hunting one day."

"Doubt you'll live long enough," McCanty snarled.

Waters laughed. He sipped coffee from a tin cup and made a show of tying knots in two ropes, while smiling at McCanty over the camp fire.

"No one ever believes they're gonna die," Dickie Waters said, his eyes taking on a faraway look as he stared into the fire. "They just can't believe it's gonna happen to them."

He looked over and grinned at McCanty.

"See...even you, right now," Waters said, knowingly. "You think there's some way out of this. That something'll happen and you'll get to carry on through another day."

Waters laughed and McCanty had to admit the man was right.

"We all think that," Waters nodded sagely. "That's because those of us sitting here breathing can't imagine we won't always be doing it. And when the day comes, when the moment comes, it's such a surprise! You can see it in a man's eyes when they're gut shot. And when they hang, you can see it in that very instant when the horse moves out from under 'em. When the rope tightens around their neck. When the breathin' is over..."

Waters drew a deep breath and winked over at McCanty.

"It only lasts a second though, so you got to be watching carefully," Waters said, knowingly. "Because after that second, the dying starts. The eyes bulge out, big as hen's eggs. A man's face turns red, then redder, then finally black, almost like a nigger. The tongue sticks out, a man shits and pisses hisself. The smell is something terrible...but you'll find all that out for your own self, right soon. I'll hang Bullis first, so you can see."

Waters smiled again. There was the first, faint light of approaching dawn in the horizon. McCanty felt a shiver run up his back.

"John Bullis didn't kill your friend," McCanty said, casually. "Was just me done that."

Dickie Waters shrugged his shoulders, as if that fact was of little consequence.

"Joe Bottom was a big mouth bully, from what I could tell," McCanty tried another tact.

Surprisingly, Dickie Waters laughed and nodded. "He was," Waters agreed, almost good naturedly. "But you still kilt him."

McCanty nodded at that fact. "I did, but he picked the fight," McCanty grinned back. "Joe Bottom thought he was tough. He weren't tough at all. You tough there, Dickie Waters?"

The low talk among the Bar-T boys stopped abruptly. Dickie Waters was not a man who got challenged often, but when he did the results were always quick and predictable.

"Tough enough," Waters said, putting his rope aside, staring at McCanty from under the brim of his hat.

"Want to find out how tough you are?" McCanty said softly, drawing himself to his feet. The men behind him cocked their weapons, but took an involuntary step back.

Dickie Waters looked at the man carefully.

"You are built heavy as an ox," Waters acknowledged, nodding amiably. "But you got a few years on you, for sure."

"That's because I ain't easy to kill," McCanty said, grinning now, judging the distance between himself and the men with the guns at his back, coming to the unfortunate conclusion that he could not get to them before they pumped a bunch of lead into his body.

"No, I bet you ain't," Waters said, judging how best to kill this big-talking old man.

Dickie Waters stood, dusting off his pants, adjusting his gun belt. He had decided that he would shoot the old fuck in one or both of his knees, then hang the son-of-a-bitch with the dawn light shining fully in his eyes.

"Now, you ain't suggesting a hand-to-hand fist fight, are you?" Waters asked, looking slyly over at the mountain man. "I mean, that don't hardly seem fair, you being so overly large and all..."

"And you not being overly large at all..." McCanty drove his advantage into Waters like a fist.

The shorter man looked up at him, rage working its way across Dickie Water's face. McCanty smiled, watching the man's eyes harden in the firelight, his mouth curling into a snarl. McCanty knew he might still die, with so many guns pointed at him, but he would not hang, and he would have the opportunity to fight for his life.

"How about we make it weapon of choice?" McCanty suggested. "It's said that Sam Colt made every man the same size, and Bullis said you call yourself a shootist. You any good with that pistol on your hip?"

Dickie Waters laughed, and John Bullis was interested enough to poke his head out of his blankets.

"You gonna shoot with me?" Waters asked, the confidence obvious in his voice.

"Naw, weapons of choice," McCanty said easily. "I'll bet my knife against your gun."

McCanty bent down and picked his blade out of the ground. The guns behind him took another step back, further away from McCanty's dangerous wingspan.

"You'll be betting a whole lot more than that Arkansas Toothpick," Waters laughed.

"You can kill me, if you're man enough, and hang Bullis at daybreak," McCanty offered the terms, ignoring Bullis' yelp of protest.

Dickie Waters laughed again, looked at his men, who stared back at him. He had been challenged and he knew enough about the laws of the pack to understand that when the Alpha Wolf is challenged, he must answer in no uncertain terms. Waters stared back at McCanty, who stood loosely on the other side of the fire. Waters was firmly confident. The opponent was big and strong, but Waters had his pistol, for God's sake. What was the other thing they always said? Don't bring a knife to a gun fight. Dickie Waters put McCanty's chances firmly at zero. He would shoot the big man in his knees and hang the both of them within the hour.

"I surely will," Waters said, a glint in his eye.

Bullis was sitting up, staring intently. Gauging how he could help gain the upper hand, once Daniel McCanty killed the little prick. Which he was certain was about to happen, although he couldn't say how, exactly.

"You really any good with that revolver?" McCanty asked, twirling the big knife on the end of his fingertips, the blade shining in the firelight, as he threw it from hand to hand.

"Hell, yes!" Dickie Waters snarled again, drawing his weapon, twirling it through the air, making the gun almost dance in his hands. In a final flourish, the gun flashed in the firelight like

McCanty's blade, before starting the return trip to Waters' holster.

And even John Bullis had to admit that it was a pretty impressive display. Or would have been, if McCanty had not stepped across the fire as the Colt was making its last pass through the air. The blade of the long knife flashing once again, an instant before it disappeared into Dickie Waters' sternum. The look in Waters' eyes, McCanty saw, was one of astonishment, confusion, and downright terror. McCanty had moved in a blur, driving the knife into Waters' chest, whose body jerked once under the impact of the blow, then seemed to crumble and fold around the blade. A gasp came from Waters' mouth as if all the air had been let out of him. Which it had, Bullis realized, struck by the hollow, gurgling sound Waters made as he died.

"Breathin' is over," McCanty whispered into Dickie Waters' ear.

McCanty had the man's gun. Bullis reached behind his saddle for his Henry rifle. The Bar-T cowboys looked as astonished as Dickie Waters himself.

"What?" McCanty said belligerently, pointing the Colt at the nearest group of men. "Did you think I was gonna let the son-of-a-bitch walk off ten paces and start shooting at me?"

Bullis almost laughed, even though the situation was still dire. But it became less so moments later when the Bar-T cowboys lost their nerve and faded into the gathering light of day.

"Should we bury him?" McCanty asked, pulling his knife from Dickie Waters' body, wondering if the man's friends would be coming back for him.

"Fuck no! The prick was gonna hang us!" Bullis growled, kicking the body aside, pouring himself a cup of half-baked coffee. "Dumb bastard! I couldn't believe he let you pick up your knife. I admit, I was a might worried until then."

"Me, too," McCanty laughed.

CHAPTER TEN

Rockville

A sudden hush fell over the Silver Strike Saloon. Jim Warner looked up from his conversation with Three-fingered Rolly Jenkins, a cowboy who had the first two fingers of his right hand blown off when his sidearm malfunctioned. He was shooting at a rattlesnake at the time and got so mad, he leaped off his startled horse and beat the snake to death with his split-barreled Navy Colt.

"Them fuckin' conversion kits ain't worth a shit," Jenkins was scratching his mangled hand, retelling his story for probably the hundredth time, Warner figured.

He was nodding agreement with Three-fingers about the unreliability of cap 'n ball weapons turned into cartridge guns, when Big Ed Grimes walked through the doors, throwing the saloon into an unexpected hush. Big Ed had been brought to trial several times in surrounding towns for assault and cattle rustling and the like, but nobody had ever put together a jury brave enough to convict him.

"The Sheriff ain't here," Jim Warner said, trying to keep the fear out of his voice as the man walked to the bar and ordered whiskey.

"I guess I can see that," Ed Grimes grunted, watching his back in the bar mirror, as the Silver Strike slowly regained its normal noise level. Bad men like Grimes coming in for a drink was not unusual, and everyone thought the best line of defense was to resume normal activities and hope nothing disastrous happened. Warner nodded to the piano man, who picked up his tempo.

"We don't want no trouble," Warner said. He kept a scattergun under the bar, but knew he had little chance against a man like Ed Grimes.

"Ain't here for trouble," Grimes threw down his whiskey and nodded for another, rattling some coins on the bar. His eye caught Skeet Miller hanging at the faro table. "You're the deputy, ain't ya?" he said loudly.

"I am," Skeet admitted, looking confused and a bit afraid, Warner thought.

"Well, there's no warrants on me," Grimes said roughly. "And I don't guess there's any law against a man having a drink."

"There ain't," Skeet said, trying to put a rough edge to his voice.

Ed Grimes chuckled at the effort. "Good," he said, in what Warner considered passed for amiable in Grimes' world. "Then I'll have my drink, maybe poke one of them Upstairs Girls, and be on my way. If nobody's got any objections?"

It appeared no one had, at least none they were willing to speak up about, so the Silver Strike took a long, collective breath. Bad men had come and gone before. Maybe this was one of those lucky times when danger blew through town like an ill-wind, leaving only stirred up sand in its wake. Maybe. The piano man played, the faro dealer turned cards, Skeet Miller thought it might be a good idea to do a patrol walk, and everybody else tried to ignore the bad man drinking at the bar.

"What'd you do?" Ed Grimes noticed Three-finger Jenkins standing next to him. "Stick your fingers in the wrong hole?"

"You might say that," Rolly, who was drunk enough not to sense the barely contained violence beside him, launched into his snake and busted gun story.

Jim Warner returned to his bartender duties. A cowboy or two took a couple of the Upstairs Girls to their rooms, and an edgy normalcy returned to the Silver Strike. Big Ed Grimes laughed roundly at Three-fingers' story, working his way down the bottle in front of him.

"Ought to get you a good Smith and Wesson Scofield," Big Ed said, lifting his pistol from its holster, slamming it loudly on the bar. Grimes looked around at the scrambling that ensued when his weapon cleared. Then he grinned and returned the .44 to its holster. "Didn't mean to alarm nobody," he said, shrugging. "Jumpy in these parts, ain't they?"

Rolly Jenkins agreed that they seemed to be, as he came to his senses and casually edged away from the bar.

Another hour or so passed before Grimes proclaimed loudly, "I guess I'll have me one of them whores now! If there's one around who ain't afraid of a real man!"

Lizzie, who was easily the most bold and brash of the Upstairs Girls, particularly when she had a few drinks in her, shook off Kate's restraining arm.

"What?" Lizzie shrugged. "Like I'm supposed to be afraid of some bad man?"

Ed Grimes laughed, hooked her arm, and started upstairs.

"That's good," he said, his words slurred from the whiskey. "I like 'em feisty."

"Wait a minute, mister," Jim Warner said, standing in the general vicinity of his scattergun. Ed

Grimes turned from the girl and stared back at the bartender. "No guns allowed upstairs. We got a rule."

"Well, I'll take my gun off to fuck," Grimes said, with more than a trace of menace in his voice. "But I believe I'll keep it on me until the festivities start."

There was a moment, as Jim Warner frowned, wondering if he could pull the scattergun before Ed Grimes could draw and shoot. Grimes raised an eyebrow, watching him closely. But Lizzie, seeking to avoid the confrontation, shook her head and pulled Grimes along. Warner shrugged as the bad man and the whore disappeared upstairs. Kate, he saw, was looking at him in disgust. Warner shook his head and ignored her. The piano man hit his keys, the faro dealer turned his cards...and it was a few minutes before the loud banging noises filtered down from upstairs. A few minutes more before there was slapping sounds and Lizzie began to scream.

"That son-of-a-bitch!" Kate growled, moving around the bar for the scattergun. Warner grabbed her arm and silently shook his head. "You fucking coward!" Kate yelled, glancing around the Silver Strike for help. Finding none...

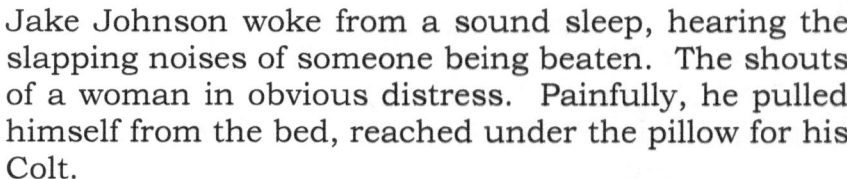

Jake Johnson woke from a sound sleep, hearing the slapping noises of someone being beaten. The shouts of a woman in obvious distress. Painfully, he pulled himself from the bed, reached under the pillow for his Colt.

Limping down the hallway, he heard the pain induced cries coming from the room where he knew Lizzie conducted her business. He shouldered open the door, and the sight disgusted him. Lizzie was naked, cowering on the bed, a large, mean looking man standing over her, about to swing his belt again.

"That's enough of that, mister!" Johnson growled.

"Who the fuck do you think you are?" Ed Grimes swayed drunkenly. "I paid for this whore, and I'm damn well gonna get my money's worth!"

"I don't think so," Johnson mumbled, feeling the floor sway under him, like a boat in choppy seas. His vision blurred. He heard the big man in front of him laugh. Saw that Lizzie was terrified.

"Is this the best they got around here?" Ed Grimes laughed some more. "They send up some sick old man? Come on in and join the party. You can have some of the same!"

Johnson saw the man lunge at him, raised his pistol. Too late, he thought, through the blur of his vision. Too slow...before he knew it, the man grabbed the barrel of his Colt...and Jake Johnson dropped the hammer. The explosion loud and stunning in his ears. The big man got a strange, confused look on his face...and dropped to the floor, gushing blood from a powder-blackened wound in his chest.

"Have some of that, you bastard!" Johnson said, turning calmly, making his way back down the hall. He almost got to Jenna's bed before he fell over. Then there were more sounds. Confused running, shouting, hands lifting him back under the covers. Later when he woke, his ears were ringing, but he couldn't remember why, exactly.

The shovels and picks began ringing. Doc Watson was somehow able to drag himself out of his tent and down to his worked-out claim on the Whitefish River.

Owen Scales decided that three days spent drunk in the mining camp was quite enough. He saddled his horse and began the ride back to town, his head jumbled and confused. Pack mules worked their way up the trail to the camp. A teamster, who swayed on his buckboard seat like he had passed the night in much the same manner as Doc Watson, Charlie Wells and himself, drove by with a wagon full of supplies. There were other men on the trail to the camp; so many that Scales convinced himself Doc Watson had to be mistaken. The camp looked to be thriving. Still, Doc seemed to know what he was talking about, even if Charlie Wells had laughed off the idea of the camp shutting down as foolish. And when he topped the hill leading to Rockville, he saw the bustling, growing town. Scales couldn't believe that it might all end. That the shops would close, the people would move on, the buildings would become abandoned. It just didn't seem possible. Not with the breeze blowing fresh and sharp, cleaning the whiskey fumes from his head, bringing with it the sounds of new construction. Every day, the wooden buildings of Main Street pushed further into the canvas tent settlements set up by the new arrivals. Every day the town got bigger, more permanent, becoming a solid fixture on the landscape. That all of this could suddenly grind to a bitter halt was impossible...or so he forced himself to believe.

There was something wrong. Scales sensed it, even before he saw the crowd gathered outside the Silver Strike Saloon. If there was a crowd, even this early in the afternoon, they should have been inside the saloon. He rode in on Main Street, tied his horse to the hitching rail, noticed several cowboys and townspeople glancing at him with strange looks in their eyes. Before he could even mount the steps to the Silver Strike, Jim Warner came out, and Scales could see the concern on the man's face. Concern mixed with what? Fear...anger?

"Where the hell have you been?" Warner asked, in an almost accusing manner. "We sent Billy Jolin up the mountain to find you!"

"Never seen him," Scales said, frowning. "What's going on?"

"What's going on is Skeet Miller is dead!" Jim Warner said.

Scales tipped his hat back, trying to digest this information.

"Dead? How?" Scales asked, feeling like a dog hearing a high-pitched, distant sound he could not identify.

"Two of them Grimes boys rode through town yesterday and shot Skeet where he sat in front of the jail!" Warner said, shaking his head.

"What'd they shoot Skeet for?" Scales asked.

"For what you and Jake Johnson done to their brothers," Warner explained, as if this was the most obvious thing in the world.

"Jake Johnson? Look, can you slow down and tell me what's going...from the start?" Scales said, trying to understand.

Jim Warner sighed, indicating he had bigger problems, which irritated Owen Scales somewhat.

"A couple days ago Ed Grimes came here looking for you," Warner shook his head. The townspeople behind him nodding, grumbling. "He got drunk and used Lizzie real bad. Jake Johnson got up from his sick bed and shot Big Ed right in the heart, from about two feet away. Kilt him dead. Next morning, the other two Grimes rode through town and shot Skeet Miller."

"Dead before he hit the ground," Slim the barber said, authoritatively.

"Good Christ!" Scales heard himself say. The news was surreal and shocking. Skeet Miller had been the Rockville deputy for years, even before Scales became sheriff. "Where are those goddamned Grimes?" he growled angrily.

"They high-tailed it out while poor Skeet was still warm," Warner explained. "But they said they'd be back, to deal with you and Jake Johnson the same way!"

"Well, I guess they can try, if they got the sand for it," Scales said belligerently, now understanding the fear and confusion in everyone's eyes. "Where's Skeet?"

"He's sharing the ice house in back of my place with Big Ed Grimes," Slim said sadly. "One of the carpenters is putting together a box for him. Some of the boys are up at the cemetery digging two graves."

"Those bastard Grimes!" Scales growled, spitting into the dust.

Jim Warner grabbed his arm and pulled him aside.

"That ain't all," Warner said urgently. "Kate's upstairs with Lizzie and the girls. Says she's leaving and taking them with her! They're packing their things right now. You got to put a stop to this, Owen. She's serious!"

"All right...all right," Scales said, the information coming too quick for him to properly process. "I'll talk to her. But, really, I'm not sure what I can do..."

"Well, you can stop her from stealing my whores!" Jim Warner seemed outraged at the possibility.

Scales, feeling his world crumbling at the edges, pushed past the bartender and stomped up to the Upstairs Rooms, where he found a flurry of activity. The bedroom doors were all open, clothes being thrown into traveling trunks, his presence largely ignored until he made his way into Kate's room at the end of the hall.

"Kate..." he began. She turned, stared at him, shaking her head.

"Told you I was leaving," she said, almost sadly, he thought.

The familiar trappings of the room, looking dingy and dusty in the light of day. Old and used, particularly with Kate's things removed from the dresser, packed into an open trunk on the floor.

"I thought we was going to talk about this some more," Scales said weakly.

"We talked," Kate said quietly.

"I don't want you to go," Scales heard himself say, knowing how pitiful it sounded.

"Then come with us," Kate said abruptly. "Because I won't spend a minute more than I have to in this smelly excuse of a town!"

"I can't just up and quit my job," Scales shook his head.

"Well, I can!" Kate said angrily. "I won't stay in a place where my girls are treated worse than animals."

Lizzie, he saw, was limping down the hallway. Her appeal spoiled by blackened eyes and an obviously broken nose.

"Those Grimes'll be back...and they'll bring the rest of their clan with them. I don't plan to be around when they show up," Kate snapped, turning her back on him, sweeping up an armful of dresses, throwing them into her trunk.

Knowing he wasn't going to win the argument, Scales backed out of Kate's doorway, looking across to Big Jenna's room, where the bed was empty and Jenna was hurriedly packing her own belongings.

"Where's Jake Johnson?" he asked, as Jenna looked up at him.

"I think he's at the livery stable," Jenna shrugged. "He's supposed to be getting a wagon for us."

"Appears you got better in a hurry," Scales said, standing outside the stall where Jake Johnson was rubbing the big roan's nose, feeding the horse from a bag of grain.

"Circumstances called for it, I guess," Jake said, not turning from his horse.

Harv Gorman, owner of the livery stable, stuck his grizzled head through the wide entry doors of his establishment.

"Got that wagon," he called out. "She's an old Conestoga, but in pretty sound shape. I greased the axles for ya. The mules are a strong team."

"Thank you, Mr. Gorman," Jake Johnson waved from the stall. "If you'd be good enough to bring it around to the Silver Strike...and throw my saddle in the back, if you would."

"You bet," Harv nodded, pleased that his business with such a famous killer of men had gone so smoothly. "That horse of yours sure does drink a lot of beer," Gorman said, casually.

"He does," Jake Johnson agreed. "But only when he's in town. He's sober as a judge on the trail."

"You ain't seen many of our judges," Harv said, shouldering the famous killer's saddle.

"So you're taking the girls out of here?" Scales asked, watching Johnson's slow movements, the way he winced as he brushed down his horse. In truth, the man's wounds seemed to have aged him ten years. Scales had seen that in gut shot victims before. Some, he knew, never fully recovered. "Didn't think you'd be able to ride yet. Doc Watson didn't believe so, neither."

"Not taking them," Jake replied carefully. "They're leaving, and I'm just hitching a ride." The man paused, rubbed his heavily bandaged side. "You're right, though. I'd probably fall off my damn horse, before I got ten miles. But I believe I can ride shotgun on the wagon for 'em."

"That's good," Scales nodded. "It can be rough country for women traveling alone."

"They're pretty tough women," Johnson commented dryly.

"They are," Scales agreed. "But there's still some of that Grimes gang out and about."

"Well, I guess we're working our way through the bastards one at a time," Jake commented.

Scales chuckled. "I guess we are," he said agreeably. "Your Winchester's still over at the jail. I'll drop it by the Silver Strike."

"Appreciate that," Johnson nodded.

"Take good care of them, Mr. Johnson," Scales said, turning away, as the old gunman nodded, putting a bridal lead on the big roan.

"You take care of yourself, Sheriff," Johnson called, as Scales stepped out into the sunlight.

A good sized crowd gathered around the Silver Strike, cowboys and miners helping the Upstairs Girls with their trunks and bags. Jim Warner watched the proceedings grimly from the front doors of the saloon.

"I can't believe you're letting Kate steal my whores," he said forlornly.

Scales shrugged, equally grim. "Once Kate gets her mind set..." he said, not feeling up to finishing the thought.

"I believe we fought a war about that," Doc Watson said, having run into Billy Jolin, who had stopped off to spark a girl at a sod buster's house. Well, not exactly spark, as she took most of young Billy's money for what was an altogether too quick encounter. But Billy had finally delivered his message, if to the wrong person. Doc, seeing there was very little metal coming out of the ground, drifted down from the camp to say goodbye to some of his charges.

"We fought a war over whores?" Warner frowned.

"Over slavery," Watson seemed exasperated that he had to explain his comment.

"Slavery, shit..." Warner grumbled. "Where am I gonna get more whores?"

"Where'd you get these?" Watson asked, assuming that was a fair question.

"They come with the place when I bought it," Warner said disgustedly.

It didn't take an hour, from start to finish, Scales guessed. The wagon packed, some tearful goodbyes between the Upstairs Girls and their favorite customers. Kate came down the long stairs of the Silver Strike for the last time, went over and shook Doc Watson's hand.

"Thanks for taking care of all us," she said.

"My pleasure, ma'am," Watson tipped his hat.

"Sheriff, I hope to see you again," she said, offering her hand.

Scales brushed it aside and hugged her. "I hope so, Kate, I truly do," Scales whispered.

She pushed herself away, dabbing her eyes.

"No hard feelings, Jim Warner?" she asked hopefully.

"No hard feelings, my ass," Warner growled, shaking his head, yet glancing quickly at Owen Scales to see if he had crossed the line into insult. But the Sheriff seemed to be paying little attention to him.

Kate shrugged, set her jaw, squared her shoulders and went to the wagon, where the girls were being lifted into the back of the canvas-topped Conestoga wagon. Lizzie, Sara, and Little Anne. Jenna disdained any help and pulled herself up inside. Kate looked around at the town, as if taking a picture of it in her mind. She installed herself up on the front bench, where Jake Johnson waited, the Winchester across his lap. She flicked the reins, the four mules dutifully began leaning into their traces, and the wagon, with the big roan tethered to the back, rolled out of Rockville. Behind them, the crowd of cowboys and miners drifted into the Silver Strike, to drink and recall the Upstairs Girls with genuine fondness.

"I bet it's gonna get real quiet in here, real soon," Doc Watson said casually, which seemed a strange statement, given the general ruckus of the place at the moment.

Lucky for Watson, Jim Warner was too busy to hear the comment, or he might later have taken great offense.

CHAPTER ELEVEN

Town Cowboy

"Changeable weather in these parts," McCanty said to Bullis, who was stirring the ashes of last night's fire to warm some coffee. In truth, it was a lot warmer than it should have been at this time of the year, in McCanty's mind.

Bullis looked up at the clouds and grunted, dismissing the weather, which McCanty thought unwise.

"Can rain like hell in these parts, when it gets its mind to it," McCanty said.

Bullis shrugged, indifferent.

"You ain't much of a morning person, are ya?" McCanty joked, laughing when his riding companion grunted again, sounding like a sleeping bear poked with a stick. "Guess not," McCanty shrugged, knowing enough not to poke a sleeping bear with anything other than the Sharps.

"Don't sleep good out in the open," Bullis admitted, as they saddled up for the day's ride. "Guess I've gotten too used to walls and a bed."

"This ride'll cure you of that," McCanty chuckled. "Ain't a wall or a bed for miles around."

"No soft-backed horses, neither, I suppose," Bullis joked back, in a better mood now that he'd had his coffee.

In truth, Bullis considered himself to be as brave as the next man, but he was having some serious second thoughts about this particular venture.

"So how and where are you planning to acquire these rifles to trade for them women?" Bullis asked, as the day brightened and the wind rippled the grass. "What'd you say their names were?"

"Didn't," McCanty responded, sniffing the air, not liking the feel of it, despite the sun poking through the clouds in long lances of light. "My woman's called Blackbird Woman and her sister is Yellowbird. There's some half-white children. Jake Johnson's mostly...but I feel obligated to keep 'em from getting kilt by the Blue Coats."

Bullis nodded. Of course, McCanty wasn't the first white man he'd known to have an Indian woman. But he was the first Bullis had encountered who'd ride hundreds of miles in what even McCanty had to realize was a trip with a low chance of success. Not to mention that trading guns to the Indians could get you killed in any number of ways.

"And the guns?" Bullis asked again, when it seemed that McCanty was lost in a span of remembering.

"I know a fellow who steals from the Army on a regular basis," McCanty said casually. "Getting the guns won't be a problem. The Army is somewhat lax with its accounting."

Bullis laughed. Truth was, just about everyone in the West had supplied themselves at one time or another with Army material, mostly in the form of food and horses.

"So this fellow will risk his neck to supply rifles to the Indians?" Bullis asked.

"No," McCanty replied, shaking his head. "But he'll risk his neck for money. He'll sell the guns for gold or currency."

"And you've got gold or currency?" Bullis asked.

"Naw," McCanty shook his head again. "Not enough for a wagon or guns. But not to worry. Something will come up. It always does."

Bullis shrugged, riding along quietly for a while. Ahead of them, the clouds began rising out of the horizon like smoke. The old mountain man might be right about the rain, Bullis considered, once again missing walls...and a roof.

"This plan, if I'm hearing it right, is to get guns from the Army, repeating Winchesters and such, and trade 'em to these wild, warpath painted Cheyenne, in the hope that they'll give you back your Indian wife and her sister?" Bullis asked, mostly for clarification, since he was pretty sure of the facts.

McCanty nodded. "That's about the size of it."

"And you think this Small Bear will make that kind of a deal?" Bullis couldn't help sounding skeptical.

"Well, if he's going to fight the Army, he's going to have to even the odds a little," McCanty said. "He's got to see that going up against soldiers with guns, he'll need more firepower than bows and arrows and war lances."

"So you plan on supplying this war chief with cannon and Gatling guns?" Bullis asked. "'Cause I never seen an Indian fire a cannon. Might be worth the ride just to see something like that..."

"No," McCanty admitted, somewhat sorrowfully, Bullis thought. "Won't be able to get no cannon nor

Gatling guns. Although, believe me, if I could even the odds that much, I surely would. I can give Small Bear some Winchesters and maybe a few hundred rounds of ammunition, but that's about all. That's why the Tribes can't hope to win in any prolonged conflict with the Bluecoats. It's just not a fair fight."

"Not to mention that there's probably ten Army regulars to every Indian on the plains," Bullis added. "With supply trains reaching back a thousand miles, while the government sends out shooting teams into the Territories to exterminate the buffalo. They mean to starve the Tribes, before the troops even take the field."

"You'd have made a proper general," McCanty glanced at the gunman. "That's Sherman's strategy, exactly. The Indian is already defeated, although most of 'em don't know it yet. Their land is going to be taken, their way of life pushed aside, as the white man comes on like a swarm of locusts. Sometimes, I admit, it shames me some to be a white man," McCanty admitted.

"A white man?" Bullis laughed. "Sometimes I'm down right ashamed to call myself a human being! Besides, you ain't that much of an actual white man. You're more a cross between an Indian, a wolf, and maybe a grizzly bear. I ain't exactly sure."

"It's the Irish in me," McCanty said, shrugging. "We mix with just about anything, and the result is some kind of mongrel."

"Mongrel...yeah, that's it," Bullis decided. "But if you somehow manage to avoid the Army with your gun running scheme, how come the Cheyenne don't just kill you and Jake Johnson, and take the damned guns? I mean, since this Small Bear hates whites so much?"

McCanty hesitated for a moment. "Well, they ain't done so yet," he said, and Bullis found this profoundly unsettling.

"I am also mighty tired of this uncertain weather," Bullis took off his hat and poured some water over his head. He figured since he was complaining, he might as well have all his concerns noted. "One day a man is dealing with the prickly heat, next mornin' it's frostbite."

McCanty grunted in agreement. The contrary winds seemed to blow one minute from the south, next minute from the north.

"A man could get his face sunburnt, and his butt froze, both at the same time, depending on which way he's facing," Bullis shook his head.

"It is vexing," McCanty agreed, studying the sky, trying to decide if it intended to rain or snow. But maybe it wouldn't matter. "With a little luck, we'll reach Rockville in a day...two, at most."

"I surely hope there's soft beds, whiskey and whores," Bullis said critically. "This rough living ain't for me. I believe I've become a town cowboy."

McCanty couldn't help but laugh.

CHAPTER TWELVE

Rockville

Doc Watson proved right, Scales later thought. It did get real quiet, real fast in the Silver Strike. As the days passed, and word of the Upstairs Girls' departure spread, many of the cowboys and miners found other places to spend their wages. Places where, it was said, the whiskey wasn't as good and the whores weren't nearly as pretty, or clean...and a breeze might suddenly blow up from a canvas flap when a man's pants were down. But there were whores and whiskey, so they made do. Even the faro dealer packed up his table and moved on to one of the canvas tent saloons at the far end of Main Street.

Owen Scales felt the loss more deeply than he would have imagined. He found himself short-tempered when dealing with the drunk cowboys and miners. And knew that he was drinking more than he should. Many a morning he woke up in his bare hotel room with blistering headaches, until even Doc Watson stopped giving him powders to kill the pain.

"You don't need more powders," Watson warned. "You need less whiskey."

Poor advice, Scales figured, from a man who was drunk most of the time himself. Yet, he knew Watson was right, and he made an effort to pull himself together.

Jim Warner fared little better. Business was so bad, he had to let the piano man go and now the Silver Strike stood mostly quiet, even on Saturday night.

"I told you not to let her steal my whores," he complained to Scales, who was trying to reform and some days drank only beer. It was the only bright spot in Jim Warner's life at the moment.

"Weren't my fault," Scales shook his head. The silence of the Silver Strike, without the piano man, the faro dealer, and all the Upstairs Girls had become depressing. Men talked, but the words, it seemed, passed through holes in the air without being heard.

"Maybe not," Warner sounded unconvinced. Lately, he had been given to rethinking past events and wished now that he had had the nerve to shoot Ed Grimes himself that night when the bad man had taken Lizzie up the now deserted stairs. A cold wind brushed against the swinging doors of the Silver Strike and Three-fingered Jenkins shoved a log into the Franklin stove in the middle of the mostly empty room.

"Go easy on the wood there," Warner said angrily. "Long winter coming. We'll be burning the tables and chairs before it's over."

"I'll bring you some coal down from the camp," Doc Watson said, warming his hands by the meager fire. He, Jenkins, and the mute half-breed hunter, LaBonty, had their chairs inches from the Franklin.

"Coal?" Scales asked.

"Yeah, the Stony Creek outfit hit a vein of the stuff before they left," Watson replied. "Those that remain are poor, but warm up on the mountain."

It went unsaid that in a few weeks the ground and the Whitefish River would be freezing over. Also that most of the miners had packed up their belongings and had already moved on. Scales felt the cold, felt his town freezing up, coming to a stop. There were no longer any new buildings going up, as Rockville waited for word from the railroad, and perhaps more importantly to see if anybody from Redeye Baker's outfit would return to root around for the vanished silver vein. Rockville wasn't simply hunkering down for the winter, Scales realized. It was dying.

"I heard this place was a growing concern," Bullis said, as they made their way down a quiet, mostly deserted main street.

"Don't look all that prosperous at the moment," McCanty agreed.

Buildings stood with their construction seemingly halted in mid-nail. Pieces of canvas tent hung from wooden frames, where their owners had torn them down in obvious haste. The owners no longer in sight, the wooden frames looking like bones somebody forgot to bury. Rockville already had a ghost-town appearance to it, despite the few dogs and chickens still poking around.

They pulled up in front of the Silver Strike Saloon, the sign above the door promising: Liquor, Girls, Gambling. All of which turned out to be bald-faced lies, except for the liquor part. Indeed, McCanty noted, the place was mostly deserted, with the exception of a few men jawing around a belly stove. The saloon had the sound and feel of a funeral parlor, he thought.

"Who the hell are you?" a nervous sheriff touched his gun, tipping down from a chair in which he seemed to have been half asleep.

"We're thirsty men. This here's a saloon, ain't it?" John Bullis said, not liking nervous men with guns, sheriff or not. The two men stared at each other for a moment.

"It is," Jim Warner stood to the bar, wiping down the dust with a rag, as if he wasn't used to actual customers. "You'll have to forgive Sheriff Scales. He ain't been himself since his town went bust. Whiskey, gents?"

Bullis nodded, as if he was still deciding whether or not to ignore the Sheriff's outburst. In truth, Owen Scales looked embarrassed to have fallen asleep following his after lunch beer. He found himself more than a little relieved that these strangers did not appear to be associated with the Grimes family. They could have shot him easily, he realized, vowing to be more vigilant.

"Sorry..." he mumbled, tipping his head in the strangers' direction. The men at the bar largely ignored him.

"Why'd the town go bust?" McCanty inquired, feeling the invigorating burn of the whiskey in his throat. He looked closer for the women and the gambling, finding neither.

"Mine played out," a man identifying himself as Doc Watson stood to the bar. "Place went to hell in a heartbeat."

"Just a few weeks ago, people were building on this street day and night," Jim Warner said, sadly. As if remembering the good times, like they were yesterday. Which they mostly seemed to be, McCanty thought. "Now those same people have picked up and moved on, quick as they could load their wagons."

So that's why the place had the feel of a funeral parlor, McCanty thought. It was a town in its death throes.

"Reckon we'll be moving on right soon," McCanty said. Everyone at the bar and around the belly stove nodded sadly, as if they wished they could do so themselves. Although McCanty did not see anything that seemed to be holding anybody here. "We're looking for a pard of mine rumored to be hereabouts...Jake Johnson. Anybody know him?"

At that, the room took on a surprising change in character. Some people were cursing, some laughing. The Sheriff seemed to have woken from a dream and walked to the bar with a look in his eye that could only mean trouble. McCanty was afraid Bullis might shoot the man.

"Jesus Christ, are you planning on hanging anybody?" Bullis said instead. McCanty followed the gunman's glare and saw, to his astonishment, Rufus Gates sitting at a table in the corner, over by the empty piano. Gates saw them staring and raised his glass in greeting.

"No," the Sheriff said, blinking in confusion. "Not that I'm aware of..."

Owen Scales realized that he was drinking altogether too much these days.

"Good," Bullis said, sounding almost relieved. In truth, he had had enough of hangings to last him a while.

"Gates passes through here on his way to the Territorial Prison in Clayton," Jim Warner said. "Although a good hanging here might be just the thing for business."

"Or a poor hanging," Doc Watson put in.

"Amen to that," Warner said, recalling the good old days of only a few weeks past.

"Ol' Rufus liked the Upstairs Girls," someone by the belly stove said. "He'd stop by even if there weren't nobody to hang."

"We all liked the Upstairs Girls," a man next to him said. And next to him, a wild looking fellow grunted in agreement.

"Those Upstairs Girls, they were the crux of the economy around these parts," Doc Watson said, authoritatively.

"Well, where the hell are they?" John Bullis asked, his third whiskey settling in nicely.

"Jake Johnson took them to Hayes City," Jim Warner said bitterly. "That son-of-a-bitch..." he started to say, before looking up at the cold eyes of the big man with the Sharps. "Well, it was mostly the girls' doin', I suppose," Warner amended.

"What do you men want with Jake Johnson?" the Sheriff asked, using his best authoritative voice. To his chagrin, both strangers ignored him again.

"So there's no Upstairs Girls about?" John Bullis asked. Both Jim Warner and Doc Watson shook their heads.

McCanty walked over to the piano, next to which Rufus Gates sat quietly. He had a whispered word with the hangman, during which several gold pieces were exchanged.

"Make sure he knows it was me who paid you," McCanty said. Rufus Gates pocketed the coins and nodded.

"What was that about?" Bullis asked, when McCanty returned to the bar.

McCanty chuckled. "That Gates fellow is gonna hang a man named Philionus Lonzo at the Territorial Prison in a couple of weeks," McCanty said, with a wink. "I happen to know a couple of the people Phil murdered. Wanted to make sure that son-of-a-bitch gets the time to think properly on his crimes. My only regret is that I won't be there to see the look in Lonzo's eyes when Mr. Gates measures him for the drop."

"Damn..." Bullis winced, reaching for the whiskey bottle.

It was all settled over whiskey. Apparently the entire town had already moved elsewhere, or was thinking about joining the exodus. It was confirmed that Jake Johnson had escorted the Upstairs Girls to Hayes City. Red Eye Baker had been the next to go, marching his men off the mountain, down the road to somewhere. The rest of the miners, suspecting a new claim had been discovered, followed Baker's crew to somewhere. The eastern dandies from the Russian Tea Room had packed up their cups and saucers, catching the stage heading in the general direction of San Francisco. The owner of the Livery Stable, Harv Gorman, had moved to Fort Lincoln. Billy Jolin stole the money Jim Warner owed him and had lit out in search of that sod buster girl. Doc Watson was heading to California...or Mexico...or the Black Hills. Jim Warner and Owen Scales were waiting on word from the railroad, in the forlorn hope that a cattle shipping railhead might still be established. Rufus Gates left for Clayton, there to hang one Philionus Lonzo. And John Bullis was greatly distressed to learn there really were no Upstairs Girls. So after only a single day of too much whiskey, he and McCanty moved on, in search of Jake Johnson.

The words, Owen Scales discovered, found even more holes in the air to disappear into.

Part Two:
The Prairie

Lo, I took a journey.
It was long and hard...
And mostly flat.
    -George Wellman,
    The Prairie Poems

"The wealth of the tall grass
prairie was its undoing."
    -John Madison

"Civilization is the plow."
    -Anonymous

CHAPTER THIRTEEN

Tall Wind

"You gonna try and catch up with that wagon?" Bullis frowned at the seemingly endless span in front of them. It seemed like they could wander around for weeks and see nothing but grass.

"Naw," McCanty shook his head, staring into the distance, as well. He could see the meandering, mostly over grown trail. "They got to follow that trail with them wagon wheels and axles. We just got hooves on the ground. We can cut across the plains and meet Jake Johnson in Hayes City."

The land spread out now, in a series of hills and ridges, holding long, grassy expanses. Late in the afternoon Bullis sat atop his horse, scanning the meadow below with a small telescope.

"What ya looking at?" McCanty asked, riding up beside him. McCanty realized that whatever Bullis saw, couldn't be dangerous, as the man was taking no precautions to hide himself, allowing his silhouette to be plainly outlined to anyone watching below.

"Supper...maybe," Bullis grinned, handing the long eye to McCanty, who grunted, following the casual movement of a small herd of deer feeding in the high grass. "Your eyes still see as far as that Sharps can shoot?" Bullis asked, skeptically.

"They might," McCanty allowed, dismounting, pulling the big Sharps from its saddle holster. He handed the reins to Bullis, the mule following along as it always did. McCanty judged the wind, which was not blowing too bad at the moment, despite the still troubling sky. It seemed like it wanted to rain, but didn't for some reason, the clouds just building and building in the distance. It was a curious thing, McCanty thought, before turning to the business at hand. He flicked the long range sights up on the gun, cocked the hammer, took aim and the heavy gun roared. Time seemed to slow down to a crawl. Bullis felt his heart thump once, twice...then one of the animals dropped cleanly into the high grass. The rest of the deer scattered, unlike buffalo, both men knew.

"Shit," McCanty said, staring at the smoking gun.

"What?" Bullis asked, confused. It was by any standards an outstanding shot, but McCanty seemed upset.

"Not the one I was aiming at," McCanty said, sheepishly.

"Huh?" Bullis asked, then understood the joke and laughed, a deep, ringing laugh. McCanty winked at him. "You are a funny old coot," Bullis said, as they rode down the ridge to collect their kill.

McCanty studied the sky. The dark, foreboding clouds that had been hugging the far horizon for days were now inching closer.

"We're gonna need shelter soon," McCanty said.

This time Bullis nodded in agreement. They field-dressed the deer, a fair sized buck, and added the meat to the mule's burden. The mule, used to being overloaded, only protested mildly, nipping at

Bullis and his horse, both dancing out of range, one more gracefully than the other.

"Damn mule!" Bullis looked angrily back at the animal, who bared its flat, heavy teeth. Bullis checked his pants, and noted a tear. "Thought that son-of-a-bitch liked me," Bullis complained.

"He does," McCanty said. "That weren't a flesh bite. He just wanted somebody to know his load was getting heavy. If he didn't care for you, he'd have taken a hunk out of your leg," McCanty chuckled.

Bullis still looked annoyed. "Well, if we shoot any more deer, tell the damned mule that I'll carry the fuckin' carcass myself," Bullis said, grudgingly.

"I believe that's what the mule already said," McCanty chuckled.

He was glad they had fresh venison, but McCanty didn't like it one bit that they were riding toward the gathering clouds. Nor that the day had turned unusually hot. He had seen what the Indians called the Tall Wind and knew that when one blew by, it was wise to hunker down. He couldn't shake the feeling that those were some bad ass clouds.

There were lightning strikes now on the far parts of the western skyline. They leaped out of the black, billowing clouds, like living things hurtling themselves to the Earth.

"Time for us to hunker down," McCanty said, in a tone that booked no argument. The wind was rising, the clouds hurrying toward them.

Bullis did not seem inclined to disagree. "There's a rock outcropping up ahead," he shouted back. "We can hole up there for the night."

McCanty urged his mount forward. They made the outcropping just as rain began falling in large drops, so big you could follow them with your eyes, watching as they swooped down like bird droppings to land with a splat that kicked up dust. The rain hurried the men on as they stripped the horses' saddles, the mule's meat and packs. Bullis found enough dry wood for a fire and McCanty let the animals drink from a nearby stream and graze a bit, horses and mules being largely unaffected by rain, McCanty knew, hoping that was all there was to this incoming storm.

Bullis had venison cooking over the open flames, and there weren't too many better smells in the whole world, both men agreed. Bullis even had a bottle in his saddle bags, bought off the bar in Rockville. Now that they were high and dry in the back of the rock outcropping, which hung over the fire and the men like a strong lean-to, McCanty began to relax, figuring they could ride out most any storm within this three-walled cave.

"I still got your telescope," McCanty said, handing the long eye across the fire.

"Took this off a genuine Confederate officer," Bullis said, pointing to the CA stamped on the side, for Confederate Army. There was a further engraving that McCanty took to be the officer's name and regiment.

"Kilt him?" McCanty asked. He had no idea where Bullis' sympathies lay and just assumed the telescope to be a prize of war.

"Nope," Bullis said smiling, pulling at the bottle. "Stole it from the son-of-a-bitch when I deserted back in '63. Actually, it was in the saddle bags of the horse I stole, when I realized the bastards were just trying to get me killed. That war was the stupidest damn thing..."

McCanty, who was living with Blackbird Woman in a Cheyenne village at the beginning of the war, had nevertheless been dragged into it. He did agree that it was the stupidest damn thing.

"I grew up in Jackson, Mississippi," Bullis explained, passing the whiskey across the fire, both men eyeing the sky outside and the venison inside. The clouds darkened, both from the approaching sunset and their growing proximity. The mule, McCanty noticed was now grazing closer to the rock outcropping. "So it was natural for me to join up and fight the Union...or so I foolishly thought. I mean, everybody else was enlisting, so I guess I followed the crowd. I wasn't overly fearful at being shot at, and I could shoot back pretty well. But after a little bit, it just didn't seem to make no sense. Here we were, soldiers marching along, led by officers who rode horses and ordered us to charge into the face of cannon fire and volleys fired from entrenched positions...and for what? Slaves? Hell, I never owned a slave. Hardly any of the infantry I marched with ever owned slaves. But the officers, you see, the ones on the horses, waving their swords, telling us to 'Charge!'...well, they did own slaves and plantations and merchant ships. Didn't take me long to figure out why they were yelling at us to 'Charge!' So they could keep their slaves, their plantations and merchant ships. So I said, to hell with this. I stole a horse and rode west. Didn't stop until I hit the frontier. Found that telescope in the saddle bags, along with a watch, some letters and a cameo of a pretty little wife. After the war was over, I sent the letters, the watch and the cameo back to Mississippi. Kept the long eye as a souvenir."

"Sounds like you did the fellow a favor, returning his possibles like that," McCanty observed.

"Well, I did sell his horse and saddle down in Mexico," Bullis admitted. "I didn't send him none of those proceeds."

McCanty laughed, and at that moment a clap of thunder echoed in his ears, like a cannon shot. So loud, he was stunned for a moment. Bullis was saying something, pointing, but McCanty could only hear the ringing in his ears. Outside the rock outcropping, the sky seemed to be boiling. Dark, ominous clouds twisting over one another. Spatters of rain falling from the eerie sky. Another clap of thunder, another bright bolt of lightning...and the mule was running toward them, McCanty saw. Its black hide shining, glistening in the aftermath of the nearby lightning strike. The animal's ears were laid back, its eyes wide with fear. The mule pounded up the short incline to the rock outcrop, pushed past a startled McCanty. The mule shouldered Bullis aside and installed itself against the rear wall of the three-sided enclosure. It stood there, shaking, with its head down.

"What the hell..." Bullis began.

But the thunder came again, like cannon fire, stripping his words away. The sky was dark as midnight now and still the clouds boiled toward them. McCanty watched, frozen, as the clouds became even darker, taking on an almost green hue. Bolts of lightning leaped between the dark splotches of cloud, looking almost like a fire-breathing dragon opening its maw. And McCanty was struck with the sudden realization that this was where the myths about such fire-breathing beasts came from, because one could well believe that there were dragons in the clouds rushing toward them. Or that the Gods themselves were throwing thunder bolts down from unimaginable, unseen heights.

Then the rain came. Sudden, pelting waves, that drenched the fire inside the rock outcropping. Increasing in its intensity, until McCanty could not see beyond their poor shelter. The horses, huddled beneath a tree, vanished in what looked like a wall of water roaring down from the sky. It was as though a river was suddenly flowing around them. The wind whipped the cascading water, reaching in, taking the remnants of their smoldering fire away into the watery world of the storm. The wind sweeping the rain away, as quickly as it had come. And for several moments, the world grew strangely quiet, as if the sky above was somehow holding its breath. McCanty made out the forms of the two horses, heads down, huddled together under the solitary tree...and then the roaring began. Distant, at first, then louder with each passing second, as if a herd of buffalo, thousands strong, were stampeding across the sky. The roaring shook the earth, and McCanty's eyes widened as he saw the towering, swirling funnel cloud that the Indians called the Tall Wind. He heard Bullis curse, the mule bray...then the wind was upon them and the outside world became masked by dust, rocks, and debris flying across their limited field of vision.

The wind reached in, pulling at McCanty, until he was forced down between two large stones, shielding his head, clinging to the earth as the wind tried to drag him out into oblivion. He closed his eyes against the sharp, stinging dust and waited...either for the storm to pass, or the wind to blow him away. He had no idea which would happen first...

He came to awareness sometime later, for some reason laying beneath the still shaking, but upright mule, which stood firmly against the back wall of the outcrop shelter. Bullis, looking dazed, was stumbling out from behind a large boulder, where he had dug himself a small trench to escape being carried away.

"Jesus Christ," Bullis mumbled, trying to find his balance. "What the fuck was that?"

"The Indians call it the Tall Wind," McCanty said, patting the side of the mule, in an attempt to comfort the terrified animal. "Tornadoes, they're called. I've seen 'em from a distance. First one I've been up close to."

"Last one I ever want to see," Bullis said, shaking his head, rubbing the dust from his eyes.

Both men then thought the same thing, at the same time: the horses. The air was quiet now, although the clouds seemed to be rushing by faster than ever. Rain dripped from the low sky, falling into the rushing streams left by the terrible storm. They stumbled out into the trashed landscape, which indeed had the look of a valley through which millions of buffalo had run. The tree where the horses had sheltered was gone. A ragged stump in its place. The two animals were nowhere to be seen.

"Jesus Christ," Bullis said again, walking aimlessly around the shattered ground, even as nightfall came, and there was still no sign of their horses.

It was a bad thing to lose one's horse in the middle of the wilderness, McCanty knew all too well. Men died from such misadventures, if a horse grew sick or stepped in a gopher hole and broke its leg. But there was nothing to be gained by stumbling around in the dark looking for lost animals, so the men returned to the rock shelter, rolled in their wet robes and tried to sleep. In reality, both man and mule stayed awake in the dark, nervously waiting for first light.

Bullis found them, a few hundred yards down the valley, where the two horses had been swept, either by the wind or the river of rain. They were dead, as both men had feared.

"Damn, I really liked that horse," Bullis said, sadly, running a hand over the cold, broken flank of the animal.

"*Wiconi* weren't a bad critter, neither," McCanty rubbed an uncomfortable bit of dust from his eye. "We ain't gonna be able to bury them."

"No, suppose not," Bullis agreed.

It was bad, both men knew, but at least they had the pack mule, their weapons, and most of their supplies.

"That's one smart mule," Bullis acknowledged, although he was still trying to come to terms with the death of his horse.

"Too bad he wasn't smart enough to get the damned horses to follow him," McCanty said, fanning the smoking fire, trying to heat up some coffee and maybe cook a bite or two of the soaked venison. "It's gonna be a long walk to someplace."

"Yeah," Bullis agreed, watching as the mule grazed on the wet grass, seemingly oblivious now to the loss of its companion animals. Although it did glance at the sky nervously, from time to time. Bullis had the sudden thought that the mule knew it was walking to wherever anyway, so the situation really hadn't changed that much.

"We'll have to cache the saddles and harness," McCanty said, achieving a small victory when the coffee boiled over the wet, smoldering wood. Bullis winced at that suggestion, he saw. "Unless you want to carry your saddle out?" McCanty asked.

"Too bad one of us can't ride that overly smart mule," Bullis said, wincing again at the bitter, half-cooked coffee.

"He'll have to haul our supplies," McCanty said. "Besides, he ain't a riding mule. I sure as hell would rather walk than try to ride that mean son-of-a-bitch."

"I guess," Bullis agreed. The mule stopped its grazing for a moment and looked at the men. As if knowing, somehow, that he was the subject of conversation. "I sure hate to leave my saddle behind."

"We'll cache the whole of our riding gear in them rocks," McCanty said, knowingly. "I done it with fur packs countless times. You can bet it'll be here when we come back for it."

"*If* we can get back for it," Bullis said, gloomily.

"That's an entirely different bet," McCanty agreed. "But I've known men who have walked out of worse."

Bullis nodded. It could be a lot worse, he understood. Hell, it probably would get a whole lot worse before it was over.

"How far, you figure?" Bullis asked, wondering why he had ever left the safe haven of walls and beds and saloon girls.

"Army fort below the Missouri Falls, I guess," McCanty said. "A week, ten days, maybe..."

"Well, it ain't getting any closer, is it?" Bullis said.

"Guess not," McCanty agreed.

Leaving their saddles, tack, and other equipment they could not carry, McCanty and Bullis packed the mule with food, water, ammunition and the basic trail supplies, and began walking westward. McCanty carried his Sharps, Bullis his rim-fire Henry, also his Colt, which he took off only to bathe and sleep. At first, McCanty held a rope tie to the mule's harness, but after a few miles it became obvious the animal would simply follow along without unnecessary encouragement.

"I think there's an Army supply road somewhere up ahead," McCanty said, studying the sky, which was thankfully clear. "We should cut that in a couple days, maybe. There's likely to be a homestead or ranch along that route."

"You got money to buy horses?" Bullis asked, as he himself had a mostly empty pouch.

"Nope," McCanty shook his head.

And Bullis thought that for a potential gunrunner, McCanty seemed awful short on cash. Not for the last time, he was left to wonder if all this was a mistake.

CHAPTER FOURTEEN

The Trail

Jake Johnson felt like he had perhaps made a mistake, as well. Earlier, when Rockville had barely disappeared in the distance, Jake came to the conclusion that bouncing along on a wagon seat all the way to Hayes City was likely to turn his insides to jelly. The road, if it could be called such, was little more than a bumpy path, and he found the jerking motion of the mule team even less to his liking. This realization came on the heels of looking at himself in the mirror, after one of the girls had trimmed his hair and scraped off several weeks' worth of beard. Underneath all that, Jake Johnson had seen only a barely recognizable gaunt, lined face that looked like the reflection of an old man. Truth be told, he never expected to see an advanced age, but it was plain that the years were catching up with him. He had been shot before, with bullets and arrows, as every trapper and gunman he had ever met carried the scars of those trades. Still, Doc Watson had marveled at the number of puckered up holes in his hide. Yet none had taken the starch out of him like this last round of lead poisoning. It was, of course, as he had joked to Watson, only the last one that counted, because that was the one that put you under. But he guessed he would prove tough enough to weather this particular storm. Hickok had once said of him:

"That Jake Johnson is so thick-skinned, you'd have to kill him two or three times, just to make sure he stayed kilt."

The statement made largely in jest, when he and Wild Bill had been drinking together in Abilene. It was generally considered by those who speculated about such things that Wild Bill was one of the few men in the West who was a better shot than himself. Jake never paid much attention to any of that, knowing there was a little spit of a girl he'd seen shoot one time at a county fair, who was a better shot than any of them. Of course, she was only shooting at targets. It was different, he knew, when there was a gun on the other side shooting back. Then it generally came down to whose hand shook the least. Jake always knew he had the advantage then, because he had the talent, or lack of imagination, to consider the men across from him to be merely targets. Hickok had the same ability, he knew, although it was rumored that Wild Bill's eyesight was fading. But you never knew...one time he and Daniel McCanty had been in Fort Dodge, when a bullet came out of nowhere and killed a man named Herman Wright. Old Herman just fell over dead with a hole in his head. It was usually ill luck and surprise that did a man in.

"You all right, Mr. Johnson?" Kate's voice came to him out of the fog of his thought.

He blinked at the bright light, heard the Upstairs Girls laughing and giggling in the back of the covered wagon. Realized that, no, he was not all right. He had been half asleep, day-dreaming, just waiting for ill luck and surprise to come out of the shadows.

"I believe I've had about enough of this damned laudanum," he said, reaching under the seat, tossing the cork stopped bottle into a nearby field. "Makes your head thick and heavy as an anvil."

Kate smiled at him, and the simple act of throwing the bottle away made him feel better.

"You're still poorly?" she asked gently.

"Ma'am, I'm out of that dammed bed, riding in a wagon full of pretty girls," he said brightly. "If that don't make a man feel lively, I don't guess nothing will."

Kate smiled again, believing his lie. "Well, we're pleased you came with us on our little journey," she said kindly.

"Least I could do to repay your kindness," he said, feeling the sun warm his bones. But he knew, also, that it was no little journey. That it would take a week to ten days to reach Hayes City, and even though the sun was warm, when the seasons changed on the prairie, they often did so in a fury.

Yet for all that, he heard the girls jostling one another. Like kids freed up from Sunday school, he considered. That had to make a man smile.

On the second day out of Rockville, Kate's arms grew heavy as tree limbs on the reins, so Jake took over. Later, Jenna said she could surely keep a few mules on track, so he gave up his seat to her and saddled the roan to ride ahead a bit. He jumped a small herd of whitetail deer, and returned with one slung over his saddle. They cooked venison that night, sat around the campfire wrapped in blankets against the chill, watching the stars blink overhead. Wolves howled in the distance and several of the girls, who had spent most of their young lives in cities and towns, grew frightened. Jake had stories he could tell them, but wisely kept quiet. He did, however, tether the mules and the roan close to the wagon and fed the fire most of the night, while the girls slept inside the Conestoga. Sometime before dawn, Kate came out and sat beside him.

"I'll stand watch for a while, Mr. Johnson," she said quietly. "You get some sleep."

He began to protest, but she reached over and set his Winchester on her lap.

"I've been keeping wolves at bay most of my life," she said firmly. "And I promise you'll hear me scream if anything's amiss."

"Yes, ma'am," he said, surprising himself by giving in so easily. He laid his head on his saddle and was quickly asleep, dreaming of sunshine, warm breezes and butterflies. Which was indeed strange, he considered upon waking, because he had certainly never dreamed of butterflies before. But he had also never before traveled with a company of females before, either. He had the odd thought that maybe he was going soft. Wild Bill certainly would have a laugh...

They spent the next night at a farm cut out of the prairie by a tall, bearded man, his wife and five children. The woman, haggard and ill-tempered, made a point to keep her man and half-grown sons away from the Upstairs Girls. In the morning, she sold them eggs and charged to use the well, which seemed to embarrass the bearded man to no end.

They were five days out of Rockville when Jake saw the first Indian sign. Tracks from a group of unshod ponies, maybe six or seven, he thought, cut across the winding path they were following. A hunting party, most likely, he considered. There had been buffalo sign, as well. Wide trails cut through the high grass, as if a trackless train had passed by. The herds, of course, were nothing like they were in years past, as the hide hunters worked the plains, killing the great beasts by the thousands. Stripping the hides, leaving the meat to rot. An atrocity in the minds of the plains Indians, for whom the buffalo was life itself. But it was part and parcel of the white invasion, Jake knew. As inevitable as it was tragic.

Later that day, as if to give voice to Jake's thoughts, a distant, booming echo rode the north breeze, sweeping down from the even more distant mountains.

"Is that thunder, Mr. Johnson?" Kate twisted her head at the faint sound. Unable to relinquish her role, Kate had rested her arms briefly, stubbornly retaking the reins. Jenna sat happily next to her, seeming to enjoy this outside adventure.

It was not an unreasonable question, Jake thought, as a band of dark clouds had been hanging on the horizon to the west of them for the past couple of days. After cutting the Indian sign, he had closed up ranks, riding the roan beside the wagon, the Winchester ready across his saddle, his sharp eyes scanning the horizon.

"No, ma'am," he said carefully, keeping any sign of menace out of his voice. "That's a heavy gun you're hearing. A Sharps fifty, I'd guess. Buffalo hunters, a few miles due east of us."

But later that night, it was thunder that woke them. Lightning so bright and fierce, Jake was reminded of artillery fire during the war. The wind came up, and with it the rain and hail. It came down so hard, he abandoned his place under the wagon and crawled into the canvas covered Conestoga, for fear of being washed away. The sweet, musty smell exuded by the covey of Upstairs Girls provided him with little comfort, however, as the wind rocked the wagon like it was a run-away horse. The sky boiling and angry, even with the dawn.

"Well," Jake Johnson said, embarrassed to be seen standing in his still wet long johns. "That was as banging a storm as I care to see."

Around him, the Upstairs Girls giggled.

CHAPTER FIFTEEN

Encounter

"Guess somebody will just have to trust us," Bullis said, although that seemed unlikely. In truth, he had resigned himself to walking for the foreseeable future.

And so they walked. The landscape rolled slowly beneath them, and Bullis got a new appreciation for the mule's life. Although the critter did have four legs to move himself, Bullis allowed.

They were on the second day of a march that reminded Bullis too much of his brief time in the Rebel Army, when he noticed that McCanty had stopped at the top of yet another in a series of rises. Also that the big man was keeping himself and the mule below the ridgeline, so their silhouettes could not be easily seen. Oh shit, Bullis thought, feeling his stomach roll.

"Got that telescope?" McCanty asked, and Bullis could not help but hear the note of concern in the man's words.

"What is it?" Bullis asked, unconsciously keeping his voice quiet, as he fished the long eye out of his back pack.

"Not sure," McCanty matched his voice level, scanning the far horizon with the Confederate officer's once prized telescope. "Got dust rising out there...yup, Indians. I was afraid of that."

"How many?" Bullis asked, looking around for a place to fort up.

"Ten or twelve," McCanty responded. "Can't rightly tell...looks like a mixed band. Some Sioux, a couple Comanches, and at least one Cheyenne brave. Renegades likely."

We're in for it now, Bullis thought to himself. Renegades were outlaws from their own tribes, with nothing left to lose. They could be counted on to do unspeakable things to their enemies, among which white men were at the top of the list these days.

"We'd better get ready, if they've seen us," Bullis said seriously. "If we can set up a proper ambush, maybe we've got a chance..."

"Naw, we'll light a fire and have a smoke with these here braves," McCanty said, grinning. "I know a couple of those boys. Hunted with some of 'em a time or two," McCanty said, reassuringly.

Bullis knew that when it came to Indians, one could never be assured of anything, but he would try to trust the old mountain man. Which became extremely difficult a half hour later, when a dozen warriors, painted and whooping, rode up to the small knoll where McCanty had set a fire, and stood passively, the Sharps in the crook of his arm, while the wild horsemen of the plains rode in a circle around them, raising dust and creating a scene of general chaos.

"Jesus Christ," Bullis mumbled, as one of the horseman came seriously close, the man leaning across his pony to inspect him.

"Stay calm," McCanty whispered intently. "They're just playing."

Finally the band wheeled to a stop and one of the Indians, a tall fellow, made taller by a slough hat, with black paint streaking his face, dismounted with a flourish and stood menacingly before McCanty.

"How fairs my old friend, Two-Tongues?" McCanty asked in surprisingly passable Cheyenne.

The Indian grinned, much to Bullis' surprise, and shouted something back, raising his arms, which curiously held a war club and an old musket. The others in his party responded in the same manner.

"What are they saying?" Bullis demanded, wondering if he was about to be gutted and skinned, like some fish pulled out of the water.

"My name...what the Tribes call me," McCanty said quietly. Bullis frowned. "It's hard to translate... means Hide Man Hunter."

By now the Indians had all dismounted, chatting among themselves, looking over the mule and Bullis with an equally detached manner.

"They admire the mule and they like your rifle," McCanty explained, as Bullis pulled the Henry away from a brave, who he thought was inspecting the gold finish of the gun a little too closely.

"For God's sake, don't make any quick movements," McCanty warned. "These are painted warriors and they're as high strung as elk in rutting season!"

"They know you," Bullis protested.

"But they don't know you," McCanty repeated his warning, smiling at the brave called Two-Tongues.

Two-Tongues was the son of a Cheyenne chief, Black Kettle, who had been sent to the French school in Canada to learn the language, writing, and customs of the white man. Which Two-Tongues did all too well, returning to the tribes, telling them of the white soldiers' plans to declare war and exterminate the Indian way of life.

"Now grin back...that's right," McCanty said pleasantly, if tersely. "Go stand by the mule now while I parlay."

"But..." Bullis began to argue.

"They know the mule," McCanty explained quickly. "If the mule accepts you, they'll take that as a sign of respect."

Bullis shrugged, went over to the mule and scratched its ears until the animal relaxed and began to graze, ignoring the men and horses milling around. The Indians, seeing that the mule was friendly toward the white stranger, turned their attention back to Two-Tongues as he sat and smoked with the Hide Man Hunter.

Bullis, who knew some of the signs the plains Indians used to speak to other Tribes, tried to follow what was going on, but it was so jumbled he could only catch bits and pieces. Finally McCanty left the fire and came over to Bullis.

"They're a war party, but I guess we knew that," McCanty said, indicating the painted faces of the dozen men milling around the ponies. "Renegades, led by a Sioux outcast by the name of Grey Wolf. That's him over there staring at you. The one with the wolf skin cap. Smile at him...good. Now, I told him about losing our horses in the Tall Wind. They don't have any spare ponies, but they know where we can get mounts."

"Well, that's good news, I guess," Bullis said, already tired of walking, and taking some offense that the Sioux called Grey Wolf did not return his good-natured grin. He just stood there, with the wolf sitting atop his head, the skin itself hanging off his shoulders. In truth, the Indian's snarl looked downright provocative. "Who do we have to kill?" he asked, jokingly.

"There's a party of buffalo hunters a day or two to the north," McCanty said, not taking Bullis' words as a joke at all. "They're working a large herd over that way, killing forty or fifty shaggies a day. Grey Wolf tried to attack them, but the hunters' long rifles held them off. They want me...us, to go and help them wipe out that bunch. And we can keep two of the horses for our trouble."

"Kill white men for the Indians?" Bullis shook his head. "Not sure about that..."

"I kilt white hide hunters before," McCanty reminded his companion. "Do it again when I come across them. Greedy, evil bastards, pure and simple. They're killing the herds the Indians rely on, stripping the hides and taking the tongues to sell back East. They're doing Sherman's dirty work, starving the Tribes into submission. I'd kill the bastards, whether there was horses involved or not. The question is...are you coming along?"

Bullis considered the question for a moment. What were the choices, really? Go along with the heathens' plan, or be left alone out here on the prairie. Like those young bucks wouldn't circle back, kill him and claim his Henry rifle for their own.

"Guess I'm coming along," Bullis shrugged.

"Good," McCanty grinned. "There's six or seven of the bastards. Could use a little help, I reckon."

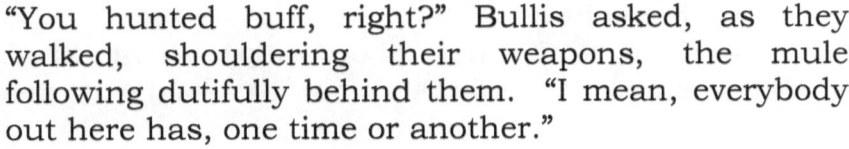

"You hunted buff, right?" Bullis asked, as they walked, shouldering their weapons, the mule following dutifully behind them. "I mean, everybody out here has, one time or another."

"'Course," McCanty grunted. "Ate tongue and fat cow 'til I couldn't hold no more. When I lived in Two Eagle's village, we kilt dozens at a time."

"Well then..." Bullis said carefully, glancing at his companion, trying to judge how riled he might get. Daniel McCanty riled was not particularly safe to be around. "How come them hide hunters perk you up so much?"

McCanty walked in silence for a few minutes, all the while testing the wind, watching the tops of the ridges.

"We et what we killed," he said slowly. "The women dried the meat, made pemmican against the winter. The bones were cracked and scraped for marrow. The hides were used for clothing and shelter. Tools were made from the bones, the hooves were boiled for glue."

He stopped, looked at Bullis to see if the man understood.

"Them hide hunters cut the coats off the shaggies and hack out their tongues," McCanty growled. "They ship the hides and the tongues back East, and leave the rest to rot. You can smell the stink for miles."

McCanty sighed, shaking his head. "It's one thing to make meat," he said finally. "But you don't kill off whole herds. You don't kill every living thing...for hides and tongues. It ain't right!"

They walked on a while longer. The sun touched the far hills. Both men looked for a place to camp for the night.

"And it ain't just about money, neither," McCanty growled. "I know what the bastards are doing..."

They camped in the open. McCanty gathered some old buffalo chips for a fire. They ate biscuit and dried venison, drinking sparingly from their dwindling water supply.

"They done the same thing to the Irish, in my Da's day," McCanty said, his normally loud voice soft, like the whisper of a breeze.

Above them, the stars cut a walkway of light in the dark sky. McCanty thought that it was indeed possible to believe the old ones' tales that those lights were a path to the Great Spirit.

"Who's 'they'?" Bullis frowned across the small fire.

"The people with power," McCanty growled. "The politicians...rich bankers, lawyers, businessmen who own them. They starved the Irish farmers when the potato blight hit. They shipped grain and meat and milk out of the country every day, while the constables threw families off their land and set 'em out to starve. My dad, he told stories about seeing women and children, hardly more than bones and eyes, laying in the ditches at the side of the road, their mouths ringed with green from trying to eat grass. All to get rid of the 'Irish problem'. So the English landlords could graze their fucking sheep. My dad got out...caught a famine ship to New York, but the English starved a million people to death so they could take their land."

"Jesus," Bullis said, although he truly did not understand the number and the references were vague to him. He was reacting mostly to the deep sadness in McCanty's voice.

"They're gonna use the same trick here," McCanty said, anger now dancing at the edge of his words. "Them hide hunters, they're doing Sherman's dirty work. Slaughtering the buffalo in order to starve out the Tribes. Then they're going to send the Army in to deal with anyone who's left. Anyone who refuses to be confined to the reservations will be rubbed out. And that's why I kill those bastard hide hunters, wherever I find them. That's why I aim to get Blackbird Woman and her sister out of harm's way before Butcher Grant orders his Army to kill everything in their path, just like he and Sherman done in Georgia during the war."

Bullis was silent, understanding now. It was not an argument he could dispute.

"The South couldn't beat the Blue Coats," he said carefully, after considerable thought. "The Tribes will lose, too."

"I know," McCanty nodded. "People from the East are going to pour into this country like a wave. There's already rumors of gold in the Black Hills. The railroad's cutting the country up. Settlers with plows are right behind, ranchers with cattle pushing up from Texas."

"So..." Bullis ventured.

"So, I can't stop the Army or the railroad or the plowmen or the ranchers or the miners," McCanty said bitterly. "But I can stop those fucking hide hunters when I find them. Then maybe some village won't starve this winter."

Then they'll starve next winter, or the one after, Bullis didn't say. Or the Army will come hunting them, under orders from Grant and Sherman. Or the whiskey will poison them, or the smallpox will take them, like it did the Blackfeet...spread, some said, by traders with infected blankets. The buffalo and the Indians who depended on them, were both doomed, Bullis knew. But he said none of this. McCanty, after all, knew it, as well. Bullis only nodded his understanding.

At first it was the wolves howling in the night. In the morning, it was carrion birds, flocks of them, vultures and crows, sweeping the air over a far ridge. Finally, it was the yipping of foxes and coyotes, just before the smell hit. It was the stench of death. A putrid, befouling of the air that traveled on the wind like a stinking, unseen fog.

"Damn," Bullis grumbled, pulling his bandana up over his nose. "Makes your damn eyes water."

McCanty nodded, covering his own mouth and nose. At the next ridge line they came upon the carnage. Dozens, maybe hundreds of buffalo carcasses, stripped of their hides, great mounds of flesh rotting under the sun. The bodies stretched as far as either man could see. To Bullis, it looked like a battle field he had seen at Antietam, near Sharpsburg in '62. Only the stink, if possible, was greater.

A green haze seemed to be hanging over the bodies of the butchered animals. A green light, almost, Bullis saw.

"Blow flies," McCanty answered, when his companion pointed.

"Good Lord," Bullis whispered. Each animal was lying in a pool of dried blood, the grass around the carcasses yellowed and withered, as if poisoned.

In the distance, there was the faint booming sound of a heavy caliber rifle being fired. It was methodical, like a measured drum beat. And Bullis knew the slaughter was continuing, just over the next ridge. He had been wondering how he might react when McCanty started killing the men responsible for the buffalo slaughter. Now he knew. He grimly checked the loads in his Henry as McCanty went to the mule, rummaging through the packs for more ammunition for the Sharps.

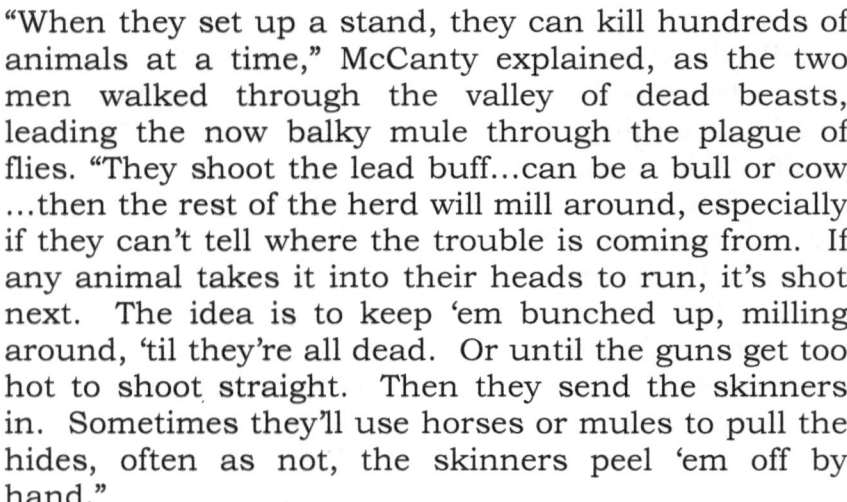

"When they set up a stand, they can kill hundreds of animals at a time," McCanty explained, as the two men walked through the valley of dead beasts, leading the now balky mule through the plague of flies. "They shoot the lead buff...can be a bull or cow ...then the rest of the herd will mill around, especially if they can't tell where the trouble is coming from. If any animal takes it into their heads to run, it's shot next. The idea is to keep 'em bunched up, milling around, 'til they're all dead. Or until the guns get too hot to shoot straight. Then they send the skinners in. Sometimes they'll use horses or mules to pull the hides, often as not, the skinners peel 'em off by hand."

"A bloody business," Bullis grimaced, as they picked their way around the rotting beasts.

"A crime, pure and simple," McCanty growled.

He picketed the mule, which seemed unusually jumpy at the distant noise of the big guns, before he climbed the ridge top. Below, the booming continued. God knew how many more dead buff they'd find here, Bullis found himself thinking. The mule, reluctantly it seemed, bent his head to graze.

"Keep low," McCanty said quietly. "I'll take out the big guns. They won't have more than one or two. They got range...that's why the Indians have trouble gettin' close enough to do damage. But this here will do the trick."

McCanty patted the stock of the heavy .50 caliber Sharps, which he used to great effectiveness at distances the Henry could not hope to reach. The two crawled forward, inching over the rise...and Bullis, who was known by most as a hard man, felt his bile rise in the back of his throat. Below, the grass was littered with dead and dying buffalo, some in their final death throes, breathing out spouts of thick, ropey blood, as they tried to rise, bawling, from their knees. And below them a figure lay next to a wagon, already piled high with skins, a forked stick holding the long barrel of his heavy gun, as he fired round after round into the confused, milling animals. Around the shooter, two other men leaned against the wagon, drinking, watching. A fourth was bringing more ammunition from a crate in the wagon. It looked to Bullis, for all the world, like a battlefield. And it was, he supposed, as McCanty lay prone, sighted down the barrel of the Sharps and pulled back the hammer. The men below may not be firing into an Indian village, but they were killing the people of the Tribes just as surely...

McCanty's weapon roared and Bullis was up, running toward the startled men. He hadn't even stopped to check that McCanty had hit his target, so sure was he of the man's marksmanship. The Sharps boomed again and a second man fell where he stood. When he got within range, Bullis knelt and fired at the man carrying the ammunition, as he frantically tried to bring his partner's buffalo gun to bare. The man jerked, fell, twitched, much to Bullis' satisfaction. The two skinners had panicked and were running...first toward the horses hobbled away from the wagon. Then when the horses shied, they turned down into the valley, where the buffalo, catching sight of the enemy, were now fleeing. Some several hundred of the shaggies, by Bullis' quick estimate. The buffalo, he realized, shook the ground, even from this distance. They were soon only a haze of dust on the horizon.

Another man crawled out from under the hide wagon, throwing up his hands.

"I give up! Don't shoot, by God! I surrender!" he shouted.

Bullis held his rifle on the fellow, who looked drunk, as he swayed and tried to keep his balance. Up on the ridge, McCanty jerked another shell into his Sharps.

"Don't recall offering surrender terms," McCanty yelled down. The Sharps boomed again and the fellow's chest exploded like a gourd, the surprise evident in his eyes.

"What the hell?" Bullis called out.

"What are we gonna do?" McCanty shrugged. "Bring the son-of-a-bitch to Hayes City so he can testify against us?"

"I guess not," Bullis admitted. Then he looked beyond McCanty to where the mule had stood on the ridge. The animal had collapsed into a heap, he saw. "Your mule..." Bullis said, pointing, believing that the mule must have caught a stray bullet, although he didn't recollect one being fired in that direction.

"Damn..." McCanty whispered, having genuine feelings for the beast. But as he ran toward the animal, the mule twitched and pushed to its feet, shaking, staring down at the grass, as if surprised to have found itself on the ground. McCanty checked the mule over and it appeared to have no injuries. Bullis had come up by now.

"Not shot?" he asked. McCanty shook his head, puzzled. "I believe the damn mule fainted," Bullis said, patting the mule's muzzle, looking into its white-rolling eyes.

"Fainted?" McCanty asked in disbelief.

"Startled by the loud noise...your Sharps," Bullis said. "I have seen such a thing in goats. My

Aunt Gertie had a goat that if you snuck up behind it and shouted loudly, the critter would stiffen and fall over. Much like your mule here."

"The mule's never been gun shy," McCanty scoffed.

"Maybe not gun shy, but he sure got the devil scared out of him by that Tall Wind," Bullis said, knowingly.

"Suppose that's true," McCanty admitted. "Still..."

"Your mule is not gun shy, but tornado shy," Bullis said, authoritatively.

The two surviving skinners were running down the valley, disappearing into the fog of dust thrown up by the stampeding buffalo. They were already beyond the accurate distance of the Henry, Bullis thought, so he waited for McCanty to come up with now upright mule. He wasn't sure that the skinners presented any danger, since they couldn't have been near enough to identify either himself or McCanty. Bullis was inclined to let them escape, provided they could make their way back to civilization without mounts or weapons, which seemed unlikely.

In fact, it got a lot less likely a minute later, when the Indian war party, led by Grey Wolf, came whooping over the horizon.

"Figured they wouldn't be far away," McCanty said casually, leading the mule. "They'd love to come in and do the job themselves, but they got no answer for the big buff guns the hide men carry."

McCanty nudged the shooter with his boot, analyzing the shot that took him square in the chest. It was much the same with the man who tried to give himself up. The ammunition hauler that Bullis had shot lay sprawled out beside the hide wagon, a big block Remington in the bloody grass.

"Got any use for a buff gun?" McCanty asked. Bullis shook his head, indicating he had enough fire power between the Colt and his Henry rifle. "Then we'll leave it for Two-Tongues," McCanty nodded. "He'll have a surprise for the next hide hunter he comes across."

"I guess," Bullis said, noncommittally. He still wasn't sure about this business of providing Indian war parties with modern weapons. They did damage enough, in his mind, with the bows, lances, and smooth bore guns they already had...not to mention the pistols and repeater rifles they took in battle. When they could get ammunition for the weapons, of course. But there seemed to be quite a few cartridges for that Remington.

Down in the valley, still obscured by the dust, there were suddenly screams rising above the war party whoops.

"Looks like they found them skinners," McCanty said.

Bullis winced at the sounds.

"Them boys ain't innocent in this," McCanty said.

"Still, they're only fifty dollar a month hired hands," Bullis said, quoting the standard pay for skinners in the hide business, who were usually drifters or out of work ruffians.

"Grab the Remington," McCanty frowned. "We best claim our horses and git!"

There wasn't much to claim, in Bullis' mind, but anything had to beat walking.

"What are they doin'?" McCanty asked.

He and Bullis had pulled up on the next ridge. Across the valley, there was a massive amount of screaming and yelling, but it was difficult to tell what was actually taking place. John Bullis had his long eye out, surveying the situation.

"Grey Wolf's bunch has got a fire going," Bullis said. "Those skinner fellows is tied to the wagon wheels. Don't look good for them."

"Damn it," McCanty spat. He didn't mind shooting buffalo runners, but he didn't care to be responsible for two skinners being tortured to death. "They're gonna burn those boys," he shook his head.

"That'd be my guess," Bullis agreed.

Bullis offered the telescope, McCanty declined. He could hear the proceedings well enough from where he stood. As the screaming intensified, Bullis raised an eyebrow in his direction.

"Shit..." McCanty said, hefting the Sharps, jerking a shell into the chamber.

"I don't know..." Bullis said, measuring the distance, which looked to be half a mile or better. It would be a difficult shot, even for a marksman like Daniel McCanty.

McCanty looked down the barrel and shook his head. There were figures running back and forth in his line of sight.

"Can't draw a clear bead," he said, shifting the barrel.

"Let's get the hell out of here," Bullis shook his head. "There ain't nothing to be done..."

McCanty knelt to steady himself. In a moment, the Fifty roared. Bullis quickly put his long eye back on the far ridge, but before he could sight, the Sharps roared again, startling him. It was another second

before he saw one of the skinners jerk as an ounce of
lead struck his chest. The other boy was already
slumped over against his restraints. The Indians, he
saw, were stunned and outraged.

"That might be the best shooting I ever seen!"
Bullis exclaimed, but McCanty didn't seem to care.
Behind them there was a thump. The mule had once
again collapsed into a stiff-legged heap.

"I'll be damned," McCanty said, even as the
mule recovered and staggered to its feet.

"Having a falling down mule will be a trial, I
suspect," Bullis said, secretly pleased that he had
been right about the mule's affliction, not so pleased
when McCanty looked about ready to shoot the
critter. "We'd better get the hell out of here," he
suggested, diverting McCanty's attention by pointing
at the goings-on over at the hide wagon, where
members of Grey Wolf's band were pointing in their
direction.

McCanty looked from his gun, to the still
recovering mule, to the Indians milling around the
wagon. "I really don't want to kill all of them," he
said, agreeing with Bullis that they should ride as
quickly as possible.

"I believe you could kill all of them," Bullis said,
catching hold of his horse, not mentioning that it
would be an extraordinary feat.

"I could," McCanty agreed. He especially did
not want to shoot Two-Tongues, whom he considered
something of a friend. "But I doubt I would feel good
about it in the morning."

Bullis laughed, swinging into saddle. "We might
be in for it now," he said, hearing the Indians shout
their anger from the distant ridge. "The Blue Coats
will be after us for shooting white men, and that Grey
Wolf will be angry at us for the same reason."

"We got a pretty fair lead on 'em," McCanty said, confidently.

Across the valley, the renegade Indian band came to much the same conclusion, and had to content themselves with burning and cutting the already dead men.

McCanty and Bullis loped away, the mule in tow.

CHAPTER SIXTEEN

Two-Tongues

For days, since leaving the prairie farm, they had not seen another human being. Jake hoped to keep it that way. The news of buffalo hunters in the area caused a stir of excitement among the girls, and several poked their heads out of the wagon, no doubt seeking a look at such wild, unpredictable men. Hide men were uncommon visitors even in a frontier town like Rockville. The hunters, unusually raw and rough men, seemed to disdain all the trappings of civilization, other than whiskey and women, and made only rare appearances for those. Of course, they came into towns with railheads to sell their hides, but they were not often seen in mining towns like Rockville. When they did occasionally come in off the prairie, Kate always made them visit the barber baths before their introduction to the Upstairs Girls. And although they were, even by their own admission, harsh men, widely known for their gargantuan appetites, they always grudgingly obeyed the small slip of a woman, who had no qualms about standing up to them. Kate, who was certainly not prudish by any standards, drew a hard line against the unwashed hide men and their inevitable companions, fleas and ticks. In the end, she and the occasional buffalo hunters who frequented Rockville, had entered into a peaceful understanding, and they generally showed up at the Silver Strike in reasonable states of cleanliness. But in truth, it was no less than the standards she demanded of the cowboys and miners.

"Are we going to encounter them?" Kate asked, echoing the giggling questions that arose from inside the wagon.

"Not if I can help it," Jake said firmly. And there was some sounds of regret from within the Conestoga. They were, he reminded himself, whores, as much as he had grown to like and even admire them.

"Good," Kate replied, as the girls let their displeasure known. "Hush back there! You've only seen those men at their best in town," Kate reminded her charges. "Out here, there are no civilizing elements, other than our own Mr. Johnson."

Jake had to chuckle at that. It was unlikely that he had ever been considered a civilizing element. Seemed to show, he thought, just how far out on the edge of the frontier they were. But the plain fact was, Jake admitted to himself, he was nervous. Because, of course, if he could hear the sounds of the buffalo hunters working their disagreeable trade, so might the Indian hunting party, if they were still in the area. The Tribes despised all the hide men, and for good reason. And once those warriors got blood on their hands, no white person in the general vicinity was likely to be viewed in a friendly manner.

As they moved slowly through the rolling hill country, dominated by the tall grass, an occasional spiny tree, and large boulders the size of the Conestoga wagon itself, the distant booming continued, with unceasing regularity. Shot after shot after shot...

Kate frowned. "How many buffalo will they kill?" she asked.

All of them, Jake thought, but didn't say. Which was why the Indians took such great offense at the presence of the bloody hide men.

"As many as they can," he said instead, shaking his head at his own statement. Kate glanced at him, silently asking for an explanation. "Big as they are, buffalo are pretty much defenseless against determined men with heavy guns," he said quietly. "The buff have poor eyesight and have never been hunted in such a manner. The hunters, you see, will set their stand upwind of a herd, maybe three or four hundred yards away. Easy range for a .50 caliber rifle. Then the shooter will start picking the animals off, one by one. The buffalo can't see or smell any threat, so the herd will generally just continue to graze, thinking that the dead animals have maybe laid down to sleep. I don't know. It can go on for hours sometimes, until the hunters' guns get too hot to fire, or something happens to startle the herd and they move out of range. A team in a good stand can kill a hundred, two hundred animals at a time."

"My goodness," Kate said, frowning again. "But then..."

"Then the skinners go down to the kill site, usually with mules or horses that are used to the smell of death, and strip the hides," Jake said. "The meat...well, it's left to rot, for the scavengers to pick over. Look there..."

Jake pointed. Vultures had begun to gather, circling in the air several miles distant. Many, many of them, he noted. If those hide men weren't careful, they were going to attract unwanted attention. Probably already had, he considered. A prospective camp site presented itself a dozen yards or so off the trail.

"We'll stay there for the night," Jake said.

Kate glanced up at the sun, which wasn't yet halfway down the horizon. "We could make a few more miles, Mr. Johnson," she said critically.

"And maybe run into something we want no part of," he replied firmly. "Those hunters, whoever they are, aren't careful men, and they might be attracting the wrong sort of attention."

"Wolves?" Jenna asked, curiously.

"Wolves if they're lucky," Jake shook his head. "We'll settle in here. Keep the horse and mules close. And no fire tonight, I'm afraid. We'll try and make ourselves as inconspicuous as possible."

Kate looked at him and raised her eyebrows.

"Indians," he said quietly, not wanting to cause a stir. Causing one anyway.

Before they got the mules unhitched, the distant guns went silent. Their sound echoed, fading into the distance. The animals were watered in a nearby stream, Jake keeping a sharp eye on them. In the aftermath, as darkness spread out like a shadow across the land, the quiet was large and uncomfortable. The girls curled up together after a cold supper and slept, nervous as prairie dogs with a coyote sniffing around.

In the morning, when the sun swept the darkness away and nothing terrible had happened, the night fears seemed foolish and largely forgotten. Jake even allowed a small fire for coffee and bacon, which was gratefully eaten after last night's cold beans and jerky. The girls, Jake noted, had long since lost the allure of camping out, and now looked for the adventure to be over. Which was unfortunate, since they were, by Jake's reckoning, still several days'

travel to Hayes City. This news was greeted with some bitterness. But the sun brightened the morning, and the girls' spirits improved. Jake, however, could not shake his ill feeling and rode close to the wagon as they made their way slowly across the undulating plains. The tall grass had gone brown and in the wake of the storm, a chill wind could be felt from the north. The time between the blazing heat of late summer, to the first blizzard, could sometimes pass in the blink of an eye, Jake knew.

The smell came to them first. A harsh, sharp smell of offal. Faint, in the beginning. The big roan's nostrils flared, his ears laid back. Jake drew the hammer on the Winchester that lay in front of him, across his saddle, a shell already in the firing chamber.

"What is that awful stench?" Kate asked, as they climbed a ridge, and the wind brought whispers of what lay on the other side. Beside her, Jenna drew a handkerchief from her sleeve, holding it up to her nose. The girls whispered quietly inside the wagon. The mules grew balky.

"Dead buffalo," Jake said quietly, hoping that was all it was.

"No vultures," Kate commented.

They're too fat to fly, Jake knew, but didn't say.

"No matter what, just keep the mules moving," he ordered.

Kate nodded, slapping the harness reins across their dark backs. They were in a shallow valley, pulling uphill to the top of the ridge. When they swung over the rise, the smell came like a bitter, choking fog. Inside the wagon, the girls shrieked and gasped. Below them, the valley was filled with the carcasses of slaughtered buffalo.

"Oh my goodness," Kate whispered, her stomach rolling at the smell, her eyes barely able to process the sight of so many dead animals.

A hundred or more, Jake counted quickly, scanning the valley, the surrounding horizon. The girls poked their heads out of the wagon at this gruesome, amazing sight.

"Ahhh, there!" Jake slapped the rumps of the mules to keep them pulling in their traces.

The wagon rolled downhill. Dozens of vultures flapped and screeched, trying to gain flight at the wagon's approach, but they were too heavy with carrion to lift into the air. Flocks of blackbirds swept through the fouled air like dark, waving hands. Foxes and wolves pulled at the dead lumps, each weighing a ton or more. Meat that would feed a dozen Indian villages, rotting on the plain. And in a distant corner of the valley, he saw the buffalo hunters' wagon...and several other animals, some that looked like mules, laying among the field of dead buffalo.

"Keep them moving, no matter what!" Jake growled to Kate, spurring the roan forward.

There was no movement around the hunters' wagon, and as he rode down into the valley, he saw the reason. The slaughter that had taken place here was not limited to the dead buffalo herd. A thin trail of smoke rose into the air from the partially burned wagon. Arrows here stuck in the hide men's mules, and as he grew closer, his worst fears were realized.

"Mother of God," he whispered.

There were half dozen men who had found the same fate as the animals they hunted. The vultures, knowing only the rules of carrion, flapped around them, as well. It was hard to tell exactly what had opened their insides to the glaring sun. Many were punctured with arrows; all had been mutilated in some grotesque way. They had all been scalped. Two of them, tied to the wheels of the smoldering cart, looked as though they had been turned inside out, before being set on fire. Yet, one at least, looked to have been shot. The hole in his skull seemed to be from a heavy caliber weapon. Maybe killed with his own buffalo rifle, Jake wondered? On closer inspection, a couple of others looked to have died by gunshot, as well.

Strange for Indians to kill in such a manner. Although, admittedly, it was hard to pinpoint a cause of death, with vultures and other carrion eaters at work. Further down in the valley two men had been caught stripping the hides from their kill. The mules, dead themselves, were still tied to ropes that were designed to pull the hides off the slaughtered buff. The half-skinned carcasses of the shaggies open to the sun and the scavengers. Several of the men looked to have been staked out and tortured. Their bodies only barely resembling human beings. Oddly, Jake was reminded of something Daniel McCanty had told him, in another lifetime, it seemed now...of poachers taking deer in the King's forest.

The arrows, he saw, had both Comanche and Sioux markings. A mixed band, most likely renegades thrown together out of necessity, making them all the more dangerous. The hunting party had obviously heard the thundering echo of the hide men's guns, and had descended on the group as they went about their bloody work. Yet...it was hard to tell, but there looked to be boot prints approaching from up above, from where the wagon was now approaching. No shod horses, but boot wearing white men. That, and the heavy weaponry used to kill some of the hide men raised Jake's suspicions. But still, there was nothing to be done. No time to bury the dead, even if he was so inclined. Which he wasn't. The hide men had poached the King's game, and had paid the price. They were greedy men, and the Indian hunting party had merely reacted to these poachers as if they were taking food from the tribe's mouth. Which was exactly the case, Jake knew. It was a grim, bloody business, to be sure. The hide men gambled and lost. Jake had no time for sympathy. He kicked the roan into a lope.

Kate looked to question him as he rode up beside the lumbering wagon. He merely shook his head, throwing a rope around the head of the lead mule, gently urging the team through this valley of death. Hoping that if they were quick...and lucky...they might avoid the same fate as the hide hunters. The sun danced high on the horizon as the mules grudgingly pulled the Conestoga forward. The grass shimmered in the breeze. Flies in uncountable swarms filled the valley; the vultures cackled and screeched at their passing. The smell stuck to them like pine sap. In the wagon, the girls gasped and whispered. Kate, he saw, had tears running down her cheeks. The mules balked and Jake had to keep the roan in front, pulling them through this terrible field of slaughter...

They finally topped the rise, and the breeze blew down from the distant mountains, washing the stench away. And even as they left the horror behind them, Jake Johnson's blood turned to ice. Down in the next swale, a campfire burned. Horses, Indian ponies grazed in the tall, yellow grass. The renegade hunting party, fresh from their own victory, had stopped to cook meat and celebrate.

"Dear Jesus," he whispered, halting the mule team, which wanted to run, now that they were free from the valley of death.

They were outlined against the horizon. From below, he saw the warriors staring up, shielding their eyes against the sun. There was nothing else for it, he knew, but to go forward. No place to run, no place to hide. He heard Kate curse behind him. Glancing back, he saw her pass the reins to Jenna, reaching under the seat for the shotgun.

She was a fighter, he acknowledged, and wouldn't sell her life or the lives of her charges cheaply. He pulled the roan up beside the wagon.

"Keep the girls quiet and don't shoot unless I fire first," he said, trying to keep his voice steady. "There's nowhere to go, so we're just going to have to ride past them."

To her credit, Kate nodded. Then, to his utter surprise, as they started down the hill, he heard a voice shout:

"Son-of-a-bitch, if it ain't Jake Johnson!"

The voice, which was high and flighty, came to him like a swarm of swallows on the wing. The words themselves were tinged with an odd accent, like a French priest he had once heard say Mass. Despite the imminent danger of the situation, Jake felt himself smile. He knew the voice, knew the man behind it. By now the Indians had caught their ponies, were whooping and preparing to make their way to this unexpected apparition coming down the trail toward them. But the man who had yelled out the greeting waved his rifle in Jake's direction, shouting something to his companions, a mix of Sioux and Comanche it looked like, which caused them to hang back. He was large by Indian standards, made bigger still by his buffalo robe coat.

He swung aboard one of the ponies and galloped toward Jake.

"Hi-ya, Two-Tongues!" Jake returned the big man's greeting, although he kept his finger on the trigger of his rifle, hammer back, resting across the neck of his horse.

The Indian, a heavily painted Cheyenne warrior, even though he rode with the Sioux and Comanche band, stopped some way off, just at the edge of the Winchester's effective range. Jake allowed the roan to take a couple of steps forward. Still, the Indian known as Two-Tongues continued to smile at him, as if the two had just crossed paths at a mountain rendezvous. Jake made sure to keep the Winchester in full view, to try and avoid any miscommunication on either side. Even though Two-Tongues smiled engagingly, the man was known on the plains for his wanton, savage violence, usually directed toward the much hated whites. Still, oddly enough, Two-Tongues could be pleasant, even generous, to those he considered his friends. Which Jake was, at least the last time they had met up, in a winter camp along the Powder River. Behind him, Jake heard the mule team come to a disjointed stop. Two-Tongues was distracted for a moment by the sound of female voices coming from the wagon.

"That your work back there?" Jake asked, the edge unmistakable in his voice. Two-Tongues hated the hide men, as did just about every Indian west of the Mississippi.

"Some of it," Two-Tongues admitted casually. "But mostly them," he nodded back toward the rest of the Indian party, who seemed to be at odds with themselves over what to do about this unexpected development. "That would be Grey Wolf and his renegade band."

Down in the valley, the Indian party stood near their ponies, watching as the two men parlayed. There were seven of them, Jake counted, eight when you figured in Two-Tongues. Jake doubted he could get them all before they overwhelmed him and got to the wagon behind him.

"And a white man or two, I'm guessing," Jake spat tobacco juice into the ground.

Two-Tongues laughed appreciatively. "Yes, the Sharp shooter McCanty, also his friend with the fast pistol and the name like a bull buffalo," the Indian nodded. "Grey Wolf won't like me telling you, but he did not want to charge the big buffalo guns."

"Sensible," Jake allowed. "So McCanty and John Bullis, what were they doing here?"

"Looking for you, I believe. They had lost their horses in the Tall Wind storm and were afoot. Now, you know all," Two-Tongues said, respectfully. "The Sharp shooter has no love of the hide men. He agreed to kill the hide men's big guns in exchange for their horses. His own horse was killed, but luckily his mule survived. Both McCanty and the fast gun have ridden on."

It was Jake's turn to laugh at the mention of the West's most ornery mule, but it was a short laugh, as the renegade war party had mounted their ponies, moving slowly toward them.

"So..." Jake said, deciding to wait and see how this largely untenable situation played out.

"So the rumors were true," Two-Tongues grinned, glancing back at the wagon, where Kate and Jenna sat in full view of all concerned.

"What rumors?" Jake asked.

"That someone was escorting a wagon full of white women across the prairie," Two-Tongues shrugged, turning his attention back to Jake and the

Winchester across his saddle. "Word travels faster than the crow flies out here. You know that, too, I guess."

Jake sat quietly on the roan. The war party, fresh from their massacre of the hide men, inched closer.

"It appears we have what you whites call, a situation," Two-Tongues said, glancing back, shaking his head.

"Best tell them to stay where they are," Jake growled, pulling the Winchester up to rest on his leg.

"There is no need for that," Two-Tongues said quickly, turning, shouting something to their leader, Gray Wolf, that Jake didn't understand. The Indian party stopped and milled about, talking loudly among themselves.

"Where do we stand here?" Jake asked, keeping his voice level, even as his eyes measured the distance, knowing he would have to dismount to keep his weapon steady once the skirmish began.

"You have history with me. You have history with my father, Black Kettle," Two-Tongues shrugged.

That was true enough, Jake considered. He had wintered in the old chief's village a time or two on the Snake River, and had hunted buffalo with them often over the years. It was also an unfortunate fact that Black Kettle had been killed at the Washita River by Custer back in '68, when Two-Tongues had been a young man. Black Kettle, unlike his son, sought peace with the white man...for all the good it did him, Jake thought.

"I do not wish to see a friend go under before it is necessary," Two-Tongues said solemnly. "My father liked you and would not have wished it, either."

"Me neither," Jake said coldly. He had already decided that English speaking Indian would be the first man he'd kill, if it came to that.

"Good...good," Two-Tongues nodded and smiled, knowing well that Jake Johnson with a cocked and loaded Winchester was a very lethal man, indeed. He knew enough, also, to keep his hands in plain sight and to choose his words carefully. Two-Tongues had heard about the famous Abilene shooting, but did not put much stock in it. In his mind, the three men Jake Johnson shot down were either drunk or stupid...or both. Simply because when the Rattlesnake, as Jake was called by the Tribes, pointed his Winchester at them with obvious ill-intent, they did not run or ride away, as quickly as possible. Still, there were almost a dozen riders in Grey Wolf's band.

"It is doubtful that even you can get all of them," he said quietly.

"Maybe not all...but most," Jake replied.

"You see, that's the kind of talk that should be avoided in a situation like this," Two-Tongues said, nervously. "But I would expect nothing less from you."

"So, again...where do you stand in all this?" The sun was starting its downward swing and would soon be in his eyes, Jake knew.

"Right in front of you, of course" Two-Tongues turned and nodded toward the other Indians. "You know who Grey Wolf is?"

Jake's eyes settled on a lean Indian wearing a wolf skin, circling his pony at the front of the band.

"I know he'll be the second one to die," Jake said, feeling the tension work up into his shoulders. To his surprise, the comment caused Two-Tongues to roar with laughter.

"That I am sure he understands!" Two-Tongues said, with obvious delight. "I am also certain that is the only thing holding him back. He knows who you are, my friend. He knows your strong medicine. You kill white men, mostly. And you hate the Blue Coat soldiers. The Cheyenne and the Sioux kill mostly white men these days. And we, of course, hate the Blue Coat soldiers, as well. So we are all bothers, you see?"

Jake doubted that and was about to say as much, when Two-Tongues grinned again.

"I am going back to Grey Wolf and his warriors, and see what I can work out, to extract us from our situation," he said, amiably. "Would the Rattlesnake agree if a non-killing solution can be found?"

Jake nodded and saw a quick look of relief pass over Two-Tongue's normally stoic face.

"Why don't you take the wagon with the white women and fort up in those trees, and I'll get Grey Wolf to agree to a peace council," Two-Tongues said, backing his big buffalo horse away from Jake and his Winchester. "But just so you know, I have no ties to Grey Wolf. He was exiled from his village. I do not especially care for him, if the truth be told."

When he was out of comfortable firing range, Two-Tongues turned his horse and galloped back toward the waiting war band. Seeing little choice in the matter, Jake rode back to the Conestoga and directed the women into the stand of birch and oak.

A stream ran through rocks that poked up like old teeth. And they had the high ground, if it came to that, Jake thought, surveying the trail that led downward into the valley. He set the women to gathering as much wood as they could and to fill the water barrel, even as the sun began to set behind the far mountains. He hobbled the livestock as close to the wagon as possible and checked the loads on his weapons. Waiting for trouble you knew was coming was the worst part. Once their tasks were completed, Jake gathered the women together. In the distance, he could see the flames from the Indian camp.

"We're in trouble here, aren't we?" Kate asked.

Jake knew it was useless to deny it.

"It's not good," he admitted. The girls, he saw, were rightfully frightened, although they worked hard not to show it. Upstairs Girls were plucky by nature, he knew. "We've got an ally, I think, in Two-Tongues, the big Indian I was talking with. He's a Cheyenne riding with Grey Wolf's renegades. I knew his father, Black Kettle. That might work in our favor."

"They're the ones that killed those buffalo hunters, Mr. Johnson?" Big Jenna asked.

He nodded, glad now that he had not stopped to bury those dead men. It was better that the women didn't know the particulars of that slaughter. They were, after all, scared enough as it was.

"No one leaves the camp," he said, even though it was obvious to everyone that would be a really bad idea. "We'll keep the fire up; keep the horse and mules close to the wagon. Kate has the shotgun, Jenna will take my pistol. We three will share the guard duties. The rest of you girls stay in the wagon, no matter what happens. But first, we're going to set up some of these fallen logs against the rocks to give us cover. If they come at us in force...well, we'll make them pay."

Kate gripped the shotgun and nodded. Jenna checked the loads on his Colt, as if she'd done it every day of her life. The other Upstairs Girls worked through their fear. Lizzie and Sara hauled logs, Little Anne made coffee and put on a pot of beans. They were brave, he had to give them credit.

"With luck, we'll get through this," he said, encouragingly. And saw, to his dismay, that they trusted him, believed him. In his heart, he had to wonder if any of them would see the sunrise. Of course, he couldn't bring himself to tell them that. It was most fortunate, he understood, that they hadn't seen the carnage visited upon the hide men. But he had...

Sunset came and the darkness outside of the fire circle was complete and daunting. The moon would rise in a couple of hours, Jake thought, and that would give him some advantage. He was willing to die for the girls. The question was: Would Grey Wolf? Would Two-Tongues? As if in answer, a single horse clomped up the trail. The heavy step of Two-Tongues' buffalo pony, Jake recognized, squinting out into the darkness, the Winchester like a sword in his hands.

"Coming in!" Two-Tongues shouted, the high voice with its French accent at odds with the hulking figure, nearly as big as a grizzly. "I'm alone!"

"Come ahead," Jake called, and he heard the big man dismount with a grunt, leading his horse into the firelight. Two-Tongues grunted again, throwing off a haunch of buffalo meat.

"A peace offering," he grinned, surveying the campsite, the women especially, with obvious pleasure. "Grey Wolf thought you might be hungry. Although, God knows, there is plenty of meat in these parts."

Two-Tongues laughed at his joke, spread his hands, stained with buffalo blood, to show Jake he was unarmed. The women, hungry for fresh meat, began cutting up the buffalo haunch, setting it to cook on the campfire. The sizzling meat setting everyone's mouths to watering, Jake's included.

"Grey Wolf wants to come and smoke with you," Two-Tongues said, wiping his hands on his leggings, settling his bulk on a log near Jake.

"Doubtful," Jake said, cautiously.

"You might want to reconsider," Two-Tongues sounded disturbingly like a white politician. "To smoke with a powerful man like yourself would help Grey Wolf's status among his people. It might help him ride away peacefully. You know his story, don't you?"

Jake nodded. Grey Wolf had been driven from his father's camp, for the surprising reason of killing too many whites. In Many Horses' view, his upstart son had caused the Army to pay too much attention to the Sioux band. And it hadn't helped Grey Wolf's cause any that the young brave thought he should replace his father as War Chief. Now, oddly, with the white encroachment on Indian land, with Sherman's insistence that the tribes submit to the reservations, Grey Wolf was gaining in popularity, as people were realizing that killing too many whites was now a good thing.

"It is true that Grey Wolf has a powerful hatred for most white men," Two-Tongues conceded. "But you are the Rattlesnake, killer of many white men, so he is willing to look past your unfortunate color and smoke with you. It might help with our...unpleasant situation."

Jake thought about the proposal for a while, as the girls served up steaming hunks of mostly cooked buffalo hump. Two-Tongues was wise enough to let him think, as he smiled politely at the Upstairs Girls in the manner he had been taught at the Jesuit school. His attempts to put them at ease, failing for the most part. Finally, seeing no other way around it, other than killing all the Indian band, and probably Two-Tongues as well, Jake agreed, around a mouthful of buffalo meat.

"He can come in," Jake grunted, thinking that at least he would be able to fight on a full stomach. "We'll smoke."

"That will be a good thing," Two-Tongues said, nodding. "Grey Wolf mostly hates hide men and the Blue Coats."

"Can't blame him much for that," Jake grunted again. It was, after all, the hide men who operated with the full knowledge and protection, such as it was, of the Army and the U.S. government, killing the buffalo, destroying the Plains Indians' way of life. Before too much longer, Jake knew, Sheridan and Sherman and Bad Hand McKenzie would have their way. All the Tribes would be starving or holed up in one of the government reservations, eating scrawny beef and sending their children to the white man's school. It was as inevitable as the changing of the seasons, as inexorable as the railroad's push across the rapidly dwindling wilderness.

"No, you cannot blame him for that," Two-Tongues conceded. "I will fire my weapon once to signal Grey Wolf," he said, carefully reaching inside his buffalo robe coat for an ancient, long barreled cap-and-ball pistol.

"Wait a minute," Jake said, motioning for the girls to finish their meal and to go into the canvas-covered wagon.

"I'm not sticking my head in the sand for anyone," Kate said belligerently, the scattergun laying across her lap.

"Me neither," Jenna spoke up, cradling Jake's pistol.

Unable to help himself, Jake had to laugh at their bravado.

"Maybe seeing you two armed females wouldn't hurt none," he acknowledged. "Just don't go shooting anybody unless I say. The rest of you, in the wagon. And keep your heads inside!"

There wasn't much of an argument from Sara, Lizzie, or Little Anne, although Jake doubted that they would be able to resist poking their heads out for a look at real, wild Indians.

"Shoot your gun, big man," Jake said, remembering something McCanty said, quoting some ancient Chinese general: Keep your friends close, and your enemies closer. Jake found himself hoping he wasn't making a terrible, fatal mistake.

Two-Tongues pointed his oversize pistol skyward and let off a round, sparks and gunpowder filling the air.

"If you shoot that thing off again, it better not be pointed in my direction," Jake said, after the booming sound of the Civil War weapon faded.

Two-Tongues nodded solemnly. Which Jake took to be something of a handshake across the campfire.

A few minutes later, Grey Wolf and another of his renegades came whooping and hollering toward the light.

"He's loud enough," Jake commented, pulling the hammer back on the Winchester.

"He's afraid of your medicine," Two-Tongues said tensely. "Keep that in mind..."

Grey Wolf and his witness to this haphazard peace council, one of the painted Comanche warriors, reined their ponies up and dismounted with a flourish. The Comanche had half his head shaved, his body painted bright red from the waist up. When he hit the ground, he raised his arms to the sky and shrieked out what sounded like a prayer to some strange god. Then, with squared shoulders and jutting chins, the braves entered the circle of light reflecting off the shadowy trees and the rock ledge, looking pointedly at where the Conestoga and the animals were tethered.

They didn't seem all that afraid, Jake thought, keeping the barrel of the Winchester down, but his finger on the trigger.

Jake's horse startled at this intrusion and Jake murmured a quick snort. The big roan quieted, and Grey Wolf nodded appreciably at this sign of training. The Indian ponies huffed and puffed for a moment after their gallop, but were soon quiet themselves. Grey Wolf shouted something, loud and curt. Jake sat passively, the Winchester laid in his lap.

"Grey Wolf thanks you for allowing him to share your campfire," Two-Tongues translated.

Jake, to everyone's surprise, welcomed the brave in his own language, directing the women, Kate and Jenna, to offer up the remains of the buffalo hump. The Indians, he noted, brought their particular smell with them — smoke and paint and blood. The latter from their slaughter in the valley of death beyond the ridge.

"I recall a bit of Sioux," Jake said to Two-Tongues, reinforcing his words with the universal sign language of the Plains Indians.

"Enough, I think," Two-Tongues said quickly, watching his comrades' suddenly subdued demeanor. They obviously had not expected to be treated with such respect.

After they had eaten a mouthful or two, just to be polite, Jake realized, Grey Wolf made another loud speech, producing an intricately carved pipe and the particular tobacco and sage mixture favored at such occasions by the tribes.

"Grey Wolf says that he is pleased to smoke with a person of such importance as the Rattlesnake," Two-Tongues continued to translate for some reason, as the ceremony progressed and the carved pipe was passed among the men. "But he also says that he is not pleased that so many white people are to be found on the plains these days."

Kate and Jenna, understanding the situation, returned to their places, guns across their skirted laps. While Grey Wolf did not even glance in the women's direction, his companion did. The weapons the women cradled made a suitable impression, Jake thought. Jake accepted the pipe when it came to him, blew smoke in the direction of the Four Winds and passed the smoldering pipe back to Grey Wolf, locking eyes with the formidable Indian.

"Grey Wolf, while I understand your hatred of the hide hunters, I cannot condone your method of killing these admittedly unjust men," Jake said slowly.

Grey Wolf listened for a moment, the muscles in his jaw clenching. The Indian responded, loud and intimidating.

"Grey Wolf says that it is not for you to say how he takes his vengeance on those who would...take his tribe's way of life," Two-Tongues said uneasily. "No, take his tribe's life. Exterminate them, he means."

"As a man, as a human being, it is for me to say," Jake responded. "But as a friend of the Indian people, I understand his anger."

Grey Wolf glared for a moment, then his eyes turned, briefly, less hard. The Indian pulled deeply at the pipe, passing it back to Jake.

"Grey Wolf says, the Rattlesnake has struck and killed many white men himself, and for this Grey Wolf extends his respect," Two-Tongues said quickly. "But Grey Wolf says that a clean and honorable death is not given to those who would disregard the sanctity of the Earth."

Jake drew on the pipe. Without blinking, he met the brave's eyes.

"In my heart, I cannot argue with that," Jake said, simply.

Two-Tongues, using sign and words, translated. Grey Wolf nodded, accepting the pipe and the peace it symbolized. In the depths of the night, wolves howled, the stars swirled overhead, and the Upstairs Girls poked their heads out of the canvas top of the Conestoga. Grey Wolf then said something, seemingly offhandedly, that caused Two-Tongues to catch his breath.

"What?" Jake asked into the sudden silence, wondering if he heard correctly.

"He wants one of your women," Two-Tongues said slowly. "Grey Wolf says..."

Jake waved the big Indian silent, resting the butt of the Winchester on his knee, the barrel pointing upward, for the moment. He had been expecting something like this.

"They ain't mine to give," Jake said, calmly, in English.

Two-Tongues dutifully translated, and the renegade warrior smiled coldly; the wolf atop his head seemed to smile, as well.

"Then Grey Wolf says he's sure you won't mind if he takes one or two of them, since you have so many," Two-Tongues said, uncomfortably.

"They ain't mine to give, they ain't his to take," Jake replied menacingly, meeting Grey Wolf's dark eyes squarely across the campfire.

"He says, then just one," Two-Tongues repeated, nervously. "He isn't likely to let this be..."

Jake shifted uneasily. As the two Indians talked loudly to one another, Grey Wolf continued to gesture toward the wagon.

"What happens if I kill him?" Jake asked quietly.

"I don't know," Two-Tongues said, glancing around at the darkness outside the firelight. "The others are out there. They might run, they might decide to kill everybody. I can't say..."

"No women!" Jake growled, leveling the Winchester at Grey Wolf. "Tell him unless he leaves now, I'll kill him."

Hearing the translation, Grey Wolf stared at Jake, apparently convinced the white man was speaking the truth.

Without another word, Grey Wolf and his companion moved quickly to their ponies and galloped away, hooting and hollering as soon as they disappeared into the darkness.

"I shoulda killed him," Jake shook his head.

"You might have started a bloodbath," Two-Tongues said, letting out a long sigh, his body relaxing. "You got any whiskey? That was a near thing."

"You're not getting any whiskey," Jake said, one part of him relieved, another part wondering if the confrontation was truly over. Two-tongues looked so distraught, Jake relented. "All right, one drink," he said. Jenna fetched a bottle; the other girls came out of the wagon, huddling by the fire. Grinning, Two-Tongues drank deeply, Jake took a quick, short slug. The Upstairs Girls, well used to strong drink, passed the whiskey around like it was a peace pipe, Jake noted.

"Is it done?" he asked Two-Tongues.

"Who can say?" the Cheyenne shrugged. "Grey Wolf needs no trouble with you...and surely he does not need the trouble of a white woman. I will remind him of both those things."

Feeling the effects of the whiskey, Two-Tongues grinned at the girls, the girls grinned back.

"'Preciate that," Jake nodded, even though he knew Two-Tongues was not acting solely on his good nature. When the bottle came around again, Jake corked it, much to Two-Tongues' dismay. The Upstairs Girls didn't seem all that pleased, either. "We'll all need our wits about us," Jake said, and Two-Tongues grudgingly agreed. "You girls get in the wagon now. Kate, you too, but keep that scattergun close. Get some sleep. Me and Two-Tongues will keep watch and swap stories you don't want to hear."

Two-Tongues laughed, the girls piled into the Conestoga, whispering among themselves.

"I heard you were shot dead," Two-Tongues said.

"Almost," Jake said, feeding the fire, listening to the prairie night. In the next valley over, wolves howled, the carrion eaters feasting in the dark. Overhead, the stars turned. Toward dawn, Two-Tongues fell asleep. Jake watched the fire, making occasional, silent rounds about the perimeter of their camp. To his relief, the night passed quietly.

With the dawn, Two-Tongues swung onto his horse and prepared to ride off.

"Take care, Jake Johnson," Two-Tongues said. "If I find Grey Wolf and his bunch shadowing you, I'll try to fire off a warning shot."

"Make sure it's in the general direction of the Wolf himself, if you don't mind," Jake said, only half joking.

Two-Tongues grinned, touching a finger to his battered slough hat, trotting off, whistling a tune only he heard in his grizzled head. Being sent off to the Jesuit school had made Two-Tongues a half-breed of sorts, Jake considered. Even though he was full-blooded Cheyenne, Two-Tongues sometimes seemed to have a foot in both worlds, even though he well understood what the white man had in store for his people.

Kate was beside him, scattergun in the crook of her arm.

"Are we still in danger, Mr. Johnson?" she asked plainly.

He looked down at her, admiring her toughness, knowing she deserved nothing less than the truth.

"We are," Jake said simply. "Until we livery those mules in Hayes City, we are in danger. But for the moment, I'd say the immediate peril is past."

The Upstairs Girls piled out of the wagon, yawning, blinking at the bright morning sun, whispering among themselves. Jake felt a deep sense of responsibility toward them, these whores who had tended him so protectively while he was healing. Silently, he vowed to get them to their destination, or die trying.

"All right," he said, forcing a smile. "You girls are going to stick together like a covey of quails. Nobody goes anywhere, even to gather wood or do your business in the bush, without me or Miss Kate with you."

That brought a smattering of giggles and a couple of inappropriate offers that Jake pretended not to hear. These were not school girls, he reminded himself for the hundredth time. He stared at the sun, looked out at the lay of the land. With luck, he figured, they were less than a week out of Hayes City. With luck...

Jake hitched the mules, took a cup of coffee and chewed on some of the left-over buffalo hump. They were rolling not long after the sun began to warm the undulating prairie. There was a touch of chill in the air, even at noon. The tips of the far mountains were white with clouds and dusted with snow, even though it was still early in the fall season. The trees would soon be getting that washed out look to them that heralded the coming cold. Jake was glad they only had a week's travel left. It surely wouldn't do to get caught out in the open with a wagon full of women when winter closed in. Down in the valley, they passed the remnants of the Indians' fire, but saw no fresh sign. Except for the knot in Jake's stomach, the trouble of the previous night might not have ever happened. He rode next to the wagon all day, his eyes scanning the skyline, but if Grey Wolf's band was still in the area, they were being careful not to be seen. Jake remembered something Bridger had once said:

-When you don't see no Injins, there they are.

Good advice, he considered. Then, just before nightfall, he thought he glimpsed a puff of dust far behind them. Of course, it could have been anything...buffalo moving, deer or elk, a dust devil. But somehow, he knew it wasn't.

Two days later, as they crossed the muddy Platte River, their luck ran out...

CHAPTER SEVENTEEN

Platte River

The lead mule let out a baying, surprised yelp, as its front feet sank into deep mud, just off what looked like a firm sandbar. The other leg followed, and before Jake could react, both lead mules were up to their haunches in sucking mud and swirling water. Kate yelled, the wagon tipped dangerously.

"Get out!" Jake shouted, pushing the roan forward, jamming the Winchester into the saddle sheath, grabbing his rope, tossing it over the head of the nearest mule. "Get out of the wagon!"

By then, the girls were jumping free, as the Conestoga lurched dangerously. Cursing, Jake tried to pull the lead mules free of the enveloping mud, but the animals had panicked as the weight of the listing wagon drove them into the muddy water. Shrieking, the mules fought to find their footing. An impossible task, as the heavy Conestoga rolled into deeper water, floated for a single, terrifying moment, then turned slowly onto its side. Jake pulled his hunting knife, leaped from the roan, and cut the struggling mules free of their traces.

"Haw! Haw!" he yelled, slapping the mules on their rumps. Without the weight of the wagon, they were able to pull themselves free of the mud and struggle to shore, where they stood, heads down, panting. The Upstairs Girls splashed their way through the waist-high water and mud to stand with the animals.

Kate was in the overturned wagon, pawing frantically through the ruin of waterlogged trunks, scattered clothing and blankets. Jake grabbed his horse's reins, made his way to the back of the Conestoga.

"Get out!" he shouted. "Come on, before it washes away!"

"Not without this!" Kate yelled back, fumbling in her trunk, pulling out a locked metal box. Her strongbox, Jake realized. Her life savings. She was not about to leave without it, he saw.

"Give it here!" he said, reaching inside, grabbing her shoulder. She thrust the box into his arms. "Fetch the scattergun," he said, as calmly as he could, with water pouring into the rear of the wagon.

Kate fell out of the back of the wagon, into the swirling water. He caught her, tossed her up onto the saddle of his horse, where she held onto the saddle horn with one hand, the shotgun clasped firmly in the other. Carrying the surprisingly heavy strongbox, Jake staggered to the far shore, leading the big roan.

"jesus..." he panted, feeling the old wound in his side like the snap of a whip across his middle. He fell into the damp grass, turning as the wagon collapsed under the weight of mud and water. They were in for it now, he knew. The girls cried and comforted one another. Kate beside him, her red hair in wet, ropey strings, trying to squeeze the water from her sopping dress. Reaching out, he put an arm around her, wondering how long he would actually be able to protect her and her charges.

"We're alive, anyway," he said.

Behind them, as the sun began its downward swing, he caught another glimpse of the dust cloud he had seen earlier. Grey Wolf and his band, still on the other side of the river, but stalking them, he knew instinctively. Pulling himself to his feet, Jake realized he had to somehow get control of this situation. Otherwise...well, he didn't care to think about that.

"Night'll be on us soon," he said, more calmly than he felt. He knew a fire would mark their position, but didn't feel as though he had any choice. "We'll set up camp over in those cottonwoods. We need to get a fire going, get dried off and warmed up before it gets cold. Kate, you and the girls drag some wood over. I'll get the animals settled."

Twilight, that all too brief time on the plains, between light and dark, found them hungry and shivering around a fairly good fire. Jake set some fishing lines out in the river, but as yet had nothing to show for his efforts. The girls, frightened and in ill spirits, kept glancing at the canvas top of the Conestoga as it flopped in the muddy current. Sleeping and riding in the wagon had once seemed to be a trial, but the girls now seemed to recall living in the close confines of the protective wagon with bitter fondness, he suspected.

"What are we going to do?" Kate asked, as the darkness spread like a fog, surrounding them.

Jake took a moment to respond. The Winchester, safe in its saddle scabbard, had required only a light greasing. The scattergun, apart at his feet, had taken a big gulp of water and mud, but would be fit for service when he finished cleaning and put it back together. Shells for the shotgun were going to be a problem, as they only had a half dozen or so that happened to be loose in his saddlebags.

His Colt, too, was going to require some attention. But with the Winchester in proper order, wet guns were the least of their problems. They had his trail kit to cook with, the girls were now passing his tin cup around, drinking water from a spring they'd found back in the cottonwoods. He could provide fire with his flint and steel tinderbox, but other than that, the rest of their supplies were encased in mud at the bottom of the Platte River. They had the clothes on their backs, although two of the girls had lost their shoes in the mud. All-in-all, it was a grim situation, he knew. But he'd seen worse.

"We've got the mules and my horse for transportation," he said, nodding toward the hobbled animals, who at least had found supper in the thick grass along the riverbank. "There'll be fish on the line for breakfast, I guess," he predicted confidently. "Anything else, we can buy at the General Store with what's in that strongbox you risked your neck to get."

He glanced over at Kate, belatedly wondering if he should have joked with her in the midst of their troubles.

To her credit, Kate laughed. "If you can find a General Store, I'll see if I can locate the key, Mr. Johnson," Kate returned his jest.

Jake grunted, pushing a gun rag through the twin barrels of the scattergun.

"In the morning, I'll go out and cut the canvas off that damn wagon," he said. "We'll rig some horse blankets for the mules and get enough to make a passable tent for night shelter. And I'll see if any of the provisions are salvageable, although I doubt it. If necessary, I'll hunt us across the rest of these plains to Hayes City. Your girls will be sore as the devil, but we'll make it. Here..." he said, snapping the oiled scattergun back together, slipping two shells into the chambers, handing the weapon over to her. "You're armed, anyway."

Kate smiled. "We'd be in dire straits without you, Mr. Johnson."

Jake nodded, although he knew they were in dire straits with him.

"You may think it was foolish to risk going into the wagon for that strongbox," she said, nodding at the metal box between them. "But there's almost ten thousand dollars in paper and gold in that box. It'll be all we have to set us up in Hayes City. I couldn't leave it."

Jake raised an eyebrow at the amount. "For that kind of money, I might have risked my neck, as well," he said.

"I'd appreciate it if you'd see that box into Hayes City for me," she said.

"That's mighty trusting of you," Jake said.

"I'm a pretty fair judge of character, Mr. Johnson," she replied. "In my business, you have to be."

"It'll be in my saddlebags when we hit town," Jake nodded, and she touched his arm in appreciation. The warmth of her startling to him.

"I'd better go tell the girls about your plans," Kate said, smiling. "I'm sure they'll take some comfort, knowing we're in such capable hands."

The Upstairs Girls, their clothes dried, if somewhat caked with river mud, began to dress themselves, their mood improving as Kate explained the plan. Jake, tending to his Colt, stole fleeting glances in their direction. He chuckled to himself, thinking about the strange twists and turns a life might take. Ten thousand dollars lay at his feet, a sound horse munching grass behind him. Some of his old partners would surely have a laugh at his expense, that he didn't simply saddle up and ride off into the night. And at one time...in the long ago days of his wild youth, he might have done just that. He tried to tell himself that he wouldn't have, but knew that was a lie. In truth, he had killed men for less ...for a lot less. And even to this day, he remembered each and every one. Still, he tried to convince himself, he had never killed anyone who didn't deserve killing. Another lie, he understood. But one he felt compelled to tell himself, if only to keep reasonably sane.

Strange, how killing came so easy to him. You cocked the gun, aimed and fired. Then you walked away. That's how easy it was. Hickok told him once that he'd encountered only a handful of men like himself and Jake, whom he considered natural born killers. Wild Bill had meant it as a compliment, although Jake himself wasn't so sure about that. But in his heart, he felt he could justify most of his killings. Most...but not all. He supposed that was the way all men justified the taking of life. Sometimes it was necessary, if you wanted to keep on living yourself. Yet, it shouldn't be so easy to do, he considered, wondering if there was something wrong inside him. But violence...it had just become a way of life, somehow.

He poked at the strongbox under his feet. The girls were bedding down, clumped together like baby rabbits for warmth. Perhaps this challenge, this test of his will, his strength and honor, was a way for making up for those few who, perhaps, hadn't deserved to die at his hand. Maybe, in getting these girls to their destination safely, he might find some salvation for all the ruin he'd inflicted.

Jake Johnson laughed at his own foolishness. He was an old trapper, turned bounty hunter. There was no salvation, no penance, no justification. There was only life and death, and the harshness in between. He greased the Colt, spun the chamber, loaded shells. Killing was what he knew how to do. Did it better than most. That was why he still walked the Earth. There were no great mysteries, no fate, no damming God to judge right or wrong. There was only life and death.

Then why didn't he saddle up and ride off, strongbox and all, while the whores slept and the fire burned low and the stars turned overhead? Because there was life and death...and honor, he knew. A man couldn't live without honor. God or no God, judgment or no judgment, a man had to do what he thought was right. So he walked the parameter of their lonely campsite, in the middle of a lawless wilderness. Because, in the end, it was the right thing to do. And God or luck or fate kept his enemies at bay. For this night, anyway.

Prairie dogs tasted like dirt and dust, and there surely wasn't much meat on them. But it was the only game he found, limited in his hunting range by the need to stay close to the women, as they walked and rode the mules, sharing shoes and drinking from his canteen, which hardly held enough water for the six of them. Unfortunately, the water barrel on the Conestoga had been crushed in the spill, but he had gotten enough canvas to rig a tent of sorts, and the girls huddled beneath it on this, their second night without the protection of the wagon. They hadn't made nearly as many miles as he had hoped, but the mules, after balking a bit, had allowed the women to ride in shifts for most of the day.

The plains, in the dying light, looked flat and featureless, but Jake knew that was an illusion. The land undulated, like the frozen waves of a great, dusty sea, providing any number of draws and ravines for anyone trailing them to hide. Especially Indians, who were most adept at using the landscape to their advantage. The animals, resting now, fed on the meager sage brush and sand grass of this current, largely empty part of the prairie. Jake had seen a snake or two, and lizards basking on rocks, but decided they weren't that desperate yet to eat such fare. The prairie dogs, along with a couple of scrawny rabbits, were skinned and roasting over a buffalo chip fire. Even though the dry buffalo dung burned into a fine ash that had an unfortunate tendency to blow into food and coffee, the meat would provide enough nourishment until something better happened along. If there were such things as God or fate or luck, now would be a good time for such entities to send a stray buffalo cow their way, Jake thought, spitting sand and grit between mouthfuls of charred meat. He was tired. Bone weary and doubted he'd be able to stand guard another night without sleeping. Perhaps if he just closed his eyes and rested a moment or two...

Jake woke up with a start. It was pitch black, although his senses told him there should have been a moon rise. No stars, either, he noted. Clouds and a west wind starting to tickle the air off the far mountains.

"It's all right, Mr. Johnson," Kate whispered beside him. As his eyes adjusted, he saw there was still a faint glow from the buffalo chip fire. He could make out the bunched up figures of the girls, asleep in their canvas lean-to.

"You were exhausted, so we thought it best to let you sleep," Kate said quietly. "Jenna and I took turns on guard. It's been uneventful."

"Good...good," he mumbled, slowly regaining his wits. "The animals..." he began.

"They're hobbled over near the tent," Kate smiled in the dim light. "We're not quite helpless, you know."

He managed a grin back. "Never once thought that," he said, amiably. "And I guess I did need to sleep some."

"Why don't you get back to it for a while more?" Kate suggested.

The temptation was there, all right, but Jake knew the dangers of cloudy, moonless nights. To an Indian, this kind of night was an invitation to steal horses...or mules.

"No, I'm fine now, thank you," he said, rising up, stretching, feeling his bones crack, his body sighing with age. Too many nights spent on hard ground in bitter weather, he knew. Too many years altogether, he thought glumly, hardly believing that he had fallen asleep like that. In his youth, such a dereliction of duty would have been unthinkable. But now, it seemed, sleep had become a necessity.

"You go rest," he said to Kate, trying to judge how much of the night was left. Only a few hours, at most, he decided, although it was difficult to gauge with no sky above.

Somewhat reluctantly, Kate did as he'd requested. The wind ruffled the canvas, masking the night sounds of critters and their own animals, so he moved casually behind the tent. Something had startled him awake, he thought. Some muted sound echoing into his brain, riding in on the breeze. The big roan nickered at his approach, the mules ignoring him. He moved among them, patting the horse's nose reassuringly. Kate was right, he decided, it did seem uneventful. Still, something bothered him. He stood quietly beside the horse, blending into the darkness, trying to push his senses out into the night, as his ancestors had for many thousands of years.

He smelled the faint hint of rain and feared they might get some weather in the morning. He blinked. Had he caught some hint of movement, beyond the close limits of his eyesight? He couldn't be sure. Might be anything, he told himself...then the roan's ears picked up and a rush of alertness brushed away the last remnants of his tiredness. Quietly, he pulled the hammer back on the Winchester, the click sounding loudly in his ears. To the right, low to the ground, far out in the dark, a shape moved. Almost imperceptibly. Jake stood stone still, shielded by the roan's bulk. Did he dare chance a shot? In the dark, it would surely reveal his position. He held his breath, waiting. One of the mules grumbled, pulling at the hobble rope on its leg. The form, the shape seemed to freeze, then it melted away into the black night. A big cat, hunting? Maybe...maybe not. The wind picked up a bit. The first, faint predawn light worked its way across the far horizon behind him. Gray and dim, but bright as the street lamps of St. Louis after the pitch black of the prairie night. Rocks and scrub brush took shape. The dark hides of the mules, wet with dew.

He waited until the light brightened some, then made his way carefully a hundred yards or so out, to where his eyes told him the shape had been.

"Son of a bitch," he whispered, a chill running through him that was not entirely related to the morning cold. He saw in the flattened grass and sand where someone had laid, watching them. And a single set of prints in the dry ground. Grey Wolf or one of his band? Impossible to tell. But someone had been scouting them. No doubt to steal one or more of the animals, but had been spooked off. Perhaps sensing, somehow, that he was there. His own eyes and ears and nose, sharpened by years on the trail, were considered by some to be acute. But he knew them to be poor instruments compared to any Indian, particularly horse stealing Sioux warriors. A man had to admire them for that, he acknowledged. And be wary, if not outright fearful of their stealth.

Thank Christ Kate let him sleep, he thought, making his way back to the still quiet camp. He might be weary, but there was a difference between that and the exhaustion he had felt come over him as they ate their sandy prairie dogs yesterday evening. Now, overhead, a hawk rode the breeze, outlined in the grey, cloudy sky. Rain soon, he decided, hoping it wasn't snow, or too much of either. The Green River was ahead of them, and they had better be across that uncertain water before it swelled up.

"Morning ladies," he stuck his head inside the canvas shelter. "We need to be moving as soon as possible."

Tired grunts and groans greeted him. These were town girls, he reminded himself. But they would have a story to tell for years to come, he thought, grinning at them, deciding to keep the moccasin print a secret between himself and God...or luck or fate.

CHAPTER EIGHTEEN

Prairie Hotel

Rain caught them again, as he feared, before midday. The mules accepted their riders best if they were strung together by rope leads, tied to the roan's saddle horn. It gave them something to follow, and mimicked the traces they were used to, Jake thought. Anne, the lightest, rode doubled up with their supplies, with Kate up behind him on the roan. She was his 'behind eyes', keeping watch on the girls and the mules, freeing him to study the landscape in front. The girls let out a collective, cursing mutter when the first splashes of rain hit them in large, bloated drops. It would be a soaker, Jake thought, watching the clouds rush overhead, boiling off the far mountains. He tipped his hat down, forced the roan into a steady pace, feeling the rope lead tighten as the mules, with their shorter strides, tried to keep up. The girls, bad mouthing the weather in no uncertain terms, pulled shawls over their heads, or ripped off pieces of petty coat to tie as scarfs.

"I'm afraid it's gonna get worse, before it gets better," Jake called out, garnering even more foul curses. These, somehow, aimed at him, rather than the cold rain now soaking them all. The water making the mules' backs slippery and hard to ride, even with the admittedly poor canvas saddle blankets. And it wasn't long before the trail, such as it was, went from dirt to mud. A shout behind him, and even more savage cursing. The lead rope jerked against his saddle horn.

"Mr. Johnson, I'm afraid Lizzie has fallen off," Kate said quickly.

Pulling up the roan, glancing back, he saw the fiery Mexican girl stamping angrily in the mud, kicking at the mule, which luckily ignored her.

"I wouldn't try to outkick a wet mule," Jake called back, cautiously. Even he was taken back by the storm of Spanish curses pouring out of the angry girl. This, of course caused the other Upstairs Girls to laugh uproariously, ignoring their own wet misery. All of which served to further infuriate Lizzie, in what she no doubt considered the latest in a long series of outrages. She picked up a handful of mud, flinging it at her tormentors. And, as Jake sighed, things only deteriorated from there, until Kate had to dismount and bring a semblance of peace to her angry gaggle of charges. Muddy and soaking wet, the Upstairs Girls turned their glares in Jake's direction, as he couldn't help but burst out laughing himself.

Lizzie gave one last futile kick at the unoffending mule.

"I will walk to Hayes City, I swear to the Virgin Mary herself, before I'll ride that fucking mule again!" she shouted, wiping mud from her face, which still showed the marks of her recent encounter with Big Ed Grimes, then trudging off down the trail by herself.

Jake hopped off the roan, scooping Lizzie up before she got past him, swinging the startled, angry woman into his saddle.

"Ride up there for a bit, Miss Lizzie," Jake said, soothingly. "I don't mind walking some, myself."

He slipped Kate up behind, and once the other girls got settled again, Jake began leading the roan and his motley mule train up yet another of the undulating prairie hills. The rain soon slacked off a bit, and he hoped they might be through the worst of it.

The Green River was still a ways out, and now he doubted they'd reach it before nightfall. One good thing, he considered, the rain might discourage anyone who happened to be following them. Maybe...

The rain grew heavier again, water running off the brim of his hat like a waterfall. The usually sure-footed mules were finding the going difficult. The mud sucked at his boots, and Jake was soaked through, even with his slicker on.

"What's that ahead?" Kate called from her position high on the roan.

Jake squinted through the veils of rain. Down in the next valley, he saw what looked like a bump on the prairie. As if a boulder had grown out of the ground, to be covered again by dirt and grass. Although closer inspection, as they trudged through what now seemed to be a wall of water, showed what might have once been a pole fence of sorts. Definitely man-made, he thought, his spirits rising.

"Looks like a hotel to me, Miss Kate," he called back, laughing under his breath. The bump was, he now knew, a soddy. A sod house cut out of the prairie by some settler. No smoke, no movement from the structure and from the poor condition of the split log fence, long deserted, he guessed. Picking up the pace, Jake led them down to what he hoped might provide some shelter from this storm, which didn't seem likely to abate anytime soon.

Pushing aside a crumpled gate, Jake guided his party toward what appeared to be a dirt cave hacked out of the ground.

"Like I said, a hotel," he said, jokingly, helping the two women off the high back of the roan. "Or at least what passes for one in these parts."

Jumping off the mules, the girls made for the entrance like a line of wet ducks. The door, such as it was, leaned on broken hinges. A window, cut in the stacked sod, stared at them like a dark eye, the torn remnants of a curtain flapping in the breeze. Jenna had already pulled the broken door aside, leading the charge out of the torrent of water that had turned the dusty front yard of the place into a shallow pond.

"Yug!" someone shouted from inside, as Jake led the animals up to somewhat drier ground.

"Dear God..." he thought he heard Kate's voice.

"All right, so it's not exactly a hotel," Jake said, standing in the doorway, surveying the dim interior.

Water dripped from the dirt ceiling. The interior of the sod shack was indeed as damp and gloomy as a cave. Cobwebs everywhere, the remains of an old bed in one corner, a busted up table and two homemade chairs. A nest of some sort built into what appeared to be an old cabinet. He poked at the nest with the tip of his boot. It seemed empty, except for a few old bones. The Upstairs Girls, he saw, were looking at him in mute horror.

"Well, it ain't much," he admitted, wiping the rain from his face, catching sight of an old broom nestled among the cobwebs in one corner. "But it might clean up some." And there was what looked to be a still serviceable fireplace cut into the far wall. "If someone wants to sweep a bit, I'll see if I can light a fire..." he suggested amiably.

At which point Sara screamed.

"What?" he shouted, looking for a direction to point the Winchester. Then something flapped by and he saw chickens roosting under the rafters above the bed. Grabbing the fleeing, squawking bird before it made good its escape, he cradled it roughly in his free arm.

"Room service," he said, winking at Kate. Several more half wild birds glared down at him warily. "Supper ladies, and there might just be some eggs up there, too."

Lizzie, always the boldest of the Upstairs Girl, went after the small flock in a flurry of feathers and dust. An hour later, after breaking apart the table and chairs, Jake had a fire going, Kate had swept out the worst of the cobwebs, and Lizzie held a plucking party with Sara and Little Anne, after deftly wringing the chickens' necks.

"In my village, we ate chicken every Sunday," she explained her expertise to the two other girls, who watched her casual brutality with something approaching amazement.

Outside, Jake threw up a lean-to against one corner of the soddy for the animals, using the split rails from the broken fence and canvas taken from the Conestoga wagon. He brought the canvas strips they had cut for mule blankets and his own saddle blanket inside to lay on the dry parts of the dirt floor. On rope lines strung inside, dresses and petty coats and other female paraphernalia dripped dry, barely concealed bottoms and bosoms warmed themselves by the glow of the fire. The pleasant smell of chicken cooking in the pots and pans of his trail kit greeted him. The anticipation of food and passing of a relatively dry night had improved the girls' disposition considerably. A rag doll, stuffed with hay, had been found in one corner, prompting questions, largely unanswerable, about who had once lived here, in the middle of the prairie.

"Some man, an immigrant probably, thought it would be a good idea to come west and get a new start for his family," Jake said, studying the construction of the soddy. "There're places like this dotting the plains. Some make a go of it, most don't."

He thought for a moment about the kind of man who would be bold, or foolish enough, to cart his family out into an Indian infested prairie, to try and pull a living of this inhospitable land. A hopeful sort, not afraid of hard work, who dreamed of owning his own little piece of the Earth. The east was full of such men, he'd heard. Had seen them for himself on the crowded streets of St. Louis.

"Some say there'll come a day when this prairie is full of settlers," he said, skeptically. "When the buffalo are gone, and the Army has forced the tribes onto reservations. Then the grass will be plowed under and the ground planted with corn. And who knows, they might be right. When I first came out west, towns like Hayes City and Rockville didn't exist. Trading posts here and there, but mostly this was empty country, populated with Indian villages and buffalo herds. The herds so big, they sometimes took days to pass by, and no one could count them. Now, the railroads are pushing in from the east and the west. Wagon trains leave St. Louis every week, packed with the very people who built this soddy. In a way, they're like the old buffalo herds. So many, nobody can count them."

The Upstairs Girls, eating chicken, sitting on canvas blankets, stared at him. Hearing something in his voice, something forlorn...something they did not understand. The rain hammered down on their little shelter, swelling the Green River, he knew.

"You make it sound like a sad thing, Mr. Johnson," Kate ventured.

"Oh, I don't know, Miss Kate," Jake chuckled. "I'm just an old man, I guess. And an old men don't like to see things change. But that don't matter none, because things change anyway. It's the way of the world. I guess you could say that I'm not real big on civilization, since I've spent most of my life avoiding it."

"I wouldn't rank this real high on the civilization scale," Lizzie observed, drawing a laugh from everybody, Jake included.

"Well, I didn't say we were there yet," Jake responded lightly. "Guess I'd better check the animals."

Jake pushed himself to his feet, feeling the ache in his bones that bad weather produced these days. What he really wanted to do was look at the smoke from their fire, which he hoped was pretty much blotted out by the rain. It was slacking off some, but the fog and the clouds would probably keep them hidden from any of the closest observers. Inside, he could hear the girls whispering in his absence.

"They say he's killed at least twenty men," someone said.

"Hush now, he's a good man."

"He don't look so old to me...and he's thoughtful..."

"You just keep your skirts down, girl!"

"I ain't wearing any skirts...and I'm only saying."

"The line between saying and doin' ain't a big one for you."

"Well, I might just *do*, once we get to Hayes City!"

Laughter, giggling. A strange sort of silence when he came back inside. Jake Johnson, surprised to find himself oddly uncomfortable. Amazed, again, at the odd twists and turns a life can take. He mumbled an embarrassed good-night, knowing that ahead of them the Green River was rising. And while civilization might be coming, it surely hadn't arrived in these parts just yet.

It was then that Little Anne began to sing. The slow, melancholy notes of the old Civil War ballad, *Dixie*:

"Oh, I wish was in the land of cotton,
 Old times there are not forgotten
 Look away, Look away,
 Look away, Dixie Land..."

Huph, Jake Johnson thought, turning away, rolling into his blankets. He wouldn't have thought that some small girl with a big voice could bring a tear to a man's eyes.

CHAPTER NINETEEN

Spike Horn

"There's a spike horn down in the wash," Bullis said, pointing at a solitary young bull, grazing in the valley below. Buffalo under five years of age were easily identified by their short, straight horns. As they matured, their horns began to curve inward, thus they were called stub horns, or old bulls.

"We need meat," McCanty shrugged. It wasn't fat cow, but it would do.

Both men looked to the mule, which did nothing but blink back at them.

"I'll get it," Bullis said. "See if you can help the mule stay upright."

McCanty grunted and slid the Sharps out of its saddle boot. They had circled back for their saddles and tack, but were well aware of the diminished horse flesh they had appropriated from the hide hunters.

"Damn, but that is a heavy gun," Bullis said, hefting the Big Fifty. "How the hell do you carry that thing around?"

"Used to it, I guess," McCanty shrugged. "It is a man's gun, not like those six shooters you and the other quick-draws tote about."

Bullis thought he might have just been insulted, but working the Sharps into firing position convinced him otherwise. A man can't take offense at the truth, he knew. The spike horn was maybe four hundred yards off, grazing by itself in the high grass. Not a difficult shot, but Bullis understood he'd better not miss, or McCanty wouldn't be likely to let him forget it.

"Keep the mule in hand," he called back, just to take attention away from his fumbling with the shell loading, the unfamiliar twin triggers, and the weight of the weapon.

"Mind you don't shoot us...or yourself," McCanty said, taking cover behind the animals just in case, rubbing the mule's nose against the thunderous noise to come.

Bullis mumbled something under his breath, but got the heavy gun up and pointed in the right direction. He sighted carefully, pulled the triggers...

BANG! The recoil jerked his body back some, but down in the wash the buff fell, shot cleanly through the heart and lungs. Unfortunately, the mule stiffened at the unexpected loud noise, its eyes rolled white and it, too, fell over on its side.

"Damn!" McCanty said.

Bullis' elation at making a good shot was quickly eclipsed as he turned to see McCanty standing over the fallen mule with his Winchester cocked and pointing at the animal's head. An awful moment stretched out, as McCanty sighed and lowered the weapon.

"Nope, can't do it," he said, as the mule recovered its senses and struggled to its feet, looking around confused. "Must be gettin' soft," McCanty concluded.

Despite the situation, Bullis laughed. "That mule has been through a lot," he said cheerfully. "We'll figure something out."

McCanty looked doubtful but then turned his attention to the fallen buffalo.

"Got meat anyway," he said, drawing his big knife to begin the butchering.

"Do you wonder if we're eating the last one of these critters?" McCanty asked, as meat sizzled on the campfire, night settling in around them. They were yet a day or two out of Hayes City, McCanty figured, but the countryside seemed safe and quiet. At the edge of the firelight, the mule stood guard, although it was now defenseless against loud noises.

"What?" Bullis responded, the question catching him off-guard.

"Well, somebody's going to be eating the last of these buffalo," McCanty said.

"Naw," Bullis scoffed. "There'll always be some buff left, someplace."

"Maybe," McCanty shrugged. "But I don't see no others around, so maybe we're eating the last one."

"If so, at least the meat ain't going to waste," Bullis said around a mouthful of hump meat. "Not all of it, anyway. I doubt the two of us can tooth our way through a whole buffalo."

"Speak for yourself," McCanty chuckled, grease running down his buckskins. There wasn't nothing so good as fresh-cooked buff hump...unless it was warm, raw liver, dipped in gall.

"Well, not in one night," Bullis corrected himself. Still, it was a sobering thought that they might be cooking up the last of the great herds, although Bullis doubted it.

"Be a shame when no one gets to eat fresh-cooked hump or ribs over a campfire," McCanty said, with some sadness. "Did you know Congress tried to pass a law against the slaughter of the herds?"

Bullis shook his head, not knowing much, if anything, about Congress.

"Read it in the *National Republican* newspaper," McCanty said, knowingly. "Grant vetoed the law. Sherman agreed. He said: 'They should hunt, kill, skin the buffalo, until they are exterminated.'"

"Huh," Bullis said, thinking for a moment. "I guess they just about did," he said, finally.

"I guess they did," McCanty agreed.

CHAPTER TWENTY

The Green River

Dawn broke, cold and damp. Grey clouds hugged the horizon, but overhead the sky was milky white, promising sun later in the morning. As he readied the animals, Jake saw what drew the unknown settler to this patch of ground. A stream, now a torrent of water, pushed through a stand of trees that would have provided firewood and the materials for a real house. And in the back, he saw the reason for the sod farmer's failure — two graves, overgrown now, one large, one small, marked with crude crosses. Whoever the man had been, he had brought his family here, only to bury them. Or perhaps they'd buried him, he considered. The wilderness always extracted a price, he knew. And sometimes it was everything a man had, everything he loved in the world. That didn't seem fair, somehow, reinforcing his belief in God and fate and luck. Namely that God pretty much kept His nose out of the day-to-day workings, leaving a man to his fate, which found him when his luck ran out. He'd said that once to a preacher and the fellow had looked at him like Jake was the Devil himself. Still, that didn't make it any less true, Jake thought.

True to her word, Lizzie refused to ride the mules, so Kate took her animal, while Lizzie walked for a bit until Jake took pity and hauled her up behind him on the roan. Some of the girls didn't think it was fair for her to get to sit on a horse out of stubbornness, but Jake did it anyway, knowing that fairness wasn't part of the deal. If it was, they would have taken supper last night in a frame house with a man and his family, and then slept comfortably in a barn.

They heard the Green River long before they came upon it. A rushing, gurgling sound that might have been a waterfall. And as they topped the ridge leading down into the river valley, Jake heard another sound...faint, but unmistakable. A single shot from a heavy gun, echoing somewhere off in the distance behind them. He turned, staring back at the empty plains, remembering Two-Tongues' promise to warn them, if possible.

"A hunter?" Kate asked, glancing around with him.

"Maybe," he said, skeptically. There was no way to accurately judge the distance of the sound. Gunshots had a way of echoing, for miles sometimes. But one thing was certain, they had to cross the roaring Green River below, then make a dash for Hayes City, which shouldn't be more than a couple days' ride, Jake thought. The river, however, was going to be a problem.

"That's some rough water," Jake admitted, more to himself than anyone else.

The Green, usually no more than a placid stream, was raging in flood, more than a hundred yards wide. As they stood on the bank, the animals grazing, recharging themselves, an uprooted tree made a long, lazy turn around a bend in the river, then shot past them with surprising speed.

"We can't swim that," Kate frowned, her usual optimism deserting her.

"Only we got to," Jake replied. In a day or two, the river would probably sink back into its banks, returning to its normal flow. But with the possibility of Grey Wolf and his band behind them, Jake knew they didn't have the luxury of time. "The roan can make it," Jake announced, with more confidence than he felt.

If Kate thought differently, she didn't say. Jake uncoiled his rope off the lead mules. He tied one end off on a tree set back along the crumbling bank.

"I'll get across, string us a lead, and come back for you," he said, swinging himself into the saddle. And without time to think much about the decision, Jake waded his animal down into the surging water. The roan, feeling its hoofs slip on the muddy rocks, balked at entering the current.

"We got to do it," he leaned over the horse's neck, whispering confidently into the roan's flickering ears. The big horse's eyes rolled white, as Jake urged the animal into the cold, swift water. A dozen yards out, the ground under the roan gave way to several feet of water and the horse began swimming gamely. "You got it...you got it," Jake patted the animal's neck, feeling the current heavy against its flanks. The water pushing them dangerously downstream, the roan fighting the current, nostrils flaring in the effort to keep its head above water. Jake felt himself float up out of the saddle. He slipped the stirrups and clung to the roan's neck, until a few yards from shore when the horse found purchase and bolted out of the water, sides heaving. On the other bank, Jake heard the girls' cheering and waved nonchalantly, tying the rope off on a large elm. Still, it had been a near thing, he realized, testing the strength of the rope, which was taut above the surging Green. And now the hard part, he thought, kicking off his wet boots, hanging his gun belt on the saddle horn. The roan, soaked and tired, was not about to be forced back into that flood, he knew. The horse, as usual, having more sense than the man. It wasn't a thing he would do either, if he had any choice in the matter, Jake considered. And it wouldn't have been any great task if he was twenty years younger, but fate seemed to have brought him to this point. The thought made him grin some, as he went back across the Green, pulling himself hand-over-hand along the rope.

"All right, ladies," he panted, as the women stared at him, wondering if he really meant that they were to do the same thing. He did, they quickly came to realize. "I'm sorry, but this ain't a time for modesty." (And he bet to himself that the Upstairs Girls probably hadn't heard those words in many a year.) "Those dresses and petty coats will drown you for sure. Best get out of 'em now. We'll bundle your clothes up in the canvas and tie 'em to one of the mules."

There was, he noticed, some hesitation at the undressing, for reasons he couldn't fathom, but Kate led by example, and soon all the girls were shivering in their bloomers.

"It ain't hard to do, really," he lied, and with the scattergun rolled up in her dress, Kate grabbed onto the rope and plunged in, gasping at the coldness. Jenna followed, then Lizzie and Sara.

"Miss Anne, maybe you'd better hang onto me and I'll escort you across."

The little slip of a girl scowled at him. "If the others can do it, so can I," she scoffed, watching as her companions made their way slowly through the churning water, grunting, calling encouragement to each other. They were brave girls, Jake thought with admiration. Hesitantly, Anne grabbed the rope and followed.

The mules, however, had more caution. As if realizing the foolishness of what they were being asked to do, the animals balked and bayed, until Jake got a switch and all but beat them into the water. Too heavy to be tied to the rope lead, the mules quickly lost their footing and began swimming frantically, wildly for the far bank. He expected them to be swept downstream, and they were. Knowing he would have to round up the survivors later, Jake waited until the last woman had made it across the wild water.

"All right," Jake called out. "Good work, everyone!"

The women, wet and exhausted, glared at him from across the river. Now the shaky part of the deal, Jake thought, watching as the mules floundered, baying angrily at their ordeal.

"Miss Kate," he yelled from across the surging water. "I want you to untie the rope there and loop it around the saddle horn of my horse. That's right, tie it off firm, now. I'm going to take the other end here on this side, and the roan is gonna pull me across. We can't afford to leave the rope behind. OK, set now? Gently lead the horse...not too fast!"

In the water now, being pulled downstream with the floundering mules, Jake felt the rope tighten around him, yanking him through the current. He swam, keeping his head above water for the most part, hammering at the mules with his switch, forcing them on. Thirty yards downstream, the girls in their wet bloomers running along the bank, he and the mules emerged, wet and shaking, but across. Unable to find his footing, Jake laid in the shallows, as the girls waded in to pull him the last few feet to the muddy shore.

Gasping, shivering, but laughing to himself, Jake Johnson had the passing thought that his luck still held firm.

"That was a very dangerous thing," Kate came to him, helping the girls lift him to his shaky legs.

"Yes, ma'am, it was," Jake admitted, dripping wet. A wild, hastily constructed plan that had one, overriding positive factor — it had worked.

Behind them, in the distance, a second shot rang out. This one closer, more distinct, jerking Jake from his momentary victory.

"Ladies, we got to make tracks," he said, shaking himself, knowing there was no time to waste. No time for weakness or delay.

"It's not hunters, is it, Mr. Johnson?" Kate asked, looking across the Green River with fear in her eyes.

"I'm afraid it is," he said quietly. "Only they're hunting us..."

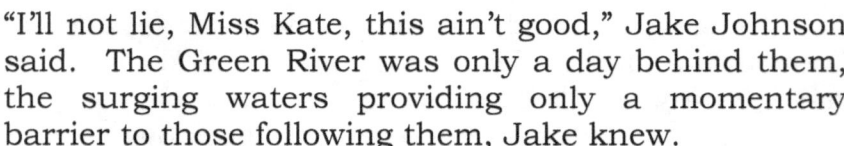

"I'll not lie, Miss Kate, this ain't good," Jake Johnson said. The Green River was only a day behind them, the surging waters providing only a momentary barrier to those following them, Jake knew.

"No, I didn't suppose it was," Kate managed to say, trying to keep her balance and hold onto the reigns as Jake led her mule into a draw, the other animals following with their female cargo. Lizzie, still refusing to ride, scrambled behind, as they all ran the length of draw, hiding in the rust colored boulders that littered the far end of the valley floor.

Behind them, Grey Wolf's band of screaming Indians blocked the entranceway, brandishing their weapons.

"What are they shouting about?" Sara asked, all of them panting, peering out from their rock enclave.

"I think they want to see your titties," Lizzie responded, with a grin. Kate scowled at the remark.

"I shot one of them," Jake admitted. "They was shadowing us and he got too close. I couldn't chance his marksmanship."

"They are mad as poked bees," Kate observed.

Jake snapped off another shot, just to remind the band to keep their distance. He knew he couldn't chance too many warning shots, however, as they had limited ammunition. His saddle bag contained a box of cartridges for the Winchester, a box for his Colt and some loose shells for the shotgun Kate now carried.

"Reserve the shotgun for when they're close," he said quietly, and Kate nodded.

The same for his pistol, he calculated, slipping a half dozen shells into his pocket to use if they were about to get overrun. It wouldn't do, he knew, to get captured alive...for any of them. Grey Wolf and his renegades were mad as hornets, as Kate correctly pointed out. He pulled the canteen of water off the mules. Not nearly enough, he knew, glancing up at the suddenly hot sun. A day, maybe two. And then...well, things would have to be settled by then.

He led the mules deeper into the enclave, along with his horse. They could drink the animals' blood and eat one or two of the mules to extend things, if it came to that. And they might have to climb higher, just to avoid being flanked, he knew. Jake stared across the dry, dusty valley, sighting down the barrel of the Winchester. Eight or nine in Grey Wolf's band, he counted. He needed to kill three or four to make the rest think twice about trying to overrun them. Might be able to do it, he thought, if he could work his way up and get closer to the canyon mouth. And he had until nightfall, he calculated, before the Indians climbed up behind them.

"Miss Kate, I'm going work my way up into those rocks. I'm thinking if I can get closer, I should be able to get some shots off," Jake said, drawing out his strategy in the dust. "When I get in position, you gals can yell and distract 'em, if you would."

Kate nodded. Jake gave his Colt to Jenna.

"Wait until Kate fires, if they get that close," Jake said, hoping there was no need for his instructions. Jenna wiped sweat from her eyes and nodded grimly. They would be in deep trouble if those Indians got that close, he knew, but didn't say. Instead, he nodded and began the climb, hoping he could keep enough cover between himself and the notoriously sharp-eyed braves.

The sun baked the rocks, although Jake knew that when night came, it would be freezing, especially with only brush wood to burn for fuel. He cursed his slowness, the manner in which his boots kept slipping on the loose gravel, the way his balance shifted. Christ, he was getting old.

Not to worry, he thought. The chances of getting too much older were slim at the moment.

The laughter caught in his throat, making him realize just how thirsty he was. But it also lightened his mood, particularly when he realized the Indians were paying no attention to him, as he crept into the rocks above them. Then he saw why. Below, at the far end of the canyon, the Upstairs Girls were indeed providing a distraction. At first, they were merely shouting and waving their arms. Then one of them, he couldn't tell who from the distance, lowered her dress and showed her ample bosom. From there, things only got curiouser and curiouser.

Two-Tongues, still riding with Grey Wolf's renegades, could not believe what he was seeing. The white women trapped in the rock filled canyon, were displaying all parts of their anatomy. Dresses were lifted, bottoms as fleshy as any he had ever seen, wagged above the boulders. Some of the shameless women showed their whole fronts, laying astride the rocks, kicking their legs in the air. All the while, shouting and waving at the much-riled Indian band.

Sioux or Cheyenne maidens could surely be lustful and wanton creatures, when in the mood to do so, Two-Tongues knew. But they were like a laced-up religious order compared to the actions of these white women. He knew they were whores, of course. Upstairs Girls, as the white men called them. Being Indian, he had never actively engaged any of them. Nor had any of his brethren, not being allowed in the saloons at any of the forts they traded at, much less the brothels. But all around Two-Tongues eyes widened, breach cloths extended at the unbelievable sights before them.

Fumbling in his saddlebag, Two-Tongues pulled out his own long eye and stared at a closer view. The long eye was abruptly snatched from him by Grey Wolf, who himself could not believe the scene taking place in and on the rocks, just out of rifle range. His braves were working themselves into a full-blown lather, their ponies circling one another, man and animal barely under control. His long eye taken, Two-Tongues blinked into the bright sun and the churning dust caused by the agitated ponies. He thought he saw something, other than bared female flesh...

A cracking sound came and one of the braves pitched off his horse. Two-Tongues shouted, but of course everyone was shouting and only the man next to the fallen brave suspected something might be wrong. Then blood flew from that man's chest also, and he went down under the ponies' hooves. By now, Grey Wolf's men were all turning away from the wanton women. Confusion was overcoming lust, Two-Tongues saw. But it was much too late. Another crack and a third brave, the red-painted Comanche, slumped over the neck of his animal. Two-Tongues saw the flash of this shot, above them in the rocks. Saw that the Rattlesnake had them all in his sights. Two-Tongues quickly decided that what the Upstairs Girls were displaying was not all that different than what could be had in any Sioux or Cheyenne village. And was certainly not worth getting shot over. He grabbed the bridal of the wounded brave and goaded his own animal into an immediate gallop.

By now, even the most distracted among them realized they were coming under fire. Unfortunately for Grey Wolf and the brave closest to him, they saw Two-tongues' movement as an opportunity to attack...to ride down the canyon mouth and capture the white women.

Later, Two-tongues would admit to himself that this was not an all-together bad idea. That with Jake Johnson, the Rattlesnake, behind them on the ridge, it might have been possible for all the surviving members of the band to overwhelm the white women, then hold them as hostages to keep the Rattlesnake at bay. It might even have been possible to use the white whores as they seemed to be desirous of being used, then trading some of them to Jake Johnson, while keeping one or two for obvious purposes. Two-Tongues thought of this much later in a Cheyenne village after a sexual encounter with a maiden both willing and experienced. Still, he could not help but compare her in his imagination with the voluptuous white whores...

But now, in this moment, Two-Tongues had no thought about changing direction and following Grey Wolf deeper into the canyon. For one thing, he and the others with him had already outdistanced the deadly range of the Rattlesnake's Winchester. Pulling up, Two-Tongues quickly concluded that he was not about to put himself back in that kind of danger, certainly not for Grey Wolf or the offered pleasures of the white women's fleshy parts.

As for Grey Wolf, he now realized that only he and one other, a brave named Buffalo Hoof, had ridden into the canyon to overwhelm the white women. He turned his pony and screamed curses at Two-Tongues and his companions for their cowardly desertion. Two-Tongues felt only momentary guilt over this development, as it had been his intention to retreat as soon as the Rattlesnake opened his deadly fire on them. It was hardly his fault that Grey Wolf, inflamed by his lust, had misread the situation.

Now, however, Grey Wolf and Buffalo Hoof both had a serious decision to make. Separated from their brethren, they could either continue their charge toward the suddenly quiet white women, or risk a run back out of the canyon mouth, under the deadly eye of the Rattlesnake. In normal circumstances, both Two-Tongues and Grey Wolf himself knew, the two trapped Indians would chance a wild gallop out of the enclosed canyon. They could lean over their horses' necks and expose very little of themselves to the Rattlesnake's fearsome Winchester. Chances were good they would both survive. But the Rattlesnake was a white man. He would simply shoot their horses out from under them, then calmly riddle them with bullets, if they happened to survive their ponies' fall. It was not easy to fight white men, Two-Tongues thought, watching his companions' dilemma. The white man had such little respect for the lives of animals. Who could forget that Badhand MacKenzie killed an entire herd, over fifteen hundred ponies he had trapped in a canyon such as this at Palo Duno? A slaughter that had been as ugly, as it was unnecessary.

Understanding all of this, Grey Wolf whooped and charged the white women, who now hid behind their rocks. He and Buffalo Hoof were beyond Jake Johnson's shooting range, so Two-Tongues and the others waited to see what might happen. There was an outside chance that Grey Wolf might be successful and the night would yet be filled with the shrieks of white women. Two-Tongues figured it was worth the wait to see. He assumed, correctly, that the Rattlesnake's attention, like the rest of them, was engaged by the small chance that Grey Wolf and Buffalo Hoof might overcome the white women's position.

The two riders, shouting and firing their own rifles, although without any hope of hitting anything from the back of a galloping horse, headed bravely down the canyon. Behind the rocks, Kate and Big Jenna leveled their weapons nervously.

"Wait...wait until they're in range," Kate said, trying to sound calm. There were two shots in the ten gauge, six in the Colt, she thought. Maybe five.

She didn't know, and that somehow increased her panic.

"I kilt the man next door to us when I was twelve," Jenna revealed. "Got tired of him stickin' his pecker in me. I believe I can kill the Indian on the right..."

"All right, then," Kate said. If she was surprised by this admission, she did not show it, but centered her barrels on the man to the left.

They were close. And they were bouncing targets, Kate realized.

"Put the first shot into the horses!" Kate shouted, recognizing the bigger targets.

Jenna fired. The horse on the right faltered. Kate let loose her first barrel, and caught both Grey Wolf and his mount. That slowed them both up considerably, she thought, pleased with the effect. Her second shot tore away Grey Wolf's shoulder and he went down. Jenna emptied her gun into the Indian on the right...

Yes, and there it was, Two-Tongues thought sadly, as the Rattlesnake walked calmly down from the rocks and put finishing shots into Grey Wolf and Buffalo Hoof, and into their writhing horses. There would be no fucking white women tonight...perhaps ever, he thought, wondering if they could possibly be worth such effort. The white men seemed to think so, he considered, as they went to great lengths to keep their women for themselves.

The wounded Comanche brave, whose lead rope Two-Tongues still held, had fallen from his horse and did not seem to be alive. Two-Tongues claimed the man's pony and rode off with the rest of what was formerly Grey Wolf's renegade band. Now a defeated bunch, haunted by white women's fleshy parts.

There was no time for celebration, less time for lamenting their actions. Jake watched as Two-Tongues and his now considerably smaller group moved off. He and the Upstairs Girls had better hightail it, too.

"Come on, ladies," he said, pushing them to action in the hope they would ignore the dead horses and men on the valley floor.

Kate seemed struck the most by the realization that pulling the triggers on the shotgun had such a terrible effect. She stared out at the brave she had helped kill with a stillness that approached shock. Jenna, meanwhile, was gathering the mules, helping the other Upstairs Girls get organized to travel.

"You know what would have happened if those two got through to you, right?" Jake said softly, standing behind Kate, knowing that everyone reacted differently to the taking of a life, no matter how necessary it might have been.

"Yes," Kate said, her voice barely a whisper.

"They would have killed or hurt you and all the girls," Jake explained, although surely Kate knew that. Sometimes, though, a person needed to be reminded about why they did what they had to do. "You and Jenna saved everybody. There weren't nothing else to be done."

"I know," Kate nodded. "It's just that..."

"You took someone's life," Jake said, knowingly, lifting the shotgun out of her arms. "But you done what was required, otherwise you and me wouldn't be moving on with all these young girls."

Jake smiled and helped Kate to her feet. She seemed stiff, sore and tired. He knew the feeling, but also knew there was nothing to be done about it at the moment. Hayes City was still two days' hard travel away.

"Come on, now," Jake said, wondering if he might need to tie her to his horse. "We got to finish what we started here."

That seemed to wake her up some, Jake thought, watching as Kate shook her head and looked to come back into focus.

"Those others?" she asked, staring out at the canyon opening, reaching for the shotgun again.

"Gone, with their tails between their legs," Jake chuckled, but prudently kept the shotgun away. "Let's get this mule train moving!"

Two days later a curious procession made its way down the crowded street of Hayes City's main thoroughfare. Jake Johnson, with Kate behind him on his big roan, leading several mules, carrying as many smiling, waving Upstairs Girls, and one walking Spanish female, who stubbornly refused to give into her swollen, bruised feet. All of them looking somewhat worse for wear, but nothing that a hot bath and some clean clothes wouldn't fix up, Kate thought.

Jake led them to a hotel, where he helped Kate down and handed her the strongbox from his saddle bags.

"As promised," he said gallantly.

"You are a true gentleman," Kate said, reaching up to kiss him on his grizzled cheek.

Jake Johnson, to his surprise, blushed as he realized that was the first time he had ever heard those words directed at him.

"Ladies, let's get some rooms and a bath!" Kate said, hustling her covey of females into the hotel lobby, much to the astonishment of some of the guests and the general amusement of the hotel clerk, who had enough experience to recognize Upstairs Girls when he saw them. Things were about to get a lot more interesting in his little corner of the world, he suspected.

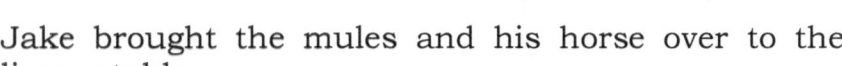

Jake brought the mules and his horse over to the livery stable.

"I'd say a beer is in order for both horse and rider," a voice said behind him.

"Good to hear your jaw moving, Dan McCanty," Jake said, turning toward his sometimes trail partner. "And you couldn't be more right!"

Once the animals were tended to and a bucket of beer ordered for his thirsty horse, Jake walked back to the hotel with McCanty, telling the story of his and the Upstairs Girls' adventures.

"Looks like they got a pretty fair boomtown going here," Jake said, as they passed through the busy street.

"They got a railhead coming," McCanty said, and both men knew that was one of the keys to success in any budding town. The railroad men controlled commerce, for better or worse, and the only thing a town could do was deliver satchels of bribe money and hope for the best.

As they walked past the hotel, Kate pulled Jake inside and insisted he take a pouch of coins and some of the folding money he'd helped to Hayes City.

"None of us would be here, much less the strongbox," Kate said, the look in her eye suggesting she was not about to accept any sort of refusal. "Besides, I got a feeling that this place is going to be my own personal gold mine."

She winked at that, and at the fact that several of the hotel guests were already taking a healthy interest in the Upstairs Girls, as they stood in line to use the two steamy bathtubs in the hotel's back room. Jake didn't doubt it a bit.

"Hey, we got us a stake!" Daniel McCanty said, as they made their way across to the Number 10 Saloon, where John Bullis was trying to win his own stake at the faro table.

"Looks like," Jake Johnson agreed, not taking any notice that McCanty had just hitched himself to his coins and folding money. Jake had done the same thing plenty of times himself. It was what pards did.

John Bullis was largely mistaken. He did not win his stake at the Hayes City gambling tables. In fact, he lost his shirt, the good one, anyway. And he almost lost his horse, before Daniel McCanty pulled him forcibly away from the faro table. That was also what pards did.

Sweet Kate, however, was not mistaken in the least. Hayes City proved to be a gold mine for her and the Upstairs Girls. At first, under the watchful eye of the desk clerk, Kate rented rooms for the girls, and as their story spread, the hotel did a booming business in short-term guests. A newspaper, The Hayes City Telegraph, featured an interview with Jake Johnson, in which he confirmed that several of the Upstairs Girls had participated in a gun battle, during which five hostile Indians had been killed. Two by the girls themselves.

After that, the hotel could no longer hold the number of customers wanting to pay for the Upstairs Indian Fighting Girls. So Kate had their own building put up just off Main Street. By then, the Telegraph story had hit the New York papers, and a dime novelist arrived to interview everyone involved. His book, *Indian Fighting Maidens*, made everyone so famous that all the Upstairs Girls involved had so many offers of marriage that it was almost impossible to sort through them...busy as they were, since every tourist visiting Hayes City wanted to take a turn or two with them, just for bragging rights, mind you. Little Anne even had a short career as a singer at the Hayes City theater, before a rancher swept her off her feet and gave her five children. Sweet Kate grew so rich, she had trouble keeping track of all her money.

That was where John Bullis turned out to be a big help. He and Kate somehow got sweet on each other; although no one could tell why, really, as is often the case in such matters. No one could tell, either, where Bullis picked up his accounting skills, but they proved considerable. Eventually, he and Kate married, started a cattle ranch outside Hayes City. With the railhead in place, the ranch was a thriving success. Sweet Kate became even richer, becoming one of the wealthiest women in the west. She and John Bullis, much to everyone's surprise, remained married for most of forty years, both of them surviving well into the next century.

Bullis even took in Daniel McCanty's fainting mule, as the once wild beast had become too old to travel very far. Plus it would fall over at the sound of thunder or loud gunfire. It was a further oddity that the mule itself became famous, and not for falling over, either. It happened when a photographer, who was traveling the west, recording the frontier before it faded away, took a picture of the mule as it stood in a meadow of yellow flowers, which it favored in the spring. When told of the mule's history by local people, the photographer titled the picture: Indian Fighting Mule. Knowing, as he did, that anyone or anything associated with Indian fighting these days had increased commercial potential. It didn't seem to matter to anyone that the mule had only fought and killed wolves. Which was a considerable feat in itself for a mule, but in point of fact, it had never actively fought any Indians.

"At least not that he's mentioned," Daniel McCanty said, when informed of the pictorial developments and the Indian fighting claims attributed to the once ornery mule.

Of course, by then McCanty was scheduled to be hung at the Territorial Prison in Clayton.

"I'm telling you boys, by spring Uncle Billy and Little Phil will have us in the field again!" The man, wearing sergeant's stripes and a blue coat was just drunk enough that he didn't care who heard him. There were several tables of cavalrymen in the Number 10 Saloon, each seeming to try and out-loud the other. The Sergeant's easy use of Sherman and Sheridan's nicknames reminding the younger men that this man might be a drunken loudmouth, but he was a veteran. "We'll get Private Collingsworth here bloodied, by God!"

Private Collingsworth, who looked like he was maybe two weeks off his daddy's farm and a year away from shaving regular, blushed under the attention of the older, more experienced man.

"It'll be like when we was with Custer back on the Washita!" the grizzled man said, winking at his other companions, draining off his beer mug. "Jesus, you remember that one, Davey?"

Davey, also wearing stripes, but slightly less grizzled, nodded and smiled. It was obviously a subject that had been visited and revisited numerous times.

"Davey here helped round up the squaws and the children after it was over. Them that was left alive, that is."

"The General used 'em as shields to get us out of there," Davey admitted, although the facts of the matter seemed not to bother the drunken, mouthy Three-Striper.

"They didn't expect us to come after 'em in the dead of winter. Mother of Jesus, it was cold, but we still managed to get us some souvenirs, didn't we?" the Sergeant laughed loudly. "Sully still has one or two that he keeps in his saddle bags."

The wink and the gleam in the man's eye brought another round of laughter from the men around the tables. Private Collinsworth looked slightly upset at these revelations, but he drank deeply and laughed with the rest.

"We best get on up to Small Bear's camp on the Powder," Daniel McCanty growled. He and Jake

Johnson were standing at the bar, where they had been for the past few days. "Get the women out of harm's way before them fuckin' Blue Coats go on the warpath. We can hunt up some hides I got cached on the way and maybe find some buff runners to harass."

There was an old bull's head above the bar. A big one, too, Jake acknowledged, knowing it would remain there even after the rest of the herds had been slaughtered.

"I heard Cody shot 250 of them critters in a single day," Jake said, as if addressing the animal itself. It was an attempt to get McCanty to pay attention to something other than the loud trooper conversation going on behind them. "What measures might you take if you seen ol' Buffalo Bill a-killing so many shaggies?"

"That dandy wants nothing to do with me," McCanty growled again, and Jake was convinced of that. "I got no quarrel with any man making meat, even for the railroad. But if they're killing just to kill, then they're doin' Sherman and Grant's dirty work. That's when they got a problem with me!"

Jake chuckled, not doubting that a bit, either. Behind them, the bar seemed to grow louder with soldiers and cow punchers and hunters.

"I do hear Cody's a pretty fair shot," Johnson allowed.

"Any damn fool can shoot into a herd of dumb beasts all day long," McCanty spat into the sawdust, eying both the cavalrymen and the rough hunters wearing buffalo robe coats. Luckily, Jake thought, they all ignored McCanty. "I never did hear of the man shootin' at anything that could shoot back."

"Me neither," Jake admitted. "Maybe an Indian here and there."

"Any damn fool can shoot at Indians from a distance all day long with a Sharps or a Winchester repeater, too," McCanty amended his statement. "But come shoot one in my direction and see what happens."

Jake chuckled again, nodding. Not even bringing up the likes of Wright Moarr or Whistling Jack Kileen, who were said to have killed more buffalo then there were Indians on the plains. The hunters were rapidly stripping the herds from the land. All planned, both men knew, to starve the tribes into submission, to open the land for the white invaders. And Jake knew there was nothing anyone could do to stop it. Although it didn't sound as though McCanty was ready yet to quit trying.

"Well, what do you say?" McCanty asked again, as more soldiers came into the bar and the noise level grew. Anyone with half an ear knew what the Army men were talking about.

The invasion of the Tribal Lands was about to commence on orders from Washington. As of 1871, Congress had declared the Fort Laramie Treaty to be essentially defunct, by passing an act that no Indian tribe should be recognized as an entity allowed to make treaties with the United States. Columbus Delano, Secretary of the Interior, had declared the government's right "to control the soil which they (the Tribes) occupy, and we assume that it is our duty to coerce them, if necessary, into the adoption and practice of our habits and customs." The Army wasn't doing much to keep their plans secret, as Cavalry troopers talked openly of the upcoming conflict. The man who claimed to have been with Custer at the Wabash continued to brag about their trophies...ears and breasts and dried genitalia from both sexes.

Disgusted, McCanty knew he had to leave before he killed one of them...or all of them, if it was possible.

Jake, who had no use for the Blue Coats or the hide hunters, took another few moments to weigh the possible consequences of McCanty's course of action. They were considerable, he knew.

"Sure," he said finally, the whiskey spinning his head, stirring up pleasurable memories of Yellowbird, Blackbird Woman's sister. "What the hell...why not?"

There were many reasons why not, as Jake later considered, but by then it was much too late to do anything about them. McCanty slapped him on the shoulder and laughed.

"But first..." Jake Johnson frowned, as if he might be having second thoughts. "We'd better be sure we've got the whiskey and whores out of our blood."

McCanty quickly agreed. There was, after all, still a bit of weight to the poke they'd been staked with, although he wasn't sure about the folding money. Also there was Jake Johnson's horse, which would undoubtedly require some sobering up before it could be safely ridden.

And there was a fight to be picked with one of those loud mouth troopers...

As it turned out, John Bullis was already smitten with Sweet Kate, and had begun counting her money for her. He swore that the money had nothing to do with turning down their offer, but his two sometimes pards were not entirely convinced.

"Money will turn your head," Jake said knowingly, when Bullis declined their offer to do some tipi living, run guns to the Indians, and maybe shoot some buffalo runners on the way. Both he and McCanty were still wearing the bruises from their altercation with the cavalrymen. Luckily, no one had been killed on either side. Officers from the Cavalry unit had dragged the troopers out under threat of a court martial. After that brawl, McCanty had still been in a fighting mood and wanted a piece of the buffalo hunters, but Jake pulled him away. Bullis had shown his gun, and it seemed that nobody wanted to die that day. All and all, it had to be said that the Number 10 Saloon had taken the worst of it. The owner had put out word that McCanty and Jake Johnson would not be welcomed back anytime soon, which definitely made it time to leave town, both men agreed.

"No, I believe I might love her," Bullis declared, even though he did understand the lure of money, particularly when it came attached to a wet, warm cunny. Still, he did do his best to make an informed decision as to his actual feelings on the matter.

"You can't bet against your heart," McCanty said, and no one present knew if he was quoting from one the books he read, or had just made the statement up. Either way, both Bullis and Johnson were fairly drunk, and so were suitably impressed. They raised their glasses and drained off the whiskey. McCanty winced. He had a broken tooth that would have to be pulled by the barber before he went on the trail. He later declared that the trip to the barber was much worse than the chair the mouthy Sergeant broke across his head.

In the end, since talk of the ranch he and Kate would own was proceeding with some regularity, Bullis took the mule and declined any payment for its upkeep.

"Money is not an issue," Bullis said, in a statement that would later have its own implications.

CHAPTER TWENTY-ONE

Rockville

Dusk was settling. There were lights winking here and there, as people clung to the final vestiges of the town. Owen Scales was walking alone down the quiet Main Street. At the far end of town, through the dust and the tumbleweeds, a coyote stared at him for a moment, then loped off to someplace that was even more devoid of humans.

Scales sighed. He had come from the livery, where he had stabled his horse for the night, along with two others that had somehow been left behind. Or perhaps they belonged to the people whose lights he saw, here and there. He had fed and watered the animals himself, as all the stable hands had gone. Now he was heading to one of the few bright lights, the Silver Strike Saloon. It was all but empty, of course. Even the cowboys from the Bar-T Ranch had driven their cows away. Presumably to somewhere there were people to buy their beef, or a railhead to ship them from. There was neither here in Rockville.

Jim Warner poured him a beer, thought about charging for it, since there was no more Town Council, no office of Sheriff anymore. But Warner had nothing to do with his beer, anyway, so Owen Scales might as well drink it up.

"Depressing out there," the former Sheriff said, stoking the belly stove. The night carried a chill that was not only a result of the changing seasons.

"Depressing in here," Jim Warner said, continuing his task of boxing up his liquor stores. He had cases of the stuff, not to mention untapped barrels of beer in the cellar. He knew he'd need help and a wagon in order to move it. Neither of which was available anyway. His inventory was worth several hundred dollars and he didn't dare to just up and leave it. There wasn't hardly anybody in the damned town anymore, but Warner knew if he left for a few days to find a wagon and some help, all his stock would somehow find itself gone before his return. Given time, of course, Owen Scales would probably work his way through most of it, but Warner did not have the patience for that. Besides which, Scales did not appear to be a likely candidate to suddenly become a paying customer.

"Listen," Warner said, an idea coming to him. "You and me, we both waited too long to leave this fucking place."

Scales nodded. That was all too true, he admitted to himself. The men sent out by the Town Council to contact the railroad never came back. But there were a couple fellows up at the mining camp, pecking the ground like chickens, convinced there was ore in the mountain that everyone had missed. It was a slim hope, but one that Scales often imagined as paying off handsomely. Sometimes he could almost see those men crashing through the swinging doors of the Silver Strike with bright metal in their hands. And then the rush would be on again. The streets filled with people, the sound of building going on day and night...

"Hey, you hearing me, Owen?" Warner asked, concerned that the once formidable Sheriff seemed to have been replaced by a rickety old man who fell asleep in the middle of conversations.

"All I got to do these days is listen," Scales snapped. And all he heard was mostly silence, he didn't say out loud. Jim Warner looked at him strangely enough as it was.

"Good," Warner said. "So we're in agreement?"

Scales blinked, not at all sure what he was in agreement with.

"I'll go for a wagon and some mules, and you'll stay here and guard my liquor stock," Warner said, saving Scales the embarrassment of asking.

"Right," Scales said, raising his almost empty glass. "Guess I'd be here anyway."

"That's the way I figured it," Warner nodded, pleased now that a plan of some sort was in effect. Maybe he'd get out of this disaster yet. Head to Hayes City himself. Open his own saloon. At least raise a stake by selling his beer and whiskey.

"You know, we could have really had something here," Scales said, shaking his head at the magnitude of the lost opportunity.

"That's surely true," Warner said, feeling jubilant enough to pour himself and Scales a measure of his labeled rye and have a drink with the former Sheriff. "It all went downhill when Jake Johnson took them whores to Hayes City."

"Naw, you can't have a town without money," Scales said, in a moment of clarity. "How are people supposed to pay for whores, or liquor, or food without money? It was Redeye Baker walking away from the mine that killed this town. What's wrong with mining coal, I ask you? Dirty work, I admit. Not as glamorous or as profitable as gold and silver. But still, it's honest work."

Jim Warner nodded, not mentioning the fact that neither he nor Scales could be said to be doing any honest work these days themselves.

"Maybe we can head to Hayes City and see how Kate and the girls are doing," Scales suggested, fondly remembering Sweet Kate in the upstairs rooms, lifting her skirts, sitting down on the shaft between his legs. Her movements like warm honey poured over his body. That seemed to be in another lifetime now. A time when he understood what it meant to be happy. Any man having his pecker warmed had to be happy.

"That's a good idea," Warner agreed, returning to his task of boxing and labeling his whiskey.

The fire in the Franklin stove burned down. Owen Scales drifted off to sleep. The beer and whiskey settling nicely in his stomach. He was dreaming that he and Kate were walking together down the street, arm in arm. Kate was laughing at something he'd said...

Then the saloon doors burst open. Scales jerked awake, thinking it was the miners, holding silver in their hands. They were smiling, looking pleased with themselves, he thought absently. But Jim Warner did not look so pleased to see the two men.

"Shit!" Warner shouted, fumbling around on the far side of the bar for his neglected shotgun.

That was the first indication to the former Sheriff Scales that something was amiss. The second was when shots were being fired in the direction of the bar. Still blinking away the fog of sleep and alcohol, Scales tried to tip his chair forward and draw his weapon. But he was too slow...too old. A man kicked the chair and the gun away from him, and Scales was left on the floor of the Silver Strike, staring up at the grinning face of what was undoubtedly a Grimes boy.

"Sheriff Scales," the voice growled. "My little brother says hello…"

And a boot came crashing down into Owen's face. Another boot, the chair maybe. He couldn't tell exactly. Not that it made much difference. After pummeling him for a bit, they jerked him to his feet and started cutting on him. He heard a scream from far away…and was surprised to realize it was coming from his own mouth.

Part Three:
The Indian Problem

"The more Indians we can kill this year,
the fewer we will need to kill in the next,
because the more I see of the Indians the
more convinced I become that they must
either all be killed or maintained as a species
of pauper."
-General William Tecumseh Sherman

"I propose, if let alone, to settle the
Indian matter in the West forever."
-General Philip Sheridan

"The only good Indians I ever saw were dead."
-Sheridan, Fort Cobb, January 1869

CHAPTER TWENTY-TWO

Cavalry Encounter

D aniel McCanty pulled his hide wagon into a stand of hackberry and maple trees, hobbled his horses out in the grass to graze. It was still an hour or so until sunset as he set up camp alongside a small stream. He was well into the Powder River drainage, with Small Bear's village some two days away at last report. While there was still some light left, McCanty figured he had spent enough time bumping along the rough prairie for one day. He carried some fresh water up from the stream, started a fire and put some coffee on to boil. He fully expected to run into some of Small Bear's Dog Soldiers, and Jake Johnson would be along shortly, returning from his afternoon scout. Jake might have come across some whitetail deer or at least a jack rabbit or two, so McCanty decided to cook up the last of the beans and dried beef. It was early fall in the high country, the maples already showing their red flags, and if Jake hadn't jumped any eatable critters, Small Bear could likely be counted on to provide a good feast when the hide wagon made its way into the Indian camp. And McCanty knew they had better be quick about it, unless they wanted to risk getting the wagon and its hidden cache of guns caught in the snows that were soon to come. McCanty didn't, for any number of reasons, not the least of which was running afoul of the Blue Coats.

It had been fairly quick work finding the cached buffalo hides and selling them at Fort Dodge. Buying the rifles had been more problematic, but finally he and Jake had come across an inventory clerk at Fort Lincoln...who had served with the rebel forces at Sharpsburg during the war. A bottle of whiskey and a good share of the hide money had bought them two cases of Winchester repeaters and several hundred rounds of ammunition. It had also bought the news of Philionus Lonzo's hanging at the Territorial Prison in Clayton. Seems the knot that was supposed to break Phil's neck mysteriously unraveled at the height of the proceedings, depositing Lonzo onto the ground some ten feet under the gallows, where he had the misfortune to break one of his legs. Howling at the pain of the broken bone and the obvious miscarriage of justice, he was carried back onto the gallows and had to be tied into a chair so the execution could be completed. Onlookers reported never having seen the like of it. McCanty figured he had gotten his money's worth.

He and Jake both planned on wintering with the Cheyenne, which was where McCanty spent most winter seasons anyway. In Small Bear's village they could ride out the winter storms in warm lodges, with Blackbird Woman and Yellowbird to romp with under the buffalo robes, to pass the long nights. Without whiskey though, as Small Bear had banned the white man's poisoned water. The chief understood the effect whiskey had on his people, who seemed to have little tolerance for liquor. In the beginning of his dealings with the Tribes, McCanty had brought a jug or two along on his treks across the wilderness, but had mostly abandoned the practice, as the liquor was invariably stolen and consumed, inciting Small Bear's anger. Not a thing an outsider cared to do.

Even today, his and Jake's place among Small Bear's villagers was hardly secure. They were, in the end, white men, and with the Blue Coat Army pressing in on their borders, the Cheyenne and Sioux leaders were hesitant to accept any whites into their community. But the Tribes needed guns. Mr. Winchester bought them a whole lot of good will.

McCanty couldn't blame the Cheyenne. As much as he was a part of the white world, McCanty suspected there was something inherently wrong in a society whose greed and self-centeredness dictated that all the land and all the available resources belonged to them, simply because they could take it. By guile, or by force. And that seemed to be the way of things, as treaties were ignored and Indian agents robbed the Tribes at will, turning the reservations into their own private fiefdoms. Stealing both outright and covertly, backed by the military presence of the Army, should anybody be foolish enough to argue. Who could blame leaders like Small Bear and Sitting Bull for not trusting a system that was rigged against them from the start?

Daniel McCanty knew that the Romans had conquered the world through the strength of their army, obliterating or enslaving anyone who stood in their way. A man could make the case that the American capital, Washington, was the New Rome, with Grant installed as Caesar. Rome became the ruler of the world by exerting its military muscle, supported by the resources of conquered territories. Here, Sherman and Sheridan were the conquering generals; their patrols were the cohorts in the larger legion...the 7th Cavalry, the 2nd and the 5th under Wesley Merritt, who defeated the Sioux at Slim Buttes, following Custer's crushing defeat. The same pattern had played itself out in the European conquest of the New World. Plundered Aztec gold funded the ruling families of Europe for generations, all at the expense of conquered nations, whose cultures were obliterated. England had conquered Ireland, McCanty's own ancestral home, and then proceeded to starve the inhabitants and steal their land. The Union had conquered the South in much the same manner, with the twin fists of economic and military supremacy. The South's culture, the good and the bad, all but vanishing in the process. And now the New Romans were about to do the same thing to the Indian tribes.

The sun settled toward the horizon. A cold breeze blew through the yellow leaves of the hackberry trees. McCanty scanned the prairie, missing the mule's sharp senses, the animal resting now in its stable at the Hayes City livery. Jake Johnson topped the rise in the west. The man came in quickly, pulled up, pointing to a dust cloud barely visible in the east.

"Blue Coats, I suspect," Jake Johnson frowned, pulling his Winchester from its scabbard.

McCanty nodded. The Roman soldiers were approaching; both men began moving quickly to make the necessary arrangements for their arrival.

They heard horses loping toward them for some time before the patrol actually came in sight. McCanty built up the fire, Jake Johnson brought their hobbled horses closer to camp. Because, of course, that was what prudent men, fearful of Indians, would do. It was expected. Dan McCanty and his partner had no fear of Indians in this part of the country, as they fell under the protection of the war chief, Small Bear, but those approaching did not enjoy that protection. Roman soldiers at the edge of the Empire would always be suspicious. As rightly they should be, McCanty considered. He and Jake drank coffee, ate their beans and jerky. And waited...

The mounted patrol topped a small ridge, just as the sun began to set.

"They're late making camp," McCanty noted.

Jake nodded, both men realizing that meant the patrol's Lieutenant was probably inexperienced, or in too much of a hurry to establish their own campsite. Neither of which were particularly good signs. A dozen riders, Blue Coat Cavalry, turned their line into a wide circle around the men, their animals and wagon. The Lieutenant rode his horse slowly toward the light of the camp fire.

"Don't be shy, come on in!" McCanty called, standing in front of the fire, his hands open and empty. Jake just sat there, looking into the flames. "Always glad to see the Army, even when I don't need no rescuing."

The Lieutenant, he saw, grinned a bit. The man dismounted, leading his horse into the line of trees.

"We've got coffee, if you don't," McCanty offered. Jake merely grunted at the invitation.

"Thank you, but we have provisions," the Cavalry man said, nodding to his patrol, as they closed ranks and moved around the campsite.

"Even better," McCanty said congenially, pretending not to notice that the Army was surrounding them.

"You wouldn't happen to have a flask of hard corn about, would you?" Jake Johnson asked. "It's been mighty dry out here..."

"No, sorry, we're on patrol," the Lieutenant shook his head, as his men circled, slowly moving inward.

"Well then, coffee and beef jerky will have to do," McCanty shrugged, although he knew that a Sergeant or two in that group would never travel far without sufficient liquid provisions. "Where you fellows out of?"

"Lieutenant Carson, from the 7th Cavalry, out of Fort Kearny," the man shook the dust out of his hat, moving into the circle of fire light.

"Joe Burk, out of Hayes City," McCanty lied easily, throwing more wood on the fire, slightly disappointed at the lack of liquor. "This here's my partner, Mickey Reilly. Sit yourselves down, cook what you got. We ain't seen no injin sign, so your boys can relax, if they want."

"You're pretty deep into Indian country," Carson commented, glancing around at the wagon and horses.

"That's where the hides are these days," McCanty shrugged. "A man's got to make a living, you know."

"We heard of some men makin' a living other ways," one of the soldiers made his way into the fire light. Another grizzled Sergeant, McCanty saw, of which the Army seemed to have an abundance.

Night had fallen quickly. The trees were bare outlines. The rest of the patrol was setting up their own camp, down closer to the stream. McCanty glanced in the Sergeant's direction, saying nothing. Jake Johnson spat a stream of tobacco juice into the fire.

"We've had reports of gunrunners bringing weapons to the Tribes," the Lieutenant said. Both men, McCanty saw, were watching them with open suspicion.

"Heard about that," Johnson sipped his coffee.

"A good way to get yourself killed, if you ask me," McCanty put in.

"A real good way," the Sergeant grunted. "You got yourself a bit of a drawl there, Mr. Berk. You fight for the Rebs during the war?"

"Our origins never leave us do they, Sergeant?" McCanty said easily. "Maine, right?"

"Portsmouth," the Sergeant admitted.

"I was at Shiloh with General Johnston and Perryville with General Bragg," McCanty said, without apology. There were those who said if Sydney Johnston hadn't gotten himself killed at Shiloh, the war itself would have had a different outcome. McCanty was not one of them. He knew the North's power. It could make more guns, put them in more hands than the South. It was the same with the Tribes. They simply could not fight the white man and win. Sometimes, he knew, courage was not enough. And sometimes being in the right was not enough, either. "My biggest regret was that I didn't go home and protect my family's holdings outside Atlanta, when that fucking Sherman came through."

"I had a friend or two with Sherman," the Sergeant growled. "And some at Andersonville. They died there. How about you, Mr. Reilly? Who'd you fight for?"

"I was at Shiloh," Jake Johnson said, his voice shaking with anger. "I kilt as many of you fucking Blue Coats as I could. I just didn't kill enough!"

Jake stood, his hands gripping the Winchester. The Sergeant glared after him. Jake was not an overly large man, but he was all muscle and tough as old leather. More than a match for the loud-mouth Three-Striper, who was used to pushing around enlisted men, McCanty thought. But it wouldn't do them any good to get into a brawl with so many Cavalry men.

"Many of my friends died, too," McCanty growled back. "You want to fight it all over again, Sergeant?"

Barely holding himself back, his right hand twitching above the knife's handle. Seeing himself, in his mind's eye, drawing the big knife from its sheath, driving it into the burly, tough talking Sergeant's chest...all before the man could blink twice. Beside the fire, Jake Johnson's eyes grew hard and cold, as though he wouldn't mind rehashing the entire conflict right here and now.

"War's over, boys," the Lieutenant said sharply, throwing a harsh glance at his Three-Striper. "Been over for a while. Sergeant, see to the guard postings. We'll be moving out at first light, after we've checked this wagon. That agreeable with you gents?"

"Check all you want," McCanty shrugged. "It's just hides. There's a panel built in the bottom, where we keep our possibles. Got a small poke of gold dust, some foofaraw and blankets we keep to trade with the Indians and to buy safe passage. I'd appreciate it if they was still there after you all leave."

"If there's no contraband, your possessions will be left alone," the Lieutenant said, nodding toward both of them. "We're the Army, not bandits. Sergeant, see to the men."

"Yes sir," the Sergeant snapped, his gaze drifting over McCanty and Jackson in obvious distaste as he went about his duties.

"The men are leery of whites who trade with the Indians," the Lieutenant said quietly.

"Then your men are idiots," Jake Johnson said, drawing a look of ire from the young Lieutenant.

McCanty laughed, shaking his head. "The white man has been trading with Indians since we landed at Plymouth Rock," he said. "And out here since the days of Lewis and Clark. We wouldn't be sitting here talking, Lieutenant, if it weren't for trade with the Indians."

"You know some history, Mr. Burk," the Lieutenant nodded, with some admiration. "One doesn't hear your average frontier man speak in historical terms."

"Then I guess you'd better talk to some of your own Army scouts," McCanty said, reaching over to stir the dried beef and bean stew, dipping his bowl into the aromatic mixture, nodding toward the Lieutenant to help himself. "I believe men like Jim Bridger could give you a reliable history of the fur trade, although the man does tell a whopper now and then. Check with Mr. Freemont or Harry Yount. All those men know some history, I believe."

"You've met Bridger?" the Lieutenant scooped beef and beans onto his tin plate. Jim Bridger was, of course, one of the legendary figures on the plains. A former mountain man, reduced now to scouting for the Blue Coat Army.

"Once, in a Sioux camp," McCanty said, casually. "Interesting fellow, but fond of spinning tall tales. What I know of history, I learned from reading and in school back East."

"Really?" the Lieutenant sounded skeptical. Jake Johnson shook his head and drifted out of the light to piss.

"Really," McCanty smiled ruefully. "My family was originally from New York. I went to school there."

Somehow it seemed necessary to explain his circumstances to this arrogant Blue Coat officer.

"We bought land in Georgia, outside Atlanta, back in the days of my grandfather. He disdained slavery, my grandfather, and paid free men to work the land. We were quite prosperous in my father's time, growing cotton, tobacco, and sorghum. My father was himself an educated man, and sent me back to New York to school...this was back in the early 50's, well before the war. I never did care for New York, or schooling, to be honest. I was supposed to read for the law, but skipped out and ran to the Shinin' Mountains."

Both men laughed a little at that admission. McCanty wished now that they hadn't insulted the Sergeant so severely, as a drop or two of whiskey seemed like a good idea.

"The old man and I kept in touch over the years, although he never did forgive me for running off like that," McCanty said, staring at the fire, as a man will do when recalling such events. "He never believed that the South would actually break away from the Union. He was a smart man in many ways, but he sure figured that one wrong."

McCanty threw some more wood on the fire. The night was growing chill, a breeze ruffled the dry leaves. Jake came back, rolled into his sleeping robes, the Winchester curled with him like a woman. Below, near the stream, the Union soldiers had a blazing fire going. Stars swept above them, like sparks across the sky. McCanty glanced at the Lieutenant, wondering if he should just shut up and go to sleep, too.

His father wrote him in the spring of '62, McCanty recalled, the memory of it flooding over him. But he figured he had shared enough with this fancy West Pointer. He had been in St. Louis at the time, and the old man had begged him to come home. But he hadn't. Instead, joined up with Johnston and Bragg. The worst mistake of his life, McCanty considered, was not running home to fight that damned Sherman.

"Your General Sherman burnt my family's farm to the ground," McCanty blurted out, surprising himself. "It killed my old man, as sure as if the Union put a bullet in his head."

"The war took a heavy toll on a lot of people," the Lieutenant said, sounding sympathetic, much to McCanty's surprise. "Even if you were there, you couldn't have done anything to stop the destruction."

"Guess I'll never know that," McCanty said.

The Lieutenant was silent for a while. Below, the troopers were talking, their voices loud, but indistinct.

"I was thirteen when the war started," the Lieutenant said quietly. "By the time I got through West Point, it was over."

"Yeah, it was over," McCanty said, his voice almost a whisper. "Sherman came through and burned everything. Killed or scattered my kin. Bobby Lee surrendered, and here I've come to this stand of trees, along this little stream, where I find myself talking to a Union Army man. You don't seem like a bad fellow, I can usually tell. But you're here with men looking for a fight. And I can tell you another thing: Once the shooting starts, it's goddamn hard to stop."

Silence spread out like a blanket between them. The Lieutenant, to his credit, did not try to justify his position, or his presence. Which, both men knew, was to subdue the Indian tribes, by peaceful means if possible, by force if necessary.

"I'll try and remember that, Mr. Burk," he said softly.

"Yes, try," McCanty said, shaking himself from his memories, knowing that the shooting had already begun. "I'd advise you to hobble your horses. The Sioux can smell horses for miles. And keep that loud mouthed Sergeant away, or by God, he'll tangle with one of us!"

McCanty saw the Lieutenant's eyes widen, but didn't care. Enough of this piddle-paddle with the fucking Blue Coats, he thought bitterly.

"There's no need for..." the Lieutenant began.

"Yes, there is," McCanty snapped. "Check my wagon in the morning, and move on. We both know why you're here, and the Tribes do, as well. It's Fort Sumter all over again. Watch your hair. Even though we ain't friendly, I'd still hate to see it hanging from some lodge pole."

Daniel McCanty, aka Joe Burk, kicked dirt on the fire, rolled into his robes to sleep. Remembering who the enemy was. Beside him, he thought he heard Jake Johnson chuckle, but it might have just been a sigh.

"If I coulda got eyes on that fuckin' Sherman at Shiloh, I mighta changed things. Maybe we coulda even got Grant, if Sydney hadn't gotten himself killed," Johnson mumbled, half asleep.

McCanty grunted back. It was true that if Jake Johnson could have could have put his sights on

Sherman, he might have been able to shoot the Union General. Both Grant and Sherman survived where the South's Albert Sydney Johnston had not. Grant, who barely escaped Shiloh with his Army intact. It had been a near thing. Grant's army vulnerable, pinned against the Tennessee River, before Beauregard foolishly called off the assault after General Johnston had been shot. It had, indeed, been a near thing. But whether or not it would have changed the outcome of the war, McCanty couldn't say.

"It just woulda been another Union general who burned through Georgia, and someone with a different name than Grant who took Lee's sword at Appomattox," he said. "The North's too strong to fight...as the Tribes will discover."

The sadness of it overtook him, as sleep came. Shiloh...it had been a near thing...

She was beautiful in his memory, as all lovers are. Passionate in her embraces, lively in her conversation. In their embraces they moaned and groaned like animals. And yet at dinner, at her family's plantation, they laughed and engaged in conversation, sipped wine from her father's cellar, poured by livery-clothed black slaves. Then they would retreat to quiet, hidden places and fuel their passion like a firestorm. It was 1849 and he was going off to school, for reasons he could not yet fathom. Even then, the slavery debate bubbled just beneath the surface. At her father's house they were served by black faces, who, on the surface, seemed well treated. Still, there was an underlying feeling in his mind that something was wrong. His own father, discussing the use of slaves on their lands, often said that slavery, holding Blacks as possessions, was a great sin against God and Nature. A practice both antiquated and impracticable, as the price of tobacco and cotton, when one examined the actual figures, did not support the practice of enslavement. One's land, in his father's mind, could be as productive without slavery, as with. And so, opposed to the practice, the Old Man had freed his remaining slaves, incorporating them into share croppers. Which, his father claimed to anyone who would listen, increased their production and freed him from providing the former slaves with the economic essentials of basic survival.

On the plantation's land, freedmen grew their own food, provided for their families by their own labor. And the system seemed to work well for all parties, much to the chagrin of their neighbors, McCanty recalled. Gardens flourished on the freed share croppers' plots. The Old Man's own fields flourished, without the need of oppressive over-seers. True, on occasion, the older McCanty would be called upon to provide medical care, or to lend tools and mules for his share croppers' use. But when you added up all the plusses and minuses, the Old Man would always say, it was obvious that slavery as an economic institution, simply did not pay. It was a practice that had outlived its time.

Still, the old Southerners clung to their traditions, despite the obvious disadvantages. Chief among these drawbacks being the North's increasing adamant objection to the practice of owning human beings.

"Free your Blacks," the elder McCanty said at every town meeting. "Indenture the immigrants, if need-be to work your land. The North will allow that.

But the Abolitionists will come to free the Black Man."

God knew there were enough Irish arriving on the famine ships to pick all the cotton in the South. But no one listened. They clung to the old ways, and would be damned for it, Devin McCanty railed.

"How foolish to fight a war over an economic system that is both immoral and antiquated," the Old Man said.

Yet, the South in its stubbornness, seemed determined to do so. And then, Fort Sumter had been fired upon, and the entire world shifted.

"Foolish...foolish beyond belief," the Old Man had shook his head, sensing that his own world, comfortable and safe, was about to be blown apart. And it was...

"Of course I know you love me," she said, hugging him, laying in the crook of his arm.

And he did, then. Only later, after he left to attend school in New York and she found other arms to lay in, did he realize how tenuous love could be. Later still, in a field of the dead, brutalized by cannon fire and musket balls, he realized how tenuous life could be. When all the humanity had been ripped from him by the cries of dying men and fire. When, in the Army of General Bragg, he had seen all his comrades blown into bloody pieces. And helpless, trapped in time and place, he had heard of Sherman's bloody march. Knowing that his family's land had been decimated. Knowing what decimation really meant: In Roman times a Century, sometimes an entire Legion, that had failed to hold a position, or failed to follow orders, was decimated. One in ten persons, picked at random, were killed by their fellow soldiers. A practice so barbaric, the memory of it survived thousands of years into the future. So, he thought, would the memory of Sherman's blood march through Georgia. Turning his family lands, and those of the lost girl, into the same stupefying, ash wilderness was an act of barbarism the Romans would have appreciated. An act both merciless and shameless, that surely brought tears to the eyes of God. Burned, buried. All that he had known and loved...destroyed.

And now, the atrocity was going to be repeated. The Blue Coats were going to decimate the Sioux, the Cheyenne, any of the Tribes who opposed them. The firestorm was going to be repeated, and again there seemed nothing he could do about it. There were simply not enough guns, not enough bullets. Even if he had a hundred years to bring them...

Of course I know you love me...for some reason the girl now spoke Cheyenne.

In his dream, Jake Johnson passed the jug and he drank from it, gratefully. Daniel McCanty, the hunter of hide men, passing his first winter with the savages. Outside, the wind blew, cold and icy. Staggering, Johnson went out to relieve himself, bringing in an armload of wood. The Cheyenne girls, young maidens called Yellowbird and Blackbird Woman, who had been assigned to tend the white men, giggled drunkenly. Small Bear would not like it, if he knew they had liquor, McCanty thought, even as he pulled one of the girls down into the robes with him. She came willingly.

There was something wrong. Something wrong with the world, but McCanty could not put his finger on it...

-You know I love you, don't you?

No one loves anyone for long. People exist together across brief moments of time that seem like forever, until death finds them. That is the true reality, he knew, as Blackbird Woman burrowed under the robes with him. The true bitterness of humanity. As Jake Johnson laughed drunkenly. As the wind blew, cold and grim, off the Shining Mountains. As time moved forward...

In the morning, the Sergeant and a few of his men tore apart the wagon, lifting the hides, tearing through the underside compartment, throwing blankets and trade goods on the dusty ground. The Sergeant, hefting the small poke of gold, glanced quickly at the Lieutenant, before throwing it on the blankets.

"They're clean," the man said, bitterly.

"Mount up, then," the Lieutenant ordered. "Move us out!"

"Lieutenant..." McCanty said, staring at their goods on the ground, which Jake was starting to reload, his rage apparent. The Lieutenant turned his horse in McCanty's direction, raising an eyebrow. "There's tribal hunting grounds a day or two north of here."

"And..." the Lieutenant frowned.

"You might want to watch yourself, is all," McCanty said, picking up blankets.

"Thank you, Mr. Burk, but the Army can take care of itself," he said, as if slightly amused at the implied warning.

"Suit yourself," McCanty mumbled, and the patrol thundered off, the Sergeant lingering behind.

"I'll see you two hide men again," the Sergeant said, grinning in another implied warning.

"We ain't hard to find," Jake Johnson sneered back.

"Just follow the smell," the Sergeant laughed, raising dust as he rode off.

McCanty shook his head at his partner, hoping the man would follow his warning. Jake snarled, but made no move toward his Winchester. Both of them watched as the patrol disappeared over a series of ridges, until the horizon swallowed them.

"Heading due north," McCanty said, shaking his head.

"Hope I get a chance to shoot that fucker before the Dog Soldiers get him," Jake Johnson said, ominously.

"They're damn fools," McCanty agreed.

The Blue Coat Army, like the Romans, thinking they were invincible. Believing, to their core, that mere savages like the Cheyenne and Sioux were no match for trained cavalry. Obviously, they hadn't seen Indian hunters ride down buffalo, sitting atop their ponies like they were part of their animals, felling stampeding buff with arrows and lances. The Sioux and the Cheyenne were among the best riders on the planet, McCanty considered. And when it came to bravery in battle, they were more than a match for any Cavalry patrol. Unfortunately, he also thought, as he and Jake went out to the far side of the tree line with shovels to dig out the buried cases of repeating rifles, the Dog Soldiers could not hope to contend with the sheer masses of men the Blue Coats could bring to bear upon them. Or their guns. It had been the same with the rebel army. In the end, they had simply been outmanned and outgunned. Small Bear's warriors could win skirmishes, but not the war.

The two men hefted the crates of rifles into the rear of the wagon, along with boxes of ammunition, covering them with blankets and foofaraw. A few dozen Henry's and a couple hundred rounds of cartridges. Hardly a match for an Army of thousands, armed with artillery, Gatling guns, and the economic strength of an industrialized civilization. It was the Romans against the barbarian hordes all over again. Cromwell against the Irish. The North against the South, McCanty thought bitterly. But the Romans fell in the end, he considered, as Jake Johnson rode out to scout and he drove their liberated hide wagon, bumping along the thin road leading to nowhere. The ancient empire, victims of their own greed and corruption. And this was McCanty's dilemma. He didn't really want his own country to end up like the Romans. A fallen civilization, poisoned by the twin plagues of corruption and greed. There had to be a way to avoid all that, he thought. At least he hoped there was, doubtful as it seemed. Power, greed and warfare ruled the hearts and minds of men. The Romans subdued all the known world. The Spanish subdued the Aztecs. The English subdued the Irish. The Europeans had been subduing the Native Tribes since the days of the Pilgrims. It had to change, somewhere, somehow.

He had read in a newspaper once about the right of white civilization to rule over the godless savages. In fact, nothing could be less true than to call them godless. They were deeply spiritual, he knew from living among them. Although they were certainly not church-going, as the laughable preachers defamed their religious beliefs. And most assuredly they could be savage. McCanty had seen that firsthand. But he had also seen the savagery of legalized justice, as applied by American courts. The Hanging Days at Rockville and Hayes City were clearly akin to bonfire justice as applied by Small Bear's village. In the end, men were men, and there was little difference between them. They loved their women, raised their children, did their best to provide for their families. And they fought their wars with brutal savagery. How interesting would it be, he considered, to bring a Gatling gun to the Dog Soldiers? A field artillery piece or two for Small Bear's village to use to keep the Blue Coats at bay?

He chuckled to himself, bouncing along the prairie, knowing that if the weapon advantage could somehow miraculously become equalized, Sherman and Sheridan would have a whole different outlook on the so-called 'Indian Problem'.

A bird, lofting high in the distance, riding the wind currents that pushed down from the unseen mountains, caused Daniel McCanty to sit up suddenly on the seat of his wagon. It was unusual for him not to be alert, but he had to admit the truth: he had been dozing. A sure sign that he was becoming lax. And lax men, he knew, did not survive long in the wild country. He had seen enough evidence of the unwary to understand that fact. Survival in Indian country called on a man to use all his senses, day and night. Even then there was a good deal of luck involved, particularly for anyone who had made his way across this mostly trackless country as many times as McCanty. Another sign that he had, perhaps, pushed his luck as far as good sense permitted.

He tucked his rifle between his knees and watched the bird, small in the distance, soaring effortlessly on the air currents. An eagle, he hoped, knowing it was probably something more ominous. The mules plodded on, requiring little attention or encouragement. The tall, dried grassland, void of almost any visible landmarks, stretched out on all sides, broken occasionally by rock formations and worn sandstone cliffs. Even though the prairie seemed, on the surface, mostly void of life, this was an illusion. Insects, grasshoppers in particular, abounded. Snakes, rabbits, prairie dogs, all manner of birds and tunneling rodents made their homes in what some deemed a wasteland. Larger creatures, especially the buffalo herds, once prominent all across the prairie, could appear suddenly, moving still in groups that numbered in the hundreds. Once, only a few short years ago, the buffalo had been uncountable in their multitudes. Their numbers would darken the landscape for miles, throwing up clouds of dust that could easily be mistaken for storms. Now, under pressure from the Tribes and the buff runners, the great beasts were more elusive, making life difficult for native populations like Small Bear's village. Soon, the buffalo would be gone. And the Tribes, no doubt, would follow. General Sherman and his henchman, Philip Sheridan, were preparing their troops to move in and finish the task of exterminating the Indian, or force them into the protective custody of the reservations. There they would still languish and die, albeit more slowly, while settlers and miners and railroad men overran their land.

Termination was the federal government's official policy now, and backed by the force of the Blue Coat army, it would probably succeed. The illusion of peaceful treaties with the Indians had been officially cast aside. Patrols, like the one McCanty had encountered, were only the first salvo in the early stages of this war. But make no mistake, he knew, the war was carefully planned, cruelly executed, and had already begun. Custer's attack on Black Kettle's village along the Washita River in '68 had killed a hundred Indians, most of them women, children, and old men. Yet the newspapers had called it a great victory. Custer, a Union Civil War hero, played it up for the Eastern newspapers, the media campaign already in full swing. The papers, once filled with news of the Civil War battles, had now turned their attention to the opening of the West. The Indians portrayed always in villainous terms, the Army heroic in its efforts to fight the savages. Even as Custer fell at the Little Bighorn, following a series of inept leadership decisions that bordered on incompetence.

Somehow, it did not matter that the federal forces were invaders into territory long held by the Tribes. It didn't matter, either, that a campaign of starvation and blatant killing, against entire populations of men, women, and children was in process. These facts, ignored or lied about in the press, went largely unchallenged. The West was opening in the wake of the Civil War. The Tribes were in the way. Progress, the newspapers reported, could not be hindered by bands of heathen savages.

It was a travesty, a miscarriage of humanity on an epic scale. That, and McCanty's desire for revenge on the Blue Coats, who had done to his own family

exactly what they planned to do to the Tribes, led him
to his current circumstance — a gunrunner to Small
Bear's warriors. True, McCanty acknowledged, he
had moments of regret. People died because of what
he did. He couldn't hide or run away from that fact.
But he knew, also, that if he did nothing, an entire
culture would perish. The Romans were in the field,
marching. Someone had to stand in their way, even
if defeat was already ordained.

Another soaring bird joined the first. And
another. Vultures, he knew now. Death waited, just
over this rise or the next. The mules plodded along,
knowing only their burden. A blessing, McCanty
thought, bestowed upon the beasts by a God, who in
other ways seemed largely uncaring and disconnected
from the world of men.

Dark shapes littered the ground. They would have
been unidentifiable from this distance had McCanty
not had some inkling of what he was seeing. Topping
the rise, leading into the next undulation of the land,
the mules hesitated. Balking at the scent of death
that remained, as yet, beyond McCanty's senses.

"Dear God," he whispered, flicking the reins,
moving the unsettled mules forward.

Men and horses lay scattered about. As he
approached, McCanty could make out the circle
pattern of the patrol's defense. They had drawn their
animals inward, no doubt caught out on the open
plain, or perhaps encamped for the night. Surprised
by an overwhelming force. Most likely Small Bear's
Dog Soldiers, McCanty supposed. As he drew closer,
the smell of the slaughter came to him, and he pulled
a bandana up to cover his mouth and nose, as if he

had encountered a dust storm. But this was a storm of another nature. Closer, he could see the extent of the slaughter. The bodies of the patrol, stripped bare, white and bloated in the sun, hideously mutilated. Revenge, he knew for the Washita Massacre, for Chivington's slaughter of surrendering Cheyenne at Sand Creek...and all the rest, past, present, and future. The circle of horses, although fewer in number than the men, adding to the stomach-churning stench. A hundred yards away, the mules halted, refusing to go any nearer. Wisely, McCanty thought, not pushing the issue as he dismounted from the wagon, in some manner almost drawn to inspect the scene. Vultures flocked around the remains, swarms of blackbirds, and hoards of flies, their buzzing audible even from a dozen yards. Cradling his rifle, McCanty walked toward the site of the fight, scanning the horizon, finding it empty. When the Dog Soldiers got their blood up, he knew, any white man could be seen as the enemy. As he approached, McCanty tried to do a body count, but could not recall, exactly, how many soldiers had been in the Lieutenant's patrol. It was also difficult to tell how many warriors had attacked the Blue Coats. Unshod pony tracks encircled the battle ground, uncountable in the churned up earth. It was equally impossible to identify the specific soldiers whose faces he recalled. The elements had already begun their work of disassembling the bloated, naked bodies. Three days, perhaps, had passed since the slaughter. McCanty was all too familiar with what happened to the unburied dead, having seen it on too many battlefields. Still, the condition of the bodies sickened him. They were all scalped, of course, the tops of their bare skulls dried by the unrelenting sun. The vultures, many of whom were too full to fly, scattered at his approach, squawking their ungodly anger in his direction. Many of the corpses had been eviscerated, their genitals cut away. Truly, he hoped, the men had been dead before the desecrations. Hollow eyes stared up at him, lips curled back in grotesque death snarls. Some of them, anyway, had been alive when the mutilations had taken place, he guessed. There were a few arrows, mostly in the drying hides of the horses. Some heads had been removed. He didn't care to count and match, to determine if any had been taken as trophies. But the lack of arrows told him that the Dog Soldiers had been armed with rifles, guns that may well have been supplied by he and Jake Johnson, McCanty knew.

Somehow, some way, he should feel responsible for at least a part of this, his inner voice suggested. A thought registered, then dismissed. Perhaps too casually, he wondered? No...only if Colt and Winchester and Henry bore responsibility for the carnage their weapons produced. Only if the metal workers who made the Roman gladius or the armor smiths of the Middle Ages or those who rolled the steel for artillery pieces used at Gettysburg, were responsible for the weapons they made.

Savagery and killing, in its many modes and fashions, was ultimately the work of men. Work at which humanity had become most adept. It was, McCanty considered, what humanity lacked that gave them this expertise. Not owning suitable teeth and claws, men made weapons to do their killing. The club and knife, the lance and hatchet, perhaps more personal than the arrow and gun, but each progression more deadly than the last. And by separating the individual from the actual act, making it easier to extinguish the life of another living, breathing being, be it human or animal. Witness the ongoing slaughter of the buffalo, and the wars made more terrible, more horrific by this separation from the actual act. The future...only God knew what slaughters waited in the future.

The mules startled, their ears standing upright. McCanty startled also, lifting his rifle. The sound of a horse's hoofs pounding the ground. Topping the rise to the west, the solitary figure of Jake Johnson came into view. Jake, out scouting for the location of Small Bear's village, pulled up his horse, Winchester resting easily across the saddle in front of him. He came slowly, forcing his balking horse into the battleground.

"You warned 'em," Johnson said grimly.

By now, McCanty had recognized the Lieutenant, split from neck to crotch. And the Sergeant, the hard look on the man's face now turned to one of horror. Meat, what looked like genitals, stuffed in his gaping mouth. McCanty swallowed the bile in his throat.

"Warned 'em, but they didn't listen," McCanty said, grimly.

"Well, they made their own end," Jake Johnson said, grimacing. "They jumped a hunting party and killed two braves. Then the Dog Soldiers came. Caught the Army boys in the open. Them Blue Coats didn't have no place to run."

The wind blew up, bringing a chill into the valley.

"Guess you better know who you're shootin' at, before you open fire," Jake Johnson said solemnly.

"There's gonna be hell to pay for this," McCanty said. "You know these cavalry people. They'll come hard."

"Small Bear thinks the same," Johnson nodded. "Met up with him this morning. He's moving his village further up the Powder to winter. I'm guessing those rifles in the wagon will make us welcome. The Elders still seem to recognize the difference between us and the Blue Coats."

"I hope so," McCanty said, more calmly than he felt.

Jake was poking through the bodies. Almost, it seemed, in a professional manner. He was, as were most men of his time, something of an expert, having seen bodies littered across battlefields in both the North and South.

"You know," he said, nudging a body with his foot. "It was the English and the French who started this scalping business. They paid a bounty for every dead Indian. Back in the early trapping days. French voyagers, mostly. They couldn't very well cart the bodies back with 'em, so they took the hair and a piece of the scalp. Collected their bounty on that. And the English didn't much care whose hair it was...man, woman, or child. The Indians took up the practice as revenge."

"Does it matter who started it?" McCanty said, horrified at the carnage.

"Guess it did to them Indians who first got scalped," Johnson shrugged, slightly amused that a man as tough as Daniel McCanty would get peeked over a little killing. "Anyway, too many of these boys to bury, and no time to do a proper job of it."

"The Army ain't going to take kindly to this killing," McCanty commented.

"Small Bear didn't take kindly to it neither, when these Blue Coats shot up his braves," Johnson shrugged again, shouldering his Winchester walking back toward his horse, grinning.

"I guess not," McCanty shook his head.

"Probably best if we just move on," Johnson seemed to read his mind. "Too bad we can't sneak some whiskey in with us."

"Yup," McCanty replied, pulling himself up on the wagon seat. The mules, for once, seemed glad to be moving.

"You know, I hear there's a buffalo runner camp up on the South Platte," Jake Johnson winked. "We might find us a couple of jugs in their wagons, after them bastards didn't have no more use for it." Jake chuckled at McCanty's snarl, knowing they would be hunting those hide men before too much longer.

McCanty flicked the traces and the mules plodded on. The two of us, McCanty thought, bumping along after his partner, traitors to our race.

"Dear Lord, look at that!" Jake Johnson said, pointing to a figure staked out on the sandy ground.

McCanty blinked, his eyes hardly registering what was in front of them. A body stretched out, pegged to the ground. A white man, it appeared, although his skin was so burned and tattered, it was difficult to tell. He was naked and had so many holes burned in him it looked like he had been next to a shell burst on some battlefield. But, of course, the burns had been inflicted on him by the group of Indians surrounding the body. One of the troopers from Lieutenant Carson's doomed patrol, McCanty assumed, although there was no real way to tell. At first, it appeared that the man was dead, until he unexpectedly turned his head and groaned pitifully. His eye sockets were empty, mouth bloody where his tongue had been cut out.

"Jesus," McCanty whispered, reaching for his Sharps, than realizing the folly of such a mercy killing. There was nothing he or Jake could do to help the man.

The Dog Soldiers whooped and hollered at their arrival, knowing that the white men's appearance meant more guns and ammunition for their cause. Small Bear himself rode up to McCanty's wagon, honoring him with this personal acknowledgement. Small Bear sat high on his pony, his head straight, pointing his long, wide nose at the horizon. While he might be considered small for a bear, he certainly wasn't for an Indian. He was almost as tall and wide-shouldered as McCanty himself, his face leathered and worn, his eyes exceptionally sharp. McCanty showed the man three hands, to indicate the number of repeating rifles he had brought. Small Bear grunted and nodded in the white men's direction, although McCanty knew the kindness was strained. He then spoke some quiet words to one of the Dog Soldiers riding with him; the Guardian, who always stood between Small Bear and white men. Because, Small Bear thought, no one could tell when a white man might go crazy and start killing Indians. McCanty thought there was a much better chance of the Dog Soldiers going crazy and killing white men.

"Small Bear greets you," the Dog Soldier said, his voice a low snarl. There was no real need for a translator. McCanty understood the language well enough. But it was another of the chief's quirks that Small Bear did not speak directly to white men, rather through the Guardian, a fierce looking man with black face paint, his hair woven with feathers and quills. Small Bear did not speak to whites because he had been lied to many times...at Fort Kearney, at Fort Lincoln, even in Washington, where he had gone to visit the Great White Father, riding the stinking, smoking Iron Horse. "He says you are a man of honor and have kept your word. That those who said to kill you have been proven wrong. He says that we have taken many buffalo and stolen many horses from the Crow, thanks to your rifles. He invites you to winter again in the Cheyenne lodges. And he thanks you for the gift of the Blue Coat patrol that you sent to him."

"Tell him I didn't send them," McCanty shook his head, as the Cheyenne chief and his warrior rode off to inspect the staked-out prisoner. "We warned them, in fact, that there would be Indian hunting parties to the North."

"Small Bear don't need to know that," Jake laughed. "Cheer up, McCanty. We'll spend the winter in snug lodges, with our injin women to warm the nights. We'll fuck and drink our corn liquor, if'n we get any. We'll eat pemmican while the cold wind blows. In all God's world, it don't get much better than that!"

Jake Johnson whooped and waved his Winchester in the air. He rode his horse in a wild circle around the camp. Even Small Bear grinned a bit at the man's antics, hardly noticing that Johnson rode close enough to the staked trooper, to be sure he was dead. All the while, McCanty thought, dead men's bones were being gnawed by wolves, vultures, and coyotes. The price of their winter refuge. A larger, more deadly price was in the offing, he suspected. The Blue Coat Army was relentless. A fact he knew as well as anyone.

It had been many winters since he had first come visiting. She was older, of course, as was he. She smiled when he rode up to her, her long dark hair touched now with grey, her skin crinkling as her mouth curled. In truth, she did not mind that her man came only during the winter season. He always brought her gifts – beads and brightly colored stones, which she wove into her clothes and hair; bracelets and necklaces, which she shared with Yellowbird and the wives of Small Bear. Blackbird Woman was never without a sharp, new knife or warm blanket. And, in the best kept secret of all, she had her own gun. A small pistol, with cartridges, which she kept hidden in a deer skin bag under her sewing kit. This she did not reveal to anyone, not even Yellowbird, as the gun would have been quickly taken from her if Small Bear even heard a whisper of such a thing. McCanty took her far from the village for her to practice, so she might shoot straight when the time came.

"Use it only to protect yourself," McCanty made her promise. And she agreed, but secretly Blackbird Woman could not wait to shoot a Blue Coat soldier.

There were other advantages to being the Hide Man Hunter's part time wife. Because McCanty brought rifles, Small Bear treated her like a daughter. She was never without food, unless the entire village was starving, and she had her own pony, a small mustang she called Soaring Bird. Although there had been no children, other than a small babe who died of fever in the first month of life.

She watched with pleasure as he dismounted, stretched his back and smiled at her. Blackbird Woman reached out and touched McCanty in the way she understood white men liked, putting her arms around his shoulders, pressing her body against his. In the end, she understood, men were men, white or red. McCanty returned her greeting, but it was an all-too-brief interlude.

To McCanty's disappointment, there was no rest, no feast or celebration when they arrived at Small Bear's village. Blackbird Woman hardly had time to greet him. The women and children were breaking down their pole and hide dwellings, packing up the dog and horse travois. The men were rounding up the pony herd, ready to push further into the Powder River Range, to a secondary wintering valley.

Small Bear's village packed up their meager belongings as the sun rose, throwing the last of its warmth across the land. The leaves had turned from dull, translucent green, passing through the colors to yellow and gold, brilliant bright red and orange. Water fowl, ducks and geese, called to one another across the meandering waterways. The great Shining Mountains loomed in the distance, as Small Bear's band moved deeper into the wilderness, further from the reach of the Blue Coat soldiers. A chill rode the night breezes, miles of frost laid across the tall grasses in the dawn light. Rain turned from a cold mist, to hard pellets, then to the first flakes of snow. At a stand of trees, a deep valley running with rivulets of water, a hole in the encroaching mountains, Small Bear called a halt to the village's migration. The lodges were erected, the pony herd set out to graze. McCanty and Johnson joined the hunting parties that rode out to make more meat before the snows closed in. And Daniel McCanty understood, if others were able to ignore it, that a whole world existed beyond this simple village.

The snows came, and the cold descended. Outside, the wind slapped their faces like an icy hand. In a way, it felt invigorating after the smoky closeness of the tipi, which McCanty and Jake Johnson shared, enjoying the company of Yellowbird and Blackbird Woman. When they had been young women of marriageable age, both had been given or lent to them (it was never really clear which) by the families whose warriors had received the gifts of repeating rifles.

Shouldering their axes, the two men went out into the stand of woods and cut firewood for their dwelling, and for Small Bear's lodge, as well, as a sign of respect. There were still many in the village who resented their presence, McCanty knew. They were, after all, white men and their race was responsible for the growing encroachment on Tribal lands. Which would do nothing but grow worse in coming seasons, he understood. Sherman and his Blue Coats will see to that. And they will not stop until all the so-called savages were prisoners of the reservation, at the mercy of the Indian Agents...or dead.

It made little difference either way, he suspected, to Sherman. The great general who burned the South into submission, now turning his bloody, heartless policies toward the Red Man. And in the end, Sherman would succeed. The Tribes, whether they knew it or not, were out-manned, out-gunned...and no matter what anyone else might think, out-savaged by Sherman's relentless tactics. Back East, those few who understood that an entire culture was on the verge of being destroyed, were shouted down. The indomitable machine that is white civilization, gathered its forces, preparing to assault the Tribes in the same ruthless manner they employed in destroying the South.

McCanty did his best to convince Small Bear to flee north in the spring, to move his people across the border into Canada, the Grandmother Country as it was called because of the British Queen, where they might find some protection against the coming onslaught. But Small Bear and the other War Chiefs believed it was possible to fight the Blue Coats. They were encouraged by Fetterman's defeat at Fort Kearney, by the Dog Soldiers' slaughter of Lieutenant Smith's patrol on the plains of the Big Horn Mountains, and by the defeat of Longhair on the Greasy Grass. But these encounters, McCanty tried to explain, even the victory over Custer, were but small skirmishes to the Blue Coats, whose numbers were like a vast, stampeding buffalo herd, unstoppable, impossible to turn aside.

Small Bear shook his head at McCanty's description of the Blue Coat numbers, unable to believe that such a force existed. McCanty explained once more that he had fought against the Blue Coats, and had seen them wage war in all their ruthless savagery. Around the winter fires, he told of Sherman's March, in which the bloody general burned cities that dwarf all the Cheyenne and Sioux villages together. Small Bear listened, then shook his head, discounting such talk as gross exaggeration.

"Bring us more guns, Hunter of Hide Men, and we will defeat your enemy," he said through his translator, believing that it would be so.

McCanty agreed that he would continue to bring him guns, but that Small Bear should realize how few they were, compared to the endless supply available to the Blue Coat Army.

McCanty knew that when they came in force, nothing would stand in the Blue Coat's way. A good death, he thought, echoing Jake Johnson's words, is all that would be available when the Army comes in force. And even that, in and of itself, was an unlikely outcome.

Blackbird Woman also heard McCanty's stories, as had many others in the village. Blackbird Woman, who helped him understand the Cheyenne language, at least sometimes, asked uncommonly straight-forward questions and told him the village gossip in her sing-song voice. Which, he found, was quite pleasing to the ear. Just as Blackbird Woman was quite pleasing herself during the long winter nights. She told him that he was known not only as Hide Man Hunter, but also as Ice Tongue, for his chilling stories about Sherman's March through the South.

"There are those who think you seek to frighten Small Bear," she said quietly, cradled against him in the smoky tipi night. "That you are a Blue Coat in disguise, trying to push Small Bear onto the Reservation..."

"Small Bear is much too brave to frighten," he whispered in her ear, knowing well that the whispers beneath the robes would be repeated to all within her circle of friends.

The Cheyenne women, he discovered, were much like their white counterparts. They gossiped incessantly, and could be relied upon to relay information to all quarters of the village. Thus, he knew for a fact that what he whispered in Blackbird Woman's ear would at some point be whispered into Small Bear's ear beneath the robes in his own smoky tipi.

"I speak only what I know to be true," McCanty said, in all seriousness.

"Then the soldiers will come, even to this far place," Blackbird Woman said, a catch of fear in her voice.

"As surely as spring will come, the Blue Coats will follow," McCanty replied, knowing that his words fell upon Blackbird Woman like the winter chill.

She wrapped herself closer around him. And he marveled at her strength, this passionate, beautiful, dusky-skinned woman. She trembled against him, and McCanty felt a terrible sorrow that he had to burden her with such a dreadful reality. She was truly unlike any female he had ever known. Independent to the point that she could easily fend for herself in any circumstance. She rode like a warrior, was quick with her fletching knife as she was with her tongue. Yet she gave herself to him, willingly and freely, unashamed of her passions and desires.

And she knew that he was serious when, in their first winter, he had offered her father, a great warrior in his own right, her bridal price in ponies and guns, to make her his permanent mate.

How Jake Johnson had laughed when McCanty had told him of his plans.

"Don't forget...you're still a white man," Jake said.

"That's true," McCanty agreed. But as a white man, he had lived in befouled cities. Had seen the piles of buffalo bones, raised up like some obscene cathedral to misbegotten gods. Had seen the devastation brought by agents of the federal government. He had seen what his so-called civilization was capable of...his family home, fired and destroyed. The people he loved, scattered and killed. What loyalty did he owe the men who would do such things?

None, he knew. None...

With a few horses and repeating rifles, he could bring Blackbird Woman to him forever. They could flee north, into the Grandmother Country. They could start a new life together. Gently, he brought this up to Blackbird Woman, who had said:

"Where my people go, I go," she touched his forehead, brushing back his thick hair.

The terrible sadness washed over him again. Sherman and his Blue Coats were coming...again. Again they will burn and scatter and kill what he come to love. Like all the People, Blackbird Woman was tied to her tribe, her extended family, in ways that whites can barely comprehend. To separate her from all that she knows and loves, would be like cutting off one of her limbs. Unfortunately, he thought bitterly, all that she knows and loves is doomed.

Still, he gave her family the horses and many repeating rifles. Knowing that eventually he would have to fight again. And that he would lose...again. The knowledge of it turned his heart as cold as the winter winds blowing through the mountain passes.

"Tell me again of your other life," Blackbird Woman asked gently, resting against McCanty's body, as the coals of the fire cast their shadowy spells, their smoking intoxication, as the wind blew and the night deepened. "I wish to know of your people. Where you came from," she whispered.

"Why?" he asked. "I have already told you." It was a tale he repeated every winter.

"What you were makes you what you are," Blackbird Woman replied, as if this were the most obvious thing in the world. "I like hearing of it."

How does one explain Ireland and the Atlantic Ocean and New York City slums to a Cheyenne girl who has lived her entire life on the Western Plains? She moved against him, needing his story it seemed, as much as she needed him. So he tried, staring into the fire embers, warm beneath the robes, as the winter wind wrapped itself around the sleeping village.

He spoke again of the vast water, so deep and wide, it is impossible to see across or walk around or swim over. Water that was bitter with salt, so it cannot be drunk. Water wider than all the land upon which the Cheyenne dwell.

Here, Blackbird Woman laughed as she always did, snuggling against him, thinking he was telling another wild, fantastic tale.

"No, it is true," he said softly.

And spun the story of men crossing this water on ships, bigger than a hundred canoes. Ships that are powered by the wind blowing into sheets of cloth larger than any tipi. And of Ireland on the other side of this vast ocean. A green land, filled with rivers and bogs and farms, where sheep and cattle graze, where his people lived for more generations than either of them have fingers to count.

"You were chiefs there?" she guessed, her eyes wide in the fire light.

"No," he chuckled. "We were farmers, working the land. In that place, the land is handed down from father to son...or rather to the oldest son. My grandfather, for whom I am named, had the misfortune to be the fourth son. So when his father died, there was no land for him to inherit. My grandfather, being an adventurous man, packed up his wife and children and moved across the vast water to America, to this land. To a city called New York, which is far to the East. This city is a place...how do I explain it? A place where there are more people than there are buffalo on the plains. And they live crushed together in wooden and stone houses that are taller than the highest trees."

She giggled against him. "You are making this up. You are being Ice Tongue again," Blackbird Woman chided him. "People do not live like that."

"Oh, they do. More people than an honest man can count," he said seriously, using a phrase she might understand, because to the plains Indians any number too large to relate was designated in this manner. Even Small Bear, upon seeing Washington had declared that he now understood the whites. That they lived like ants crawling over one another, and it was little wonder that they longed to come west, where men could breathe without borrowing the breath of their neighbors.

"What do they hunt?" she asked curiously. "How do they feed themselves?"

"That is a good question," he acknowledged. "They do not hunt or farm, most of them. They work in factories, great closed houses that produce all the goods, all the clothes, all the weapons that the Blue Coat soldiers use. And for their labor, they are paid in coin and dollars, which they use to buy food and shelter. Outside the city, there are people who farm and raise animals, which they sell to those working in the factories. And others still, who labor on the railroads, bringing the Iron Horse across the whole of the Americas. The ships, with their tipi-sized sails, carry goods and people around the whole of the earth. It is a thing called commerce, and it runs the world. Some men become rich, having more gold and goods than they could possibly use, while others are barely able to feed themselves and their families."

"It sounds strange...and terrible," she shivered beside him.

"Yes, and it is even worse than I can describe," he said, sadly. "The air is befouled with smoke from the factories, and the stench of waste, both human and animal, hangs like a fog over the buildings and the people. My grandfather, seeing all this, realized it was not a fit place to live, and so packed up his family again and moved to a place called the Carolinas. There it was more like the green of Ireland, with farmland and pastures. There in the Carolinas, my grandfather worked for others, sharing his knowledge of growing and caring for animals, until he was able to own a plot of land and work it for himself."

This, he knew, was alien to her. She was silent for a moment.

"No one owns the land," Blackbird Woman said finally.

He pulled her close, knowing that this was the fatal flaw in the Indian culture. That even now, the railroads, the miners, the settlers were laying claim to the West. Establishing ownership, no matter what her own culture thought.

"In the white man's world, a man is defined by what he owns," he said carefully. "By the land or property he lives on and works. We even fight wars over land and property."

"We know of your wars," Blackbird Woman said solemnly. "It is said that there is death beyond counting."

Blackbird Woman also knew what Small Bear said: That it was too bad all the white men did not have a war and kill themselves off. She did not say this to McCanty, since he was a white man.

"That is true," he said. "And I fought in such a war. It was the most terrible thing I have ever seen. Men died in numbers greater than all the Cheyenne and Lakota villages combined. I fought because the North was trying to take my family's land. In the end, they did. Sherman burned and killed my entire family. There was nothing left, nothing to return to, once the war was over. So I stayed in the west and ended up here, in these robes, beside you on this winter's night."

"And you bring us guns, hoping for revenge," she offered.

"And I bring you guns, hoping for revenge," he admitted, quietly.

"I am glad you are here," she whispered. "Even though the path was difficult."

"I am glad, as well," he whispered back. "At least for this time with you."

The wind blew, they held one another under the buffalo robes. She was quiet for a while, as if digesting all that he had told her.

"There was another woman..." she ventured.

"Yes," he said, the pain of remembering like a soft knife in his side. "But no longer."

In the silence, the embers of the fire caught her dark hair, her half-closed, sleepy eyes.

"And even as we lay here, the Blue Coat soldiers gather to make war on us," her voice soft and quiet, like the barest hint of a breeze on a warm summer day. "The factories make weapons. And after the soldiers, the people in the cities, more than all the buffalo herds, will come here to our lands?"

"Yes," he said, sorrow like ashes in his throat.

"Then we will be no more," Blackbird Woman whispered. "We will be swept away like dust."

Yes, he thought, but couldn't say.

Outside, the wind blew and he felt her tears, wet upon his shoulder.

Winter still held its grip in the upper reaches of the Big Horn Mountains. Below, in the lowlands to the east, the snows had turned to rain, grass sprouting on the prairie. And with that, the cavalry units would begin their push into the Tribal lands. Small Bear understood this fact as well as he did, Daniel McCanty knew. The war council was meeting in Small Bear's lodge, and to his surprise, he and Jake Johnson were invited to attend. Unusual, of course, because the white man was rightly considered to be the mortal enemy of the Cheyenne and their allies the Sioux, those bands who refused to surrender to the reservation. There was angry grumbling among the hard knives in the lodge regarding the whites' inclusion at the council, even as the pipe was passed around the fire. McCanty frowned at the grumbling, understanding that Small Bear's invitation had angered many. Especially those like Buffalo Rider and Iron Hand, who felt that all white men fell into the enemy camp. After the pipe had made its rounds and Small Bear's women had departed, the Cheyenne chief addressed the issue.

"I have asked the Hide Man Hunter and the Rattlesnake to sit with us," he said, glancing at McCanty, even as the Dog Soldier Guardian, placed himself between his chief and the white men. Small Bear made a point to use their Cheyenne names, reminding all present of the men's service to the tribe. "They have wintered with us and provided meat for our lodges. They bring guns, and so they have both proven themselves to be the enemy of our enemy."

"Still, they are snow people," Iron Hand said, referring not only to white men's skin color, but also to the general belief that they had hearts and minds as cold as winter.

"These men understand the Blue Coat soldiers," Small Bear said carefully. "Hide Man Hunter has killed many white men, many buffalo hunters. While I do not speak to him, I include him and his friend in our council because they know how white men wage war."

At that, some of the grumbling ceased, although the long entrenched animosity remained. McCanty felt the hard eyes of the warriors on him and saw that Small Bear was fighting a mutiny within his own ranks. Broken Antler, a medicine man, came to the Chief's rescue.

"I have had a vision," the old man said softly. That caught the attention of the entire council, as Broken Antler was a respected seer, whose visions of the future were generally regarded as fact among the entire Cheyenne tribe. Broken Antler's dark eyes peered out from a lined, weathered face, as he tapped an owl feather on his knee. "It was a dream that repeated itself many times over the winter. In this dream, the Blue Coats came. They dragged big guns on wheeled carts. Horns blew, as the Blue Coats gathered in a long line. The mouths of their big guns turned toward our village. Hide Man Hunter stood before them and raised his hands to the sky, and the mouths of the big guns were silenced. More horns blew and the Blue Coats rode toward our village. Hide Man Hunter raced forward and the Blue Coats scattered. There was water. The People walked across the water, scattering in many directions, while white men died hiding behind rocks."

Broken Antler tapped the feather against his knee and grew silent. The silence spread through the tipi as the members of the war council stared at one another, then at McCanty.

"Do you know how to make the Blue Coat guns go silent?" the Guardian Dog Soldier asked, as Small Bear whispered in his ear.

"No," McCanty said, shaking his head in dismay. The vision was obviously some sort of hopeful fantasy.

"Well, you will learn to do so," the translator spoke through Small Bear's grunts, both men accepting the medicine man's dream as a factual rendition of an upcoming battle.

The others at the council apparently did, as well. Even Iron Hand and Buffalo Rider nodded in his direction.

"Really, there is no way such a thing might be accomplished," McCanty protested, stunned that any rational person could believe that to be true.

Small Bear, however, seemed to take no notice of his protest, moving on to an inventory of horses and weapons, discussing when and where the camp might move, and what preparations would be necessary to protect the women and children in the upcoming conflict with the Blue Coats.

Jake Johnson, McCanty saw, winked at him, as if he believed the tale, as well.

"I can't..." McCanty began again, but by now the warriors were standing, exiting the lodge, whooping and shaking their weapons, as if victory were already assured.

Even Jake, he felt, failed to appreciate his dilemma, as the two walked together outside Small Bear's lodge.

"You know that vision is impossible," McCanty said, miserably, as the wind blew off the Big Horn Mountains, carrying with it a mixture of snow and sleet.

"A medicine man's visions ain't necessarily facts," Jake said, carefully, studying the sky, pulling his heavy coat around him. "We're gonna have another snow before winter lets go, I guess. It's the end result that counts, not the way a particular thing happens. The old man, he was just saying that you would find some way to beat back them Blue Coats."

"But I don't..."

"Think on it some," Jake advised. "That Broken Antler is right smart. Might be he was challenging you to come up with something...something you ain't thought of yet. Small Bear and his boys put a lot of stock in that old man's dreams. You want to beat back Sheridan and his Blue Coats, don't ya?"

"Of course," McCanty said vehemently.

"Well, then, there you have it!" Jake Johnson said amiably, as if that was all there was to it. "Wonder if them gals got any of that pemmican left?"

With that he walked away, seemingly unconcerned, leaving McCanty to stare at the mountains and the gathering clouds, as if the answer to his sudden problem might somehow magically appear.

Eventually spring came, even to the high country of the Yellowstone. The snows melted, filling the drainage basins of the Powder River and its tributaries. Water flowed and with it the plains sprang to life. The grasslands, which sustained all who lived on or near the great ocean of grass, pushed their green shoots up from the warm earth. The horses grazed, losing their winter gauntness, elk and deer roamed the high plateaus, and the buffalo herds spread across the newly reborn plain, like dark, living clouds. Hunters filled the village with meat, until even the camp dogs grew fat on the scraps left from the feasting.

Into this time of plenty, stragglers came, thin and poor, carrying tales of starvation from the southern reservations. So terrible were these stories that old disputes between the free hunting bands and the reservation Indians were largely forgotten, and all Cheyenne and Lakota made peace with one another. The pipe was passed among all the tribal leaders in the shadow of the Shining Mountains, and it seemed the Blue Coats had accomplished the impossible, joining old adversaries together against their common foe, the white man. Although McCanty noticed, the pony herds of each band were guarded with more than usual scrutiny. But despite this minor tension, there were few violations of the temporary peace proclaimed between the various groups, who were usually hostile to anyone who was not blood kin.

"They've had a good taste of the government's so-called friendship," Jake Johnson commented dryly, as he and McCanty passed the reservation tipis, packing meat into Small Bear's camp. "Still, I wouldn't turn my back on 'em, and I'd keep a close eye on my horses and guns."

McCanty nodded, feeling the eyes of the agency refugees on them as they rode the outskirts of the encampment. The braves wondering at the presence of two white men living among the Cheyenne.

"They don't seem overly friendly," McCanty commented.

"They ain't," Jake agreed. "Doubt I would be either, if I was in the process of being exterminated. Washington considers the Red Man to be a hair or two above vermin. Odd, ain't it? The Union fought a whole war to free the black man, but they're bound and determined to rub out the Indians. Don't seem to make a lick of sense."

"The black man didn't have any land with gold on it," McCanty spit the dust out of his mouth.

"Ain't that God's own truth!" Johnson shook his head. "There's a lesson for ya. When the white man shows up, you'd better not have anything they'd want...furs or gold or silver. Else your powder had better be dry."

"Makes a body shamed to be a white man, sometimes," McCanty said.

"Most times," Jake chuckled. "We ain't a likeable people, I got to admit. We got too many guns and not enough sense. I mind a time when there weren't a hundred white men between the Missouri River and the Rocky Mountains. Know what I call that?"

McCanty shook his head.

"The good old days," Jake Johnson laughed at his own joke.

McCanty laughed with him. Unfortunately, he thought, there were several million people on the other side of the Mississippi, just waiting to push into the West. And they were on the way now, with the U.S. military in full support, leading the charge.

"They even got old mountain men, like that little weasel Jim Bridger, scoutin' for 'em," Jake said sadly. "Crows and Pawnee, too. Mark my words, they'll be here afore too long."

Jake sighed, pulling the pack horse loaded with meat up to the tipi the men shared with Yellowbird and Blackbird Woman.

"These fat times ain't gonna last," he said, as the women turned out to begin processing the buffalo hump and ribs Jake hefted off the tired pack horse.

Yellowbird and her children, Red Shell and Sky Eyes, praised his hunting skills. Blackbird Woman came out, as well, smiling happily at McCanty. Damn, but she was still a pretty thing, he thought, smiling back at her. Long black hair framing her brown skin. Thin and willowy, she moved like reeds in the wind, seeming to float along the ground like the bird for which she was named. Her dark, dancing eyes caught the sun, her fringed buckskins, worked with beads, shining stones, and porcupine quills, framed her body. Red ochre lips grinned at him. Her subtle body always inviting, warm beneath the robes on the coldest nights. This was a sweet time, he thought, reaching out, touching her dusky skin. A man could be happy forever, living like this.

But, of course, there was no such thing as being happy forever. He knew that off in the distance, the Army was gathering. Readying themselves to march at the forefront of a wave of miners, settlers, land speculators and railroad men. Readying themselves to destroy this idealistic existence. The sadness of it all was almost too much for him. He had seen it before...the killing, the burning, the carnage of war. And now, he knew with certainty, it was coming again.

"You are sad," Blackbird Woman said, frowning.

"Not when I am with you," he said, willing them both to believe his lie. To her credit, he saw, Blackbird Woman did her best to believe him.

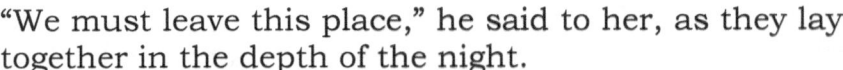

"We must leave this place," he said to her, as they lay together in the depth of the night.

"We will leave soon," she replied. Callers had come through camp, announcing that the village would move in two days' time, to hunt buffalo along the Tongue River. The Cheyenne, like all Plains Indians, were nomads. Packing up their villages, their possessions, moving with the seasons to various hunting grounds.

"No, we must move north, to the Grandmother Country," he said again, carefully urging her, knowing that the suggestion to leave her people would be a foreign idea. For a Cheyenne female it was all but impossible to leave the tribe, her extended family. "Into Canada, above the Milk River, away from the Blue Coats."

"Small Bear says we will not fight the Blue Coats," she said firmly. "We will treaty with them, or avoid them altogether. My sisters have told me."

Blackbird's other sisters, Flows-like-water and Fox Tail, were married to Dog Soldiers close to Small Bear.

"The Blue Coats will not treaty with Small Bear, and it will be impossible to avoid them," McCanty said, fighting the urgency inside him. "They will demand that Small Bear go to the reservation, or they will rub him out. I know the Blue Coats. They are savages."

Blackbird Woman laughed quietly. "That is what the white man says about us," she chuckled. "That we are savages."

"They tell themselves that, to make it easier for their soldiers to kill you," McCanty tried to explain.

"Why would they do such a thing, if we make peace with them?" she asked.

"You cannot make peace with savages," he said.

"I have made peace with you," she said, curling against him.

"We got to go!" Jake Johnson stuck his head into the tipi.

Early morning mist obscured the sun; the open flap brought a blast of cold air. There was still snow in the mountains, although the spring thaw was well under way along the Powder River basin. McCanty stuck his head out of the warm buffalo robes, Blackbird Woman stirring beside him.

"What the hell?" he murmured, blinking into the smoky dawn light.

"We got to go!" Johnson repeated, urgently.

McCanty knew the tone and hurriedly pulled on his buckskins and boots. His rifle, always loaded, was in the crook of his arm before he had fully discarded the fog of sleep. Outside, he noted, there was unusual noise and activity, for this early in the day.

"What is it?" he asked, gathering up his possibles. Blackbird Woman was sitting up now, wondering at the intrusion.

"A band of Small Bear's braves had a run-in with some cavalry scouts yesterday, not twenty miles from here!" Jake said, the frown apparent on his face. "They killed a couple of Crows, two or three troopers...and captured one of them."

Now McCanty saw the reason for his partner's concern. A white captive in camp was real trouble.

"The Army'll be coming for him," McCanty nodded.

"It was south of here, so most likely the column is out of Fort Kearny," Jake said, thoughtfully. "We might be able to get out in front of 'em and point the patrol west, along the Tongue."

"Maybe," McCanty frowned. "How bad off is the trooper? Can we talk to him?"

"He's all right for now," the other man shrugged. "Small Bear's got him trussed up and the women are sharpening their skinning knives."

"Things'll get ugly right quick, no doubt," McCanty agreed. "But maybe we can get some direction from the fellow before it does."

Signaling Blackbird Woman that he would return, McCanty went out with Jake, and found the morning awash with chaos. Ponies and men running every which way. Dogs barking, women huddled in groups around the cooking fires, dust everywhere.

"We got to be gone when the cavalry comes," Jake said urgently. "Unless you plan on fighting the Blue Coats today?"

McCanty shook his head. This was not the time or the place to make such a stand. He hoped to be able to convince Small Bear of this, as well. The Army would shoot he and Jake Johnson on sight, along with everyone else, McCanty knew. No, far better if he could talk Small Bear into moving the village, especially the women and children, out of the path of the on-coming column. And perhaps, as Johnson suggested, he and Jake could misdirect the cavalry, buy Small Bear's people some time to flee. Providing everyone involved would listen to reason, he reminded himself, as they approached a heavily guarded tipi. The guards, with lances, trying to keep a group of armed women at bay. The women brandished their knives, chanting loudly, demanding revenge for all the misery, all the deaths inflicted on the tribe by the Blue Coats. They were mad, all right, and had plenty of reason to be so, McCanty thought.

Johnson pushed their way inside, where they found a white trooper, his blue coat and trousers in tatters, all trussed up like a Christmas goose. The soldier looked no more than twenty years old, McCanty thought. The man stared at them, blinking, as if greatly surprised to see white men in an Indian village. The fellow was also wide-eyed with fear, as well he might be, with what was waiting for him outside, McCanty considered. He was bleeding from several places, but both men knew that was only the beginning of what the squaws had planned.

"There's not much time," McCanty said, offering the trooper water from his canteen. The soldier drank gratefully, then remembered to glare up at them.

Jake stood guard by the entrance, on the off chance that the women broke through before they finished questioning the trooper.

"Where's your column?" McCanty asked. "How many men?"

"I ain't telling you squaw fuckers nothing!" the kid spat into the dirt at McCanty's feet. "My Captain, he'll be here soon, and then you bastards will be dead or in chains."

"Hear that noise out there?" McCanty asked quietly, trying to get the trooper to trust him. Although, granted, the man had little reason to do so. "Those women lost a lot of their men folk and children to the Blue Coats. They want to take your hide off a piece at a time."

"My Captain'll save me!" the kid said, sounding confident, as though he actually believed such a miracle to be possible.

"Nope, he won't," McCanty said frowning. "The Indians have scouts of their own. They've been alerted. They'll know long before your Captain can get here."

That sobered the trooper up some, McCanty saw, although he still shook his head and closed his eyes, refusing to give them any information.

"I recollect when the Cheyenne caught a trooper last fall," Jake said slowly. "The squaws, they're right mad over the Washita massacre, Sand Creek and the like. They're fierce ones for revenge, you know. They cut that poor bastard, just a little, right here..."

Jake drew a line over the right side of his belly. He smiled coldly at the kid, holding the young man's eyes.

"What they do is reach inside with a finger and fish out of bit of intestine," Johnson said, his voice hard and cold. The trooper's eyes got bigger. "Just a piece, mind you. Enough to make a man howl some, but not to do no major damage. But the major damage...it ain't far behind."

By now, the trooper's eyes were wide with fear. The sounds from outside the tipi growing louder, more chaotic. Despite his lack of clothing and the chill in the air, the trooper's forehead glistened with sweat.

"They take this piece of gut, all grey and slimy, straight from a man's belly, and tie it with a loop of rawhide," Jake said, grinning, his own eyes alight with the cruelty of story. Which happened to be all too true, McCanty knew. And certainly it appeared as if the trooper believed it. "They tie the other end of the rawhide to a stake in the ground if it's a bonfire dance, or around a tree, if one's handy. Then they poke and prod their victim with knives and spears, dancing him around the tree or the bonfire. Make the man pull out his own insides. Oh, I tell you, it is a fearsome thing to see. More fearsome, I imagine, to have it happen to you!"

The young man looked terrified now, McCanty saw. The noise outside was growing in intensity, as the squaws demanded their rite of revenge.

"Once enough gut is out, they'll let the camp dogs start gnawing away," Jake continued his tale, sounding almost casual at this point. "To the dogs, buffalo gut and man gut is pretty much the same."

The wiry man paused, leaning on the butt of his rifle, working on a chew of tobacco.

"Now, a brave man...a really brave man, will just start himself to running, once his gut is tied off," Jake said, winking at the young trooper. "He'll understand the hopelessness of the situation, and rip his insides out right quick, to end it. Because for sure, a man don't want to be on the receiving end of those squaw blades, particularly with the camp dogs chewing on his guts and all. Sometimes running hard will work, if a man is strong enough, determined enough. But sometimes, even though he wants to do it more than anything in the world, to end the torment, sometimes the agony of it is just too much and a man's courage fails. He stumbles, he falls, and the squaws are on him with their skinning knives. The dogs fighting over his entrails. Sometimes it ain't even his fault. A Dog Soldier might think it's a good joke to reach out and trip him, as he's trying to tear his own guts out. Just out of spite, or to make the entertainment last longer. And there he is, sprawled on the ground, his intestines all over the place, as the squaws skin him and stick his cut-off dick in his mouth. Anyway, it's an ugly way to die. Wouldn't want no part of it, myself."

The trooper looked like he didn't want any part of it, either. He looked like he might get sick, or start crying, McCanty thought.

"Tell me where the column is," McCanty leaned in, whispering. "How many men?"

"You'll take me with you, if I tell?" the trooper asked, hopefully.

"Can't," McCanty said, nodding toward the tent flap, where the women shouted calls for justice for all the Blue Coat killings. "You ain't my prisoner. You're theirs..."

The trooper's lip began trembling, desperation etched onto his twisted features.

"But I'll leave you a weapon," McCanty whispered, holding out what must have seemed to be a glimmer of hope. "You can use it as you think best."

The trooper nodded, understanding McCanty's unspoken words. That he would leave the means for the man to spare himself the unspeakable torture Jake Johnson had described.

"They're coming in from the west, from the Belle Fourche River," the trooper said, closing his eyes against his betrayal. "Two columns under Captain Hardy."

"Good, good," McCanty said, reaching into his boot for a small skinning knife, driving it into the ground at the trooper's feet.

He stood quickly. He and Jake strode out, pushing their way through the increasing crowd of women, children and old men.

"Hey, wait!" the trooper yelled from inside the tipi, but the two men were already gone in search of Small Bear.

"Thought you might be giving that boy a gun," Jake said, casually.

"Don't want him hurting nobody," McCanty shrugged. "Knife will do the job, if he uses it right."

"I suppose," Johnson replied, his tone indicating that he didn't care much one way or the other.

Small Bear was in front of his tipi, giving hurried instructions to groups of agitated men. A normally calm, quiet man, Small Bear looked uncommonly agitated himself, McCanty thought. All of the other Cheyenne cast ominous glances in the two white men's direction. Small Bear waved them quickly into his tipi, stepping in with his ever-present Guardian a few minutes after them. McCanty knew the Chief to be a mostly reasonable man, but he surely looked to be at the end of his patience today.

"The young men wish to go and fight the Blue Coats," the Dog Soldier translator said, his eyes hard and cold. "Small Bear may have to allow them to do so."

"There are two columns of soldiers," McCanty shook his head gravely. "As many as forty Blue Coats, all of them with repeating rifles. They are too many for your young men to fight alone."

"They'll likely have field artillery," Jake put in. "You can't fight cannon."

Small Bear grunted, shaking his head. "We have guns," the Dog Soldier said, staring at the two whites.

"Give us four or five of your young men," McCanty said. "If they can follow our instructions, perhaps we can lead the Blue Coats west to the

Tongue River. You can move the village further up the Powder, out of harm's way."

"It would be but a momentary escape," Small Bear's Dog Soldier said, doubtfully. "We will have to fight the Blue Coats eventually."

"Not with women and children in the path of the columns," McCanty said, urgently. His fear for Blackbird Woman almost palpable. He wanted desperately to lead the soldiers away, believed that he and Jake could do so...but certainly not if Small Bear allowed his braves to fight. A fight they would almost assuredly lose.

"Tell him to give me the young men and we will decoy the Blue Coats away," McCanty said. "I will not put them in danger, they will return safely to you."

At that, Jake frowned at him. Small Bear took a few moments to consider the proposal.

"And you agree to watch over Blackbird Woman until I return," McCanty said.

"Yes, she will continue to be like my own daughter," Small Bear's translator nodded, an oath that McCanty knew the Chief took seriously, even though Jake Johnson looked mostly skeptical.

From the far end of the village, a scream echoed. It stretched out, long and pain-ridden. The sound of it sent a shiver up McCanty's spine. The young trooper, it seemed, had not used his weapon to proper advantage. The shrieks continued, loud and sharp, as the two white men mounted their horses and rode toward the pony herd, where four of Small Bear's young men awaited them.

They rode all day, east toward the Little Missouri River. At night, around a camp lit only by moonlight, McCanty explained his plan to Hawk, one of the Dog Soldier's sons, who in turn told his mates. They were all young men on the verge of manhood, thirteen or fourteen, McCanty guessed. They were, of course, good riders and anxious to be engaging the Blue Coats, if only from a distance, as McCanty explained. They all appeared excited by the plan, yet he knew they were apprehensive, taking instructions from a white man. And he couldn't blame them. Whites had been the enemy for all their short lives, and would likely remain so for however long the young men lived. But they did understand the necessity of protecting their people, so McCanty hoped they would listen.

It was a decoy plan, McCanty explained, careful in his instructions, as decoy plans often went astray when young men could not control their excitement. In the world that these boys grew up in, bravery and counting coup on one's enemy was the ultimate prize of war. In the thick of battle, a brave would gain glory by riding up and physically touching the opponent with a bow, spear handle, or coup stick. For the Blue Coats, of course, killing one's enemy was the ultimate goal, so the soldiers simply shot anyone who got close to them. Thus, the Tribes and the Army fought on entirely different grounds. It was critical that Hawk and his companions follow their part in the plan, otherwise... well, McCanty did not want to explain to the Dog Soldiers how their sons had gotten killed or captured.

"When we find the Blue Coats, the Rattlesnake and I will ride toward them quickly, as if we are being chased," McCanty explained. "You and Little Horse and the others will be hidden in an arroyo. When you hear us yelling, you will ride your ponies as quickly as possible to the southwest. But do not let the Blue Coats get too close to you! That is very important. Understand?"

Hawk nodded, as his father had told him to pay strict attention to what this white man told him. "We will drag blankets and tree limbs to make much dust, so the Blue Coats think we are many and give chase," he said.

"But take no chances," McCanty implored. If the decoy plan went bad, he knew, the young men would not only be put in harm's way, but also give away the ploy to divert the Army columns. If that happened, Small Bear would not have time to move his village further up the Powder, away from the immediate danger. "Once you have led them to the south, pull in your blankets, cut the tree limbs free, and separate. Then when you are away from the Blue Coats, ride to your village on the upper Powder. Do not allow the Blue Coat scouts to sight you. Your bravery is already assured, so you need to take no further chances. Yes?"

Hawk nodded again that he understood. That, in fact, he had been told the same thing by his father.

"Good," McCanty said, hoping his plan would work.

"Might work," Jake shrugged. "Unless the Army shoots us outright when we come ridin' toward 'em."

McCanty grunted, then rolled over into his robes to try and get some sleep.

When he woke in the predawn light, the young braves were painting their faces. Jake Johnson was coming down into the arroyo where they'd dry camped.

"One of them young bucks smelled smoke," Jake said, point to the west. "Sure enough, campfires yonder. Must be the Blue Coats."

"That's them," McCanty said, turning his long eye telescope on the twin Cavalry columns riding confidently, with the morning sun at their backs. Twenty men in a line, with mules trailing in the dust, carrying equipment and pulling two small field pieces. "We'll get them boys set up, then ride into 'em like we've got the whole Cheyenne nation at our backs.

Jake Johnson squinted into the sun, as if the idea suddenly held little appeal to him.

"Hi-ya!" McCanty yelled, riding hard off the ridge above the approaching column. For effect, he took off his hat and slapped his saddle, deftly avoiding the horse's flanks. They were coming at the column fast enough to be convincing, he figured. No sense taking a chance of having his horse break a leg in a gopher hole or something. Behind, he heard Jake's horse right on his tail. The cavalry columns had stopped, the Captain watching them through his field glasses.

"Indians!" McCanty shouted, waving his hat, making sure the troopers took them for white men. "Indians!" he said again, panting now, pulling his lathered mount to a halt beside the Captain and his second Lieutenant at the head of the troopers.

"How many?" the Captain asked, as his Lieutenant scanned the ridge and the Sergeants milled around, awaiting orders.

"A passel of 'em!" McCanty shook his head. "They jumped us while we was hunting down by the Tongue."

"Cheyenne and Sioux, I took them to be," Jake Johnson said, almost too casual to McCanty's ear.

"Yeah, Sioux! Maybe some Cheyenne!" McCanty gulped, injecting a note of fear in his voice. "Had to be twenty braves."

This was a fine line, McCanty knew. He had to make it sound like a credible threat, yet one that the cavalry could easily subdue. He must have figured the right number, because the Captain began snapping orders.

"Sergeant Mills, take half a dozen men and scout that ridge! Lieutenant Harris, spread the men out in closed battle formation! You men..." the Captain pointed his freshly shaved chin at McCanty and Jake Johnson. "Follow my scout patrol and point out the direction of the hostiles!"

"The direction of the hostiles?" McCanty asked, all but shouting his panic. "Why, it's the direction we just run from! You'll know 'em when you see 'em. They'll be the ones with the war paint, screaming for your scalp!"

The Sergeant rode up, pointing with his rifle toward the ridge.

"Scouts seen dust rising," he said, glancing in disgust at the open fear in McCanty's face. "Looks like they've spotted us and are runnin'."

"Very well, Sergeant," the Captain nodded toward his Lieutenant. "Have the bugler sound the charge. We will pursue in close order formation. Gentlemen, you'll be joining us?"

"Not on your life!" McCanty said sharply. "I don't get paid to kill Indians, or get kilt by 'em!"

With that, McCanty gave his horse its head and rode off. Jake Johnson shrugged in the Captain's direction and followed his fleeing partner.

"I'm guessing they bought it," McCanty glanced back at the disappearing Cavalry men, as they dutifully followed the young Cheyennes' dust trail.

"Hey, you was pretty convincing back there," Jake chuckled. "Might be you could join ol' Buffalo Bill on the theater stage, in one of his play-acting adventures."

At that, McCanty looked gravely insulted, to the point where Jake Johnson almost fell off his horse laughing.

"Don't know about you, but I'm circling back up the Powder," McCanty said.

Jake Johnson stopped laughing and followed.

CHAPTER TWENTY-THREE

Powder River Basin

Blackbird Woman let her pony, Soaring Bird, run freely through the flat grassland. Behind her, McCanty rode his bigger, lumbering Army horse. They were racing, although Blackbird Woman suspected McCanty was letting her win. Little did he know that her mare could keep this pace for hours, while his overgrown mountain of horse flesh was already breathing heavily, like an old man in heat, she thought smiling. Soaring Bird, which was her secret name for herself, moved easily beneath her. The sun was bright and warm, reflecting off the yellow grass of summer. And best of all, her deerskin pouch, holding the gun and cartridges was tied to her belt, bouncing against her thigh. Soon she would load the bullets into the chamber, spin the cylinder deftly around, pull the hammer back, and feel the kick of the weapon against her wrists and forearm. It was Blackbird Woman's favorite thing. Even better than riding McCanty while the cold wind blew and the warm fire caressed her breasts. Blackbird Woman smiled again and hummed a song of happiness.

"You must be careful with that!" McCanty cringed, as she spun the loaded chamber and pointed the barrel of the pistol into the air.

Blackbird Woman laughed away his concern. There was such a feeling of power in the act. She now understood why the white men were so exuberant in their wars.

"I cannot wait to shoot a Blue Coat soldier," she said, instantly regretting her words, as McCanty glared at her. It had been a month or more since the Hide Man Hunter and Jake Johnson had led the Army patrol away from the village, still her man would not let it slip into the past. "But only if they are about to rape me," she said, demurely, looking up at Hide Man Hunter with sorrowful eyes.

"I hope you heed my words," McCanty said, with tenderness in his voice. "It is better for you to run and hide, than to fight."

"Of course, my husband," Blackbird Woman dutifully nodded that she understood. Although, in truth, she wondered why one would run and hide if they had the power of a gun.

McCanty walked off twenty paces, reminded her again of the gun's workings. She then gleefully emptied the pistol twice into a fallen log he stood upright to represent a man. Most of her shots sent bark flying into the air.

"Not bad," the Hide Man Hunter said, and Blackbird Woman felt the sun hit her face more forcefully than before. She was about to ask for more shells, when he turned, his head tilting.

"Hear that?" he asked. She shook her head, and then a faint rumbling came to her ears. "Buffalo?" McCanty asked, even though there was no way of knowing.

He took her arm and swung her up on Soaring Bird.

"We better go see what's what," he said.

There was dust in the distance, a half day's ride away, McCanty saw. Maybe buffalo, he hoped...

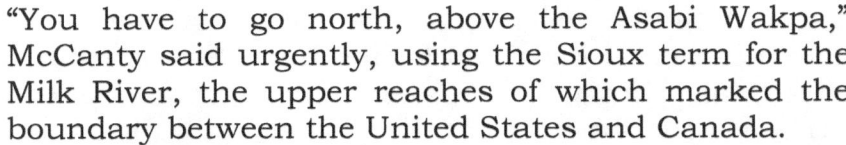

"You have to go north, above the Asabi Wakpa," McCanty said urgently, using the Sioux term for the Milk River, the upper reaches of which marked the boundary between the United States and Canada.

Small Bear shook his head uncertainly, as the Dog Soldier Guardian stepped between his Chief and the obviously agitated white man. The other Elders of the village also looked skeptical.

"The Blue Coats will not follow you there," McCanty said, hoping it was true. He doubted Sherman cared much for the border, but also didn't think that a General with such close personal ties to the Washington politicians would risk an international incident, just to chase down a few retreating Cheyenne.

"There's buffalo on the northern plains," Jake Johnson said, as if he knew that for a fact, which he did not. In actuality, the hunters up north had killed almost half a million buffalo by this time. He did know that if Small Bear's village stayed here along the Yellowstone, the Blue Coats would come and kill all they could - men, women, and children. Then they would march any survivors off to the reservation.

"Many of the Lakota will be going north, as well," McCanty said. There were rumors that leaders like Sitting Bull were leaning toward a tactical retreat above the Asabi Wakpa.

He reached outside the tipi to grab Blackbird Woman and bring her inside the Council. The Elders would not like this, he knew, but was past the point of caring. They would listen, or they would be slaughtered. It was as simple as that.

"If you stay here, you will die," McCanty said, pushing Blackbird Woman toward the fire. "Tell them what we saw," he said to her.

Blackbird Woman shrugged and did as he asked.

"The Blue Coats are coming," she said simply. "We saw them on the trail above the Tongue River. Many of them, marching in long lines. They are more than you can kill, also they have big guns."

"Cannon, artillery pieces, along with repeating rifles," Jake said, nodding encouragement toward Blackbird Woman.

"Yes, all of those things," she said, looking down at her feet now, remembering her fear when she and McCanty looked through the telescope at the long lines of soldiers. "Hide Man Hunter speaks true. No matter how brave you are, no matter how hard you fight...your women, your sons and grandsons will all perish," she said, trying to keep her voice level and calm. She knew now why people with small guns would run and hide from the Blue Coats.

"Perhaps they will stay south of here," Small Bear tried to reason with himself. "They have done so in the past. Perhaps the Tribes will come together as they did at the Greasy Grass."

The old man, like all the war chiefs of the Plains Indians, recalled fondly the time and place where they defeated Custer and the 7th Cavalry back in the summer of '76. McCanty shook his head. It was that battle, a small victory in a larger war, that had perhaps sealed the fate of the Cheyenne, the Sioux and their allies, when they wiped out the famous Long Hair. That slaughter had galvanized the politicians in Washington into unrestricted action.

The generals, Sherman and Sheridan, had quietly been given orders to take any measures they deemed necessary to eradicate the Indian threat. To open the land for settlers, miners, cattlemen and the like. There was land, there were riches, and the Indians were in the way.

"A column of Blue Coats out of Fort Sully has already passed the Black Hills," McCanty said, revealing information Jake Johnson had gotten from a trader in Bozeman. He simply had to make Small Bear see the only option he had left, other than to die here, in this place. "Another will be coming up the Yellowstone shortly. They will be along the upper Powder and the Rosebud River before summer passes. There is nothing else, but to retreat above the Asabi Wakpa to the Grandmother Country."

Small Bear nodded.

"The Council will consider all that has been said," the Dog Soldier Guardian spoke Small Bear's words. Small Bear sat down in front of the fire, into which someone threw some sage and cedar wood chips.

Jake grabbed McCanty's arm and pulled him outside, before the big man did something foolish. Blackbird Woman followed.

"You have to give them old buzzards time," Jake said. "It ain't an easy decision for them to make."

"I know," McCanty said, knowing Jake was right. "But if they wait too long..."

"Yeah," Jake said, watching as the day came to a slow, comfortable end. Women were cooking, men tending their weapons and ponies. Boys and dogs ran about wild. It was hard to imagine that this peaceful village might soon be the site of fire and slaughter. That this entire way or life would soon end.

"I ain't waiting," McCanty said suddenly, turning to Blackbird Woman. "We're leaving in the morning. Get up to the Asabi Wakpa anyway. Make it so we can get across to safety quick, if it comes to that."

Blackbird Woman looked sad, then defiant for a moment. But remembering the long line of troopers, she moved off to pack up their few possessions. Indians traveled light, of necessity, McCanty knew. Now it was more necessary than usual.

"You're welcome to join us," McCanty said to Jake. "Bring Yellowbird along."

"Not a bad idea," Jake said. "You know what the Army'll do if they catch us on the wrong side of this, right?"

McCanty nodded. "You probably got time to fade into the mountains," he said, encouragingly.

"What...and miss a good fight, like this one's shaping up to be?" Jake laughed loudly. "I ain't got that many good fights left in me. Don't care much to be sittin' around on a porch somewhere in my dotage, wishing I had stuck around to pot some Blue Coats," Johnson said, sounding enthusiastic about the possibilities. "Shoot, any damn fool can get old and sit around on a porch."

The Asabi Wakpa, or the Milk River, didn't look like much from where they stood. Maybe a couple hundred yards of open water to cross, not much depth or current. Of course, it was a whole other story in spring, when melt from the heavy snows spilled the river over the flat plain. The Milk was named by Lewis and Clark on their legendary exploration back in the early 1800's. Meriwether Lewis had said: "Being the color of tea with the admixture of a teaspoon of milk...from the color of its water we called it Milk River." Not milk, but clay sediments along its bank claimed the color of the water, McCanty knew, as he debated sending Blackbird Woman and her sister across to the safety of the Canadian border. It didn't make sense, exactly. The land on the upper reaches of the Asabi Wakpa was mostly woods and fields, grass and boulders, with the Shining Mountains in the distance. You might as well be on one side, as the other, he considered. Yet for reasons that seemed mostly imaginary, far side was safe from the Blue Coats, and this side was not. Still, McCanty figured they'd have enough notice if the Army was on its way. Some deer moved downriver on their particular side of the water, so he decided they'd camp here in the maples and cottonwoods. Wait and see what developed, he thought.

Jake Johnson had also seen the deer moving through the tall grass, toward water, and slipped off to get them some venison. Blackbird Woman and Yellowbird set up camp, the children walked off to collect enough wood for the night. McCanty hobbled their horses, stripped their packs and saddles, the Indian women using only riding blankets and horse hair bridles. He looked over the trail they had come up, working out firing angles from the various stands of trees and collections of boulders. It was defensible, he thought, as a shot downriver startled him. He smiled at his reaction to Jake Johnson making meat. He hoped they made it through the next few days without throwing too much lead around.

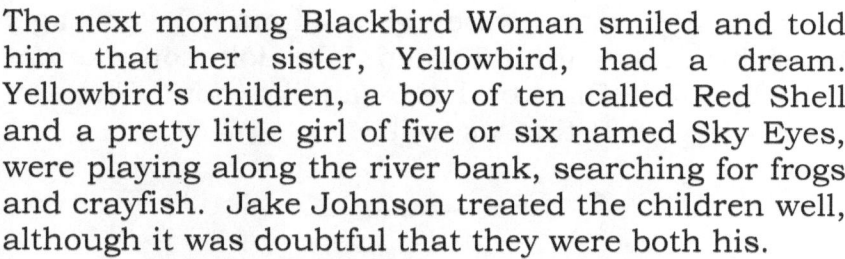

The next morning Blackbird Woman smiled and told him that her sister, Yellowbird, had a dream. Yellowbird's children, a boy of ten called Red Shell and a pretty little girl of five or six named Sky Eyes, were playing along the river bank, searching for frogs and crayfish. Jake Johnson treated the children well, although it was doubtful that they were both his.

"I spent a lot of time away, running with the likes of you," he joked to McCanty. "Can't expect a young woman of breeding age not to follow her instincts."

As to Blackbird Woman's instincts, McCanty thought it best not to ask, especially since their own babe had died of fever some years back. McCanty had been off trapping and only learned of the tragedy later.

"Tell me about her dream," he said, smiling back.

"A runner, a boy from Small Bear's village, will come up that path," she said, pointing. "He will be in a great hurry and he will tell us that it is safe to return to the Powder River camp."

McCanty looked at her kindly, hoping the dream was a true one. He put his arm around her shoulder.

"I would be glad for this to happen," he said, gently. "Still, we should dry some of that venison, in case we have to travel quickly."

Blackbird Woman nodded, pleased that this large white man, who came into her life so infrequently, was still protective of her, even though she was past the age to give him sons. There were others in the village who could, and she tried to encourage him in their direction, but he remained fixated on her. Secretly, Blackbird Woman liked this. She and Yellowbird giggled at that foolishness when their white men were gone from the village. Yellowbird slept around when Jake Johnson was not with her, but Blackbird Woman did not. The two sisters giggled at this, as well.

On the second day, Yellowbird's dream came true...or mostly true, McCanty later thought.

A boy came running up the trail toward their camp. Yellowbird saw him and was overjoyed.

"Look! It is Red Shell's friend, Antelope! We will return home!" she said, hugging her sister.

But Blackbird Woman saw the panic, the fear in the boy's eyes. Her sister's dream had happened, she knew, but not exactly in the way either of them hoped.

McCanty saw the fear, as well, and was calling out the alarm, even before the boy started shouting.

"The Blue Coats have attacked the village," Antelope said, gasping, even though he ran like the animal for which he was named. "Many dead...many fleeing!"

"Get packed and across the river," McCanty said quickly to the women. "Ride far enough away to be out of rifle range. Set up a camp and we'll send people to you! You, boy, help these women and children across that river!"

The boy, perhaps twelve years old, was only too pleased to have something useful to do. The fact that it involved moving to safety in the Grandmother Country only enhanced the opportunity. The land was flat, rolling hillside, with valleys and cut-backs up beyond the spring flood line. The Asabi Wakpa was a slow, meandering ribbon of water this late in the season and the women had no trouble crossing. The boy helped move them to higher ground. Once on the far side of the water, Blackbird Woman sat on a rock, with her loaded pistol on her lap. She refused to move, no matter how much Yellowbird pulled at her. No matter how much McCanty yelled and waved from the American side.

Finally, convinced their women and the children were safe at least, Jake and McCanty set up in the rocks, with the river at their backs, giving them clear shots down the trail. There was a lot of brush along the riverbank, some ash and cottonwood stands, but the main feature in this part of the country was the wide, open grass fields, with the mountains etched against the horizon.

"They won't be able to get behind us, anyways," Jake Johnson said, looking down the barrel of his Winchester. "And if they move through that grass to flank us, they'll show themselves pretty quick."

McCanty nodded, setting up the Sharps, with all the reloads he had at hand. He leaned his own Winchester against the rocks, within easy reach for when things got closer.

"They'll be too many of 'em for us to hold off very long," McCanty stated the obvious. "And they'll have field pieces, no doubt."

"No doubt," Jake reluctantly agreed. "But we can maybe keep the bastards back long enough for the rest of the women and children to get across to safety. Then we can skedaddle our own selves."

It went without saying that the fleeing Indians would be women and children, as Small Bear's surviving warriors would be fighting in the delaying action.

"That'd be my thought," McCanty nodded, although both men knew it would take plenty of luck for things to break that way.

"And we get to shoot some of those fuckers," Jake said brightly, as if he actually looked forward to doing so.

McCanty glanced over at his friend, who winked and smiled back at him.

"You really do want to shoot with them, don't you?" McCanty asked.

"'Course," Jake said, as if there was ever any question about it. "Them Blue Coats destroyed the South. Then they proceeded to destroy the buffalo herds. And now they're after the Tribes themselves. Who wouldn't want the chance to shoot some of those fuckers?"

"Well...when you put it that way," McCanty shrugged, sliding a shell into the Sharps.

But it wasn't until midday before the first group of people came up the trail toward the Asabi Wakpa and the Grandmother Country. And it wasn't Blue Coats, but Cheyenne women and children in desperate flight.

"The ford is just ahead," McCanty said, ushering them along like he was a theater ticket taker. There were maybe thirty or so, but they were followed quickly by hard riding warriors, who were escorting an even larger group of fleeing survivors.

To McCanty's surprise, Two-Tongues was among them. The Indian pulled up his pony, nodded at the white men, as if nothing out of the ordinary had passed between them. He waited for a moment, to see if the Rattlesnake was going to shoot him.

When he did not, Two-Tongues nodded in his direction. The Rattlesnake did not nod back, but neither did he open fire, which Two-Tongues took as a sign of temporary peace between them.

"The Blue Coats are behind us," Two-Tongues said, his face and eyes set hard. In the distance, a cloud of dust bore out his words. "Small Bear and the Dog Soldiers are trying to slow them, but the Blue Coats are stopping only to kill anyone they find."

"Go and set your warriors along the trail," McCanty said, trying to figure the best way to save as many Cheyenne as possible, while inflicting the heaviest casualties on the Cavalry men. This might give them pause and discourage them from crossing the Milk to pursue the fleeing villagers. "Funnel the Blue Coats into us here at the rocks. Give me half a dozen men with rifles, and we'll make them pay!"

Two-Tongues moved quickly to follow the white man's instructions. The Hide Man Hunter and his friend, the Rattlesnake, were great killers...of Indians, Blue Coats, and white men. Two-Tongues was glad that the Rattlesnake was able to put aside past grievances without a lot of ceremony and focus on what needed to be done in the here-and-now. There would undoubtedly be some sort of reckoning at a later date, assuming both men survived the coming encounter. Which, at the moment, Two-Tongues deemed unlikely and not worth worrying about. He quickly sent six young men with repeating rifles McCanty had brought them into the rocks, instructing them to follow the Hide Man Hunter's orders.

"He knows how to kill Blue Coats," Two-Tongues said to his charges, who were not happy to be dismounting their ponies, but did so because Small Bear had given them the task of saving as many of the women and children as possible. And it was true that the line of women and children were moving quickly across the Asabi Wakpa, into the safety of the Grandmother country.

They were also not pleased to have been placed under the direction of a white man...Hide Man Hunter or otherwise. Two-Tongues understood this, as well. Had it not been only a few moons back when he himself was trying to kill the Rattlesnake with Grey Wolf? He remembered well the fear that rose up in him, when the Rattlesnake's sights had been drawing down on him. Now the Rattlesnake stood, Winchester cradled in his arms, a feather in his slough hat, spitting tobacco juice as his eye fell upon Two-Tongues. To his surprise, the half-wild white man winked at him, and then proceeded to turn his back and began placing the young men where they could best fire into the approaching Blue Coats.

This was the strange puzzle of white men, Two-Tongues thought, as he headed for the brush and the high grass, to ambush the enemy Cavalry. In truth, it made little or no sense to him. White men like the Hide Man Hunter and the Rattlesnake would fight to the death to protect their own women and children. And for some reason, they would fight equally hard to protect Cheyenne women and children. In fact, they would both die during this engagement, Two-Tongues was sure, having seen the attacking force of Blue Coats. Who, incidentally, were made up almost entirely of white men. So there were white men who would kill women and children, as easily as one might shoot a deer or a buffalo. Yet there were white men who would stand and point their guns, saying: No, this is wrong. Two-Tongues did not understand. Any more than he understood how white men could stand above a buffalo herd, and kill *all* of them, taking only the hides, leaving meat that would feed everyone to rot. And other white men, like the Hide Man Hunter, who would stand with their own big guns, and say: No, this is wrong. White men, it would seem, were both good and bad, benevolent and cruel, as the situation and their mood dictated. Two-Tongues truly did not understand. The real truth was that he feared to come under their guns. There was no fighting the white man's cannon, their artillery, or fast-firing rifles, he knew. The only reasonable thing a man could do was flee. Which was what Small Bear's village was trying to do. But some of the white men were trying to exterminate them. While other white men were trying to save them. Two-Tongues wanted to know how the white men decided which side to be on.

The Indian rider wheeled, twisting to fire down the trail at a still unseen attacker. There was dust, shouting, chaos, and the sound of close, snapping gunfire. McCanty braced himself against the rocks, sighted down the big fifty-caliber Sharps. When a shadowy, ghost-like form appeared out of the fog, he took a breath and squeezed the double triggers. The gun roared. Behind the Cheyenne brave, a Blue Coat was knocked from his horse.

The Dog Soldier continued up the trail, hollering, waving his weapon. In front of him, the Big Fifty roared again and down in the dust cloud another uniformed soldier lurched from his saddle. No women or children had appeared in the last few minutes, only warriors closely pursued by Blue Coat Cavalry. The pursuers, however, pulled up now that they were taking fire from fortified positions in the rocks above the trail leading to the Asabi Wakap. McCanty caught sight of an officer forming the troopers into a fighting line, but couldn't get a clear shot. The Blue Coats had mostly dismounted by now, which was the entire purpose of this delaying tactic. McCanty allowed himself a quick smile. He knew that the women and children, along with a few surviving Elders and some warriors to protect them all, were escaping across the river, running for the nearby Canadian border. He did not think that the Cavalry, once they broke through, would follow them. For one thing, the fleeing Cheyenne had a pretty fair head start. For another, the safety of the border was only a few miles away. But he needed to be sure. Once the Army's killing blood was up, it was hard to tamp down. Besides, as Jake Johnson had said: 'Who'd pass up the chance to shoot some of these fuckers?'

And Jake was getting his shots in. Most of the troopers had moved up into reasonable rifle range, although the rocks were currently taking most of the damage on both sides. While the trail head was the primary focus point, the retreating Indians had fanned out, scattering as the Blue Coats overran their main party. These stragglers now splashed across the Asabi Wakpa, scrambling through the brush, and down the river bank. Two-Tongues and the warriors from Small Bear's village harassed and harried the soldiers following these groups in what was becoming a horse-to-horse encounter, at which the Cheyenne riders excelled. The odds were leveled even further, given the fact that many of the Dog Soldiers were armed with repeating rifles, courtesy of McCanty and Johnson. They whooped and hollered, sweeping in behind the Blue Coat pursuers, as the Cheyenne women and children rode and ran up the ridges that led to the Grandmother Country. As the Blue Coats took causalities and broke off this pursuit, McCanty felt his thin line of defense being fortified.

"Them Blue Coats don't like fightin' so much, unless they got five or ten times the advantage," Jake observed, his voice a snarl. "Or unless it's women and children they're chasing..."

McCanty wasn't so sure about the numbers, but didn't say anything, as Jake Johnson seemed to be in a furious mood. He snapped off two rounds and down on the trail, a Blue Coat let out a strangled shout.

"I'd be dangerous if I had one of them big Sharps," Jake said with a chuckle.

McCanty made to hand him the Fifty, but Jake declined with a grin.

"I ain't got the bulk to fire off such a cannon," Jake scoffed, as Two-Tongues came up beside them.

"The Blue Coats are coming up through the tall grass," Two-Tongues pointed off to the right, where there was indeed movement on the wide, mostly flat ground.

"Shit," Jake frowned. It was one thing to have an eyeball-to-eyeball stand-off from behind fortified positions, but the damn Blue Coats did have too many numbers on them. As McCanty suggested, if the Army got close enough to put fire on them from two sides, it was all but over.

McCanty sniffed the wind. "Burn the fields," he said, directing Two-Tongues to take some of the Dog Soldiers and set fire to the high, dry buffalo grass. "That'll back 'em off some."

"What'll we do about them cottonwood stands on the other side?" Jake asked, pointing his nose to their left flank. "Reckon those'll burn, too?"

"Nope," McCanty shook his head. He had already sent some of the younger men out in that direction to act as sentinels. "When the Blue Coats get into them woods, we best be off across that water. We got enough guns to defend one front, but not two. They'll net us, once they get around that side. But it'll take 'em a bit. It's swampy ground out that way, I'm told. Our people will be on the far side of the border by then. That's the best we can do."

"Well, I can at least shoot at these bastards for a little while longer," Jake said, swinging his Winchester around, looking for likely targets.

To their right, smoke began to rise from the brush along the riverbank. Flames could be seen licking the edge of the tall grass. There were shouts in the distance, as the Blue Coats realized which way the wind was blowing. McCanty grinned, hoping the breeze held direction.

It was not unlike a North/South standoff, McCanty thought, as the day progressed and pot shots were taken on both sides. The Blue Coats were hunkered down at either side of the trail in front of them. A sheet of smoke rose like an ashy dust storm to their right. It was still relatively quiet in the cottonwoods on their left. Although it would not remain so, McCanty thought.

"When night comes, we skedaddle across that river," he said to Jake, as they lay in the rocks, squeezing off the occasional round. He'd like to leave right now, but knew that any retreat in daylight would only invite pursuit. And he had no idea what the Blue Coat officers might do if the troopers started chasing them across the Milk.

McCanty had no way of knowing that behind the Blue Coats, dead Cheyenne lay scattered for miles. The survivors of Small Bear's village had made it across the Asabi Wakpa, but others sadly had not.

"I guess," Jake reluctantly agreed. He doubted that there would be much more shooting of Blue Coats on this day, anyway. He took a sip from his canteen and grimaced, hoping the water in Canada was better than this silty caulk water. "You could drink this with a spoon," Jake said, frowning...

And the first explosion roared from somewhere far in front of them. A whistling shell passed overhead, exploding in the brush behind them.

"Oh-oh," Jake said, eyeing the trail with his telescope. "Looks like they brought up the artillery."

A second shell came in closer, as the gunners got their range. Two-Tongues hesitated only a minute, before McCanty nodded, releasing them from their obligation.

"Blackbird Woman's sitting on a rock on the other side of the river," McCanty said, pointing in her direction. "She ain't likely to move, but put a rope on her if you have to...oh, and she's armed, so be careful."

"She will be safe with us," Two-Tongues promised.

The Cheyenne warriors broke and headed across the river.

"If I can get a shot at the wheels, I might be able to knock that damn cannon out of commission," McCanty said, taking the long eye, pulling the Big Fifty up to balance on the rocks.

"And if I could get a shot at Sherman, I'd be the most famous ex-Rebel ever," Johnson said urgently, pulling at his friend's arm. "We got to get..."

The whistling sound of an approaching sounded overhead.

"Shit!" Jake Johnson said, knowing what it meant, diving for cover.

Behind them, Two-Tongues and the Dog Soldiers splashed across the Milk River. McCanty was sighting down the barrel of the Fifty, even as the shell fell on them.

It was an hour, or a minute, or a day later. Time had become impossible to determine. McCanty lay on the ground, feeling as though he had been dropped from the clouds. Broken like a doll he had seen once in a village along the Washita. He tried to put movement back into his body... failed. And the light turned dark again.

"Are those white men?" someone asked.

"One of them might be," someone else replied. "The other one's crow food."

"Wait a minute, I know that son-of-a-bitch," the first man said, and McCanty felt a boot poke his side. "By God, that's Daniel McCanty. He shot up a gang of hide men out by Dodge."

The boot kick grew rougher. Then someone grabbed him by the shoulders. He felt warm, bitter breath in his face.

"You're Daniel McCanty, ain't ya?" the voice asked harshly, sounding slightly afraid, for reasons McCanty couldn't begin to understand. "Runnin' with the injins, huh?" the voice laughed, and McCanty tried to find the strength to spit in the man's face. Tried to put his fingers around the haft of his blade.

"He's a feisty old bastard," the other voice acknowledged. "I'd watch out for that knife, if I were you, even though he does seem to be blowed up pretty good..."

CHAPTER TWENTY-FOUR

Territorial Prison, Clayton

"You bastards!" the shout echoed down the corridor of the cell block, followed by the banging of chains against steel bars...then silence. A long, deep silence that was somehow worse than the shouting. Some unknown man in the throes of anger and despair. McCanty understood both.

An entire season had come and gone since Daniel McCanty's capture. More weeks had passed since his trial...since the verdict and sentencing. And now the waiting. Better, he thought, to have been blown to bits like Jake Johnson, instead of only being half blown-up. His eyes were the worst part. Vision still hazy around the edges, bright sunlight all but blinding him. Not that there was much sunlight here. Just what filtered down the corridor, and what found its way through the small barred window set high in the brick wall of the cell. Probably for the best, he considered. Just as it was probably for the best that he end his days here, as he would be of little use half blind like he was.

And so the waiting...for his eyes to get better...for the hangman to arrive. Wondering which would come first. The latter, as it turned out.

Another shout of anguish from down the corridor...

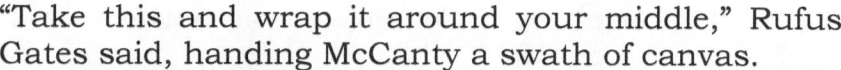

"Take this and wrap it around your middle," Rufus Gates said, handing McCanty a swath of canvas.

McCanty stared at the man, uncomprehending.

"Like a baby nappy," Gates made a motion indicating underwear. "It's so you don't soil your britches," he said, shaking his head.

"Oh," McCanty said, nodding.

"Be wise to empty your bladder before," Gates counseled. "And tie your boots on so they don't slip off. Nothing more undignified than a man's bare feet or filthy socks dangling in the breeze."

McCanty nodded again, the reality of the situation failing him. He was in the Territorial Prison, condemned by a judge to be hanged. Probably rightfully so, he admitted, but still could not bring himself to believe it was going to happen. Dickie Waters' prophetic words came to him:

-Nobody believes they're gonna die, Dickie said. They always think something's gonna save them.

And it was true. McCanty could not believe that he was going to die...here, now. But Rufus Gates seemed to believe it, as he measured McCanty from neck to heel, standing back to estimate his client's weight.

"They took my money," McCanty said, feeling a sudden rush of clarity. "I don't have any..."

Blade sharpening coins, he didn't say, realizing that Rufus Gates had probably never read any English or French history.

"That's all been took care of," Gates waved the concern away, understanding the reference, if not the actual history.

"Who?" McCanty asked, confused.

"That gunman I almost got to hang back in Rockville," Rufus Gates flashed a twinkle of a smile. "Bullshit...something. Said money was not an issue, or some crap like that."

"Aw, Bullis," McCanty nodded. He felt himself curiously separating from the place his mind and body currently occupied. A surreal effect, he thought, as if one stared at clouds too long and forgot their feet were attached to the actual ground. It was a dizzying thing, he realized, as Rufus Gates finished his measurements.

"Don't worry," Gates said. "You won't hardly feel a thing."

"No?" McCanty asked, wondering how the infamous hangman would know such a thing.

"Nope," Gates said, with such conviction that McCanty could do nothing but believe him. "You'll float free for a second, then you'll be free. It'll happen ...like that!"

Rufus Gates snapped his fingers and grinned, knowingly.

"Now, they'll put shackles on your feet, mostly for show," Rufus Gates said, chuckling. "How far do they figure a man's gonna run with his arms handcuffed to his belt? Anyway, them shackles'll help us. You got a mighty thick neck, so I'll add a bit of weight to those leg irons when we're up topside. That'll give ya a little pull downward, you see. But just enough to help snap your neck. Too much weight and your head might go flyin' off!"

Rufus Gates chuckled again. McCanty did not. The hangman looked a trifle sorry at his last remark.

"Not to worry...not to worry," the hangman said, putting away his measuring tape, writing the results down in a tiny notebook, using the barest stub of a pencil. "Feeling a little disconnected, are ya?" Gates asked, not unkindly, then nodded as if answering his own question. "That's to be expected. Actually, that's exactly what we're doing here, you and I. Disconnecting you from this lump of flesh you've been dragging around all these years. Yes..." Gates said, patting McCanty's shoulder. "That's exactly what we're doin'. Perfectly natural to feel that way. Happens to everybody, eventually. We all leave this world, one way or another. Some sooner than others, of course. But it'll be over right quick. No need to fret about it."

The old man left, walking his shuffling steps down the jail corridor. McCanty blinked, wondering at the exchange. Wondering, also, at the fact that he did somehow feel more at ease. Who would have thought that strange old man seemed to know what he was talking about. But did he...really?

"Guess I'll find out," McCanty said to himself, shrugging.

They came for him one chilly morning. A Marshall and four guards. Big men, all of them. They approached McCanty as though expecting trouble, like he was armed and dangerous. Which, in his current state, he was neither. When they finished, his hands were pinned neatly to a chain belt around his middle, shackles on his ankles. He had taken the hangman's advice. Drained his bladder, wrapped the canvas cloth under his pants, tied his boots on. All of which did little for his appreciation of the proceedings, but he did feel somewhat prepared for them.

Outside, he found the sun surprisingly bright. McCanty looked up, blinking. Still half-blind, but the warmth, it felt comforting. Making him feel...alive, somehow. A curious feeling to be having at such a moment, he thought. The Marshall was surprised to hear the condemned man chuckle. That was a first, in his experience.

Behind them, some preacher was reading Bible verses, which irritated McCanty some, but he decided not to bother complaining. Wouldn't matter much in a few minutes, he considered. Thirteen steps, although he only counted twelve. Did they short-step him? Would that somehow affect the all-important drop? He was about to ask, when the smiling face of Rufus Gates greeted him.

"A fine morning, Mr. McCanty," the hangman said cheerfully. A little too cheerful, in McCanty's mind. But to his surprise, Rufus Gates broke out a flask, took a slug, then put the flask to McCanty's own lips, all before the guards, the Marshall, or the preacher could object. Gates grinned, took another big pull himself before the liquor disappeared.

"Helps keep everyone calm," Gates said, as the Marshall glared at him. "Go on now, read your law paper, whilst I get ready."

At that, the Marshall seemed to recall his purpose, unfolded the death notice from his vest pocket and began reading. The man droned on and McCanty found himself barely listening. Events moving quickly around him, as though he was seeing everything from a great distance.

"Right over here, if you will," Rufus Gates was saying, directing McCanty to stand on the trap door, like they were all going to have their picture taken. "All of this won't take but a minute."

"Take your time," McCanty managed to say and Rufus Gates let out a quick, barking laugh.

"No, no, best to get these things over quickly," he said, adjusting his knots, adding a small amount of weight to the ankle shackles. He produced a stool from one corner of the gallows' platform and stood on it behind McCanty. Gates brought the noose down and placed it gently around McCanty's neck. The big man could not help but flinch at the touch, but Rufus Gates put a reassuring hand on his shoulder. "Don't worry about a thing," the hangman whispered. "We'll be done here in just a minute."

The Marshall droned on, the preacher rattled off words.

"They make such a production out of this," Rufus Gates mumbled, shaking his head. "Like everybody ain't gonna die someday. Now, I'm going to put the hood down in a second and I want you to take a deep breath, hold it, and count to ten...softly in your head."

McCanty could see the crowd now. Mostly silent, their faces a blur to him, as were the words of the Marshall and the preacher. He thought he might have seen John Bullis near the back, but couldn't be sure. Thought for a brief moment that Bullis had come to rescue him...that the gunman would rush the gallows, guns blazing and somehow spirit him away to waiting horses...that he would flee to the Grandmother Country and be with Blackbird Woman again...

Rufus Gates brought the hood down, winking at him at the last moment.

"Don't worry about a thing," Gates whispered.

As instructed, McCanty took a deep breath.

-Breathin' is over, the thought came, startling him.

Can't be...can't be, he thought. Not yet. He managed another deep breath...began counting. Got to five before there was a noise behind him and the floor fell away. He dropped, jerked to a stop...and then there was nothing.

People said it was the cleanest hanging Rufus Gates ever did. The hangman did not even sell pieces of the rope afterward.

The End

Historical Note:

By the 1880's the hide business was as dead as most of the buffalo. Mountains of bleached bones dotted the plains. Poor homesteaders, with wives and children working beside them, gathered cartloads of the bones. They were shipped back east, following the trail of hides and tongues. The bones were ground into fertilizer and used to make charcoal and glue. Many of the Sioux and Cheyenne who fled into Canada returned to settle on the reservations. Even the great Sitting Bull, who was murdered by reservation police in 1890 at the Standing Rock Indian Reservation in South Dakota. The dispute over the Native Americans' confiscated land continues to this day.

The buffalo, once numbering in the millions, hunted to the brink of extinction, have made something of a comeback. There are said to be some 15,000 free range buffalo living in the wild today. Another half million of the creatures are kept on private farms and ranches.

Bad Men

Bad Men

Michael Kanaly

Bad Men